"*Santiago: A Myth of the Far Future* is (Resnick's) best yet.

"Mike says he likes to tell fables. That makes him a fabulist, and his stories and characters fabulous. *Santiago*'s certainly fit. There is the tale's hero, the Songbird, former revolutionary, a bounty hunter with a heart. There is ManMountain Bates, gambler and avenger of fraudulent markers. There is the Angel, deadliest of men, and journalist Virtue MacKenzie, and the pulpit-pounding Father William, who collects scalps and uses the bounties for good works. Outrageous. Preposterous. Fabulous, all.

"You can already sense a strong flavor of the American frontier, of mountain men and gunfights, of Paul Bunyan and Mike Fink among the stars. And that's what you'll find. From the enchantment of page one onward, the book reads like one of those compendia of myth and legend on which we all cut our literary teeth. Where Resnick has previously contented himself with single legends, centering on only one or a few of his trademark fabulous characters, here he invents them wholesale, endlessly and delightfully."

—*Analog*

SANTIAGO

A Myth of the Far Future

Mike Resnick

ARROW BOOKS

Arrow Books Limited
62-65 Chandos Place, London WC2N 4NW

An imprint of Century Hutchinson Limited

London Melbourne Sydney Auckland
Johannesburg and agencies throughout
the world

First published in Great Britain 1986
© Mike Resnick 1986

Printed and bound in Great Britain by
Anchor Brendon Limited, Tiptree, Essex

ISBN 0 09 944600 6

To Carol, as always

And to my agent, Eleanor Wood,
For advice, encouragement, and money

Table of Contents

PROLOGUE

They say his father was a comet and his mother a cosmic wind, that he juggles planets as if they were feathers and wrestles with black holes just to work up an appetite. They say he never sleeps, and that his eyes burn brighter than a nova, and that his shout can level mountains.

They call him Santiago.

Far out on the Galactic Rim, at the very edge of the Outer Frontier, there is a world called Silverblue. It is a water world, with just a handful of islands dotting the placid ocean that covers its surface. If you stand on the very largest island and look into the night sky, you can see almost all of the Milky Way, a huge twinkling river of stars that seems to flow through half the universe.

And if you stand on the western shore of the island during the daytime, with your back to the water, you will see a grass-covered knoll. Atop the knoll are seventeen white crosses, each bearing the name of a good man or woman who thought to colonize this gentle world.

And beneath each name is the same legend, repeated seventeen times:

Killed by Santiago.

Toward the core of the galaxy, where the stars press together so closely that night is as bright as day, there is a world called Valkyrie. It is an outpost world, a place of ramshackle Tradertowns filled with dingy bars and hotels and brothels, where the explorers and miners and traders of the

Inner Frontier congregate to eat and drink and embellish a few tall tales.

The largest of Valkyrie's Tradertowns, which isn't really very large, also has a postal station that stores subspace messages the way the postal stations of old used to store written mail. Sometimes the messages are held for as long as three or four years, and frequently they are routed even closer to the galactic core, but eventually most of them are picked up.

And in this postal station, there is a wall that is covered by the names and holographs of criminals who are currently thought to be on the Inner Frontier, which tends to make the station very popular with bounty hunters. There are always twenty outlaws displayed, never more, never less, and next to each name is a price. Some of these names remain in place for a week, some for a month, a handful for a year.

Only three names have ever been displayed for more than five years. Two of them are no longer there.

The third is Santiago, and there is no holograph of him.

On the colony world of Saint Joan, there is a native humanoid race known as the Swale. There are no longer any colonists; they have all departed.

Near the equator of Saint Joan, very close to where the colony once lived, there is a blackened swath of land almost ten miles long and half a mile wide, on which nothing will ever grow again. No colonist ever reported it, or if any of them did, the report has long since been misplaced by one of the Democracy's thirty billion bureaucrats—but if you go to Saint Joan and ask the Swale what caused the blackened patch of ground, they will cross themselves (for the colonists were a religious lot, and *very* evangelical) and tell you that it is the Mark of Santiago.

Even on the agricultural world of Ranchero, where there has never been a crime, not even a petty robbery, his name is not unknown. He is thought to be eleven feet three inches tall, with wild, unruly orange hair and immense black fangs that have dug into his lips and now protrude through them. And when youngsters misbehave, their parents have merely to hint at the number of naughty children Santiago has eaten for breakfast, and order is immediately restored.

*   *   *

Wandering minstrels sing songs about him on Minotaur and Theseus, the twin worlds that circle Sigma Draconis, and always he is portrayed as being exactly 217 years old, taller than a belltower, and broader than a barn, a hard-drinking, womanizing Prince of Thieves, who differs from Robin Hood (another of their favorites) primarily in that he takes from rich and poor alike and gives only to himself. His adventures are legion, ranging from his epic hand-to-hand struggle with a chlorine-breathing Gorgon to the morning he went down to hell and spat full in Satan's burning eye, and rarely is there a day that does not witness the addition of a few new stanzas to the ever-evolving "Ballad of Santiago."

And on Deluros VIII, the huge capital world of the race of Man, the nerve center of the Democracy, there are eleven governmental departments and 1,306 men and women charged with the task of finding and terminating Santiago. They doubt that Santiago is his given name, they suspect that some of the crimes attributed to him were committed by others, they are almost certain that somewhere in their files they possess his photograph or holograph but have not yet matched it with its proper identity—and that is the sum total of their knowledge of him.

Five hundred reports come to them daily, two thousand leads are followed up each year, munificent rewards have been posted on half a million worlds, agents are sent out armed with money and everything that money can buy, and still those eleven departments exist. They have outlived the last three administrations; they will continue to survive until their function has been fulfilled.

Silverblue, Valkyrie, Saint Joan, Ranchero, Minotaur, Theseus, Deluros VIII: interesting and evocative worlds all.

But an even more interesting world in the strange tapestry of Santiago's life is the outpost world of Keepsake, at the heart of the Inner Frontier; for Keepsake is the home, at least temporarily, of Sebastian Nightingale Cain, who dislikes his middle name, his profession, and his life—not necessarily in that order. He has fought what he believes to have been the good fight many times over, and he has never won. Not much excites his imagination anymore, and even less surprises him. He has no friends and few associates, nor does he seek any.

Sebastian Nightingale Cain is by almost every criterion a nondescript and unremarkable man, and yet our story must begin with him, for he is destined to play a major role in the saga of the man known only as Santiago. . . .

Part 1

The Songbird's Book

1.

Giles Sans Pitié is a spinning wheel,
With the eye of a hawk and a fist made of steel.
He'll drink a whole gallon while holding his breath,
And wherever he goes his companion is Death.

There never was a history written about the Inner Frontier,
so Black Orpheus took it upon himself to set one to music.
His name wasn't really Orpheus (though he *was* black). In
fact, rumor had it that he had been an aquaculturist back in
the Deluros system before he fell in love. The girl's name
was Eurydice, and he followed her out to the stars, and since
he had left all his property behind, he had nothing to give her
but his music, so he took the name of Black Orpheus and
spent most of his days composing love songs and sonnets to
her. Then she died, and he decided to stay on the Inner
Frontier, and he began writing an epic ballad about the traders
and hunters and outlaws and misfits that he came across. In
fact, you didn't officially stop being a tenderfoot or a tourist
until the day he added a stanza or two about you to the song.

Anyway, Giles Sans Pitié made quite an impression on
him, because he appears in nine different verses, which is an
awful lot when you're being the Homer for five hundred
worlds. Probably it was the steel hand that did it. No one knew
how he'd lost his real one, but he showed up on the Frontier
one day with a polished steel fist at the end of his left arm,
announced that he was the best bounty hunter ever born,
foaled, whelped, or hatched, and proceeded to prove that he
wasn't too far from wrong. Like most bounty hunters, he only

touched down on outpost worlds when he wasn't working, and like most bounty hunters, he had a pretty regular route that he followed. Which was how he came to be on Keepsake, in the Tradertown of Moritat, in Gentry's Emporium, pounding on the long wooden bar with his steel fist and demanding service.

Old Geronimo Gentry, who had spent thirty years prospecting the worlds of the Inner Frontier before he chucked it all and opened a tavern and whorehouse on Moritat, where he carefully sampled every product before offering it to the public, walked over with a fresh bottle of Altairian rum, then held it back as Giles Sans Pitié reached for it.

"Tab's gettin' pretty high," he commented meaningfully.

The bounty hunter slapped a wad of bills down on the bar.

"Maria Theresa dollars," noted Gentry, examining them approvingly and relinquishing the bottle. "Wherever'd you pick 'em up?"

"The Corvus system."

"Took care of a little business there, did you?" said Gentry, amused.

Giles Sans Pitié smiled humorlessly. "A little."

He reached inside his shirt and withdrew three Wanted posters of the Suliman brothers, which until that morning had been on the post office wall. Each poster had a large red X scratched across it.

"All three of 'em?"

The bounty hunter nodded.

"You shoot 'em, or did you use *that*?" asked Gentry, pointing toward Giles Sans Pitié's steel fist.

"Yes."

"Yes *what*?"

Giles Sans Pitié held up his metal hand. "Yes, I shot them or I used this."

Gentry shrugged. "Goin' out again soon?"

"In the next few days."

"Where to this time?"

"That's nobody's business but mine," said the bounty hunter.

"Just thought I might offer some friendly advice," said Gentry.

"Such as?"

"If you're thinking of going to Praeteep Four, forget it. The Songbird just got back from there."

"You mean Cain?"

Gentry nodded. "Had a lot of money, so I'd have to guess that he found what he went looking for."

The bounty hunter frowned. "I'm going to have to have a little talk with him," he said. "The Praeteep system's got a Keep Out sign posted on it."

"Oh?" said Gentry. "Since when?"

"Since I put it up," said Giles Sans Pitié firmly. "And I won't have some rival headhunter doing his poaching there and picking it clean." He paused. "Where can I find him?"

"Right here."

Giles Sans Pitié looked around the room. A silver-haired gambler on a winning streak, decked out in bright new clothes made from some glittering metallic fabric, stood at the far end of the bar; a young woman with melancholy eyes sat alone at a table in the corner; and scattered around the large, dimly lit tavern were some two dozen other men and women, in pairs and groups, some conversing in low tones, others sitting in silence.

"I don't see him," announced the bounty hunter.

"It's early yet," replied Gentry. "He'll be along."

"What makes you think so?"

"I've got the only booze and the only sportin' ladies in Moritat. Where do *you* think he's gonna go?"

"There are a lot of worlds out there."

"True," admitted Gentry. "But people get tired of worlds after a while. Ask *me*—I know."

"Then what are you doing on the Frontier?"

"People get tired of people, too. There's a lot less of 'em out here—and I got me my fancy ladies to cheer me up if ever I get to feelin' lonely." He paused. " 'Course, if you want to hear the story of my life, you're gonna have to buy a couple of bottles of my best drinkin' stuff. Then you and me, we'll mosey on out to one of the back rooms and I'll start with chapter one."

The bounty hunter reached out for the bottle. "I think I can live without it," he said.

"You'll be missing out on one helluva good story," said Gentry. "I done a lot of interesting things. Seen sights even a killer like you ain't likely ever to see."

"Some other time."

"Your loss," said Gentry with a shrug. "You gonna want a glass with that?"

"Not necessary," said Giles Sans Pitié, lifting the bottle and taking a long swallow. When he was through, he wiped his mouth with the back of his hand. "How long before he gets here?"

"You got time for a quick one, if that's what you mean," said Gentry. "Just give me a minute to check and see which of my frail flowers ain't working this minute." Suddenly he turned to the doorway. "Whoops! Here he is now. Guess you'll have to go loveless a little longer." He waved his hand. "How're you doin', Songbird?"

The tall, lean man, his face angular and almost gaunt, his eyes dark and world-weary, approached the bar. His jacket and pants were a nondescript brown, their many pockets filled with shapeless bulges that could mean almost anything on the Frontier. Only his boots stood out, not because they were new, but rather because they were so demonstrably old, obviously carefully tended yet unable to hold a polish.

"My name's Cain," said the newcomer. "You know that."

"Well, it ain't what they call you these days."

"It's what *you'll* call me if you want my business," replied Cain.

"But Black Orpheus, now, he's got you all written up as the Songbird," persisted Gentry.

"I don't sing, I'm not a bird, and I don't much care what some half-baked folksinger writes about me."

Gentry shrugged. "Have it your way—and while we're on the subject, what else'll you have?"

"He'll have Altairian rum, like me," interjected Giles Sans Pitié.

"I will?" asked Cain, turning to him.

"My treat." The bounty hunter held up his bottle. "Come on over to a table and join me, Sebastian Cain."

Cain watched him walk across the room for a moment, then shrugged and followed him.

"I hear you had pretty good luck on Praeteep Four," said Giles Sans Pitié when both men had seated themselves.

"Luck had nothing to do with it," replied Cain, leaning back comfortably on his chair. "I understand you didn't do too badly yourself."

"Not so. I had to cheat."

"I don't think I follow you."

"I had to shoot the third one." Giles Sans Pitié held up his steel fist. "I like to take them with *this*." He paused. "Did your man give you much trouble?"

"Some," said Cain noncommittally.

"Have to chase him far?"

"A bit."

"You're sure not the most expansive raconteur I've ever run across," chuckled Giles Sans Pitié.

Cain shrugged. "Talk is cheap."

"Not always. Suliman Hari offered me thirty thousand credits to let him live."

"And?"

"I thanked him for his offer, explained that the price on his head was up to fifty thousand, and gave him a faceful of metal."

"And of course you didn't then take thirty thousand credits off his body without reporting it," said Cain sardonically.

Giles Sans Pitié frowned. "The son of a bitch only had two thousand on him," he growled righteously.

"I guess there's just no honor among thieves."

"None. I can't get over the bastard lying to me!" He paused. "So tell me, Cain—who will you be going out after next?"

Cain smiled. "Professional secret. You know better than to ask."

"True," agreed Giles Sans Pitié. "But everyone's allowed a breach of etiquette now and then. For example, you know better than to make a kill in the Praeteep system, but you did it anyway."

"The man I was hunting went there," replied Cain calmly. "No disrespect intended, but I wasn't going to let four months' work go down the drain just because you think you own the deed to an entire solar system."

"I *opened* that system," said Giles Sans Pitié. "Named every planet in it." He paused. "Still, it's an acceptable answer. I forgive you your trespass."

"I don't recall asking for absolution," said Cain.

"Just the same, it's freely given. *This* time," he added ominously. "But it would be a good idea for you to remember that there are rules out here on the Frontier."

"Oh? I hadn't noticed any."

"Nevertheless, they exist—and they're made by the people who can enforce them."

"I'll keep it in mind."

"See that you do."

"Or you'll brain me with your metal hand?" asked Cain.

"It's a possibility."

Cain smiled.

"What's so funny?" demanded Giles Sans Pitié.

"You're a bounty hunter."

"So?"

"Bounty hunters don't kill people for free. Who's going to pay you to kill me?"

"I've got to protect what's mine," replied Giles Sans Pitié seriously. "I just want to be sure that we understand each other: if you go poaching on my territory again, we're going to come to blows." He slammed his metal hand down on the table, putting a large dent in it. "Mine are usually harder."

"I imagine they are," said Cain.

"Then you'll steer clear of Praeteep?"

"I'm not aware of any pressing business engagements there."

"That's not exactly the answer I was looking for."

"I'd suggest you settle for it," said Cain. "It's the best you're going to get."

Giles Sans Pitié stared at him for a moment, then shrugged. "It could be years before anyone hides there again, maybe even longer. I suppose there's no law that says we can't behave cordially in the meantime."

"I'm all for living in peace with my fellow man," said Cain agreeably.

Giles Sans Pitié looked amused. "You picked a mighty strange profession for a man who feels that way."

"Perhaps."

"Well, shall we talk?"

"What about?"

"What about?" repeated Giles Sans Pitié mockingly. "What do two bounty hunters *ever* talk about when they meet over a bottle of rum?"

And so they fell to discussing Santiago.

They spoke of the worlds where he was most recently thought to have been, and the crimes he was most recently

thought to have committed. Both had heard the rumor that he
had robbed a mining colony on Bemor VIII; both discounted
it. Both also had heard that a caravan of unmanned cargo
ships had been plundered in the Antares region; Cain thought
it might well be the work of Santiago, while his companion
felt he was far more likely to have been on Doradus IV at the
time, masterminding a triple assassination. They exchanged
information about the planets they themselves had been to
without finding any trace of him, and of the other bounty
hunters they had encountered who had added still more planets to the list.

"Who's after him now?" asked Giles Sans Pitié when their
tallies had been completed.

"Everyone."

"I mean, who most recently?"

"I hear the Angel has moved into the area," answered
Cain.

"What makes you think he's come for Santiago?"

Cain merely stared at him.

"Stupid remark," said Giles Sans Pitié. "Forget I made
it." He paused. "The Angel's supposed to be just about the
best."

"So they say."

"I thought he worked the Outer Frontier, somewhere way
out on the Rim."

Cain nodded. "I guess he decided Santiago's not there."

"I can name you a million places Santiago *isn't*," said
Giles Sans Pitié. "Why do you suppose he thinks he's on the
Inner Frontier?"

Cain shrugged.

"Do you think he's got a source?" persisted Giles Sans
Pitié.

"Anything's possible."

"It's more than possible," he said after a moment's consideration. "He wouldn't move his base of operations halfway across the galaxy if he didn't have hard information.
What planet is he working out of?"

"How many worlds are there out there?" replied Cain with
a shrug. "Take your choice."

Giles Sans Pitié frowned. "Still, he might know something
worth listening to."

"What makes you think he'll talk to you, even if you find him?"

"Because the one thing bounty hunters never lie about is Santiago; you know that. As long as he stays alive, he makes all of us look bad."

"Maybe the Angel does things differently where he comes from," suggested Cain.

"Then I'll just have to explain the ground rules to him," said Giles Sans Pitié.

"I wish you luck."

"Interested in throwing in with me until we catch up with the Angel?"

"I work alone," said Cain.

"Just as well," said Giles Sans Pitié, suddenly remembering his rum and taking a long swallow of it. "Where did you hear about him?"

"In the Meritonia system."

"I think I'll head out that way later this week," said Giles Sans Pitié, rising to his feet. "It's been an interesting conversation, Cain."

"Thanks for the rum," said Cain wryly, staring at the empty bottle.

"Any time," laughed his companion. "And you *will* make an effort to keep out of the Praeteep system from now on, won't you?" He flexed his steel fist. "I'd hate to have to give you an object lesson about trespassing."

"Would you?"

"Not really," was the frank answer.

Cain made no reply, and a moment later Giles San Pitié placed the empty bottle on the bar, left enough money to cover another one he ordered for Cain, promised Gentry he'd be back to sample some nonalcoholic wares later in the evening, and walked out into the hot, humid night air of Moritat in search of some dinner.

Gentry finished serving the girl with the melancholy eyes, then brought the bottle over to Cain's table.

"What is it?" asked Cain, staring at the clear liquid.

"Something they brew out Altair way," replied the old man. "Tastes kind of like gin."

"I don't like gin."

"I know," replied Gentry with a chuckle. "That's why

I'm just dead certain you're gonna invite me to sit down with you and help you drink it.''

Cain sighed. "Have a seat, old man."

"Thank you. Don't mind if I do." He lowered himself carefully to a chair, uncorked the bottle, and took a swallow. "Good stuff, if I say so myself."

"You could save a hell of a lot of money by not supplying glasses," remarked Cain. "Nobody around here seems to use them."

"Savin' money ain't one of my problems," replied Gentry. "And from what I hear, makin' it ain't one of yours."

Cain said nothing, and the old man took another swallow and continued speaking.

"Did old Giles Without Pity warn you off the Praeteep system?" he asked.

Cain nodded.

"Gonna pay him any heed?"

"Until the next time I have business there," replied Cain.

The old man laughed. "Good for you, Songbird! Old Steelfist is gettin' a little big for his britches these days."

"I'm getting tired of telling you what my name is," said Cain irritably.

"If you didn't want to be a legend, you shouldn't have come out here. Two hundred years from now that's the only name people'll know you by."

"Two hundred years from now I won't have to listen to them."

"Besides," continued Gentry, "Songbird ain't on any Wanted posters. I seen Sebastian Cain on a flock of 'em."

"That was a long time ago."

"Don't go gettin' defensive about it," chuckled the old man. "I seen posters on just about all you bounty hunters at one time or another. Ain't no skin off my ass. Hell, if Santiago himself walked in the door and asked for one of my sportin' gals, I'd trot him out the prettiest one I've got."

"For all you know, he already has," remarked Cain.

"Not a chance," said Gentry. "He ain't that hard to spot."

"Eleven feet three inches, with orange hair?" asked Cain with an amused smile.

"You start huntin' for a man who looks like *that* and you're going to be out here a long, long time."

"What do *you* think he looks like?"

The old man took a small swallow from the bottle.

"Don't know," he admitted. "Do know one thing, though. Know he's got a scar shaped like this"—he traced a crooked S on the table—"on the back of his right hand."

"Sure he does."

"Truth!" said the old man vigorously. "I know a man who saw him."

"Nobody's seen him," replied Cain. "Or at least, nobody who's seen him knew it was him."

"That's all *you* know about it," said Gentry. "Man I used to run with spent a couple of weeks in jail with him."

Cain looked bored. "Santiago's never been arrested. If he had been, we'd *all* know what he looked like."

"They didn't know it was him."

"Then how come your friend knew?"

" 'Cause Santiago's gang broke him out, and one of 'em called him by name."

"Bunk."

"Here I am, offerin' to do you a favor, and you turn your nose up at it," said Gentry. "Damned good thing for you I'm an old man who ain't got the wherewithall to give you a thrashing for insulting me like that."

"What favor?"

"I thought maybe you might be interested in knowing who my friend is and where you can find him."

"There are half a dozen bounty hunters who frequent this place," said Cain. "Why give it to me?"

"Well, now, *give* ain't exactly the term I had in mind," answered Gentry with a grin. "Name like that, name of a man who actually spent some time with Santiago, it ought to be worth a little something now, shouldn't it?"

"Maybe."

There was a momentary silence.

"I didn't hear no cash offer yet."

"Let's get back to my question," said Cain. "Why *me*?"

"Oh, it ain't just you," said Gentry. "Sold it to Barnaby Wheeler a couple of months ago, but I heard on the grapevine that he got killed chasing down some fugitive or other. And I offered it to Peacemaker MacDougal just last week, but he didn't want to come up with no money. And I'll see if I can't tempt old Steelfist with it before he takes advantage of one of my poor innocents tonight.'' He smiled. ''I got to be fair to *all* my customers.''

''People have been after Santiago for thirty years or more,'' said Cain. ''If you have any information worth selling, why did you wait until now to put it on the market?''

''I ain't got anything against Santiago,'' said the old man. ''He ain't ever done me any harm. Besides, the longer he stays free, the longer you guys'll stay on the Frontier lookin' for him, and the longer you stay out here, the more money you'll spend at Gentry's Emporium.''

''Then what caused this change of heart?''

''Hear tell the Angel has moved in. Wouldn't want no outsider picking up the bounty fee.''

''What makes you think he will?'' asked Cain.

''You know what they say about him,'' replied Gentry. ''He's the best. I'll bet you Black Orpheus gives him a good twenty verses when he finally gets around to meetin' him. So,'' said the old man, taking yet another swig, ''I'm hedging my bets as best I can. The Angel collects that money, he'll be back on the Rim before he has a chance to spend it. But if *you* get it, you'll spend a goodly chunk of it on Keepsake.''

''If I don't retire.''

''Oh, you won't retire,'' said Gentry with assurance. ''Men like you and Sans Pitié and the Angel, you like killing too damned much to quit. It's in your blood, like wanderlust in a young buck.''

''I don't like killing,'' replied Cain.

''Gonna give me that bounty hunter guff about how you only kill people for money?'' said the old man with a sarcastic laugh.

''No.''

''That makes you the first honest one I've met. How many men did you kill for free before you found out there was gold in it—two? Three?''

''More than I hope you can imagine,'' replied Cain.

''Soldier?''

Cain paused before answering. ''I thought so once. I was wrong.''

''What the hell does *that* mean?''

''Never mind, old man.'' Suddenly Cain sat erect in his chair. ''All right—how much do you want for the name?''

"What kind of currency can you lay your hands on?"

"What kind do you want?"

"Credits'll do, I suppose," replied Gentry. "Though I'd be real interested in Bonaparte francs or Maria Theresa dollars if you got any."

"I haven't seen a Bonaparte franc in ten years," said Cain. "I don't think they're in circulation anymore."

"I hear tell they're still using 'em in the Binder system."

"Let's make it credits."

The old man did a quick mental calculation. "I think ten thousand would do me just fine."

"For the name of a man who might or might not have seen Santiago ten or twenty years ago?" Cain shook his head. "That's too much."

"Not for a man like you," said Gentry. "I saw the poster for the body you brought in. I know how much you got for it."

"And what if this man is dead, or if it turns out he didn't see Santiago after all?"

"Then you got a free pass to fertilize my flowers for a full month."

"I visited your garden last night," said Cain. "It needs weeding."

"What are you quibbling about?" demanded Gentry. "How long have you been on the Frontier, Cain?"

"Eleven years."

"In all that time, have you ever met anyone who's seen Santiago? Here I am offering you what you ain't never found before, for maybe a tenth of what you just picked up on Praeteep, and you're haggling like some Dabih fur trader! If you're gonna just sit there and insult the most beautiful blossoms on the Frontier and haggle with an old man who ain't got the stamina to haggle back, we ain't going to be able to do no business."

Cain stared at him for a moment, then spoke.

"I'll tell you what, old man. I'll give you twenty thousand."

"There's a catch," said Gentry suspiciously.

"There's a condition," replied Cain. "You don't supply the name to anyone else."

Gentry frowned. "Ever?"

"For six months."

"Make it four."

"Deal," said Cain. "And if you're lying, may God have more mercy on your soul than *I* will."

"Ain't got no reason to lie. Only two more of you fellers due in here in the next four months, which means one of 'em's probably dead, and there's only a fifty-fifty chance the other'd come up with the money. Not everyone makes out as well as you and Sans Pitié."

"All right. Where do I find this man?"

"I ain't seen no money yet."

Cain pulled out a sheaf of bills, peeled off the top twenty, and placed them on the table. Gentry picked them up one at a time, held each up to the light, and finally nodded his head and placed them in his pocket.

"Ever hear of a world named Port Étrange?"

Cain shook his head. "Where is it?"

"It's the seventh planet in the Bellermaine system. That's where he'll be."

"And his name?"

"Stern."

"How do I locate him?"

"Just pass the word you're looking for him. *He'll* find *you.*"

"What's he like?" asked Cain.

"A real sweet feller, once you get used to a couple of his little peculiarities."

"Such as?"

"Well, he drinks too much and he cheats at cards, and he ain't real fond of people or animals or aliens, and he out-and-out hates priests and women, and he's been known to have an occasional disagreement with the constabularies. But taken all in all, he's no worse than most that you find out here, and probably better'n some."

"Should I use your name?"

"It ought to get him to sit up and take notice," said Gentry. "When are you planning on leaving?"

"Tonight," said Cain, getting to his feet.

"Damn!" said Gentry. "If I'd of known you were that anxious, I could've held out for thirty!"

"I'm not anxious. I just don't have any reason to stay here."

"I got seven absolutely splendid reasons, each and every

one personally selected and trained by Moritat's very favorite son, namely me.''

"Maybe next time around."

"You got something better to spend it on?"

"That depends on whether you told me the truth or not," said Cain, walking to the door. Suddenly he stopped and turned to Gentry. "By the way, I assume your friend Stern is going to want to be paid for this?"

"I imagine so. Man sells his soul to the devil, he spends the rest of his life trying to stockpile enough money to buy it back." Gentry chuckled with amusement. "Have fun, Songbird."

"That's not my name."

"Tell you what," said Gentry. "You bring in the head of Santiago, and I'll hold a gun to old Orpheus until he gets it right."

"You've got yourself a deal," promised Cain.

2.

He's Jonathan Jeremy Jacobar Stern,
He's got lust in his heart, and money to burn;
He's too old to change, and too wild to learn,
Is Jonathan Jeremy Jacobar Stern.

They say that Black Orpheus caught Stern on an off day, that in point of fact Stern never stopped changing and learning, until he'd changed so much that nobody knew him any longer. He began life as the son of a miner and a whore, and before he was done he'd set himself up as king of the Bellermaine system. In between, he learned how to gamble and did a pretty fair job of it; he learned how to steal and became more than proficient; he learned how to kill and did a bit of bounty hunting on the side; and somewhere along the way he learned the most important lesson of all, which was that a king with no heirs had better never turn his back on anybody.

Nobody knew why he hated priests; rumor had it that the first time he'd gone to jail it was a priest who turned him in. Another legend held that he'd once trusted a couple of priests to keep an eye on his holdings while he was fleeing from the authorities, and when he'd finally come back there'd been nothing waiting for him but a note telling him to repent.

It wasn't all that difficult to figure out why he hated women. He grew up in a whorehouse, and the women he met once he went out on his own weren't much different from the ones he'd known all his life. He was a man of enormous appetites who couldn't leave them alone and couldn't con-

vince himself that their interest in him wasn't as cold and
calculating as his interest in them.

A lot of people whispered that that was the real reason he'd
set up shop on Port Étrange, that since he couldn't control his
passion for women he'd decided to do without them and had
hunted up a world with a humanoid race that willingly allowed him to commit terrible crimes of pleasure for which
nobody had yet created any words.

Port Étrange itself had a long and varied history. Originally
a mining world, it had since been a glittering vacation spa,
then a low-security penal colony, and finally a deserted ghost
world. Then Stern had moved in, set up headquarters in a
once luxurious hotel, and turned a small section of the human
habitation into a Tradertown, while allowing the remainder to
linger in a state of disrepair and decay. Despite reasonably
fertile fields which sustained the native population, the citizens of the Tradertown imported all their food and drink from
a pair of nearby agricultural colonies. When the men began
outnumbering the women, they imported the latter, too, until
Stern put a stop to it.

All this Cain learned during his first hour on Port Étrange.
He had landed his ship at the local spaceport—only huge
worlds like Deluros VIII and Lodin XI possessed orbiting
hangars and shuttle service for planetbound travelers—and
rented a room at the larger of the two functioning hotels, then
descended to the ground-floor tavern he'd spotted on the way
in.

It was crowded, and despite the chrome tables and hand-
crafted chairs—leftovers from the hotel's halcyon days of
glory—it felt as dingy and seamy as any other Tradertown
bar. The only chair available was at a small table that was
occupied by a short, slender man who sported a shock of
unruly red hair.

"Mind if I sit down?" asked Cain.

"Be my guest," said the man. He stared at Cain. "You
new around here?"

"Yes. I just got in." Cain glanced around the room. "I'm
looking for somebody. I wonder if you can point him out to
me?"

"He's not here now."

"You don't know who I'm looking for," said Cain.

"Well, if it isn't Jonathan Stern, we've got a hell of a news story breaking here," said the man with a chuckle. "He's the only person anyone ever comes to Port Étrange to see."

"It's Stern," said Cain.

"Well, I suppose I can pass the word. You got a name?"

"Cain. Tell him Geronimo Gentry sent me."

"Pleased to meet you, Cain," said the man, extending a lean white hand. "I'm Terwilliger. Halfpenny Terwilliger," he added as if the name was expected to mean something. He watched Cain for a reaction, discerned none, and got up. "Back in a minute."

Terwilliger walked over to the bar, said something to the bartender, and then returned to the table.

"Okay," he said. "He knows you're here."

"When can I see him?"

"When he's ready."

"How soon will that be?"

Halfpenny Terwilliger laughed. "That all depends. Does he owe Gentry money?"

"I don't think so."

"Then it'll probably be sooner rather than later." He pulled out a deck of cards. "Care for a little game of chance while you're waiting?"

"I'd rather have a little information about Stern."

"I don't doubt it," said Terwilliger. "Tell you what. You bet with money, I'll bet with pieces of Stern's life. I'll match every credit with a story."

"Why don't I just pay you twenty credits for what I want to know and be done with it?" suggested Cain.

"Because I'm a gambler, not a salesman," came the answer.

"At a credit a bet, you're not likely to become a very rich one," observed Cain.

Terwilliger smiled. "I got into my first card game with one New Scotland halfpenny. I was worth two million pounds before it was over. That's how I got my name." He paused. "Of course, I lost it all the next week, but still, it was fun while it lasted, and no one else ever had a run of luck like that one. Been trying to do it again ever since."

"How long ago was that?"

"Oh, maybe a dozen years," said Terwilliger with another smile. "I still remember how it felt, though—like the first time I was ever with a woman, except that it lasted longer: six days and five nights. That's why I always start small—out of respect for times past. If you want to raise the stakes later, we can.''

"If I raise the stakes, what can you bet to match it?"

Terwilliger scratched his head. "Well, I suppose I can start betting rumors instead of facts. They're a lot more interesting, anyway—especially if they're about the *fali*."

"What's a *fali*?" asked Cain.

"It's what the natives call themselves. I don't suppose it's the best-kept secret in the galaxy that our friend Stern's got a couple of tastes that are just a bit out of the ordinary."

"Let's stick to facts for the time being," said Cain. He nodded toward the cards. "It's your deal."

They played and talked for more than an hour, at the end of which Cain knew a little bit more about Stern, and Terwilliger was some forty credits richer.

"You know, you still haven't told me why you want to see him," remarked the gambler.

"I need some information."

"Who do you plan to kill?" asked Terwilliger pleasantly.

"What makes you think I want to kill anyone?"

"You've got that look about you. I'm a gambler, remember? My job is reading faces. Your face says you're a bounty hunter."

"What if I told you I was a journalist?" asked Cain.

"I'd tell you I believed you," replied Terwilliger. "I don't want no bounty hunter getting mad at me."

Cain laughed. "Can you tell anything from Stern's face?"

"Just that he's been with the *fali* too long. Not much human left in it."

"What do these *fali* look like?" asked Cain.

"Either pretty good or pretty strange, depending."

"Depending on what?"

"On how long you've been alone," answered Terwilliger.

"You still haven't told me what they look like."

Terwilliger grinned and ruffled the cards. "Shall we up the stakes a little?"

Cain shook his head. "They're not worth more to me than Stern is."

"They might be, when I tell you what they do."

"Hearsay?"

"Experience."

Cain cocked an eyebrow. "I thought you disapproved of them."

"Anybody's allowed to try something new once or twice, just to get the feel of it," explained Terwilliger. "What I object to is addiction, not experimentation."

"I don't plan to be here long enough to do either," said Cain. "You can put the cards away."

"Oh, we can always find a little something to wager about," said Terwilliger. "For fifty credits a hand, I could tell you where to find the Suliman brothers."

"You're too late. They were taken a week ago."

"All three?"

Cain nodded.

"Damn!" said Terwilliger. "Well, for a hundred, I might tell you about some competition that's moved into the area."

"I know about the Angel."

"News sure travels fast," commented Terwilliger ruefully.

"Tell you what," said Cain. "I'll play for a thousand a hand if you have any information about Santiago."

"You and five hundred other guys." The gambler shook his head. "It beats me how he can still be free after all these years with so many people looking for him."

Just then the bartender walked across the room and came to a stop in front of their table.

"Are you Cain?" he asked.

"Yes."

"He wants you."

"Where do I find him?" asked Cain.

"I'll show you the way," offered Terwilliger.

The bartender nodded and returned to his duties.

"Follow me," said the gambler, getting to his feet.

Cain stood up and left a few bills on the table.

They walked out through a side door, across the dusty road that had once been a major thoroughfare, and into the smaller of Port Étrange's two functioning hotels. Terwilliger led him through a lobby that had once been quite elegant but was now showing the signs of age and neglect: sleek chrome pillars were now tarnished, the ever-changing choreopattern of colored lights was out of synch with the atonal music, the front door remained dilated for almost a full minute after they passed through it.

They approached a bank of elevators and walked to the last one in line. Terwilliger summoned it with a low command.

"This'll take you right to him," he announced.

"Has he got a room number?"

"He's got the whole damned floor. Take one step out and you're in the middle of his parlor."

"Thanks," said Cain, stepping into the elevator as it arrived. As the doors closed behind him he realized that he didn't know the floor number, but then the elevator began ascending swiftly and he decided that it only went to one floor.

When it came to a stop, he emerged into a palatial penthouse. It was fully fifty feet by sixty, and filled to overflowing with objets d'art gathered—or plundered—from all across the galaxy. In the center of the room was a sunken circular tub with platinum fixtures, and sitting in the steaming water was an emaciated man with sunken cheeks and dark, watery eyes. His narrow arms were sprawled over the edges of the tub, and Cain noticed that his fingers were covered by truly magnificent rings. He smoked a large cigar that had somehow avoided becoming waterlogged.

Standing on each side of the tub were a pair of humanoid aliens, both obviously female. Their skins, covered with a slick secretion that may or may not have been natural, glistened under the lights of the apartment. Their arms seemed supple and boneless, their legs slender and strangely jointed. Each had a round, expressive face, with a generous, very red triangular mouth and pink eyes that were little more than angular slits. Both were nude and were devoid of any body hair. They had no breasts, but their genitalia, thus exposed, seemed close to human. There was a supple, alien grace to them, which Cain found fascinating and mildly repugnant. Neither of them seemed to notice him at all.

"You're staring, Mr. Cain," said the man in the tub.

"I'm sorry," said Cain. "I had heard about the *fali*, but I hadn't seen them before."

"Nice, useful pets," said the man, reaching up and giving a friendly pat to a bare *fali* buttock. "About as bright as a potted plant, but *very* pleasant in their way." He took a puff of his cigar. "I understand that you wish to see me."

"If you're Stern."

"Jonathan Jeremy Jacobar Stern, at your service," he said. "Is this going to take long?"

"I hope not."

"What a shame," he said with mock regret. "If it was, I'd invite you to join me. There is absolutely nothing like sitting in warm water to relax a man and help him shed the cares of the day. I'll be with you in just a moment." He turned to one of the *fali* and extended his arm. "Give me a boost up, my pretty."

She reached down, grabbed his hand, and pulled him to his feet, while her companion walked to a closet and returned shortly with a robe.

"Thank you," he said, slipping the robe on. "Now I want both of you to stand over there and not bother us for a while." He pointed to a spot near the farthest wall, and both *fali* immediately walked over to it and stood motionless.

"They seem very obedient," remarked Cain as Stern led him to a grouping of chairs and couches.

"Obedient and docile," agreed Stern, sprawling on a couch and staring at them with unconcealed desire.

"That oil on their skins—is it normal?"

"Why should you suppose that it isn't?"

Cain shrugged. "It just seems rather unusual."

"It is," replied Stern, smiling at the *fali*. "It smells like the finest perfume." He turned to Cain. "Go over and experience it for yourself."

"I'll take your word for it."

"As you wish," said Stern with a shrug. "It *feels* exquisite, as well—soft and sensual. Actually, I'm convinced that it's a secondary sexual characteristic. It doesn't do much for Men, of course," he added with marked insincerity, "but I imagine it drives their boyfriends right out of their minds. Seductive odor, sensual feel." He stared admiringly at them again. "It makes them look like a pair of alien mermaids emerging from the water." Suddenly he tore his gaze away from them and turned back to Cain. "So Geronimo Gentry sent you here?"

"Yes."

"I thought he'd be dead by now."

"Not quite," said Cain, finally taking a seat.

"How is he getting along?"

"He's got a bar and whorehouse out on Keepsake," replied Cain. "I guess he's doing all right. Talks too much, though."

"He always did." Stern paused. "Why did he send you here?"

"He told me that you might have some information I need."

"Very likely I do. I know an inordinate number of things. Did he also tell you that I'm not a charitable institution?"

"If he hadn't, I would have figured it out after seeing some of your trinkets," said Cain, nodding toward a number of alien artifacts that were prominently displayed.

"I'm a collector," said Stern with a broad smile.

"So I gathered."

"You haven't yet told me what business you're in, Mr. Cain."

"I'm a collector, too," replied Cain.

"Really?" said Stern, suddenly more interested. "And what is it that you collect?"

"People."

"There's a good market for them," said Stern. "But unlike *my* collection, they don't increase in value."

"There's one who does."

"So you want to know about Santiago." It was not a question.

Cain nodded. "That's what I'm here for. You're the only person who's seen him."

Stern laughed in amusement. "His organization spans the entire galaxy. Don't you think any of *them* ever see him?"

"Then let me amend my statement," said Cain. "You're the only person *I* know who's seen him."

"That's probably true," agreed Stern pleasantly. His cigar went out and he snapped his fingers. One of the *fali* immediately came over with a lighter and relit it. "That's my girl," he said, giving her boneless hand an affectionate squeeze. She wriggled all over with delight like a puppy, then returned to her position across the room. "A wonderful pet," commented Stern. "Faithful, adoring, and totally unable to utter a sound—three qualities I never found in any woman of my acquaintance." He paused and stared fondly at her. "What a sweet, mindless little thing she is! But back to business, Mr. Cain. You wish to talk about Santiago."

"That's right."

"You are prepared to pay, of course?"

Cain nodded.

"There is an old saying, Mr. Cain, that talk is cheap. I hope you do not believe in it."

"I believe in paying for value received," replied Cain.

"Excellent! You're a man after my own heart."

"Really?" said Cain dryly. "I would have been willing to bet that not a single thing in this apartment had been paid for."

"They have *all* been paid for, Mr. Cain," said Stern with an amused smile. "Not with money, perhaps, but with human grief and suffering and even human life. A much higher price, wouldn't you say?"

"It depends on who was doing the paying," replied Cain.

"Nobody very important," said Stern with a shrug. "Oh, they probably all had wives and husbands and children, to be sure, but they were merely spear-carriers in my own saga, which is of course the only one that matters to me. Certainly you must share my point of view, since the taking of lives is your business."

"I value the lives I take a little more highly than you do," said Cain. "So does the government."

"And here we are, back to discussing value and money once more," said Stern. "I think I shall charge you fifteen thousand credits to continue our conversation, Mr. Cain."

"For that, I want more than a physical description of a man you haven't seen in fifteen or twenty years," replied Cain. "I want the name and location of the jail, I want to know when you were incarcerated, and I want the name Santiago was using at the time."

"But of course!" said Stern. "Do I strike you as a man who would withhold information, Mr. Cain?"

"I don't know," said Cain. "Are you?"

"Perish the thought," said Stern.

"How comforting to know that."

"I'm so glad that we understand each other, Mr. Cain. May I first see, as we say in the trade, the color of your money?"

Cain pulled out his wallet, counted off the appropriate amount, and handed it over.

"I realize that absolutely no one uses cash anymore in the heart of the Democracy," said Stern, "but it has such a nice feel to it that I'm glad we still indulge ourselves out here in the extremities.'' He quickly counted the bills, then signaled to a *fali*, who came over and took them from him.

''Hold these for me, my pretty,'' he said, then nodded his head and watched her as she walked back to her position with an inhuman grace. ''Lovely things!'' he murmured. ''Absolutely lovely!''

''We were talking about Santiago. . . .''

''Indeed we were,'' said Stern, turning reluctantly from the *fali* and facing Cain once again. ''I promise to give it my full attention. For fifteen thousand credits, you deserve no less.''

''My feelings precisely.''

''Now, where shall I begin? At the beginning, of course. I was serving a certain amount of time in durance vile on the outpost world of Kalami Three for some imagined infringement of the local laws or customs.''

''Robbery?'' suggested Cain.

''Receiving stolen goods and attempted murder, in point of fact,'' replied Stern with no hint of regret. ''At any rate, the only other prisoner at the time was a man who went under the name of Gregory William Penn. He was between forty and fifty years of age, he stood about six feet four inches tall, he was heavyset without being fat, his hair was black and his eyes brown, his face was clean-shaven. He spoke at least six alien languages—or so he informed me. I, myself, speak none, nor''—he smiled at the *fali*—''have I ever had any need to. On the back of his right hand he bore an S-shaped scar some two inches long. He seemed, overall, a pleasant and intelligent man. He didn't speak about himself or his past at all, but he proved to be an excellent chess player with a set that we borrowed from our captors.''

''How do you know it was Santiago?''

''We had shared the hospitality of the Kalami jail for eleven days when suddenly five armed men broke in, subdued and bound the individual charged with our care, and set my fellow prisoner free. They were very thorough about wiping the prison's computer clean, and I later found out they had done the same over in the courtroom. Then, just as they were leaving, one of them called him Santiago.''

''If that's your whole story, I want my money back,'' said Cain. ''There's probably a thousand petty crooks on the Frontier who would like people to think they're Santiago—

and if the prison records have been destroyed, you can't even prove that this one existed, let alone that he was who he said he was."

"Be patient, Mr. Cain," said Stern easily. "There's more."

"There'd damned well better be. How long ago did this little incident take place?"

"Seventeen Galactic Standard years. I bribed my way out about six months later."

"I understand that you've done some bounty hunting in your time," said Cain. "Why didn't you go after him?"

"We all have our obsessions, Mr. Cain," replied Stern. "Yours is obviously chasing criminals all across the galaxy. Mine, I soon discovered, lay in quite a different direction."

"All right. Go on."

"Shortly thereafter I noticed a sudden dramatic increase in my business."

"Which business was that?" interrupted Cain.

"I like to think of it as my wholesale redistribution network."

"Fencing."

"Fencing," agreed Stern. "By the time I reached Port Étrange I had a pretty strong feeling that I was dealing with Santiago, but of course I was never so tactless as to ask."

"Who would you have asked?"

"I dealt primarily with a man named Duncan Black—a large man, who wore a patch over his left eye—but from time to time there were others."

"Nobody wears eyepatches," said Cain sharply.

"Black did."

"Why didn't he just get a new eye? I've got one: it sees better than the one I was born with."

"How should I know? Possibly he thought it made him look dashing and romantic." Stern paused. "At any rate, I continued to enjoy a very profitable arrangement. Then, seven years ago, I received a shipment of goods that eliminated any lingering doubts I may have had that I was indeed doing business with Santiago."

"And what was that?"

"Do you see that paperweight over there?" asked Stern, indicating what appeared to be a small gold bar on a nearby table.

"Yes."

"Why don't you examine it?"

Cain got up, walked over to the paperweight, and inspected it.

"It looks like gold bullion," he said.

"Pick it up and turn it over," suggested Stern.

It required both hands for Cain to lift it. When he did so, he noticed a nine-digit number burned into the bottom of it.

"That number corresponds to part of a gold shipment that Santiago stole from a navy convoy."

"The Epsilon Eridani robbery?" asked Cain.

Stern nodded. "I'm sure you can confirm the number through your various sources. The numbers had been eliminated from all the other bars, but somehow they missed that one—so I kept it for a souvenir, never knowing when it might be of some minor use to me." He smiled. "Anyway, it was then that I knew for sure that Black and the others were Santiago's agents."

"That still doesn't prove the man you saw in jail was Santiago," said Cain, putting the gold bar back down.

"I'm not finished," replied Stern. "About a year after I received the gold shipment, a smuggler named Kastartos, one of the agents I'd been dealing with, approached me with a fascinating proposition. Evidently he was displeased with his salary or his working conditions; at any rate, he had decided to turn Santiago in for the reward. Being a prudent man, he decided not to do so himself, but offered to split fifty-fifty with me if I would approach the authorities on his behalf. I questioned him further, and eventually he gave me a description of the man I had seen in the Kalami jail. There were a few discrepancies, as might be expected with the passage of eleven years, but it sounded like the same man, and when he described the scar on his right hand I was sure."

"And what did you do?"

"I was making a considerable amount of money from Santiago's trade, and I had no more desire to be the visible partner in this enterprise than Kastartos did. After all, not only would I have faced the threat of reprisal from Santiago's organization, but once word of such a betrayal got out, most of my other clients would have felt very uneasy about dealing with me as well," explained Stern. "So I followed the only reasonable course of action: I informed Duncan Black of his proposition, and let nature take its course." He shook his head. "Poor little man. I never saw him again."

"Did he tell you where to find Santiago?"

"I felt my longevity could best be served by not knowing the answer to that particular question."

"Do you still deal with him?"

"If I did, I wouldn't be parting with this information," said Stern. "But I haven't seen Duncan Black in almost three years now, and while it's always possible that Santiago is dealing with me through someone else, I very much doubt it."

"Where can I find Duncan Black?"

"If I knew that, this little chat would have cost you fifty thousand credits," replied Stern. "The only thing I can tell you is that during the time I did business with him, his ship bore a Bella Donna registry."

"Bella Donna?" repeated Cain. "I've never heard of it."

"It's an outpost world, the third planet of the Clovis system. I'm sure that it must be listed in your ship's computer." Stern paused. "Do you still want your money back, Mr. Cain?"

Cain stared at him. "Not unless I find out you've been lying."

"Why would I lie?" asked Stern. "I haven't been offworld for seven years now, and I have no intention of leaving in the foreseeable future. You would certainly have very little trouble finding me." He stood up. "Shall I assume that our conversation is over now?"

Cain nodded his head.

"Then you'll forgive me if I immerse myself once again?" He let his robe drop to the floor and walked over to the tub.

"Come, my lovelies," he crooned, and the two *fali* walked over and gently helped lower him into the water.

"I think I could do with a massage," he said. "Do you remember what I taught you?" The *fali* immediately entered the tub and began massaging his arms and torso with their long, sensitive, alien hands.

"Would you like to join us, Mr. Cain?" asked Stern, suddenly aware that Cain had not yet left the room. "It isn't an invitation I extend to many of my guests, and it certainly won't break my heart if you should decline, but I suppose it's the least I can do for a man who has just spent fifteen thousand credits for a useless tidbit of information."

"Useless?"

"The Angel is after Santiago now, or hadn't you heard?"

"I know."

"And yet you paid me anyway?" said Stern. "You must be a very efficient killer, Mr. Cain—or a very overconfident one." He moaned with pleasure as one of the *fali* began stroking his left thigh. "How many men have you actually killed?"

"Pay me fifteen thousand credits and I might just answer that question," said Cain.

Stern laughed hollowly in amusement.

"I'm afraid not, Mr. Cain. What you have done in the past may eventually find its way into Black Orpheus' songbook, as I myself have done, but you are simply another spear-carrier passing through my life—and an incredibly minor one at that."

"And them?" asked Cain, indicating the two *fali*.

"They represent my fall from Grace," said Stern with a smile. "Far more important than mere supporting players, I assure you. Someday I suppose I shall even give them names." He turned to one of them. "Gently, my pretty—gently." He took her hand and began guiding it gingerly.

Cain stared at the three of them for another few seconds, then turned and summoned the elevator. The sound of Stern's voice, trembling with eagerness, came to him as the doors were closing:

"Here, my pet. Lie back and let me show you how."

Cain descended to the main floor, walked out across the dusty thoroughfare, entered his own hotel, and shortly thereafter unlocked his room. He found Halfpenny Terwilliger sitting on his bed, playing solitaire.

"What the hell are you doing here?" he demanded as the door slid shut behind him.

"Waiting for you," replied the little gambler.

"How did you know this was my room?"

"I asked at the desk."

"And they gave you the combination to the lock?"

"In a manner of speaking," said Terwilliger. "Of course, they probably don't *know* they gave it to me."

"All right," said Cain. "Why are you waiting for me?"

"Because I know who you are now. You're the Songbird, right?"

"I'm Sebastian Cain."

"But people call you the Songbird?" persisted Terwilliger.

"Some people do."

"Good. Because if you're the Songbird, you ought to be leaving Port Étrange pretty soon in search of better pickings."

"Get to the point," said Cain.

"I'd like a ride."

"I don't take passengers."

"Let me word that a bit more strongly," said Terwilliger. "I *need* a ride. My life depends on it."

"Why?"

"It's a long and rather embarrassing story."

"Give me the gist of it," said Cain.

Terwilliger stared at him for a moment, then shrugged. "When I was in the Spinos system about four months ago, I passed two hundred thousand credits' worth of bad notes to ManMountain Bates."

"He's a gambler, isn't he?"

"A very large, ill-tempered one," said Terwilliger devoutly.

"I'd say that was an unwise thing to do."

"I *intended* to make them good. I was just indulging in a little deficit spending. Hell, the Democracy does it all the time." He paused. "But I just got word a few minutes ago that he's due to land on Port Étrange the day after tomorrow— and truth to tell, I'm a little bit short of what I owe him."

"How short?"

"Oh, not much."

"*How* short?" repeated Cain.

"About two hundred thousand credits, give or take a few," said Terwilliger with a sickly smile.

"I certainly don't envy you," commented Cain.

"I don't want you to *envy* me," said Terwilliger with a note of desperation in his voice. "I want you to fly me the hell out of here!"

"I told you: I don't take passengers."

"I'll pay for my fare."

"I thought you didn't have any money," noted Cain.

"I'll work it off," said Terwilliger. "I'll cook, I'll load cargo, I'll—"

"The galley's fully automated, and the only cargo I handle doesn't need loading so much as killing," interrupted Cain.

"If you don't take me, I'll die!"

"Everybody dies sometime," replied Cain. "Ask someone else."

"I already did. Nobody wants ManMountain Bates on their trail. But I figured a man like the Songbird, a man who's all written up in song and story, you wouldn't be bothered by a little thing like that."

"You figured wrong."

"You really won't take me?"

"I really won't take you."

"My death will be on your hands," said Terwilliger.

"Why?" asked Cain "*I* didn't pass bad notes to anyone."

Terwilliger scrutinized him for a moment, then forced himself to smile. "You're kidding, aren't you? You just want to see me squirm a little first."

"I'm not kidding."

"You *are*!" the little gambler half shouted. "You can't send me out to face ManMountain Bates! He breaks people's backs like they were toothpicks!"

"You know," remarked Cain with some amusement, "you seemed like a totally different man when I met you in the bar."

"I didn't have an eight-foot-tall disaster coming after me with blood in his eye when we were in the bar!" snapped Terwilliger.

"Are you all through yelling now?" asked Cain calmly.

"I arranged for you to meet with Stern," said Terwilliger desperately. "That ought to be worth *some*thing."

Cain reached into a pocket, withdrew a small silver coin, and flipped it across the room to Terwilliger. "Thanks," he said.

"Damn it, Songbird! What kind of man are you?"

"An unsympathetic one. Do you plan on leaving any time soon, or am I going to have to throw you out?"

Terwilliger emitted a sigh of defeat, gathered up the cards from the bed, and trudged to the door.

"Thanks a lot," he said sarcastically.

"Any time," replied Cain, stepping aside to let him pass out into the corridor.

The door slid shut again.

Cain stood absolutely still for a moment, then opened it.

SANTIAGO: A MYTH OF THE FAR FUTURE 37

"Hey, Terwilliger!" he yelled at the gambler's retreating figure.

"Yes?"

"What do you know about a man named Duncan Black?"

"The guy with the eyepatch?" said Terwilliger, turning and taking a tentative step in Cain's direction.

"That's the one."

"I used to play cards with him. What do you want to know?"

"Where am I likely to find him?" asked Cain.

Suddenly Terwilliger grinned broadly. "I do believe I just booked passage out of here," he said.

"You know where he is?"

"That I do."

"Where?"

"I'll tell you after we've taken off."

Cain nodded his agreement. "I'm leaving as soon as I have dinner. Get your gear together and meet me at the spaceport in two hours."

Terwilliger pulled out his deck of cards.

"I've got all the luggage I need right here," he said happily. "And now, if you'll excuse me, I think I'll go down and find a little game of chance to while away the lonely minutes before we leave."

With that, he turned on his heel and went off in search of the three or four newcomers to Port Étrange who would still accept his marker.

3.

Halfpenny Terwilliger, the boldest gambler yet;
Halfpenny Terwilliger will cover any bet;
Halfpenny Terwilliger, a rowdy martinet;
Halfpenny Terwilliger is now one soul in debt.

"Gin."

"Damn!" said Terwilliger, slapping his hand down on the table. "You caught me with nineteen." He pushed the cards over to Cain. "Your deal."

"I've had enough for a while."

"You're sure?"

"I've played more cards during the past five days than in the twenty years preceding them," said Cain. "Let's knock off for a few hours."

"Just trying to keep you amused," said Terwilliger, shuffling the deck and putting it back in the pocket of his brightly colored tunic. "Where do we stand?"

"You owe me a little over twenty-two hundred credits."

"I don't suppose you'd take a marker?" asked Terwilliger. Cain smiled. "Not very likely."

"Mind if I mix up another pot of that coffee we broke open this afternoon?" asked the gambler, heading off for the galley. "Just as well you don't bring 'em back alive," he muttered as he searched for the coffee in the cramped confines of the galley. "This ship sure as hell wasn't built with an extra passenger in mind." He uttered a grunt of triumph as he finally found the coffee in amongst a stack of condensed rations.

"Go a little easy on that stuff," said Cain. "It's expensive."

"It *tastes* expensive. Where's it from—Belore or Canphor?"

"Brazil."

"Never heard of it."

"It's a country back on Earth."

"You mean I've been drinking coffee from Earth itself?" said Terwilliger. "I'm impressed! You do right well by a guest, Songbird."

"Thanks—and I keep telling you: my name's Cain."

"I've been meaning to ask you about that. You don't sound like you've got much of a singing voice, so how come he dubbed you the Songbird?"

"Because my name's Sebastian Nightingale Cain. He fell in love with my middle name, and I told him he couldn't use it." Cain grimaced. "I should have been more explicit."

"Come to think of it, Black Orpheus does a *lot* of dumb things," said Terwilliger. "Like that line about me being a martinet. I'm the sweetest, friendliest guy in the galaxy. He just used it to make a rhyme."

"I notice you don't object to the part about pawning your soul," noted Cain.

Terwilliger laughed. "Hell, that's the first thing a man gets rid of when he comes to the Frontier. Excess baggage, nothing more."

"Losing at cards seems to make you cynical," said Cain.

"It's got nothing to do with cards," replied the little gambler. "It's an obvious fact. You kill men for a living; where would *you* be with a soul?"

"Back on Sylaria, I suppose," said Cain thoughtfully.

"That's the world where you were a revolutionary?"

"One of them."

"You should have known better," said Terwilliger. "No matter what kind of promises a man who's looking for power makes, he's not going to turn out to be any different from the one he replaces."

"I was very young," said Cain.

"It's hard to imagine you as a callow youth."

Cain chuckled. "I wasn't so much callow as idealistic."

"Well, cheer up—the Frontier is filled with men who were going to make the galaxy a better place to live."

"So are the seats of power," said Cain wryly. "You'd think *some*body would know how."

"You keep talking like that and you're going to convince me you still believe in all that idealistic nonsense."

"Don't worry about it," replied Cain, leaning back and propping a foot up against a bulkhead. "That was a long, long time ago."

The gambler walked over to a sensor terminal, as he had done every few hours since leaving Port Étrange, and satisfied himself that there was still no sign of pursuit by ManMountain Bates.

"You know," said Terwilliger, finally pouring himself some coffee and handing a cup over to Cain, "you never did tell me why you became a bounty hunter."

"I'd been a terrorist for twelve years. The only thing I knew how to do really well was kill people."

"How about that?" said the gambler with mock regret. "And here I thought it was because you believed in justice."

Cain patted the weapon at his side. "I learned to use this gun because I believed in truth and honor and freedom and a lot of other fine-sounding things. I spent twelve years fighting for them and then took a good look at the results." He paused. "Now all I believe in is the gun."

"Well, I've met disillusioned revolutionaries before, but you're the first one who ever fought on a free-lance basis."

"Nobody paid me for what I did."

"What I meant was that you seemed to go from one war to another."

"When the first man I thought could put things right turned out to have feet of clay, I looked around for another. It took me three revolutions before I finally realized just how much clay God put into the universe." He smiled ruefully. "I was a slow learner."

"At least you fought the good fight," said Terwilliger.

"I fought three stupid fights," Cain corrected him. "I'm not especially proud of any of them."

"You must have been a very serious young man."

"Actually, I used to laugh a lot more than I do now." He shrugged. "That was when I thought one moral man could make a difference. The only thing I find *really* funny these days is the fact that so many people still believe it."

"I had a feeling the first time I saw you that you weren't just your run-of-the-mill headhunter," said Terwilliger. "Like I told you, I've got this knack for reading faces."

"Well, if it comes to that, I had a feeling the first time I saw you that you were a lousy cardplayer."

"I'm the best damned cardplayer *you'll* ever meet."

"I thought I beat you rather handily," remarked Cain.

"I *let* you win."

"Sure you did."

"You don't believe me?" said the gambler. "Then watch *this*."

He pulled out the cards, shuffled them thoroughly, and dealt out two five-card hands on the tiny chrome table.

"Got anything worth betting?" he asked.

Cain picked up his cards, fanned them out slowly, and found himself holding four kings and a jack.

"It's possible," he answered cautiously.

"How about twenty-two hundred credits?"

"Let's make it one hundred."

"You're sure?"

"That's my limit."

Terwilliger laid his hand down on the table. It contained four aces and a queen.

"Then why did you let me win any hands at all the first time we met?" asked Cain.

"Because professional cardplayers are very careful about cheating professional killers," replied Terwilliger. "Besides, I was lonely. Once word got out that I was broke, none of the amateurs would play with me—and you can't use tricks like that on the pros."

"And why have you let me win at gin since we took off from Port Étrange?" continued Cain.

"It was just my way of keeping you in a good mood, and thanking you for saving my life." He grinned. "Besides, it's not as if I have any money to pay you with."

"Well, I'll be damned!" said Cain with a laugh. "So *that's* why you wouldn't let the computer give us random hands! All right, you little bastard. Your debt's wiped clean."

"I'd rather owe it to you."

"Why?"

"I have my reasons," said Terwilliger.

"Suit yourself," said Cain. "I've got another question."

"Ask away."

"How the hell did someone like you manage to go two hundred thousand credits in the hole to ManMountain Bates?"

"Do you know what the odds are of a man drawing a straight flush against you when you're sitting with four aces?" asked Terwilliger.

"Not long enough, I'd guess," said Cain.

"You're damned right! You know, if you play cards every day, it might happen five times before you die of old age. It was just my stupid luck that the first time it happened was against the backbreaker."

"How did you get out with your back unbroken?"

"I waited until Bates answered a call of nature, told a couple of the other players that I was going to my room to get my bankroll so I could redeem my marker, and got the hell off the planet before anyone knew I was gone." Terwilliger frowned. "I'd love to see that guy's bladder preserved for science. He must have drunk six quarts before he got up!"

"Pardon an unethical question, but now that I've seen what you can do with a deck of cards, why didn't you do it to him—exercising due caution, of course?"

"Have you ever seen ManMountain Bates?" said Terwilliger with a bitter laugh.

"No."

"Well, he's not the kind of guy you'd want to chance having mad at you, especially if he was within arm's reach."

"Not even for two hundred thousand credits?"

"It wasn't worth the risk. It'd be as dangerous as you poaching on the Angel's territory."

"From what I hear, he's about to start poaching on mine," commented Cain.

"That's different."

"Why?"

"Because he's the Angel." Terwilliger walked over to the coffeepot and poured himself another cup. "Besides, everybody knows he's just here for Santiago. You can hardly call it poaching if nobody knows where Santiago is hiding. Which brings up another subject," he added carefully. "You came a pretty fair distance just to talk to Jonathan Stern. Usually a bounty hunter doesn't go that far beyond his own territory unless he thinks he can get a lead on Santiago. So my question is: Is there some tie-in between Duncan Black and Santiago, or not?"

"I don't see that it's any of your business," said Cain.

"Look at me," said the little gambler. "Do I look like a goddamned rival?"

"No," said Cain. "You look like a goddamned salesman."

"Just answer my question. I promise you I won't sell it to anyone else."

"Somehow, I get the distinct impression that your promises aren't exactly coin of the realm."

"Damn it, Cain—it's important!"

"To who?"

"To both of us."

Cain stared at him for a long minute, then nodded. "Yes, he's a link to Santiago."

"Good!" breathed Terwilliger with a sigh of relief.

"Why is that good?"

"Well, first I want you to remember that I still owe you a debt of twenty-one hundred credits, and that I can't pay it off if I'm dead."

"Get to the point."

The little gambler took a deep breath.

"The reason I know where to find Duncan Black is because I know where he's buried." Terwilliger held up his hand quickly, as if to fight off any possible interruption. "I should have told you back on Port Étrange, I know that. It was absolutely, positively wrong. But if I had, you wouldn't have taken me, and ManMountain Bates would be having me for dinner right about now."

"I may just take you back there and turn you over to him," said Cain.

"But everything's all right now!" said Terwilliger quickly. "Everything's all right," he repeated. "That's why I had to know if Black was a link."

"Explain," said Cain ominously.

"You see, if he had owed you money or something like that, you were out of luck and I was in big trouble. I mean, hell, the poor bastard has been dead for almost three years now." He paused for breath. "But now that I know what you needed him for, I can still help you out."

"How?"

"There was this woman he used to live with," said Terwilliger. "She handled a lot of his business for him. She probably knows everyone *he* knew, and can tell you what his connection was with each of them."

"And she's still alive?" asked Cain.

"She was two months ago."

"Where can I find her?"

"Right where we're heading—the Clovis system."

"On Bella Donna?"

"Not exactly," answered Terwilliger.

4.

She lives in a graveyard of shattered ships,
She floats through the void with her broken dreams;
But though she may long for a lover's lips,
The Sargasso Rose isn't what she seems.

Black Orpheus took one look at the Sargasso Rose and knew there was more to her than met the eye.

How he found her in the first place is a mystery, since he wasn't likely to have had any business up there, six thousand miles above Bella Donna. Probably it was the ships that attracted him, strung out in space like glittering fish on a line, some dying and some already dead. He named the station, too: he hated names like Station Number 14, and so he called it Deadly Nightshade, which was a fitting sobriquet for a graveyard of spaceships, especially one that circled Bella Donna.

He spent a couple of days up there, talking to the Sargasso Rose, jotting down her story the way he did with everyone he met. Some people say he even slept with her, but they were wrong; Black Orpheus never slept with *anyone* after his Eurydice died. Besides, the Sargasso Rose wasn't the type of woman who'd jump into bed with just anybody.

In fact, that may have been one of her problems. She was forty years old, and she had had only three lovers. The first two had left her for other women, and Duncan Black had left her to start working in the pits of hell a few years ahead of schedule. She'd always fought a lot with him, but she'd loved him as much as she would let herself love anyone after her

first two experiences, and when his heart finally gave out it
came pretty close to breaking hers as well.

She was still grieving a year later, when Black Orpheus
stopped by—but she took the trouble to show Deadly Nightshade off to him just the same. He went deep into the bellies
of the metal leviathans and spent almost a full day there,
scribbling down notes as her crew gutted them and set them
adrift, then watching with childlike enthusiasm as space tugs
dragged new corpses up to the station's docks. He even found
time to name Bella Donna's three tiny moons—Banewort,
Foxglove, and Hellebore—before he left for his next port of
call.

Deadly Nightshade wasn't much to look at by the time
Cain and Terwilliger arrived. Its hull was pockmarked by
small, hastily repaired meteor holes, one of its docks had
been damaged beyond repair by an errant tug, and it had
come into contact with enough cosmic dust and debris so that
the entire exterior needed refurbishing.

Still, it wasn't Deadly Nightshade that they had come to
see, but rather the woman who owned it, so Cain carefully
maneuvered his ship up to a dock, waited for an enclosed
mobile walkway to be attached to his airlock, and followed
Terwilliger to the interior of the station.

The floor curved gently away from them in both directions,
and a narrow mat of indeterminate properties seemed to grab
hold of their feet.

"You didn't tell me it was zero gravity in here," commented Cain.

"Just make sure one foot is always on the mat," replied
Terwilliger. "You won't float away."

"I've been on G-mats before," replied Cain irritably. "I
just don't like null-gravity situations too soon after a meal."

"You should have told me."

Cain was about to reply that he hadn't known that there
was no gravity inside the station but decided that he didn't
feel like repeating the entire conversation again.

Suddenly a humanoid being with a large cranium, deep-set
golden eyes, and orange, reticulated skin began approaching
them.

"What the hell is that?" asked Cain.

"An Orange Monkey," replied Terwilliger. "The Rose
uses them as security guards."

"I never saw one before," said Cain. "Where is it from?"

"Varien Four," said the gambler. "They call themselves Hagibens; we call 'em Orange Monkeys. It fits them better. They work cheap, they learn the language pretty fast, and they love zero gravity. It's a hard combination to beat— especially when you consider how many alien races won't work at all and couldn't care less about money."

The Orange Monkey stopped in front of them.

"Your business, please?" it said in a lilting voice that sounded more like song than speech.

"We're here to see the Sargasso Rose," replied Terwilliger.

"The Sargasso Rose prefers not to deal personally with our customers," replied the alien. "If you will tell me what you need, I will direct you to the proper areas."

"She'll deal personally with *us*," said Terwilliger. "I'm an old friend."

The Orange Monkey looked at him. "You are Halfpenny Terwilliger, who was forcibly removed from Deadly Nightshade for cheating various staff members in a card game." It paused. "*I* was among those who escorted you to your ship."

"You were?" asked Terwilliger, surprised but unembarrassed.

"I was."

"Sorry I didn't recognize you, but all you Orange Monkeys look alike to me."

"That is perfectly understandable," said the alien. "We are all quite beautiful."

"Well, as long as we're old friends, how about telling the Rose we're here?"

"I will tell her, Halfpenny Terwilliger, but she prefers not to deal directly with the customers."

Cain stepped forward. "Do it anyway," he said in very level tones. "Tell her our business concerns a mutual friend."

The Orange Monkey stared at him for a moment, then turned and headed off to another area of the space station after summoning a companion to keep watch on them. It returned a few minutes later and walked up to Cain.

"The Sargasso Rose has instructed me to take you to her," it said in its placid, singsong voice. If it was surprised or disappointed, it kept its feelings well hidden.

Cain and Terwilliger followed it through a trio of large storage rooms and up to a small door.

"She is in here," said the Orange Monkey.

"Thanks," said Cain. He opened the door and stepped into a cluttered office, followed by Terwilliger.

Sitting behind a chrome desk that no longer gleamed, wearing a metallic gold outfit that no longer glistened, was a rather plain woman. Her hair was a dull brown, her eyes a lackluster green, her nose prominent, her chin weak. She was neither fat nor thin, but if she had ever possessed an attractive figure, that time had long since passed. Attached to her hair was a small white rose, which Cain took to be artificial.

She stared directly at the bounty hunter.

"You wished to see me, Mr. Cain?"

"You know my name?"

She smiled. "I know many things about you, Sebastian Nightingale Cain. What I don't know is who referred you to me."

"A man called Stern, back on Port Étrange."

"Jonathan Jeremy Jacobar Stern," she said. "Now *that's* a name I haven't heard in years." She gestured to a pair of chairs. "Please be seated." She turned to Terwilliger. "I understand ManMountain Bates is looking for you."

"You have excellent sources," replied the gambler uneasily.

"Indeed I do," she agreed. "Not much goes on in this part of the Frontier that I don't know about."

"Then I assume you know why I'm here," said Cain.

"I know you're a bounty hunter," she said, "and you've told me that Stern sent you, so I can make a pretty good guess as to why you're here." She paused. "But Stern wouldn't send you to *me*. He would have told you to hunt up Duncan Black." She turned back to Terwilliger. "*You* told Mr. Cain to come here, of course. Stern doesn't know Duncan is dead, but you do."

"Well, there wasn't much sense trying to have a conversation with Duncan, rest his soul," explained Terwilliger defensively.

"And doubtless he has promised to protect you from ManMountain Bates in exchange for this information." She scrutinized Cain for a moment. "You made a poor trade, Mr. Cain. You should have stayed on Keepsake."

"What makes you think I come from Keepsake?" he asked.

She smiled again. "I've known your ship's registration number since I started tracking you two days ago. In the intervening forty-eight hours I've found out things about you that even *you* may have forgotten. I know the date and planet of your birth, I know why you left the more populated worlds of the Democracy, I know how many men you have killed and who they were—and here you are, practically denying that you work out of Keepsake. If you want *my* honesty, I should think the least you can do is offer me your own."

"I apologize," said Cain.

"There's no need to," she replied. "Deceit is no more than I expect from a member of your sex."

"Will you help me?" asked Cain, ignoring her comment.

"You're wasting your time."

"I've got plenty to waste," he said. "And I can pay for yours."

"I didn't say you would be wasting *my* time," said the Sargasso Rose. "I have every intention of selling you the information you need."

"I'm not sure I understand the distinction."

"I'm quite prepared to tell you what you want to know, but it won't do you any good. The Angel has moved to the Inner Frontier."

"I'm getting a little tired of hearing about him," said Cain with a trace of irritation.

"So, I suspect, is every fugitive within ten thousand light-years," she replied. "Mr. Terwilliger, I think it is time for you to leave the room. What I have to say to Mr. Cain is for his ears alone."

"Why?" asked the gambler.

"For the same reason that you are denied free access to the goods in my warehouse: I don't want you selling something that's mine to the first qualified buyer who comes along."

"I resent that," said Terwilliger, trying to muster a show of sincerity and not quite succeeding.

"You are welcome to resent it to your heart's content," said the Sargasso Rose. "What you are *not* welcome to do is remain in my office."

Terwilliger seemed about to protest, thought better of it, and walked to the door.

"I'll be right outside," he told Cain. "Yell out if you need me."

Cain stared at him in amusement, and a moment later the door slid shut behind the little gambler.

"If you plan to hunt Santiago, you really should choose

your traveling companions more carefully, Mr. Cain," said the Sargasso Rose, leaning back in her chair.

"Perhaps," replied Cain. "But on his behalf, I should point out that he brought me to you. Otherwise I'd be wasting my time hunting for Duncan Black, or else I'd be heading back for Port Étrange to beat my money out of Jonathan Stern."

"True," she admitted with a shrug. "May I offer you a drink?"

"Why not?" he said agreeably.

She pressed a button on her computer console, and a small, furry red alien, definitely not humanoid, entered by a different door and set a bottle and two glasses down on her desk.

"Do you have any Men at all on Deadly Nightshade?" asked Cain as the alien left the office.

"The race or the gender?" asked the Sargasso Rose. "In either case, the answer is no. Both tend to desert you when you need them the most—especially the gender."

"It must get lonely up here," commented Cain.

"Eventually one gets used to it." She filled the two glasses, and Cain stepped over and took one.

"Thank you," he said after returning to his chair and taking a sip. Suddenly he laughed in self-deprecation.

"What is it, Mr. Cain?"

He held up the glass. "I just realized that there's normal gravity in this room," he replied. "Some observant hunter I am! If I hadn't noticed that this stuff didn't float away, I would never have known."

"The Orange Monkeys like zero gravity. I find continued exposure to it a bit upsetting, so I tailor my office to my own needs."

"It must cost a fortune," he commented.

"It does. Thankfully, I've got a fortune to spare."

He took another sip. "This is pretty good stuff."

"It ought to be," she said. "It comes straight from Deluros Eight."

"You handle merchandise from that far away?"

"You'd be surprised at what passes through Deadly Nightshade, Mr. Cain," she replied. "Or perhaps you wouldn't. Exactly how much did Stern tell you about Duncan Black?"

"Only that Black handled stolen goods, and that he was a middleman between Stern and Santiago," replied Cain. "I know he had access to some of the gold that Santiago picked up in the Epsilon Eridani raid.''

"Now *that* was a cargo!" she said with a smile. "Six hundred million credits' worth of pure bullion!''

"I got the impression from Terwilliger that you decided to follow in Black's footsteps.''

"Terwilliger talks too much.''

"Most people do,'' agreed Cain.

"Besides, they were *my* footsteps to begin with,'' she continued. "I was dealing in stolen commodities long before Duncan Black ever thought of it.'' She paused. "I gave him a share of the business to insure his loyalty.'' She looked at Cain. "Does that seem manipulative and immoral to you?''

"I gave up making moral judgments a long time ago,'' he replied.

"Anyway,'' said the Sargasso Rose, sipping her drink, "Duncan liked dealing with people more than I did, so he became our front man for places like Port Étrange and people like Stern.''

"Then *you* made the initial contact with Santiago, not Black.''

"Actually, Santiago made the initial contact with *me*,'' she answered him. "Though it took a few years before I knew beyond any doubt that I was dealing with him.''

"Have you ever met him?'' asked Cain.

She shook her head. "No. Or perhaps I should say, not to my knowledge.''

"But you might have?''

"Who's to say?'' she replied with a shrug of her shoulders. "I met any number of people who delivered goods that Santiago may have stolen—though in truth I can't imagine why he would have risked exposure by coming here.''

"Do you know anyone who has actually met him face to face?'' persisted Cain.

"Yes, I do.''

"Who?''

"Before I tell you, Mr. Cain,'' said the Sargasso Rose, "there are a few things I would like to know, just to satisfy my own curiosity.''

"Such as?''

"You spent most of your young manhood fighting to overthrow various governments. Santiago, to the best of my knowl-

edge, has primarily attacked and looted those enterprises that
are owned or controlled by the Democracy, or are at least
vital to its well-being. You were branded as a revolutionary,
and once had a price on your head. The magnitude of his
actions is certainly far greater, but he might also be considered a revolutionary, insofar as most of his crimes are against
the State. You have so many things in common with him that
I'm just a little puzzled about why you want so desperately to
kill him.''

"The bulk of his crimes are committed against the Democracy simply because the Democracy has more assets than any
other potential target," said Cain. "As for his being a revolutionary, you might say the same for any train robber back on
old Earth who ever robbed a government payroll. The man's
a criminal, plain and simple.''

"Have you ever known him to kill anyone?" she asked.

"He killed seventeen colonists on Silverblue just last year,"
replied Cain.

"Rubbish!" said the Sargasso Rose. "He hasn't been to
the Outer Frontier in years.''

"You know that for a fact?" he asked sharply.

"Why else would the Angel have moved into this area?"
she replied.

"Maybe he's chasing him," suggested Cain.

"You don't believe that for a moment. The Angel *catches*
anyone he chases.''

"He's just a bounty hunter, not a superman.''

"You still haven't told me why you want to kill Santiago.''

"Why does *anyone* want to kill him?" replied Cain with a
smile. "There's a hell of a big reward.''

"That is not an acceptable answer," she said. "You are a
very wealthy man, Mr. Cain, so surely money is not your
primary objective.''

"Money is always an objective," said Cain. "And," he
added thoughtfully, "it would *mean* something.''

"What would it mean?''

"That I made a difference," he replied. "That just once,
something I did *mattered*.''

"How about the men you helped place in positions of
power?" asked the Sargasso Rose.

"They were the wrong men," answered Cain wryly. "They
won't even be footnotes in the history books.''

"And the criminals you've hunted down?"

"Even *I* hadn't heard of most of them before I went after them." He paused. "But Santiago is different. *He* matters, so the man who brings him down will matter, too."

She smiled. "So you want to be written up in song and story yourself."

"I've *been* in a song. I don't like it much." He finished his drink. "I don't care who else knows what I did—just so long as *I* know it."

"Well, it's a novel approach, I'll grant you that," said the Sargasso Rose.

"Now let me ask you a question," said Cain.

"We haven't settled on a price yet," she pointed out.

"That wasn't the question."

"Then go ahead."

"You've obviously made a lot of money off of Santiago. Why are you willing to help me?"

"Santiago took his business elsewhere shortly after Duncan died. I owe him nothing. Besides, I'm a businesswoman: everything I own is for sale—including information."

"Have you sold it to anyone else yet?"

"No one has asked—but if they do, I will."

"All right," said Cain. "What, exactly, do you have for sale?"

"I have the name, holograph, and current location of a man who dealt directly with Santiago. I have the names and holographs of four of Santiago's agents with whom I did business three years ago. I have some of the gold bullion with its point of origin listed on the packing crates. And I know who killed Kastartos."

"Kastartos?" asked Cain. "The man who tried to get Stern to turn Santiago in for the reward?"

She nodded. "From what I hear, it was a pretty dismal attempt."

"And what do you want for all this?"

"I want you to kill Santiago."

He looked his surprise. "That's all?"

"That's all."

"Might I ask why?"

"Duncan Black was a good man," she began. "Well, no, he wasn't. He was petty and undependable and weak—but he was *mine*. Then he found out that we were dealing with

Santiago, and he thought we could make a little more money by joining the organization. I don't know what sort of proposal he made to them, but it didn't work.'' She took a sip of her drink. ''He was found dead on Binder Ten two weeks later. The official cause of death was heart failure.''

''Are you telling me Santiago had him killed?''

''Santiago probably didn't even know he existed. But *somebody* had him killed, and if it hadn't been for Santiago, he'd still be here.'' She paused. ''He wasn't much, but he was all I had.'' She stared at Cain. ''Santiago didn't know Duncan, and I don't know Santiago. It will be a fair trade.''

''All right,'' said Cain. ''Let's see what you have.''

She rose, walked to a wall safe that was concealed behind a large, lightweight computer screen, punched out a combination on the lock, and opened it.

''You can take these with you,'' she said, withdrawing a number of items from the safe and returning to her chair. ''I have copies.''

''Somehow I was sure you did,'' he remarked, reaching over and taking a number of holographs from her.

''The top four are the agents I dealt with,'' she explained. ''Their names are on the backs.''

''One of them looks like a methane-breather,'' said Cain, holding up a holograph of a delicate crystalline being.

''He is,'' she said. ''I only saw him once. He was very uncomfortable in his life-support paraphernalia. I suspect after his initial trip here he found a convenient drop point for his merchandise.''

''Who's this?'' asked Cain, holding up the holograph of a very exotic dark-haired woman with chalk-white skin.

''Altair of Altair,'' answered the Sargasso Rose. ''She murdered Kastartos.''

He studied the holograph. ''She's a professional killer?''

''One of the best. I'm surprised you haven't heard of her.''

''It's a big galaxy,'' he said. ''There are a lot of people I haven't heard of.'' He looked at Altair of Altair again. ''Are you sure she's human?''

''Who knows? But I'm sure she's an assassin.''

He came to the final holograph.

''This is the man who met with Santiago?''

''Yes. His name is Socrates. I haven't dealt with him in

more than a year, but I know where to find him. We do a little business together from time to time.''

"Maybe it's not such a big galaxy after all," said Cain, staring at the pudgy, smiling face in the holograph.

"What do you mean?"

"I knew this man when his name was Whittaker Drum."

"The name's not familiar to me," said the Sargasso Rose.

"No, I don't suppose it would be."

"Who is he?"

Cain smiled ironically. "The man I helped put in power back on Sylaria."

"Will he recognize you?"

"I hope so," answered Cain.

5.

Socrates is hard to please:
He lives in the shade of the gallows-trees;
He prays for life on bended knees—
But he's bound for hell, is Socrates.

There weren't a lot of people on the Inner Frontier that
Black Orpheus didn't like, but Socrates was one of them.
You'd think that cutthroats and bandits and gamblers would
have bothered him more, but for the most part they were
pretty honest and aboveboard about what they did, and if
there was one thing Black Orpheus couldn't abide, it was a
hypocrite.

Now, there are people who say that Black Orpheus must
have had some respect for Socrates or he wouldn't have given
him even the single verse that he did, but Black Orpheus
knew that Socrates was the ruler of an entire planet back
when he was plain old Whittaker Drum—and besides, his job
as he saw it was to write up the folks that he met and leave it
to others to judge them.

Still, he was known to editorialize a little, and there's not
much doubt that he felt Socrates was earmarked for the pits of
hell. Oh, he'd said something like that about Halfpenny
Terwilliger and a few others, but you got the feeling that he
was joking—and he never said it at all about Schussler the
Cyborg, who thought he was *already* in hell, nor even about
Santiago himself. There was just something about Socrates
that rubbed him the wrong way, and since most people on the
Frontier were pretty much inclined to take Black Orpheus'

56

word about characters they hadn't met, it's probably just as well that Socrates didn't survive too long after that verse was written.

Actually, nobody knows how he got the name Socrates, but it's a pretty safe bet that Black Orpheus didn't hang it on him. He was Whittaker Drum when he wrote his revolutionary tracts, he was Whittaker Drum when he took over the reins of Sylaria's government, and he was still Whittaker Drum when they threw him out a few years later; then one day he showed up on Declan IV and suddenly he was Socrates. First he caught a particularly virulent venereal disease, and then he caught an equally strong case of religion, and neither of them stopped him from making a living as an entrepreneur who specialized in providing venture capital to what could be euphemistically termed high-risk businesses.

He probably didn't know it, but he had a lot of company on Declan IV. Nobody knew what the planet's attraction was, except perhaps that it was a last jumping-off point to the Inner Frontier, but during the seven years that Socrates lived there it was also the home of five exiled planetary presidents, two kings, and a ranking member of the navy who had resigned in black disgrace.

Declan IV was a frontier society that had outgrown its origins and was uncomfortably trying to fit neatly into the pattern of the worlds of the Democracy. It had grown from two grubby Tradertowns into six sprawling modern cities, it had first pacified and later decimated the six-legged marsupials that had once been the planet's dominant life-form, it imported—always a decade after they were out of style—the latest fashions and entertainments from Deluros VIII, it bribed the major retail chains to open outlets on the planet and practically subsidized them once they arrived, it entered teams in various interplanetary sporting leagues, and it was making impressive progress at polluting its atmosphere. It was too young a colony to have much sense of its own past, so buildings, some of them quite lovely, were constantly being torn down to be replaced by newer versions of the same things, some of them quite ugly. The citizenry had also belatedly decided that killing off the native population was perhaps not the most civilized approach to take, and suddenly every business, every school, and every landlord began fighting tooth and nail to hire, teach, and house the planet's few remaining native inhabitants, who cool-headedly and cold-bloodedly hired out to the highest bidders, swallowed any humiliation they may have felt, and became almost wealthy enough to achieve a sort of second-class respectability.

Cain and Terwilliger landed at a rather large spaceport that possessed hundreds of flashing, blinking signs proclaiming that work on an orbiting hangar would be completed within the year. They spent ten minutes passing through customs, wasted another five while Terwilliger created a completely logical and totally false story to explain why his passport card was seven years out of date, and finally caught a monorail that took them into the city of Commonweal.

"Would you believe that?" complained the gambler, sitting down beside Cain. "I've been on maybe a hundred worlds in the last ten years, and this is the first time anyone's ever asked me for my passport."

"We're not on the Frontier anymore," replied Cain, staring out the window at the cultivated fields. "They do things differently here."

"How come they didn't hassle you?" asked Terwilliger.

"Mine's up to date."

"Why?"

"I never know when someone I'm looking for may head back into the Democracy," said Cain.

He pulled out a map of the city that he had purchased and began studying it. There were twenty main slidewalks in Commonweal, eight north–south, eight east–west, and four diagonal. He pinpointed the address the Sargasso Rose had given him, figured out the easiest way to reach it, and put the map back in his pocket.

They spent ten minutes on a northeasterly slidewalk, passing through a heavily trafficked, shining metal-and-glass commercial area, transferred to a westbound one for another ten, and then stepped off the moving walkways onto a brightly tiled street.

"About two more blocks," announced Cain, checking the map once more.

"I'm starting to remember what I don't like about populated planets," said Terwilliger unhappily as they began walking through a residential section topped by hundreds of transparent spires. "Too damned crowded." He looked up at the buildings. "The streets are too narrow, and you can't see the sky."

"Yes you can."

"Well, it *feels* like you can't," persisted Terwilliger. "And it's dirty."

"So are most Tradertowns."

"That's *clean* dirt. This stuff is soot and grease and garbage."

"An interesting distinction," remarked Cain.

"It's noisy, too. There's too much traffic and too many people. Hell, even the slidewalk creaks and rumbles."

"This is nothing," replied Cain. "You ought to go to Deluros Eight sometime."

"No, thanks," said the gambler. "Visiting a whole planet covered by a single building just isn't my idea of a good time."

"Actually, there are a few million buildings. They're just packed so close together that it seems like there's only one."

"I don't know how to tell you this," said Terwilliger, "but you're not exactly piquing my interest. I was born on the Frontier, and I've got every intention of dying there."

"Especially if ManMountain Bates catches up with you," remarked Cain.

"Then I'll just unleash you, and that'll be the end of ManMountain Bates," replied the gambler with a smile. He paused for a moment. "By the way, have you figured out how you're going to get Socrates to talk?"

"The same way people have always gotten him to do things—with money."

They crossed a street and Cain checked the number on the corner building. "We're just about there," he announced.

When they came to the building they sought, a sleek high rise boasting four separate penthouse towers and taking up half a block at its base, they went to the main entrance and found themselves in a spacious foyer. A uniformed alien that resembled nothing more than a six-legged kangaroo with a panda's face approached them and spoke into a translating mechanism.

"Greetings and salutations, joy be upon you," it said. "My name is Wixtol; I am the concierge of the Tudor Apartments. How may I help you?"

"We've come to visit an old friend," said Cain. "Where can we find the building directory?"

"I will be immeasurably pleased to direct you to your party," replied the alien, "if you will only be so generous as to furnish me with its name."

"Whittaker Drum."

"Infinite sorrow, dear friends," announced Wixtol. "I prostrate myself to inform you that we have no such resident."

"He also uses the name Socrates," said Cain.

The alien gave them a delighted grin. "Joy supreme! Socrates lives in apartment twenty-nine fourteen, praise be. If you will condescend to follow your humble servant, I will lead you to the elevator."

It waddled off to the right, and Cain and Terwilliger fell into step behind it.

"Is that *him*, or is something wrong with the translator?" whispered the gambler.

"Who knows?" replied Cain. "Maybe they told him that's the way a concierge speaks."

They soon reached the elevators. Wixtol held the door open for them, pressed the button for the twenty-ninth floor, thanked them profusely for coming, and wished them a safe and happy ascent. Then the door slid shut, and a moment later they were walking down a mirrored corridor leading to apartment 2914.

When they arrived at the front door, Cain stopped and waited silently.

"I've seen you somewhere before," said a hoarse, masculine voice. "Who are you?"

"My name is Cain."

There was a pause. "*Sebastian* Cain?"

"Yes."

"Well, I'll be damned!" exclaimed the voice. "What have you been doing with yourself?"

"Hello, Whittaker. It's been a long time."

"What are you doing here?"

"The Sargasso Rose gave me your new name and told me to hunt you up. I'd like to talk to you, if you can spare me the time."

"I'd be delighted. Just move a step to your left so my security system can scan you."

Cain did so, and became aware of a soft humming noise.

"Do you think you're going to need two guns and a knife to talk to me?" asked the voice.

"No."

The door slid open a few inches.

"Toss them inside, Sebastian. I'll return them when we're done."

Cain withdrew the weapons in question and tossed them through the small gap.

"Now your friend."

"My name's Terwilliger," said the gambler, moving to the spot Cain vacated. "And I don't carry any guns."

"Okay," grunted the voice. "You're clean." There was a brief pause and then the door slid open the rest of the way. "Come on in."

They stepped into a small vestibule from which the weapons had already been removed, and walked through it to a large, opulently furnished living room. The carpeting was thick and expensive, the chairs and tables were crafted of rare hardwoods from distant Doradus IV, the lighting was discreet and indirect, a large window overlooked the city, alien art objects were displayed in abundance, and the walls were covered by literally scores of icons and gold and silver cruci-fixes. A pudgy man with thinning gray hair, clad in a silk lounge suit, stood in the middle of the room, a huge smile on his face.

"How the hell are you?" said Socrates, walking over and giving Cain a friendly bear hug. "What have you been doing with yourself since the old days, Sebastian?"

"Bounty hunting."

"Well, why not?" said Socrates. "Killing people was always one of the things you did best." He smiled. "Damn, but it's been a long time! Have a seat. Can I get you something to drink?"

"Later, perhaps," said Cain, sitting down on the couch. "How come I don't see any bodyguards?"

"What for? I'm a respectable businessman, and I don't keep any cash up here."

"There are probably some people on Sylaria who'd like to see you dead," suggested Cain.

Socrates laughed. "Even if they knew how to find me, which they don't, I very much doubt that any of them even remember me. They've overthrown four or five dictators since I left." He turned to Terwilliger. "Are you a bounty hunter, too?"

"Nope," replied the gambler, amused. "I'm just a visitor who appreciates your offer of a drink."

"What'll it be?"

"Anything that's wet."

Socrates walked to a wall and touched a particular spot on it, and a moment later a panel slid back to reveal a small but well-stocked bar.

"How about whiskey?"

"Whiskey's fine," said Terwilliger, swinging a small, straight-backed chair around, throwing a leg over it, and pressing his chest against the back of it. Socrates poured the drink and handed it to the gambler, then turned to Cain.

"Damn, but it's good to see you again, Sebastian!" said Socrates, sitting down opposite him on a beautifully hand-crafted chair. "It must be—what?—maybe twenty years now."

"Twenty-one," said Cain.

"I hope you're doing well."

"I've got no complaints."

"Neither have I, when you get right down to it. In point of fact, I've embarked on a whole new life—new name, new world, new money."

"I see you still have the same taste for life's little luxuries," remarked Cain, indicating the expensive furnishings.

"True," was the answer. "But then, what's life without a few luxuries?" He paused. "So tell me, Sebastian, why have you paid a visit to me after all this time?"

"Information."

Suddenly Socrates was all business.

"Buying or selling?"

"Buying."

"I've got someone coming by in a few minutes, so we'll have to make this briefer than I'd like, though perhaps we can have dinner later and talk about old times. In the meantime, what kind of information are you after?"

"I'm looking for someone. You can help me find him."

"If it's within my power. Who is he?"

"Santiago."

Socrates frowned. "I'm sorry, Sebastian. Ask me about anyone else, and there won't be any charge for the answer."

"I'm not looking for anyone else," said Cain.

"Then you should be. Leave him alone."

"A friendly warning?" asked Cain.

"A serious one. He's out of your league." Socrates paused. "Hell, he's out of *everyone's* league."

"Then what does he want with a loan shark?"

"I'm a *financier*," replied Socrates.

"I know exactly what you are," said Cain. "What I don't know is why he has to deal with you. He can't be short of money."

"I have, from time to time, arranged meetings between the various parties in a business transaction." Socrates smiled. "My calling, as I see it, is to match opportunists with opportunities."

"From what I can see, I would have thought your calling lay along different lines," said Cain, indicating the crucifixes and icons.

Socrates shrugged. "One does what one must. The good Lord is very understanding—especially when He sees the size of my weekly donations."

"I'll make a healthy donation myself if you can tell me what I need to know about Santiago."

"Out of the question."

"Name your price."

"There isn't any price," replied Socrates. "It's not for sale."

"Not to put too fine a point on it, Whittaker, everything you've ever owned was for sale."

Socrates sighed deeply. "You're referring to Sylaria, no doubt."

"As a matter of fact, I was," said Cain.

"That was an entirely different situation. I took over a corrupt and stagnant government—"

"And made it so much worse that the Democracy finally bought you off."

"That is an unfair and unjustified comment, Sebastian."

"Come on, Whittaker. I was there when your firing squads slaughtered ten thousand men and women."

"We all make mistakes," said Socrates easily. "I'll be the first to admit that was one of mine."

"I'm sure it's a comfort to them to know you feel that way."

"I should have killed thirty thousand," said Socrates seriously.

Terwilliger chuckled, while Cain merely stared at him.

"After a revolution," continued Socrates, "you either assimilate your enemies or you dispose of them. The one thing you don't do is leave them free to plot against you. There were too many to assimilate, so I should have gotten rid of them. As it turned out, I was too soft-hearted; I *believed* all that guff I used to spout. So I spent ninety percent of my time protecting my ass and ten percent trying to put Sylaria back on its feet. Is it any wonder that I failed?"

"You did more than fail, Whittaker," said Cain. "You left it a hell of a lot worse than you found it."

"I very much doubt that," replied Socrates. "I may have raised taxes and kept martial law in effect, but I got rid of the illegal searches and allowed some local elections."

"And assassinated the winners."

"Only some of them. Just the ones who were trying to sabotage my regime." He smiled. "Besides, in the long run they won, didn't they? I mean, hell, they're in control of the damned planet, and here I am, hiding out under an alias."

"After plundering the treasury," noted Cain.

"Travel expenses and incidentals," said Socrates with a shrug. "The Democracy didn't pay me all that much to vacate my position—certainly not as much as it should have." He leaned back comfortably on his chair. "You've got to learn to be a realist, Sebastian."

"I've become one," said Cain. "Thanks in no small part to yourself."

"You see? There's no need for this residual bitterness. We've each gone on to become better people. I have found God, as well as modest fortune, and you have become a successful bounty hunter and a realist. Obviously Sylaria did us both a lot of good."

"Did you *find* God, or did you buy Him off?"

"It's all a matter of viewpoint," answered Socrates. "I contribute thousands of credits to His churches and sing His praises every morning, and He pretty much protects me and helps take care of business. It's a mutually nourishing relationship."

"I'm sure," said Cain wryly. "But we're getting away from the subject."

"Sylaria?"

"Santiago."

Socrates shook his head. "I already told you: that subject is closed."

"What'll it cost to open it?"

"More money than you'll ever have," said Socrates. "All the Democracy could do was depose me. I assure you Santiago can do a lot worse."

"Santiago's not the only one," said Cain, reaching into one of his many pockets and withdrawing a small ceramic weapon, which he pointed at Socrates.

"How did you get that past my security system?" asked Socrates with no show of fear or alarm.

Cain smiled. "Do you think you're the only person in the galaxy with a security system? Bounty hunters see them every day. The molecular structure of this gun has been altered so that it won't show up on any detection device."

"Very ingenious," commented Socrates. "But it still won't do you any good. After all, if you kill me, how can I tell you what I know?" He slowly reached into a pocket, withdrew a cigar, and lit it.

"And if you refuse to tell me," responded Cain, "why should I let you live?"

"You're a bounty hunter," said Socrates confidently. "You kill for money. There's no price on my head."

"Don't push your luck," said Cain. "You're one man I wouldn't mind killing for free."

Socrates chuckled in amusement. "We turned out a strange crop of humanitarians back on Sylaria, didn't we?"

"I'd be a little more worried if I were you, friend," said Terwilliger. "That's the Songbird pointing that pistol in your direction."

"Is that supposed to mean something?" asked Socrates, puffing on his cigar and displaying a total lack of concern.

"It means he'll do what he says he'll do," said Terwilliger. "This is just business to him. He does it all the time."

"I'm counting on his being just a little bit brighter than you," replied Socrates calmly. "Killing me won't get him the information he wants, and you already know that I'm expecting company momentarily."

"There's no reason to let you live *unless* you tell me what I want to know," said Cain. "As for your visitor, you've been known to lie before."

"Not this time, Sebastian," said Socrates, checking his

timepiece. "She's already a few minutes late." He smiled. "She's a reporter. You kill me now and you'll make every newscast from here to Deluros."

Cain stared at him for a long moment. Then he glanced quickly around the room.

"That's a very pretty bowl," he said, indicating a delicate fluted structure. "Made by Canphorites?"

"Robelians," replied Socrates. "Why?"

"What's it worth—about twenty thousand credits?"

"Give or take."

Cain fired off a quick shot, and the object shattered into a thousand tiny pieces as Terwilliger emitted a startled yell.

"What the hell are you doing?" demanded Socrates furiously. He jumped to his feet, then sat back down just as quickly when Cain pointed the weapon at him again.

"Negotiating," answered Cain. "How much did you pay for the gold crucifix with the jeweled Christ?"

"Damn it, Sebastian! That's a priceless work of art!"

"You've got ten seconds to put a price on it," replied Cain. "And if you haven't told me what I want to know, you've got one more second to kiss it good-bye."

Socrates slumped back in his chair. "Destroy them all," he said resignedly. "I can replace them easier than I can replace *me*."

"You mean it, don't you?"

"I do."

"Maybe I've been approaching this all wrong." Cain lowered his aim a few inches. "What's the going price on a kneecap?"

"Not high enough," said Socrates defiantly.

"Courage from Whittaker Drum? Now that *is* surprising."

"I'm no hero," said Socrates. "But there's nothing you can do to me that'll compare to what *he* can do."

"I wouldn't bet my life on that if I were you," said Cain.

"That's precisely what I'm betting. Whatever else you do, you won't kill me."

Just then there was a high-pitched beeping noise.

"That's her," said Socrates, turning his head and staring at a small holographic viewscreen. "You'd better put your gun away and leave while you can."

"Not a chance," said Cain. "What does she want?"

"Probably the same thing you do."

There was another beeping sound.

"We'd better answer it," said Terwilliger, checking the viewscreen to make sure Socrates wasn't lying. "She's got to know he's here."

Cain nodded, and the gambler walked over to a small control panel on the wall just behind Socrates' chair. The first two buttons he pushed flooded the apartment with music and dimmed the lights in the vestibule, but finally he hit the proper one and they heard the front door slide open.

A moment later a blonde woman in her midthirties entered the room. She was a few pounds overweight, though far from fat, her tunic and slacks were functional rather than stylish, and she wore no makeup at all. A leather satchel was slung over one shoulder.

She took in the situation in a single glance and immediately turned to Cain.

"Don't kill him until I talk to him," she said. "I'll make it worth your while."

"Nobody's killing anybody just yet," interjected Socrates, unperturbed. "We're still in the threatening stage."

"Who are you and what's your business here?" asked Cain, getting to his feet and backing up a few steps to incorporate both her and Socrates into his field of vision.

"I might ask you the same thing," she replied.

"You might," he agreed. "But I asked you first, and I've got the gun."

She stared at him for a moment, then shrugged. "My name is Virtue MacKenzie. I'm a journalist; I make holographic documentaries."

"What are you doing here?"

"I came here to do a feature on Socrates."

"Where's your technical crew?" asked Cain.

"I do my own tech work," she said. "And I'm all through answering questions. Now it's your turn."

"I've got one more," said Cain. "Have you talked to Whittaker Drum yet?"

"Who the hell is Whittaker Drum?"

Cain smiled with satisfaction. "Okay. You've told me everything I need to know." He paused for a moment. "Terwilliger, get her out of here."

The gambler began approaching her.

"That's close enough," said Virtue menacingly.

Terwilliger grinned and took another step forward. As he did so, she lashed out with a foot, catching him just below the knee. He dropped to the floor, cursing and groaning and holding his leg tenderly. "You don't listen too well, do you?" she said contemptuously.

"Oh, my!" said Socrates, vastly amused. "This *is* getting interesting."

"You shut up!" snapped Cain.

"Are you ready to answer *my* questions yet?" demanded Virtue, ignoring Terwilliger and turning back to Cain.

"All right," he said.

"Who are you?"

"Sebastian Cain."

"The one they call the Songbird?" she asked.

He grimaced. "Yes."

"Why do you want to kill him?"

"I don't," replied Cain. "I want the same thing you do."

"And what do *I* want?"

"Information about Santiago."

"What makes you think so?"

"Because you didn't know that Socrates used to be Whittaker Drum—and the only important thing he's done since changing his name is to meet Santiago."

"I resent that," said Socrates.

"What's *your* interest in Santiago?" asked Virtue.

"Professional," said Cain. "And yours?"

"The same," she replied. "I really *do* produce documentaries. I convinced a couple of backers that I could get an exclusive feature on Santiago, and managed to wring a pretty substantial advance out of them."

"And now you have to deliver," suggested Cain, amused.

She nodded. "It's taken me almost a year to get this far; I don't want you killing him before I talk to him." She glanced at Terwilliger, who was getting painfully to his feet. "Who's this one?"

"Nobody very important," said Cain.

"Thanks a heap," muttered the gambler, flexing his leg and wincing in pain. "I think something's broken."

"If it was, you wouldn't be able to move it like that," said Virtue. "Now stop whining and shut up."

Terwilliger glared at her, then went back to massaging his knee.

"All right, Mr. Cain," she said, turning to the bounty hunter. "What now?"

"What do you suggest?"

"Our interests are parallel, but not identical," she replied. "I don't care if you kill Santiago, as long as I get my feature—and I assume you don't begrudge me my feature as long as you get your reward. I don't see much sense fighting to the death over who gets to extract the information we need."

He nodded. "Which brings us back to you, Whittaker."

Socrates smiled. "Nothing has changed, Sebastian. You can't afford to kill me, and I can't afford to let Santiago know I've betrayed him. So, while you can certainly cause me a great deal of pain, you're not going to get what you want."

"It's a possibility," admitted Cain. "On the other hand, finding out if you've got a breaking point is going to hurt you a lot more than it hurts me."

"Don't be an ass, Cain," said Virtue. "There's an easier way to do this."

"I'm open to suggestions," replied Cain.

"We'll shoot a couple of cc's of niathol into him and he'll tell us anything we want to know."

"Niathol isn't something that bounty hunters tend to carry around," Cain said wryly.

"Then isn't it lucky for you that I came prepared?" she said, unfastening her satchel.

"You expected to have to use it?"

"I anticipated the possibility," she replied, withdrawing a small package and starting to unwrap it.

"You couldn't have known I'd be here. How did you plan to get him to hold still for it?"

"The same way I convinced your friend to leave me alone," she replied, pulling out a small vial that had been wrapped in refrigerated tape. A moment later she had filled a small, sterile syringe with it.

"Well, Whittaker," said Cain, "are you going to make this easy on yourself, or am I going to have to hold you down?"

"All right, Sebastian," said Socrates with a sigh. "Skip the drug. I'll tell you what you want to know."

"That's very thoughtful of you, but I think as long as we

have the niathol we won't bother relying on the eccentricities of your memory. Roll up your sleeve.''

Socrates did as he was told, and Virtue walked across the room to him with the syringe in her hand.

''That looks like a hell of a lot more than two cc's,'' remarked Cain.

''It can't be refrozen,'' she replied. ''We'll just toss the syringe into an atomizer when we're done.''

''Terwilliger,'' ordered Cain, ''get over there and hold him still, just in case he has a change of heart.''

Terwilliger stared reluctantly at Socrates.

''Why don't you do it yourself?'' suggested the gambler.

''My job is holding the gun,'' said Cain. ''Yours is doing what I tell you to do. Go on; he won't kick you.''

Terwilliger hobbled over to Socrates very cautiously.

''I know about niathol, but I've never used it,'' said Cain. ''In my business, we're not usually after confessions. How long before it takes effect?''

''About ninety seconds,'' replied Virtue. ''Maybe a little longer.'' She had Terwilliger hold Socrates' arm motionless, jabbed him a couple of times until she found a vein, and then began injecting the niathol.

And then things happened so rapidly that even Cain wasn't sure of the exact progression.

Socrates casually removed his cigar from his mouth with his free hand, then suddenly pressed it against Virtue's right wrist. She yelped and jumped back, letting go of the syringe, which remained stuck in his arm. Terwilliger reacted instantly, taking a roundhouse swing at Socrates. It landed on his neck, but the momentum carried the gambler's body between Cain and Socrates.

''Hit the ground!'' yelled Cain, but even as the words left his mouth and Terwilliger dropped to the floor, Socrates had forced the syringe's plunger all the way down before Virtue could stop him.

''You lose, Sebastian,'' he said with an ironic smile as Cain realized what he had done and lowered his weapon.

''You dumb bastard!'' snapped Virtue. ''You'll be dead inside of a minute.''

''At least it's painless this way,'' said Socrates, his words starting to slur.

''Well, as long as you're finally going to meet your God

face to face. I hope for your sake that He's the forgiving type," said Cain.

"Not to worry, Sebastian," said Socrates with a hollow laugh. "He's in the bag."

He slumped forward.

"Shit!" snapped Virtue. "Who the hell would have thought he'd do something like that?" She opened one of his eyelids, stared at the pupil for few seconds, then let it fall shut again. "He's done."

"He's really dead?" asked Terwilliger, staring at him.

Virtue stared contemptuously at him and made no reply.

"Thanks a lot," said Cain sardonically.

"Don't you go acting so goddamned superior!" she shot back. "If you thought he was going to do that, you should have said so."

"I should have done it my way."

"Your way wouldn't have worked, either. Don't you understand that he was willing to suffer anything you could offer up rather than let Santiago know he'd betrayed him?" She paused and stared thoughtfully at Socrates. "Just what kind of man can put such fear into people?"

"Maybe you'd be better off returning your advance and not finding out," suggested Cain.

"Most of it is spent," she replied. "I can't go back without my feature. Besides, I've already spent a year of my life on this project."

"There are men who have spent thirty years hunting for Santiago," noted Cain.

"Most of them never got this far," said Virtue. "And the journalist who actually brings back tapes or holos of Santiago will be as famous as *he* is; she'll need a warehouse just to hold her awards, and she can choose her own assignments and name her own price for the rest of her career." She paused. "It's worth the effort."

"Have fun."

"I'm not beaten yet," she said with determination. "I have other leads."

"Oh?" he replied, suddenly alert.

She nodded. "Well, Mr. Cain?"

"Well what?"

"I'll show you mine if you show me yours," she said with a grin.

He shrugged. "Why not?"

"There's a condition."

"What?"

"We keep in touch, and give each other progress reports."

"How?"

She jerked a thumb in Terwilliger's direction. "Use *him*. He's not much good for anything else, is he?"

"Now just a goddamned minute!" said the gambler hotly.

"Out of the question," said Cain. "I'd have to give him his own ship."

"Let him use yours," said Virtue. "We won't be that far apart."

"What makes you think he won't just take off with it?"

"Will you stop talking about me as if I wasn't here?" demanded Terwilliger petulantly.

"Shut up," said Virtue. She turned back to Cain. "Offer him ten percent of the reward. That ought to buy the little bastard's loyalty."

"I'm not giving him any percentage right now Why should I change that?"

"Because you don't have any information right now."

Cain lowered his head in thought for a long moment, then looked up.

"If your leads are the same as mine, the deal's off."

"Fair enough," she replied.

"Don't *I* get a say in this?" snapped Terwilliger.

"Do you want ten percent of twenty million credits enough to do what you're told, or not?" said Virtue.

The gambler glared at her, then realized what was being offered and smiled sheepishly. "I'm in," he said.

"Somehow I'm not surprised," she replied. "Well, *that's* settled. Now I suppose we'd better do something about the body."

"I'll take care of it," said Cain.

"After you visit the local post office and see if there's any paper on him?" she suggested.

"That's right."

"I think I should get half," she continued. "It was my niathol that killed him."

"Are you a journalist or a bounty hunter?" Cain asked wryly.

SANTIAGO: A MYTH OF THE FAR FUTURE 73

"Why don't we say that I'm an underpaid journalist, and let it go at that."

He stared at her and finally nodded in agreement. "Okay. If there's any reward for him, you get half."

"You know," commented Terwilliger, who had been scrutinizing her, "you could be damned attractive if you'd just go to a little effort."

"Too bad the same can't be said for you," she said, turning her attention back to Cain. "All right, Songbird—are you ready to compare notes?"

"I'm ready," he answered.

"I have a feeling that this is going to be a long and amiable relationship," predicted Virtue.

"I'll settle for its just being profitable," replied Cain.

"That goes without saying."

He smiled and shook his head. "That's the one thing that *never* goes without saying."

She extended her hand. "Partners?"

"Partners."

They shook hands over the unmourned corpse of Whittaker Drum.

Part 2

The Virgin Queen's Book

6

She can drink, she can swear, can the Virgin Queen,
And she isn't a stranger to sin.
She knows what she wants, doesn't care where she's been,
And she'll do what she has to to win.

The name was Black Orpheus' idea of a joke, because while Virtue MacKenzie was a lot of things good and bad, virginal wasn't one of them.

He met her just once, out by the Delphini system—which was as close to the worlds of the Democracy as he ever tended to go—and she made quite an impression on him. She was drinking and playing cards at the time, and she wasn't even aware of his presence; but when she accused a fellow journalist of cheating and backed it up with a couple of swift kicks to his groin and a whiskey bottle slammed down on top of his head, she guaranteed herself a couple of verses in his ongoing epic.

In point of fact, she didn't even know she'd been written up until some months later, and then she was furious about the name he'd saddled her with—but after a couple of weeks she cooled down, right about the time she decided that being in Black Orpheus' song just might open a couple of doors for her out on the Frontier.

It did, too. She had to wait until the balladeer's disciples and interpreters figured out that Virtue MacKenzie and the Virgin Queen were the same woman and started disseminating the information across the Inner Frontier, but once the word got out it helped her get into a couple of previously inaccessible places on Terrazane, where she found out about Socrates, and it got her Socrates' address from a trader on Jefferson III.

It hadn't done her much good here on Pegasus, but this was the Democracy, not the Frontier, and Black Orpheus wasn't much better known here than the outcasts and misfits that he sang about. She and Cain had traded their information in Socrates' apartment three weeks ago, each holding back a couple of tidbits—at least, she assumed Cain had withheld some information; she knew that *she* had—and it was decided that Cain was better equipped to track down a professional assassin like Altair of Altair, whereas Virtue knew her way around the Democracy better than he did and would begin her hunt among the Democracy's older, more established worlds.

She had spent the better part of a week searching for Salvatore Acosta, one of the four black marketeers who had delivered Santiago's goods to the Sargasso Rose, and had found out from her own sources that he had been murdered on Pegasus two months earlier.

Pegasus was a former mining world, rich in gold and fissionable materials, which was now a heavily populated member of the Democracy. It had been named for the planet's dominant herbivore, a small horselike animal that possessed a pair of fleshy protuberances just behind its withers. (They had never been used for anything other than balance, but they looked remarkably like vestigial wings.)

The planet itself was one of those odd scattered worlds that seemed Earth-like, but wasn't truly habitable in the normal sense. It possessed oxygen, nitrogen, and the various inert gases that Men needed, but they existed in the wrong quantities, and twenty minutes' exposure to the atmosphere left one breathless and panting; an hour could be fatal to anyone with a respiratory problem; and even the healthiest settlers couldn't breathe the air for two hours.

But for some reason—possibly it was the view, for Pegasus was a gorgeous world, with snow-capped mountains and literally thousands of winding rivers, and was possessed of gold-and-brown vegetation that made the landscape look perpetually crisp and autumnal; though more likely it was the location, for it was midway between the Spica mining worlds and the huge financial center on Daedalus II—the planet became a very desirable piece of real estate. The original miners had lived underground, artificially enriching their air while protecting themselves from the extremely cold nights; but once the world started drawing crowds of permanent residents, construction began on a domed city, then five more, and ultimately a seventh that was almost as large as the first six combined. All of the cities bore Greek names; the newest and largest of them was Hektor, named after the supposedly mythical warrior who local historians had erroneously decided was either the rider or trainer of the winged horse.

Upon reaching Pegasus and taking a hotel room in Hektor, Virtue MacKenzie had immediately contacted Leander Smythe, a newsman who owed her a favor and very begrudgingly allowed her to access the raw data he possessed on Acosta's murder from her room's computer. There wasn't much information to be gleaned: Acosta had a long record of shady dealings, and more than his share of enemies. His throat had been slit as he was leaving the Pearl of the Sea, a restaurant and bar catering to the less wholesome elements of Pegasan society, and he had died instantly. It was assumed to be an underworld murder, if only because Acosta himself hadn't associated with any noncriminals in more than a decade.

Virtue then called up the shopping and restaurant guide that every hotel possessed but couldn't find any listing for the Pearl of the Sea, invariably a signal that a local pub or restaurant had a steady clientele and neither needed nor desired any new business. She then accessed a video overview of the city and homed in on the area around the restaurant. It seemed as sleek and shining and well kept as the rest of Hektor, but she noticed that the police patrolled the area in pairs—which tended to support her tentative decision that visiting it alone and asking pointed questions wasn't worth the risk involved.

Five minutes later she tied in to the local police headquarters' press department and quickly ascertained that the authorities weren't about to hand any information over to an offworld journalist. She immediately called back, asked to speak to the homicide department, identified herself as Acosta's grieving half sister, and demanded to know what progress had been made in apprehending his killer. The answer was simple enough: There had been absolutely no progress, nor was there likely to be. From the contemptuous way they spoke about

Acosta, she got the distinct impression that the only thing they would do if they actually found his murderer would be shake his hand, and perhaps pin a medal on him.

Finally she had the computer check her message drop—a dumb terminal in the city's central post office—to see if there was any word from Cain or Terwilliger, found nothing waiting for her, and decided to spend a little more time investigating Acosta's murder before going after Khalythorpe, the methane-breathing smuggler who was next on the Sargasso Rose's list.

She asked the computer for a running total on her expenses thus far, found that she had run up almost three hundred credits in user and access fees, and told it to warn her when she reached the five-hundred-credit mark.

She then opened a bottle of Camorian vodka, filled a cup from the bathroom, pretended that there was an olive in it, sipped it thoughtfully, and decided upon her next step, which was to access the local library's main computer. She had it scan the past five years' worth of news reports, keying on Acosta's name, and came up absolutely empty. She then tried to find some similarity between his murder and other killings that had taken place in the same area, and discovered that of the thirty-nine murders in Hektor during the past year, thirty-two of them had occurred within a mile of where Acosta had been found, and nineteen were the result of stabbings. It was quite possible, she concluded unhappily, that Acosta simply had been in the wrong place at the wrong time; at any rate, there was no reason to assume that he had died because of his association with Santiago.

Dead end followed dead end, and finally she was faced with two alternatives: start questioning people who might have known Acosta, or give up and go after the methane-breather. She made her decision, then instructed the computer to patch in a visual connection to Leander Smythe's office.

A moment later a portly, middle-aged man with a sightly uneven hair transplant appeared on the small screen just above the speaker.

"I know I'm going to regret asking this," he said when he had recognized her, "but what can I do for you?"

"I'm up against a blank wall, Leander," she said.

"Who are you trying to kid, Virtue?" replied Smythe. "You've only been on the damned planet for four hours."

"That's all the time it takes to know I'm not going to get what I want through normal channels." She paused. "I hate calling in favors," she added insincerely, "but I need your help."

"You already collected your favor this morning," he reminded her.

She smiled. "You owe me a bigger one than that, Leander. Or would you like me to refresh your memory?"

"No!" he said quickly. "This isn't a secure channel."

"Then invite me to lunch and we'll talk face to face."

"I'm busy."

"Fine." She shrugged. "Then I'll just have to hunt up someone else from your network who'll do me a favor in exchange for a very interesting story about a local journalist."

She reached out to sever the connection.

"Wait!" he said urgently.

She withdrew her hand and grinned triumphantly.

"There's a restaurant on the top of my building," he said. "I'll meet you there in half an hour."

"Your treat," she said. "I'm just a poor working girl."

She broke the connection, ascertained that 493 credits for computer usage would be added to her hotel tab, entered a request (without much hope) for a ten percent professional discount, took the elevator down to the fourth floor of the hotel, walked out on a platform, and caught the Hanging Tube—the inhabitants' term for the elevated monorail—to Smythe's office building. She noticed in passing that a thunderstorm was in full force outside the dome and that the noonday sky was almost black, and wondered idly what the little herbivores for which the planet had been named did to shield themselves from the weather, since she had seen precious few natural shelters on her way from the spaceport to the city.

When she arrived at Smythe's building, she presented her credentials to a security guard at the door. The man gave them a perfunctory glance, nodded, and passed her through to the upper lobby, where she took an elevator to the roof.

The restaurant would have impressed anyone who had been born on the Frontier, but Virtue found it just a bit overdone: the tables were too small, the furniture too ornate, and there were too many very self-assured waiters hovering around. She ascertained that Smythe wasn't there yet, found that he

had reserved a table for two, allowed the maître d' to escort
her to a seat, and ordered a mixed drink from the bar.

Smythe arrived about five minutes later, walked directly to
the bar, ordered a drink for himself, and then joined her at the
table.

"It's good to see you again after all these years, Virtue,"
he said, greeting her with an artificial smile.

"How nice of you to say so," she replied dryly. "And
how well you lie."

"Let's at least maintain the illusion of civility," he said,
unperturbed. "Until we're through with lunch, anyway."

"Suits me."

He picked up his menu, pretended to study it for a moment, recommended a dish to Virtue, signaled for a waiter,
and ordered for both of them.

"It's been a long time," he said when the waiter had gone
off to the kitchen. "What is it now—five years?"

"Six."

"I've seen your byline from time to time, when some of
your features have come up for syndication. That was a very
nice piece you did on the war with the Borgaves."

"Ugly beasts, aren't they?" she commented.

"How did you manage to land with the first invasion wave?"
he asked. "That's usually reserved for senior correspondents."

"I bribed a nice young major."

"That figures," he said with a tinge of bitterness. "You
always knew how to get what you wanted."

"I still do," she said, staring directly at him.

He met her gaze for a moment, then looked away uncomfortably. "Did you ever marry that fellow you used to live
with?"

"I've lived with a number of people," she replied. "I
never married any of them."

"Pity." He pulled out a handsome cigarette case and offered one to her.

"No, thanks."

"They're very good," he said, removing one and lighting
it up. "Imported from the Kakkab Kastu system."

"I prefer my own," she said, withdrawing a distinctive
box.

"Don't you find those kind of harsh?" he asked.

"I've been smoking them since I've been on the Frontier," replied Virtue. "They grow on you after a while."

"You've been on the Frontier?"

"For almost a year."

"What were you doing out there?"

"The same thing I'm doing on Pegasus: following up a story." She paused. "I've also picked up a pretty interesting partner."

"I thought you always worked alone," said Smythe.

"This time I needed help."

"Is it anyone I know?"

"Probably not," Virtue replied. "Ever hear of the Songbird?"

He shook his head. "Is that her byline?"

"It's a him."

"I've never seen any of his features."

"That's not surprising. He's a bounty hunter."

"What the hell kind of story are you working on?"

"If I tell you, we're all through exchanging pleasantries and we start talking business."

He shifted his weight uneasily but nodded in agreement. "We're going to do it sooner or later. I suppose we ought to get it over with." He paused. "Salvatore Acosta was a small-time smuggler who died broke. He wasn't worth much more than a five-second obituary. So who are you really after?"

"Santiago."

He laughed. "You and ten thousand other journalists."

"I'm different," said Virtue seriously. "I'm going to get him."

"I wish you luck."

"I don't need luck," she replied. "I need information."

"You probably know more about Acosta than I do."

"Forget Acosta," said Virtue. "He's a dead end. I need something else."

"Such as?"

"Someone who can tell me where Santiago is."

Smythe laughed again. "Why don't you ask for a million credits while you're at it? One's as likely as the other."

"This person doesn't have to know Santiago's headquarters. He just has to point me in the right direction."

"What the hell makes you think anyone on Pegasus has any dealings with Santiago?"

"Because, with all due respect for your beautiful city, it's not exactly a vacation spa. Acosta was here to deliver some goods or some money, or else to pick something up. He probably didn't deal directly with the person I want—but that doesn't mean you can't help me find that person."

"Are you telling me Acosta worked for Santiago?" asked Smythe.

"Indirectly. I doubt that they ever met. Acosta was just a conduit for stolen goods, or perhaps money. What I need from you is the name of the biggest operator in Hektor."

"Harrison Brett," replied Smythe without hesitation.

"Does he have a criminal record?"

"Yes."

"Tell me about it."

"He's got thirty arrests."

"Any convictions?"

Smythe looked uncomfortable. "Two."

"Suspended sentences?"

He nodded.

"Who's he paying off?" she asked quickly.

Smythe shrugged. "Everybody."

She smiled. "Come on, Leander—this is Virtue you're talking to, not some slob in your newsroom. You know what I want."

"Why not just put the pressure on Brett?" he asked in a tone of voice that implied he knew the answer as well as she did.

"How do you pressure a man who knows he can't go to jail?" she replied. "The name, please."

"I don't know any other name," he said.

"Not smart, Leander," she said ominously. "Not smart at all."

"It's the truth," he replied defensively.

"*I* know another name, though," she said. "The name I know is Leander Smythe. I even know some facts to go with the name. Want to hear them?"

"No," he said, puffing rapidly on his cigarette.

"They're interesting facts," she continued. "They're all about how he falsified evidence on his first big story and helped send an innocent man to jail for eight years."

"You *covered* for me, for Christ's sake!" he hissed. "If you knew he was innocent, why didn't you block the story when you had the chance?"

"Oh, he deserved to go to jail," she said pleasantly. "He was a bastard from the word go, and the police had been trying to nail him for years." She stared seriously at him. "But the fact remains that he was innocent of the charges that were brought against him based on your information."

"Then you should have said something at the time."

"I did," she replied, finishing her drink. "I told you that you owed me a favor in exchange for my silence, and that someday I'd be by to collect it."

"You know," he said unhappily, "I never did like you much. You were always too ambitious, always scheming and plotting."

"Why should I deny it?" she said calmly. "I'll only add that it's people like you who made it easy."

"What'll you do when you finally get to the top, and there are no more bodies to climb over?"

"Mostly, I'll enjoy it," she replied. "And I'll protect myself a hell of a lot better than the rest of you ever did."

"How many other favors have you stockpiled over the years?" he asked bitterly.

"A few."

"And how many other people have you blackmailed with them?"

"I'm not blackmailing you, Leander," replied Virtue. "I have other leads. If you don't want to do me a favor, you don't have to. Just forget I asked."

"You mean it?"

"Absolutely." She paused. "Of course, I'll have to pay a visit to your superiors. After all, I'm a journalist—and what you did qualifies as news, even after all these years." She smiled. "Don't worry; you won't go to jail for it—but you'd better find a new profession."

"Have you ever done anything, even once, with no thought of a return?" he asked.

"Yes."

"How old were you? Six?"

"Younger. And I immediately decided that there was no percentage in it."

"Who did your bounty hunter have to kill for you before you teamed up with him?"

"Actually, he had to postpone killing someone," said Virtue. "But we're straying from the subject. I need a name."

He nervously lit another cigarette before his first had gone out. "You must understand: I can't be connected with it."

"You won't be," she assured him, leaning forward intently. "The name."

"This is it?" he said. "You'll never bring up that damned story again?"

"I promise."

He sighed. "Dimitri Sokol."

"How big is he?"

"Very. He's a multimillionaire, he's a director of half a dozen corporations, he's held a couple of political offices, and word is that he's about to buy himself an ambassadorship to Lodin Eleven."

"Better and better," she said with a predatory grin. "What have you got on him?"

"Officially, nothing."

"Come on, Leander. Just blurt it all out and then forget you told me. Women?"

Smythe shook his head. "Not a chance."

"Men? Little boys? Drugs?"

"Just money. He bankrolled a smuggling operation out in the Binder system, though I think it would take you a couple of lifetimes to pierce through his corporate veil. I've got a feeling that he was peripherally involved in a couple of murders six years ago—*very* peripherally—and I know he's given and taken bribes. Anyway, somewhere along the way he decided that he wanted to be respectable, and he's been cleaning up his image for the past three years."

"And now he wants an ambassadorship?"

"So I'm told."

"Okay, Leander—start giving me names and dates, and then I think we can go our separate ways."

"I don't *know* any names and dates for sure. It's all gossip and conjecture."

"I know. Now let's have them."

"Damn! I wish I could give you a suicide pill or something, just in case this doesn't work."

"I wouldn't take it."

"I know," he muttered.

Their lunch arrived, and while they ate—she enthusiastically, he totally without interest—Smythe laid out such details of Sokol's dealings as he had been able to piece together. Virtue took no notes, but he knew that she'd be able to recite the list verbatim a month later.

"I'll try to set up an appointment with Sokol for tomorrow afternoon," Virtue announced when they were finished with dessert and sipping their after-dinner drinks.

"What makes you think he'll see you?" asked Smythe.

"Turn down an interview with a journalist from Deluros with an ambassadorship in the offing?" she replied with a chuckle. "Not a chance."

"Since when are you from Deluros?"

"Since tomorrow morning."

"He'll check you out before he sees you."

"I know," said Virtue. "That's why you're going to program my new credentials into your network's computer. It's the first place he'll look if he has any doubts about me."

"The hell I will!" he exploded, then lowered his voice when he realized he was attracting the attention of the other diners. "That's above and beyond our agreement," he said, lowering his voice.

"True. I won't threaten you with your . . . ah, journalistic indiscretion again. I gave you my word, and I intend to keep it."

"Then that's settled," he said firmly. "I'm not loading false credentials in the computer."

"The choice is entirely yours," she said. "I suppose I'll just have to tell Sokol to verify my position with you personally." She shrugged. "There's always the chance that he won't put two and two together and figure out who gave me the stuff I'm going to use on him."

"You'd do it, wouldn't you?" he said furiously. "You'd really do it!"

"Nobody's going to stop me from finding Santiago—not you, not anyone. I've staked my career on it."

"Then why don't you find another career? Go raise a family or something, instead of blackmailing your old friends. Jesus, but I feel sorry for your partner!"

"He's pretty good at taking care of himself. I think your

sympathy would be better spent on a sweet, innocent girl like me."

"Innocent of *what*?" he said disgustedly.

"You *will* remember to change my credentials, won't you?" she said sweetly, pushing back her chair and standing up.

"Yes," he muttered. "I'll change them."

"And one more thing, Leander."

"What other little favor can I do for you?" he asked. "Pluck out my eyeballs so you can play marbles with them?"

"Some other time, perhaps." Suddenly she was serious. "I'm sure everything will go smoothly—but just in case I don't come back, or get word to you that I'm all right, I want you to contact Sebastian Cain."

"Who the hell is that?" he demanded.

"The Songbird." She gave him the registration number of Cain's ship. "He should be in the Altair system in the next day or two."

"What message do you want me to give him?"

"I should think that would be obvious," she replied. "I may die unmourned, but I sure as hell don't plan to die unavenged."

7.

Since Black Orpheus never returned to the populated worlds of the Democracy, and Dimitri Sokol never left them, it's only natural that he gave Sokol neither a verse nor a nickname. They never met, never crossed paths, never even knew the other existed—which was probably just as well: Black Orpheus wouldn't have liked him much. Orpheus loved the uninhibited, colorful men and women of the Frontier; Sokol was calm, calculating, and self-controlled. Black Orpheus painted his word pictures in primaries; Dimitri Sokol was a pastel.

Sokol was a civilized man, and as such he indulged in the crimes of civilization. If a man had to be killed, his hand may have held the checkbook, but it never touched the weapon. If there was smuggling or black marketeering to be done, he put so many holding companies and middlemen between himself and his hirelings that he might as well have been on Deluros VIII itself. He craved respectability, which Black Orpheus disdained; and he disdained notoriety, which Black Orpheus dedicated his career to perpetuating.

Orpheus would have considered him a hypocrite, which is certainly one interpretation; but the truth of the matter was that Sokol managed to walk a very fine line between his deeds and his expectations with a skill that even the Bard of the Inner Frontier would have admired.

He had vacation homes on Seabright and Pollux IV, and a suite of offices—which he hadn't visited in years—on Canphor VII. He made large donations to charity each year and had recently paid for an addition to a hospital in Pallas Athena, the oldest of Pegasus' seven enclosed cities. He was a patron of the arts and could always be counted upon to support the local symphony orchestra and ballet with handsome contributions; he no longer donated to the opera, but it was common knowledge that he disapproved of his daughter's liaison with one of the lead tenors, and nobody thought any the less of him for it.

He had spent most of his working hours during the past two years in his penthouse atop one of Hektor's more desirable residential buildings. There were twelve rooms in all; nine served as the family's residence—a son and two daughters still lived with him—and the other three rooms, with their own private entrance, had been converted into an office suite.

It was just after noon when Virtue MacKenzie presented herself in the building's lobby, waited while a security woman announced her arrival, and then took an elevator directly to Sokol's office suite. Upon emerging, she found herself in a small reception foyer, where a secretary told her that she was expected and ushered her into an opulently furnished study.

"He'll join you in just a moment," said the secretary, returning to his post by the elevator.

Virtue took that moment to examine her surroundings. Two of the walls were covered with artwork from all over the Democracy, most of it expensive, some of it good, none of it showing any consistency of taste. A third wall, composed of floor-to-ceiling windows, afforded a dramatic view of a blue river and a deep ravine just beyond the dome. The carpet was plush, made of some wiry alien fabric which seemed to shrink from the touch of her foot, then instantly moved back and pressed against it once she had set it down. There was a large holographic videoscreen, the controls of which were built into the arm of a leather couch. There were four matching chairs, two of them almost pristine, the other two showing some signs of wear. An alien musical instrument, bulky as a piano but of a type she had never seen before, was carefully angled into a corner. Atop it were six small cubes, each containing a hologram of a member of the Sokol family. She picked up one containing the representation of a lovely young woman and examined it.

"My youngest daughter," said a firm, friendly voice, and she turned to find that Sokol had entered the room.

He was a tall man, burly without being overweight, with a well-groomed shock of steel-gray hair and a dapper mustache.

His eyes were a deep blue, his nose absolutely straight, his chin square without being prominent. He wore an elegantly embroidered suit of a style that had recently been popular on Deluros VIII.

"She's very pretty," replied Virtue, setting the cube back down.

"Thank you," said Sokol. "I'll tell her you said so." He touched a concealed control behind a picture, and instantly a section of the carpet disappeared and a small but well-stocked bar rose from the floor. "Can I fix you a drink?"

"Why not?" she replied.

"What will you have?"

"What do you recommend?"

He reached for a strangely shaped bottle. "Cygnian cognac. A gift from a friend who recently returned from Altair."

"I thought you said it was Cygnian," remarked Virtue, filing the reference to Altair away for future reference.

"I did. But Cygnian cognac is in demand all across the galaxy." He paused, then smiled. "If you'd ever tasted the stuff they brew on Altair, you'd know why he brought me this instead."

He poured two glasses and handed one to her.

"Very good," she replied, taking a sip.

"Won't you have a seat?" he said, escorting her to a chair, then sitting down across from her. He pulled out a large cigar. "Do you mind if I smoke?"

"Not at all."

"It's from old Earth itself," he said proudly, lighting up. "They're very hard to come by these days."

"I can imagine."

"Still," he said, exhaling a streak of smoke, "they're worth the effort." He paused. "By the way, where's your camera crew?"

"I don't have one," she replied, opening her well-worn satchel and pulling out a small, metallic, many windowed device, which she placed on a table between them. "This has a pair of wide-angle three-dimensional lenses that can follow you anywhere in the room, and there's a built-in speaker that will pick up everything you say." She pressed a small activator button. "It's not studio quality, but one doesn't always know what conditions will be like in the field, and it's a pretty handy little gadget."

"Amazing!" he said, staring at it in fascination. "It covers a three-hundred-and-sixty-degree area without moving?"

She nodded. "That's right—which means I'll be in all the pictures, too. When I get it to the lab, they'll edit it to follow a standard question-and-answer format, cutting to each of us as we speak. No one except you and me and the lab technicians will know that there wasn't an entire crew on hand."

"And this will be aired on Deluros Eight?" he asked, his expression mirroring his interest.

"As well as half a dozen other systems."

"Can I get a copy of the final cut for myself?"

"I don't see why not," said Virtue. "Of course, you'll need professional equipment to play it back."

"I own some, and have access to still more."

"Fine. Shall we begin?"

"Whenever you're ready," said Sokol.

She proceeded to conduct a thorough and professional interview for the next thirty minutes, on the off chance that she might someday be able to sell it, if not to Leander Smythe's network, then to some other Pegasus news agency, or perhaps to Lodin XI if Sokol actually got himself assigned there.

"Well," she announced at last, shutting off the recording device, "I think that's it."

"It was my pleasure," replied Sokol. "You will let me know when it's ready, won't you?"

"Certainly," replied Virtue. "Of course, it all depends on how you answer the next question."

"I beg your pardon?"

"I have another question."

"Don't you want to turn the machine back on?" he asked. She shook her head. "This one is off the record."

"Okay," he said, leaning back comfortably. "Ask away."

"I want you to consider it very carefully before answering."

"I think I'm pretty used to loaded questions," he replied confidently.

"I'm glad to hear that," said Virtue, staring at him. "Where can I find Santiago?"

For just a moment he looked surprised. Then his professional politician's smile spread across his handsome face. "It's my opinion that this Santiago is just a Frontier myth. If he ever did exist, he must be dead by now."

"He's alive."

"I very much doubt it."

"If you want someone who doesn't exist, Mr. Sokol," she said, "try Sidney Peru."

Suddenly the smile vanished. "Who's Sidney Peru?"

"He's a smuggler who was murdered six years ago."

"I never heard of him."

"How about Heinrich Klausmeier?" she asked.

"The name's totally unfamiliar to me."

"They both worked for you," she said. "And they were both murdered."

"What's this—some last-minute smear campaign?" he said coldly. "Because if it is, you've come to the wrong place. Anyone who wants to can go over my record. I have nothing to hide."

"I think you have a great deal to hide, Mr. Sokol," said Virtue. "Such as a smuggling ring on Binder Ten."

"I haven't been to Binder in five years," he replied. "Besides, the press tried to pin that on me the first time I ran for office. You won't get any further with it than your colleagues did, for the simple reason that I am not a criminal."

"My predecessors didn't know what *I* know."

"What do you think you know?" he asked, unperturbed.

"I know that if you don't point me in Santiago's direction, there's going to be a very interesting piece of investigatory reporting on your videoscreen before the week is out."

He looked long and hard at her, then smiled confidently. "Do your worst. I never heard of anyone called Peru or Klausmeier."

She stared at him. There was no question in her mind that he knew exactly what she was talking about; the only question was how well insulated he thought he was. She decided to take one more shot at it.

"That's not what Salvatore Acosta told me before he died," she said.

He snorted derisively. "*Another* mystery man. Who the hell is Salvatore Acosta?"

"He used to work for you, a long time ago."

"Nobody named Acosta has ever worked for me."

"I have a tape of him in which he implicates you in the murders of Peru and Klausmeier."

"I very much doubt that."

"Can you afford to take the chance?" she said. "Maybe it

won't hold up in court, and maybe it will—but it will sure as hell cost you a post on Lodin Eleven.''

"You don't have any such tape—and if you do, then the man's a liar.''

She shrugged and walked to the door. "You're welcome to your opinion.'' She turned to him. "Our editing lab can't go to work on your interview until we have a signed release; I'll send over a blank form tomorrow morning.''

Sokol stared at her.

"You know, you could have made this much more pleasant for yourself if you'd simply been open and straightforward with me," he said at last.

She laughed. "How much more straightforward can I be?''

"If you had just said, 'Mr. Sokol, I think you're wrong about Santiago's being dead, and I'd like any information you might have that could help lead me to him,' I'd have been happy to talk to you. But I don't like being bullied and blackmailed, especially when all you've got are lies and slander.''

She stared at him for a moment, then spoke:

"Mr. Sokol, I think you're wrong about Santiago's being dead, and I'd like any information you might have that could help lead me to him.''

He smiled at her. "That being the case, I'll be more than happy to help you in any way that I can. The man you want to see is a bandit out on the Frontier.''

"What's his name?''

"I have no idea what his real name is—but he calls himself the Jolly Swagman.''

"Where do I find him?''

"He makes his headquarters on a planet called Goldenrod, out in the Jolain system.''

"What's his connection to Santiago?''

"He used to work for him.''

"So did a lot of people,'' Virtue pointed out. "What makes him unique?''

"He knows Santiago personally.''

"You'd better be telling the truth,'' she said ominously.

"Do what you want with your tape,'' he said casually. "The truth can't harm me, and lies can't help you.'' He walked to the doorway, waved his hand before a hidden sensor, and the door slid into the wall. "I'll be looking forward to seeing the interview after it's been edited."

"That's the very least I'll be showing you," she replied, walking through the reception foyer to the elevator.

Sokol stood staring at the spot where she had been standing, lit another cigar, and walked back to his supply of liquor, where he poured himself another cognac.

"Did you hear all that?" he said in conversational tones.

"Yes," replied a disembodied voice.

"I want her followed."

"*Just* followed?" asked the voice.

"Until we find out where she's got the tape, or decide that she was bluffing. And I don't want her leaving the planet until I know one way or the other. In the meantime, I want a complete dossier on her. Not the crap they dished out at the network this morning, but the real stuff." He paused. "You've got four hours."

"It might take a little longer."

"Four hours," repeated Sokol.

In point of fact, it took only three hours and ten minutes, during which time Sokol gave out another interview, this one to a local reporter, and began preparing a speech he was to give at a political fund-raiser the next evening. Finally a blond man of indeterminate age entered the room, a small notebook in his hand.

"Have a seat," said Sokol. It was not a request.

"I've put all this in the computer," replied the man. "But I thought you'd want to go over it in person, just in case you had any questions."

"What have you got on her?"

"Her name is either Virtue Patience MacKenzie or Virtue Patia MacKenzie," said the man. "The records are a little unclear. It's my own feeling that she changed her middle name from Patience to Patia when she came of age. She's thirty-six years old. She was born on Belore, grew up on Sirius Five, got her degree at Aristotle—"

"That's the university planet they created a few years ago?" interrupted Sokol.

"Right. Her grades were mediocre, but Aristotle's a pretty classy place, and she was able to hire on with a news network right after that."

"How long has she worked out of Deluros?" asked the politician.

"She's never been to Deluros in her life. She worked on salary for about ten years, mostly in the Alphard sector, then went free-lance."

"Personality profile?"

"She's always been very bright, even precocious. She drinks more than she should, and has been known to gamble— badly, I might add. She appears to have a problem forming relationships; at any rate, she's entered into six serious liaisons, none of which have lasted for as much as a year."

"That hardly sounds serious to me," commented Sokol.

"That's as serious as she gets about anything except her career."

"Then you'd better tell me a little about her career."

"She resents authority; in fact, she's been fired twice for insubordination. Her work has been pretty good, well above average, but she hasn't come within hailing distance of the kind of breakthrough story that could make her reputation. She's very success-oriented; she's afraid time is running out on her, and she's getting very impatient. About a year ago she managed to fast-talk a couple of backers into tossing almost two million credits into this Santiago project. I still don't know how; it's possible she slept with them, and more likely that she blackmailed them. She's been working on the project for about eleven months, and she's run through two-thirds of the money." He paused. "I've got a feeling that this is a make-it-or-break-it situation for her. If she comes up empty, she's through."

"Why didn't she just take the money and disappear?"

"She'd rather be rich and famous than just rich."

"I know that feeling," muttered Sokol wryly. He looked at the blond man. "Anything else?"

"Yes. She found Whittaker Drum about three weeks ago, and may even have killed him."

"What kind of half-assed statement is that?" demanded Sokol. "Either she killed him or she didn't."

"It's not that simple. While she was on Declan Four, she teamed up with a bounty hunter called Cain, who's after Santiago for the reward. From what I can tell, he's pretty good at his job. Both of them were in Drum's apartment at the same time; it's anyone's guess as to who actually killed him." He glanced at his notebook. "There's another person involved: a gambler called Terwilliger. Cain took him on at Port Étrange, and they've been traveling together ever since. I don't know if he's part of their partnership or not. My own guess is that he put Cain onto Drum, or someone who could identify Drum, in exchange for some favor or another."

"What kind of favor?"

"I don't know—but gamblers tend to make enemies. A bounty hunter is probably a pretty handy person to have nearby, especially on the Frontier."

"All right," said Sokol, lighting up a cigar and staring at the glowing tip for a moment. "Let's get back to MacKenzie. How did she get to me? Drum didn't even know I exist."

The blond man shrugged. "I don't know."

"Then I'll tell you how," continued Sokol thoughtfully. "Somebody told her—either Acosta or someone else. Who has she seen since she's been on Pegasus?"

"Just Leander Smythe."

Sokol smiled. "There's the answer. That little bastard hand-fed her all the stuff he's been trying to pin on me all these years."

"Perhaps," agreed the blond man. "But I think we'd better be sure before we move."

"That shouldn't be too hard. Who was this Acosta, anyway?"

"A smuggler. He probably did handle a little stuff for Santiago from time to time."

"Did we ever have any dealings with him?"

"Not directly."

"Could he have known my name?"

"Anything's possible."

"Let's attack it another way," said Sokol. "When was he killed?"

"A couple of weeks ago."

"Before Virtue MacKenzie landed on Pegasus?"

"Right."

Sokol smiled. "Then she never met him."

"You can't be sure of that. She didn't have to meet him on Pegasus."

"Of course she did," replied Sokol. "She'd have come straight to me the second she had that interview. She's been bluffing all the way."

"Can you afford to take the chance?"

He frowned. "Not really. She can't do any serious harm to
me, but she could screw up this Lodin Eleven appointment."
He paused, rolling his cigar between his fingers. "Trace
Acosta's whereabouts for the past year and see if the two of
them could possibly have met somewhere other than Pegasus."

The blond man was back an hour later.

"Well?" demanded Sokol.

"You were right: Acosta and MacKenzie were never within
fifty light-years of each other."

"I knew it!" said Sokol triumphantly.

"What would you like done next?" asked the blond man.

"She's got to have a message drop somewhere in Hektor.
There's a chance that she's already contacted Cain, so tomorrow I want you to find some way to get word to Santiago.
Warn him to be on the alert, just in case Cain or this gambler
actually manage to hook up with the Swagman."

"Tomorrow?"

Sokol nodded. "This afternoon you're going to hunt up
Leander Smythe and see to it that he never again spreads any
malicious gossip about me. We don't want to kill a member
of the press, but I want you to give him a lesson he remem-
bers. And don't say who sent you. He'll figure it out."

"That takes care of this afternoon and tomorrow morning," said the blond man. "What about tonight?"

"Tonight? Go home and go to sleep."

"What about Virtue MacKenzie?"

"She doesn't have the tape, so she's no immediate threat. I
don't want any harm to come to her while she's on Pegasus."

"And once she leaves?"

Sokol smiled. "That's another matter, isn't it?"

8.

His name is Father William,
His aim is hard to ken:
His game is saving sinners;
His fame is killing men.

Whenever people would sit around talking with Black
Orpheus, sooner or later the question would come up: Who
did he think was the most memorable character he had met
during his wanderings? He'd lean back, sipping his wine and
staring off into the distance, enjoying the moment and the
memories, and then, just when his listeners began to think
that they weren't going to get an answer, he'd smile and say
that he'd seen a lot of men and women on the Inner Frontier—
killers like the Songbird and One-Time Charlie, tragic figures
like Schussler the Cyborg, entrepreneurs like Descartes White
(whom he had renamed Carte Blanche, a sobriquet with
which he was inordinately pleased), good women like Silent
Annie and Blessed Sarah, bad women like Flat-Nosed Sal and
Sister Sleaze, even virtual supermen like ManMountain Bates—
but not a one of them held a candle to Father William.

It had been love at first sight. Not a physical or personal
love, but the kind of love a landscape artist feels toward a
beautiful sunset. Black Orpheus painted his word pictures on
a very broad canvas, and even so, Father William was almost
too big to fit.

The first time Orpheus ever saw him was in the Corvus
system, preaching hellfire and damnation from a pulpit, and
daring anyone in his audience—which included some pretty

notorious characters—not to make a donation to his personalized, monogrammed poorbox. The next time was two years later, out by the Quinellus cluster, where Father William was serenely blessing the departed spirits of four men and a woman he had just killed. Orpheus ran into him a third and final time on Girodus II and watched, fascinated, as he shot down two outlaws, turned in their scalps for the reward (the taking of scalps was unnecessary, but nobody felt obligated to argue that particular point with Father William), donated the money to the local church, and spent the next two days spreading the gospel to the elephantine natives of the planet.

Orpheus tried to find out more about his past, but it was a fruitless quest. The only thing Father William wanted to talk about was God, though with a drink or two in his massive belly he'd be willing to segue into a discussion of Sodom and Gomorrah. He was a fabulous figure, standing just under six feet five inches, weighing close to four hundred pounds, always clad in black. He wore a pair of black leather holsters, each equipped with laser pistols which he insisted contained the purifying fire of the Lord. He had forsworn all pleasures of the flesh except gluttony, explaining that a weak evangelist was an ineffective evangelist, and that he aimed to run through a lot of calories bringing Christianity to the godless worlds of the Frontier. It was his earnest belief that any world that played host to a wanted killer was more in need of salvation than most, and it was his intention to bring those worlds into the fold by eradicating the evil and spreading the Word among the survivors. The already damned would simply start serving their infernal sentences a little early, and the remainder, freed from their evil influence, would be snatched from Satan's avaricious grasp for all eternity—or until such time as the government issued paper on them.

Father William wasn't as famous as he might have been. Black Orpheus only gave him three verses, a third of what he'd given to Giles Sans Pitié, who wasn't anywhere near as colorful or interesting, but that was mainly because Orpheus figured the Bible-toting bounty hunter was so much bigger than life that there simply wasn't a lot more that could be said about him. And since the stanzas were brief and muted, and the ever-growing epic was now well past two thousand verses, people who hadn't heard Black Orpheus expound upon him could be forgiven for having overlooked his exploits.

Virtue MacKenzie was one of those people. She didn't know that Father William was preaching on Goldenrod, and wouldn't have cared even if she had known. Her only interest was in finding the outlaw known as the Jolly Swagman, and, through him, Santiago.

She landed her ship on Goldenrod, a temperate little world that was owned by a cartel of farming syndicates. The crops were harvested by robots, which worked under the direction of a handful of men and women who pretended that they were executives but knew in their hearts that they were only mechanics and caretakers. There was only one city, an ancient Tradertown that predated the farms and had expanded to the point where it now housed almost eight thousand inhabitants; and, like so many Tradertowns on the Frontier, it bore the name of the planet.

She had a feeling that she wouldn't be staying there long, so rather than reserving a room at a hotel, she left her gear in her ship and took a shuttlecart into the Tradertown. When the cart came to a stop, she found herself in the middle of a town square, surrounded by long, low buildings and standing next to a monument of the planet's founder.

Unlike Cain, who had spent two decades traveling from one Tradertown to the next and usually sought his information in bars and brothels, she hunted up the local news office—the world was too small to possess its own network and in fact employed only one stringer—presented her credentials, and asked for the Jolly Swagman's whereabouts.

"You've got more important things to worry about than meeting the Swagman," said the middle-aged man who had greeted her.

"Such as?" asked Virtue.

"You might start by giving some serious thought to getting off the planet alive."

"What are you talking about?"

"Well," he said, "it's not news, so we haven't released it—not that any other world would give a damn about what goes on here anyway—but the word on the grapevine is that you made a certain party on Pegasus very angry with you. He thought it might be bad for business to redress his grievances too close to home, so he chose Goldenrod as a more fitting setting."

"He's put a hit out on me?"

"I understand that he's hired three killers to see to it that you don't leave Goldenrod."

"Who are they?"

He shrugged. "I don't know."

"Wonderful," she muttered. She glanced out at the street, trying to guess which of the many people that she could see looked like hired killers, then turned back to the stringer. "How do I apply for police protection?"

The man shook his head. "You're not in the Democracy any longer: We don't *have* a police department."

"You must have *some* way of protecting your citizens," she persisted.

"Goldenrod is the Swagman's world—*he* protects it."

"I thought Goldenrod belonged to a bunch of corporations that own all the property."

"Well, legally it does. But they're all headquartered on Deluros and Earth and the Canphor Twins, and as long as the farms continue showing a profit they don't much care what goes on here. Besides, when you make an unofficial arrangement to let someone like the Swagman stay on your world, you expect something in return."

"So they give him sanctuary here, and in exchange he sees to it that nobody tries to hijack their goods or short-change their representatives. Is that it?" asked Virtue.

"Something like that," said the man. "I don't know the exact arrangement, but I'm sure you're pretty close to it."

"Fine," said Virtue. "Then let's get word to him that I want to see him, and get him to extend his protection to me."

"I thought you understood the situation," said the man irritably. "I guess you don't."

"What am I missing?"

"The hit men couldn't have accepted the commission without the Swagman's approval. That's the way things work here."

"I've never even met him," said Virtue. "What has he got against me?"

"Probably nothing. He's a very friendly man, actually. But the killers will pay him a commission in order to operate here, and it's not unfair to say that he likes money even more than he likes people."

"Then I'd better find *him* before they find *me*."

"You don't even know who they are," replied the man.

"They *could* be those three grubby-looking men standing together across the street"—he pointed out the window to a trio of armed men who were standing together a short distance away—"but they could also be three little old ladies who are out doing their shopping, or the bartenders down the block, or even some of the mechanics at the spaceport. If I were you, I'd get back to my ship as fast as I could and take off before anyone knew I was here."

"I didn't come all this way *not* to talk to the Swagman," Virtue said firmly. "Where can I find him?"

The man shrugged.

"Damn it!" she snapped. "Are you going to help me or aren't you?"

"I don't *know* where to find him!" replied the man, exasperated. "I don't even know if he's on the planet right now. It's not in his best professional interests to announce his comings and goings."

"All right. If he *is* here, where will he be?"

"He's got a place up in the hills—a real fortress—but you can't get to it. He's got security devices all the hell over—and I mean *lethal* devices."

"How do I get in touch with him, then?"

"Well, Father William's set up shop just outside of town for the next couple of days, so I imagine the Swagman will be keeping an eye on him, just in case."

"Who's Father William?"

He stared at her disbelievingly. "Just how long have you been on the Frontier?"

"Long enough," she replied levelly. "Has Black Orpheus written him up?"

The man nodded. "Did a damned sight better on him than he did on you. You're the Virgin Queen, aren't you?"

"Yes."

"Then you ought to know what's in the song."

"I've got better things to do than commit eight thousand lines to memory. Now, are you going to tell me who he is?"

"He's a little bit of everything—preacher, bounty hunter, benefactor. I suppose it all depends on who you are."

"Would *he* know how to reach the Swagman?"

"I suppose so. There's not a lot that Father William doesn't know about outlaws."

"If he's a bounty hunter, there's a chance that he's after

the Swagman himself," said Virtue. "Why would the Swagman let him land on Goldenrod?"

"Probably because he'd have a revolt on his hands if he tried to stop him. Father William's the most popular evangelist on the Frontier—and there are some who think he's the best shot, as well. He goes anywhere he wants."

"Dimitri Sokol wouldn't have hired *him*, would he?" asked Virtue thoughtfully.

"Not a chance. He's a bounty hunter, not a hired killer."

"Well," she said with a sigh, "I suppose he's the next person I have to see. Where is he?"

"He's set up his tent about a mile west of town."

She checked her timepiece. "When does he start preaching?"

"Today's sermon started about two hours ago."

"Then he should be just about through," she ventured.

He laughed. "He won't be through until nightfall."

"You're kidding!" said Virtue. "What the hell has he got to talk about that takes eight hours?"

"Anything that comes into his head," replied the stringer. "You've got to remember that he's all the flesh-and-blood religion most of these people are going to have for the next couple of years, until he passes through again, so he's got to cram a lot of hellfire and damnation into a very short space of time."

"Sounds thrilling," she said unenthusiastically. Then she stood up. "Well, I suppose I'd better be going."

"If you insist on continuing your quest, why don't you at least wait until dark?" he suggested.

"Because I don't know my way around the city," Virtue replied. "Why give them an advantage?" She paused. "Besides, they're less likely to try to kill me in the daylight. Damn, but I wish my partner was here! This is more his kind of situation than mine."

"Who's your partner?"

"Sebastian Cain. Ever hear of him?"

"The Songbird?" he said, looking at her with newfound interest. "*He's* working with you?"

She nodded.

"I agree with you. This situation is made to order for a man like Cain. Why are you here instead of him?"

"He's out in the Altair region."

The stringer looked impressed. "Allow me to hazard a guess: Is he after Altair of Altair?"

"Yes."

He let out a low whistle. "I don't know what you two are up to, but you sure aren't going about it the easy way, are you?"

"Evidently not," she said, looking out the window once more and noticing that the three men were no longer stationed opposite the news office.

"Well, I wish you luck," said the man. "You're going to need it."

"Thanks," she said, walking to the door. "One mile due west, right?"

"Right," he replied.

She pulled a small pistol out of her satchel and tucked it in her belt, then stepped out into the humid Goldenrod air. A number of people were walking down the street in twos and threes, and she stood still for a moment, scrutinizing them, trying to see if any of them seemed to be paying more than casual attention to her as they went about their business.

This is ridiculous, she thought as she watched the townspeople. *Who the hell knows what a hired killer looks like?*

She remained motionless for another minute, half expecting to hear a shot ring out or feel a laser beam searing through her flesh, then walked up to the corner and turned left. She made three more lefts, coming to a stop in front of the news office and trying to ascertain if anyone had followed her, then decided that on a world where the only law was a bandit who lived in a fortress atop a distant hill, the less time she spent presenting herself as a potential target, the better.

She headed off in a westerly direction, staying within the shadows of buildings for as long as she could. When she had traveled some two hundred yards, the town came to an abrupt end, and she could see a colorful tent set in the middle of a rolling field almost a mile away. She took one more look around, saw nobody following her, and began walking briskly toward it, checking behind her every few moments.

She had covered half the distance, and had temporarily dipped out of sight of the tent while crossing a low area of the field, when she saw an elderly couple strolling back toward town. The man was wearing a very formal suit, obviously donned in honor of Father William, and walked with a cane.

The woman carried a picnic basket and a parasol. Keeping her hand very near the butt of her pistol, Virtue stopped and greeted them.

"Is Father William through speaking?" she asked.

"Oh, goodness, no!" said the old woman, obviously amused by the suggestion. 'I'm just going home to take my medication, and perhaps a little nap, and then we'll be coming back."

"We haven't seen you before, have we?" asked the old man.

"No," answered Virtue. "I heard Father William was touching down for a couple of days, so I thought I'd come by to hear him. I'm from Salinas Four."

"Really?" said the old man. "I hear it's a lovely world."

"It is."

"We're from Seabright originally," said the old woman. "But we came out to the Frontier to make our fortunes."

"That was close to forty years ago," chuckled the old man. "Can't say we're any richer, but Goldenrod is a pretty nice place to retire to. And of course, it's on Father William's regular circuit."

"By the way, can I offer you a sandwich?" asked the woman, holding up her basket.

"No, thank you," said Virtue.

"I wish you would," persisted the woman. "I hate to see it go to waste, and we'll just throw it out once we get home. We're having dinner with friends."

"I appreciate the offer, but I'm really not hungry."

"Here," said the woman, fussing with the lid of the basket. "Just take a look at it, and maybe you'll change your mind. There are sandwiches, and tea biscuits, and—"

Suddenly Virtue saw a movement out of the corner of her eye and hurled herself to the ground.

The old man dropped the cane he had swung at her and began fumbling with his pocket. Virtue flung herself at his legs, heard something crack inside one of them, and leaped to her feet, her pistol in her hand. The old woman had withdrawn a gun from the inside of the basket—Virtue couldn't tell if it was laser, sonic, or projectile—and was pointing it at her.

"You have very good reflexes, my dear," said the old woman with a smile.

"What happens now?" asked Virtue, ignoring the old man as he moaned and writhed on the ground. "Do we kill each other or call a truce while you move the wounded warrior off the battlefield?"

"Well, I *could* wait for reinforcements," said the old woman. "I do have them, you know."

"Yes, I'd heard there were three of you."

The old man groaned again.

"But my dear husband is in a bad way," added the old woman. "He had trouble walking even before you so callously broke his leg. So I suppose I'll either have to dispatch you immediately, or else agree to your truce."

"If you shoot, so will I," said Virtue.

"Ah, but will a properly placed head shot allow you the opportunity to retaliate?" asked the woman, raising her aim from Virtue's chest to a point between her eyes.

"Then perhaps I'll shoot first," said Virtue, a tiny section of her mind wondering how Cain would handle the situation and deciding he wouldn't have gotten into it in the first place. "And then who will be left to take care of your husband?"

"There is *that* to consider," agreed the old woman regretfully. "We're really getting a little old for this."

"Have you done it often?"

"Twelve times," she said, not without a touch of pride. "People always expect assassins to look like they do on the videos—mean and powerful. We've made quite a substantial living from it." She lowered her voice confidentially. "Black Orpheus even wanted to write us up, but we explained that the only thing we really had on our side was the element of surprise, and that publicity could drive us out of business." She smiled. "He respected our wishes—but then, he was always a gentleman."

The old man tried to roll over, moaned in agony, and passed out.

"All right, my dear," said the old woman with a sigh. "You get your truce. I really must find a doctor."

"Not quite so fast," said Virtue. "Who's the third member of your team?"

"I can't jeopardize his life by telling you that," she said primly. "Besides, if he doesn't kill you, I'll have to come after you again once I get Henry to a doctor."

Virtue considered the problem, then nodded in agreement.

"All right—we've got a truce."

"Then please put your weapon away," said the old woman. Virtue smiled. "You first."

"I'm counting on your being an honorable woman," said the old woman, opening the top of her basket and tossing her gun into it.

Virtue tucked her pistol back into her belt and quickly disarmed the old man. "If I were you," she said, "I'd get Henry to the house and stay there. The next time I see you I'll have to kill you."

"Help me move him into the shade, won't you?" said the woman, indicating a tree some twenty feet away. "It may take me some time to find a doctor and bring him back out here, and I don't want to leave poor Henry out in the sun."

"You're kidding, right?" said Virtue unbelievingly.

"If we leave him here, he may die. He's a very old man."

"He's a very old man who just tried to kill me."

"That was business," said the old woman. "And as you can see, he's quite unable to present any threat to you in his present condition."

Virtue shrugged and nodded her head, struck by the lunacy of helping one of her potential murderers drag another of them to shelter. "All right—but leave your basket on the ground."

"Certainly," said the old woman, placing the basket down.

The two women walked over to the old man, bent over, and began adjusting his weight so that they could pull him by his arms and shoulders. Virtue noticed the old woman's hand snaking down toward Henry's pocket and grabbed her by the wrist just as she was withdrawing a knife.

"I thought we had a bargain," said Virtue with a nasty smile.

"Business comes first," said the old woman, red-faced and panting from her exertions. "What are you going to do to me?"

"Nothing quite as bad as you were going to do to me," replied Virtue. "Let's get dear old Henry into the shade first—and if you try anything else, or go for that gun in your basket, I'll kill you."

Once she had dragged the old man over to the tree, she turned to his wife and drew her pistol.

"I'm going to ask you once more—how can I recognize the third killer?"

"That really would be a breach of my professional ethics," said the old woman. "Besides, if you shoot me, there's every possibility that he'll hear the sound of the gun and know where you are."

"True enough," said Virtue. She landed a heavy kick on the old woman's knee, felt the tendons and ligaments give way as the woman fell to the ground and let out a scream, and stood back.

"That should keep you off the playing field for the rest of the day," said Virtue, walking over to the basket and withdrawing a storage bottle. She opened it, saw that it was iced tea, closed it again, and walked back to where the old woman was sobbing and clutching her knee.

"It's a hot day," said Virtue. "There's every chance the two of you will dehydrate before someone finds you."

The old woman kept crying but offered no comment.

"Tell me what Number Three looks like and I'll leave this with you."

The old woman stared at her through tear-filled eyes. "Do your worst," she said. "I won't betray a trust."

"Last chance," said Virtue. "I can't waste any more time with you."

The woman shook her head.

Virtue shrugged and tossed the bottle on the ground about twenty yards away from them. Then she returned to the basket, removed the weapon, put it into her satchel, and headed off toward the tent.

When she arrived, she entered at the back. There were forty or fifty rows of benches on each side of a broad center aisle, and all but the last few were completely filled. Up front, at the makeshift pulpit, there was an electronic sound synthesizer that provided a soft, continuous background of hymns.

A huge man stood at a podium, staring out at his audience with fierce green eyes. He had wild red hair and a beard streaked with gray, he was clad entirely in black, and the polished handles of his laser pistols were plainly visible atop his holsters.

"And if thy hand offends thee, cut it off," Father William was intoning in a rich, resonant baritone. "For the Lord is

more than an ideal, more than an object of affection, even
more than a Creator." He paused for effect. "Never forget,
my children, that the Lord is also a surgeon. And He doesn't
use the sword of redemption. He uses the scalpel of justice!"

Virtue took an aisle seat in the next-to-last row.

"Yes, brethren," continued Father William, "we're talking about infection. Not the infection of the body, for the
body is the province of the doctor, but the infection of the
spirit, which is the province of the Lord and such temporal
emissaries as He deigns to have represent Him."

He paused and reached for a glass that was filled with a
blue liquid, took a long swallow, and then resumed speaking.

"Now, they've got a lot in common, the body and the
spirit. First and foremost, they can bring pleasure to the Lord,
the body by being fruitful and multiplying, the spirit by
worshiping Him and singing His praises. But they've got
something else in common, too. Both of them can be overrun
with infection: they can become pustules of decay, unsightly
in the eyes of both man and God."

A gaunt man with a handlebar mustache and thick, bushy
sideburns entered the tent, looked around for a seat, and
finally approached Virtue.

"Do you mind moving over just a bit?" he whispered.

She moved to her left, making room for him.

"I meant to get here sooner, but one of my harvesters
broke down," he added apologetically. "Have I missed much?"

She shook her head and placed a finger to her lips.

"Sorry," he muttered, turning his attention to Father
William.

"Now, if the body gets a mild infection, what do we do?"
The preacher glared out at his audience, as if daring them to
answer. Nobody said a word. "We give it antibiotics. And if
it gets a major infection, we give it other drugs." He gripped
the edges of the podium with his massive hands. "And when
it gets infected by a cancer, what do we do?" He made a
slashing motion with his right hand. "We cut it out!" he
shouted.

He paused and drew a deep breath, releasing it slowly.
"But what about the soul? What do we do when *it* becomes
infected? How do we inject an antibiotic into its bloodstream?
How do we amputate a piece of the soul before the infection
can spread?"

"The answer," said Father William, "is that we can't and won't do any of those things, because there aren't any half-way measures when it comes to the soul, my children. Your body is just a suit that you wear for the flickering instant of your lives, but your soul is an outfit you're going to wear for all eternity, and you can't afford to take any chances with it. You can't give it an antibiotic and prescribe two weeks of bed rest for it, because it doesn't have any bloodstream and it can't lie down—and besides, it's too damned important to try to cure with halfway measures." His voice rose in volume and intensity. "Never forget this: There is no such thing as a *minor* infection of the soul! There's no breaking it down into serious and trivial, into fatal and nonfatal. There's just infection, and when you see it you've got to cut it out with the holy blade of the Lord!"

Suddenly Virtue felt the point of a knife prodding her rib cage.

"Not a sound, not a movement!" whispered the gaunt man.

Father William cleared his throat. "Some of you want to know: How can such surgery make the soul well again? Well, my children, it's a damned good question—and you're not going to like the answer, for the answer is as harsh as the wrath of the Lord." He paused for effect. "*Nothing* can make an infected soul well again." He looked out at his audience, his eyes blazing. "You think you can fool God with false contrition? Hah!" He bellowed the contemptuous laugh so forcefully that the speaker system emitted an ear-splitting whine.

"So why do we cut it out? Because—and here's the gist of it, brethren—we've got to act fast to stop that infection from spreading to other souls. We've got to stop the evil from creeping like a cancer from one soul to the next!"

"I could yell for help," whispered Virtue.

"It might start as a yell," replied the gaunt man. "I guarantee it'll end as a gurgle."

"There's nothing new about this," continued Father William. "What did the Lord do when the people of Sodom became infected? He cut out the cancer. He didn't sit up with his sick patient and tend to its illness. He used the knife! What did He do when He saw that the whole world was

wicked? Did He go in and perform microsurgery? Hell, no!
He flooded it for forty days and forty nights!''

He paused and wiped the sweat from his face with a black
handkerchief.

"He's due to take a break soon," whispered the gaunt
man. "When he does, get up and walk out very slowly. I'll
be right beside you." He prodded her with the point of the
knife for emphasis.

"Why should I?" she whispered back. "You're going to
kill me anyway."

"I can do it quick and easy, or I can do it so you'll be in
pain for hours," he replied emotionlessly. "That's all the
choice you've got. It's up to you."

She considered making a break for the door, but he seemed
to read her mind and suddenly grabbed her arm. She slumped
back, her mind racing, searching for possibilities of escape
but finding none. She had already decided that she wasn't
leaving the tent like a sheep going to slaughter, and that if
worse came to worst, she'd make him kill her in front of two
thousand witnesses—but since he was operating with the
Swagman's knowledge and consent, she couldn't be sure that
anyone would lift a finger to stop him—and indeed, she
suspected that they wouldn't.

"You'd think some people would learn their lesson by
now, wouldn't you?" demanded Father William, his voice
rising. "You'd think they'd learn that you can't pull the wool
over God's eyes, that you can't hide an infection from His
heavenly clinic!"

He glared out at the audience.

"That's what you'd think—but some people just never
learn."

Suddenly Father William's face was filled with fury.

"You'd think they'd at least have the brains not to try to do
Satan's work in the house of the Lord!" he roared, drawing a
pistol and firing a blast in Virtue's direction.

Several members of the audience screamed, a few bellowed
curses, and most of them—including Virtue—dove to the
floor.

There was total confusion for the next thirty seconds. Then
people began getting up, asking what had happened. When
Virtue regained her feet, she noticed that the gaunt man was
dead, his left eye socket burnt to a crisp.

"Don't touch him!" thundered Father William as other members of the congregation began noticing the victim. "There's paper on that man. He belongs to me and the Lord."

The preacher looked out over the audience.

"The Lord is my eyes and ears, and there's not a lot that escapes the two of us." Father William paused. "The Lord steadies my hand and aims my guns. Blessed is the name of the Lord!"

He replaced his pistol in its holster.

"There's an object lesson to be learned here, my children— and that is that Good can come from Evil. Once I take this sinner's scalp and turn it in, he'll have done a hell of a lot more for the Lord by dying than he ever thought of doing while he was alive." He lowered his head. "Let's say a brief, silent prayer for this poor sinful bastard's pitch-black soul, and wish Satan the best of luck with him."

He continued his sermon for another half hour, ignoring the dead body, bringing forth every reference he thought mildly appropriate to the subject at hand, from the concept of an eye for an eye to the Day of Judgment, which he promised was a lot closer at hand than most people suspected.

Finally, when he finished, explaining that he was cutting his preaching short out of respect for the dead—and also because the Democracy's post office would be closing soon—he had a young boy from the Tradertown take his platinum poorbox up and down the aisles, and he didn't dismiss the congregation until everyone had made a contribution.

"I'll be seeing you all here bright and early tomorrow morning," said Father William, signaling them that it was now permissable to rise and depart, "when the topic will be 'Sex and Sin,' for which I suggest you leave the children at home. Donations will be appreciated, and if anyone would like to bring along a couple of chocolate layer cakes with thick fudge frosting, I promise to put them to good use." Suddenly he pointed to Virtue. "You stick around, young lady. We've got some serious talking to do."

The young boy brought him the poorbox and whispered something in his ear.

"Hold it!" he hollered, and those people who hadn't yet made it to the exit froze in their tracks.

"I don't know who goes by the name of the Spike, or even

what sex you are, but I've been told on very good authority that you tried passing off some Royal Yen in the poorbox. Now, as you know, the Royal Yen isn't acceptable currency anywhere but out on the Rim, and I've got a gut feeling that the good Lord is going to take it as a personal affront. So what I'm going to do is ask this handsome young man to move among you again, and see if you can't find it in your heart to come up with some coin of the realm that'll buy food and vaccines for the poor unfortunates on Kellatra Four, which is my next port of call. As for this," he added, holding up the unacceptable currency, "I'll just hang on to it in case I should run into some God-fearing missionary whose call is leading him out to where he can use it."

The boy walked into the midst of the crowd and emerged a moment later with two crisp fifty-dollar Maria Theresa notes. Father William nodded his head in approval, and a moment later Virtue found herself alone in the tent with him.

"I want to thank you," she said, approaching him and extending her hand. "I'd have been dead meat if you hadn't spotted him."

"I couldn't have done it if you hadn't come to hear my sermon," he replied, clasping her hand between both of his. "Which is just as it should be. You come to praise the Lord, and the Lord provides for you. Looks to me like He thinks you've got mighty important business somewhere up the line."

"I do."

"So important that a man with a price on his head wanted to kill you?"

"He was hired by Dimitri Sokol."

"Well, I'm sure Satan's warming up a special seat in hell for Mr. Sokol." He paused. "By the way, he had two accomplices. What happened to them?"

"They won't be bothering me," said Virtue emphatically.

Father William nodded his head approvingly. "Good. I'm glad to see you don't need this kind of heavenly protection all the time." He released her hand, picked up his glass, and took another swallow of his blue drink. "Why does Sokol want you dead?"

"I have no idea," she said, looking him full in the eye.

"You know," he said with the hint of an amused smile, "it's a damned good thing that God's got big plans for you—

because otherwise He'd strike you mute for lying inside His house."

"I don't know what you're talking about," said Virtue.

"Come on, young lady," said Father William. "Dimitri Sokol's a smuggler and swindler who thinks he's worked out his own special brand of contrition." He laughed contemptuously. "As if he thinks he can keep everything he did a secret while he pretends to be a humble, churchgoing public servant!" He stared at her. "Let me suggest that you blackmailed him, he paid you off, and now he's trying to get his money back."

"Close, but no cigar," said Virtue. "I blackmailed him, all right—"

"Perfectly acceptable," he interrupted her. "Sometimes you've got to hold the cancer up to the light before you can cut it away."

"But not for money," she continued. "For information."

"Ah!" he said, his eyes lighting up. "What kind of information?"

"I'm looking for Santiago."

Father William seemed to find that uproariously funny. "If I were you, young lady, I'd find out where he was and run the other way. Now *that's* some information that's freely given, and as such ought to count for more than anything Sokol told you."

"He told me to talk to the Jolly Swagman."

"Did he indeed? Well, I suppose he was right. But you're not very likely to find the Swagman attending any sermons—and especially not when I'm doing the preaching."

"Where *will* I find him?"

"Up in the hills, about ten miles out of town. Anyone around here could have shown you the way."

"They also tell me he's a hard men to see."

"It all depends who you are and what you want to talk about."

"They say that *you* can get me in to see him," she said bluntly.

"I imagine I can, at that," replied Father William.

"Will you?"

"That's another story altogether," he said slowly.

"You mean you won't?"

"I didn't say that. I said it was another story." He looked

around the room until his gaze fell on the killer's body. "That heathen came mighty close to getting you a personal meeting with God," he said. "*Mighty* close. It's a damned good thing the Lord was helping keep my eye sharp and my hand steady."

"I've already thanked you. Do you want me to do it again?"

"Well, young lady," he said, withdrawing his black hand-kerchief and polishing his poorbox meaningfully, "there are thanks, and then there are thanks."

She stared at him for a moment, finally comprehending. "One thousand credits," she said at last.

He smiled. "That's hardly chapter one of that other story we were talking about."

"Just remember that it's a story and not a novel," she replied. "Two thousand."

He pursed his lips and considered the offer.

"How's your cooking?" he asked at last.

"Terrible."

"Pity." He stared at her, then shrugged. "What the hell. Between the bounty money and your generous donation, we're going to see to it that five thousand children on Kellatra Four never come down with drypox or blue fever again." He bent over, raised his left pants leg, and withdrew a long hunting knife that he had strapped to his calf. "Let me just collect the proof of the pudding for the local constabulary and we'll be off." He turned to her. "You *do* have two thousand credits, don't you?"

She pulled the notes out of her satchel. "Have we got a deal?" she asked.

He took the money from her, put it in his poorbox, and grinned. "We sure as hell have, praise the Lord!"

9.

Up pops the Swagman, out pops his gun,
Down comes the money, away he does run;
There goes the posse, seeking his den—
Then up pops the Swagman, at it again!

Considering that he ran his own planet and had pretty much of a free hand on ten or fifteen others, you'd have expected the Jolly Swagman to be backed up by a veritable army of outlaws and cutthroats, but he wasn't. He had informants, of course, and a lot of contacts inside and outside the law, but for the most part he worked alone.

And considering that he worked alone, you'd have expected him to be a giant of a man, sort of a Goldenrod version of ManMountain Bates, but he wasn't. He was an inch or two shorter than normal and about twenty pounds overweight, and truth to tell he didn't have a single memorable physical feature, except maybe for his eyes, which were just about colorless.

And considering that he wasn't an imposing physical specimen, you'd have to figure that he was at the very least a sharpshooter or a demolitions expert or a master of disguise, but he wasn't. All he really had going for him were a pretty agile mind, an offbeat notion of morality, and a hunger for things that weren't his.

Now, all of that was enough to bring him to Black Orpheus' attention—but the thing that *really* interested the Bard of the Frontier was his accent.

It was the first one he'd ever heard.

117

Men had had accents when they were still Earthbound, and they would have them again in the future, thousands of years after the Inner and Outer Frontiers had been totally settled and civilized. But during the eras of the Republic and the Democracy and even the early Oligarchy, which spanned almost six millennia between them, every Man grew up knowing two tongues: that of his native world and Terran (and more often than not, the tongue of his native world *was* Terran). Out on the Frontier, where Men changed worlds the way their brothers back on Earth and Deluros VIII changed shirts, Terran was all anybody spoke: it had been carefully devised over a period of decades to be the kind of language any Man could pick up with ease, a language that was well-nigh impossible to speak with an accent.

So when Black Orpheus hunted up the Swagman and sat down to talk with him, the conversation wasn't half a minute old before Orpheus knew that he'd been raised by aliens.

The Swagman never denied it, but he wouldn't be coaxed into giving out any of the details. He liked the creatures who'd brought him up too much to want them to be studied and exploited by the creatures of his own race, and he knew that that was exactly what would happen if Black Orpheus incorporated them into his song.

At any rate, the balladeer was absolutely captivated by the outlaw's explosive *g*'s and sibilant *sh*'s. He stayed on Goldenrod for a week or two, and some people say that the Swagman even took Orpheus on a raid with him, just to show him what it was like. They became friends, because in spite of his penchant for lawbreaking, the Swagman was a pretty friendly person. He saw Black Orpheus a few years later and didn't even mention that Orpheus had hurt his feelings by giving him only a single verse; and Black Orpheus was so impressed that he was still on the loose that, without the Swagman's requesting it, he sat right down and added another couple of stanzas, including one about the bandit's fortress (which he insisted on calling a *schloss* in order to create a rhyme).

Schloss or fortress, Virtue decided as she and Father William stood at the massive front door, it was one hell of a structure. In a less technical age its bulk alone could have withstood an army; now its incredibly sophisticated defense systems could repel attacks from above, below, or straight ahead.

Finally the huge portal swung open with a slight humming noise, revealing the Swagman, who stood in the entry foyer, hands on hips, staring at Virtue with an amused curiosity.

Whatever it was she had expected in a bandit chief, he wasn't it. His uncalloused white fingers had been meticulously manicured; his blond hair had been painstakingly styled in the latest Deluros fashion; his face was unmarked and clean-shaven; and his clothing, from the elegant velvet tunic to the sleek lizardskin half boots, seemed to anticipate the coming fashion among the Democracy's trendsetters, rather than echoing the current one.

"Ah!" he said with a smile of greeting. "The enigmatic Virtue MacKenzie, I presume?"

"And you're the Swagman?" replied Virtue.

"The one and only," he answered. "Good evening, Father William. How's the salvation business?"

"The same as always," replied the preacher. "Satan is a full-time opponent."

"I understand that you had him down for the count this afternoon," said the Swagman in his unmistakable accent. "But where are my manners? Do come in."

They followed him down a short corridor as the door swung shut behind them, and from there into a massive great hall, complete with a floor-to-ceiling fireplace wall, a number of rugs that had been hand-made on Boriga II and Kalamakii, a set of four exquisitely crafted chairs from far Antares, and numerous hardwood shelving units that housed art treasures from literally hundreds of worlds across the galaxy.

"What do you think of my trinkets?" asked the Swagman as Virtue stopped to admire a crystal globe of Bokar from the incredibly ancient days when the Bokarites were a seafaring race rather than a planet of starfaring merchants.

"They're breathtaking!" she said, turning her attention to a *praque*, the fabled torture-stick of Sabelius III.

"That's a more accurate statement than you might imagine," said Father William sternly. "A lot of good men gave their last breaths accumulating this ill-gotten wealth for the Swagman."

"Come, come, now," said the bandit with a chuckle. "You know there's no paper on me, Father William."

"There's a pile of it as high as the ceiling," replied the preacher.

"But not for murder," the Swagman pointed out. "And you leave the punishment of lesser crimes to lesser servants of the Lord."

"True," admitted Father William. "But it's immoral to flaunt your bloodstained treasures like this."

"You mean by displaying them behind locked doors in my own home?" asked the Swagman, arching an eyebrow. He paused. "Shall we change the subject? If we keep talking about my collection, we're bound to have a serious disagreement." He snapped his fingers. "Or better still, how about dinner? I had my staff start preparing it half an hour ago, when you identified yourself at the first security barrier."

"Staff?" repeated Virtue. "I didn't notice any staff."

"They're all mechanical," explained the Swagman. "And *very* discreet."

"You live alone here?" she asked, surprised.

"Is that so difficult to believe?" he replied.

"I would have thought you'd be surrounded by henchmen," she admitted.

"One of the advantages about living with nothing but robots is that you never have to count the silverware or check the display cases when they're through for the day," he said. "Besides, what would I do with henchmen?"

"Well, you do have a reputation as a master criminal."

"So I am told," he replied dryly.

"You haven't answered my question," she persisted.

"I don't know what you think a master criminal does," said the Swagman, "but in point of fact I am a large-scale employer of criminal labor, nothing more." A bell chimed twice, and he turned to Father William. "Dinner's ready. I assume you brought along your appetite?"

"I'm never without it," said the preacher heartily.

He led them into the dining hall, which was surrounded with still more displays of unique alien artifacts. The room was dominated by a table that could easily have accommodated forty people, but the three settings were all at one end of it. The chairs were all one-legged, considerably broader at the base than the top, and were much more secure than they looked.

"Won't you please sit down?" asked the Swagman, pulling out a chair for Virtue.

"Thank you," she said as Father William sat down opposite her.

"Ordinarily I'd serve such welcome guests on my Robelian dinner pieces," said the Swagman apologetically as he joined them. "But I'm having them refinished. I hope the Atrian quartz will be acceptable. It's really quite lovely in its way."

"The only thing that matters is what's being served on it," replied Father William, leaning back to allow a robot to place an appetizer of mutated shellfish before him.

"That's because you are concerned only with accumulating energy with which to fight your holy war," said the Swagman. "Those of us who are fortunate enough to be spectators at the battle of Good and Evil, rather than participants, are doubly blessed in that we also have the opportunity to admire the containers in which the energy arrives."

"Spectator, my eye!" snapped Father William, chewing and speaking at the same time. "You've got more killers working for you than Dimitri Sokol!"

"I have more bills to pay," replied the Swagman easily. "And I might add that thanks to your little fit of pique on Darius Ten, I have four less killers than I had last month." He smiled at the preacher. "You know, you've caused me so much inconvenience that I really ought to charge you for this meal."

Father William grinned back at him. "I won't ask you for a contribution to my poorbox, and we'll call it even."

"Agreed—as long as you don't make a habit of decimating my supply of menials."

"I'll take any killer who's got paper on him!" said Father William firmly, wiping the corner of his mouth with a napkin, then tying it around his neck like a bib.

The Swagman shrugged. "Serves me right for not checking them out better. Still, by taking them when you did, you cost me the possession of a shipment of art objects from Nelson Seventeen. I do wish you could have waited another week before you went on your killing spree."

"Hah!" muttered Father William, pushing his empty dish away and signaling the robot to bring him another.

The Swagman turned to Virtue. "Never don the cloth," he

said with mock seriousness. "It drains away all compassion for your fellow man."

"You don't seem especially upset about losing four men," remarked Virtue.

"They were just men; I can always get more," he replied nonchalantly. "It was losing the *pieces* that hurt. There was a hand-spun Kinrossian bowl that . . ." He sighed and shook his head, then looked up. "Still, I suppose our friend here must score points with his God from time to time."

"You keep talking blasphemy," said Father William harshly, "and I just may forget that all that paper on you doesn't mention murder."

"You don't really think you can harm me in my own house, do you?" said the Swagman, vastly amused. "Don't talk such nonsense, or pretty soon you'll start believing it and then we'll all be sorry. Especially you."

The preacher stared at him for a moment, then went back to demolishing the food in front of him.

Virtue finished her appetizer, and the instant she did a robot whisked the empty plate away from her.

"They're very efficient," she said, indicating the retreating robot as well as a trio that were bringing out the main course. "I would think that household robots would cost an arm and a leg out on the Frontier."

"They do," agreed the Swagman. "Fortunately, it wasn't *my* arm or leg that paid for them."

"Totally immoral," muttered Father William between mouthfuls.

"Totally practical," corrected the Swagman. "It's a tried-and-true business axiom: Never use your own money when you can use someone else's. I just find creative ways to apply it." He turned to Virtue. "Have we pretended that we're all just good friends long enough, or do you prefer to play at it a bit more before talking about Santiago?"

She looked startled for just a moment. "We'll talk about him later," she said.

"As you wish," replied the Swagman agreeably. "Might I inquire if there's any particular reason why?"

"Whatever you've got to say," said Virtue, "I don't want you saying it in front of a rival."

"You mean Father William?" asked the Swagman. Both men seemed to find her remark enormously amusing.

"What's so funny about that?" demanded Virtue.

"Shall you tell her, or shall I?" asked the Swagman.

Father William looked across the table at Virtue. "I don't want him," he said.

"You don't want Santiago?" she repeated incredulously.

"That's right."

"But I thought you wanted any killer with a price on his head," she persisted. "And he's got the biggest price of all. Why aren't you interested in him?"

"A number of reasons," replied Father William. "First, as long as he's on the loose, there will be a couple of dozen bounty hunters on his trail. That's two dozen less competitors for *me*. Second, he's more trouble to dig out than he's worth, regardless of the price on him." He paused. "And third, I don't know for a fact that he's ever killed anyone."

"Come on," said Virtue. "He's wanted for thirty-eight murders."

"He's been *blamed* for thirty-eight murders," replied Father William. "There's a difference."

"We've been arguing about this for years," interjected the Swagman. "I keep offering to team up with him, and he keeps turning me down." He grinned. "It would appear that God is employing very selective killers these days." He turned to Father William. "Probably you're right," he said sarcastically. "Probably he only killed thirty-two or thirty-three of those men and women himself, and hired out the rest."

"Why do *you* want to kill Santiago?" Virtue asked the Swagman.

"You mean besides the fact that I'm an upstanding citizen who finds his very existence offensive?" he replied wryly. "Let's just say that I have my reasons."

Father William, who had finished his main course, pushed his plate away and got to his feet. "If you don't mind, I think I'm going to take my leave of you before he starts expounding upon all those reasons. I don't like arguing on a full stomach."

The Swagman remained seated. "Lemon pie," he said temptingly.

"With meringue topping?" asked the preacher.

"I had a feeling you'd be coming by."

Father William seemed to wage a mighty struggle within

himself. Finally he sighed. "I'll be back tomorrow evening for it."

"In that case, I won't detain you," said the Swagman. "I'm sure you can find your own way out."

"You'll see to it that Virtue gets back to her hotel safely?" demanded Father William.

"But of course."

"Have you got all your infernal machines turned off?"

"All but the two at the bottom of the hill—and they've been instructed to let you pass."

"Be sure that they do."

"I will," said the Swagman. "And thank you for bringing this innocent young woman up to my den of iniquity."

Father William glowered at him, then turned and made his way out of the room.

"Interesting man," commented the Swagman.

"I'm surprised you two aren't at each other's throats all the time," remarked Virtue.

"That would be bad for *both* our businesses," said the Swagman with a chuckle.

"I don't understand."

"I allow him to set up shop on my worlds, and give him occasional information about various killers who are also in these parts. In exchange, he warns me whenever he hears of a bounty hunter who isn't as choosy about his targets as he himself is."

"Speaking of killers, why did you give three of them permission to hunt me down on Goldenrod?" demanded Virtue.

"It was strictly financial," replied the Swagman with no trace of remorse. "I allowed them to operate here in exchange for twenty-five percent of their fees—and Dimitri Sokol is offering a lot of money for you."

"So you just let anyone kill anyone on Goldenrod, as long as you get your cut of the action?" she said, her anger rising.

"It depends on the situation."

"What was it about *my* situation that made you decide I was expendable?"

"Oh, I knew that the Lance would wait for you in the tent, and that Father William would spot him. As for the other two—well, if you're not good enough to protect yourself from Henry and Martha, you're certainly not good enough to go after Santiago." He took a sip of his wine. "So if you made it here, you were worth talking business with—and if you didn't, at least I had been recompensed."

She stared at him, annoyed that her fury was evaporating so rapidly in the face of his straightforward and logical answer. Finally the last of it drained from her, and she shrugged.

"All right. Tell me about Santiago."

"Eventually," he replied. "But first of all, suppose you tell me about your interest in him—and your partnership with Sebastian Cain."

"My interest is strictly professional," said Virtue. "I'm a journalist, and I've been paid a hefty advance to come up with a feature on him." Her face suddenly became serious. "And I mean to get that story, no matter what it takes."

"Very well said," responded the Swagman. "I approve wholeheartedly. And what about Cain?"

"We decided to pool our resources and our information," answered Virtue. "Our interests are parallel, but not identical. We both want Santiago, but he wants him for the reward and I want him for the feature." She paused, staring at him thoughtfully.

"Have you something to add?" he suggested pleasantly.

"Just that nothing about our agreement is written in stone," she said, choosing her words carefully. "If I were to meet someone who was better able to help me . . ." She let the sentence hang.

"Wonderful!" laughed the Swagman. "A woman after my own heart!"

"Do we have a deal?" asked Virtue.

He laughed again. "Of course not—at least, not on those terms. If you'll double-cross one partner, you'll double-cross others—and in your mind Cain must certainly be a more formidable antagonist than I am. After all, he's a bounty hunter, and I'm just a harmless art collector."

"That's not the way I hear it."

"One mustn't believe every scurrilous rumor one hears," said the Swagman. "However, that's neither here nor there." He smiled at her. "Not to worry, my dear. We seem to have another case of parallel interests. I don't want your story, and while I'd certainly like the reward money, there are things I want even more."

"Such as?"

"Such as one less competitor," said the Swagman. "Did you know that I used to work for him?"

"No."

"I did—indirectly, for the most part. I actually met him on only two occasions."

"Why did you stop working for him?" asked Virtue.

"We had a falling-out."

"About what?"

"Methodology," he said noncommittally. "At any rate, although he himself is not a collector, and indeed has no interest whatsoever in things esoteric, he has a number of exquisite art objects in his possession on any given day. Should we reach an accommodation, I would regard those pieces as mine, if our little enterprise succeeds."

"How many pieces are involved?"

"I really couldn't say. But he has warehouses and drops all over the Inner Frontier. I'm sure that I would be satisfied with the spoils of conquest." He shrugged. "Let greedy, immoral men like Cain keep the blood money," he concluded deprecatingly.

"You'd only take the pieces you wanted to keep?" asked Virtue, suddenly aware of yet another source of income above and beyond her fee for the feature.

He shook his head. "I'm afraid my creditors have very expensive tastes, my dear. I keep the finest pieces that I find, but all the rest go to support my life-style, and not incidentally to pay for my menials. No, my fee for helping you is, as our friend Father William might state it, all of Santiago's temporal possessions. Take it or leave it."

"Why haven't you gone after him before?" asked Virtue.

"I have—or rather, I've sent men after him before," answered the Swagman. "None of them got very close before being eliminated. So now it appears that I'm going to have to take a more active hand."

"Why now?"

"Well, I suppose I should say that I admire your resourcefulness, or that I wish to establish a romantic liaison with you," he answered. "But while both are definitely true, the simple fact of the matter is that certain developments have convinced me that it might be foolish to wait any longer."

"What developments?"

"The Angel has moved to the Inner Frontier."

"Cain mentioned him," said Virtue.

"Then doubtless Cain is aware of his abilities," said the Swagman. "I had an intermediary offer him the same help I'm offering you, in return for the same considerations. He turned me down flat. This would either imply that he's as much of a loner as everyone says, or that he's getting so close to Santiago that he doesn't need my help. Probably it's the former, but I really don't think I can afford to take the chance." He paused. "So, have I entered into a joint arrangement with you and Cain, or not?"

"As far as I'm concerned, you have," replied Virtue. "I'll have to clear it with Cain after he finishes his business on Altair, but I don't imagine he's interested in anything except the reward. Besides," she lied, "I don't know why the subject of Santiago's personal possessions should ever arise."

"Excellent!" He arose and walked to a small cabinet. "This calls for a bottle of my best Alphard brandy."

He returned with the bottle and two crystal goblets.

"To your very good health and prosperous future, my dear," he said, clinking glasses with her after he had filled them. He stared admiringly at her, wondering just how many fabulous private art collections she had seen on the worlds of the Democracy, and how many of them she could help him locate in the future.

"And to a successful partnership," replied Virtue, studying him carefully and mentally adding up the awards and the money for the features he could help her obtain once they had established a working relationship.

"Virtue, my dear," he said, flashing her his most charming smile, "we have a lot to talk about in the days to come."

"I have a feeling that you're right," she replied with a predatory gleam in her eye.

He spent the next hour showing her some of his major pieces. Then, with a minimal amount of verbal thrust and parry, they went to bed together. Both of them found the experience enjoyable; each pretended to find it ecstatic.

10.

Along the road to Mother Lode
Dwells the Great Sioux Nation,
Which justifies its crimes and lies
As predestination.

Black Orpheus didn't have much use for aliens. Not that he was biased or bigoted; he wasn't. But he saw his calling as the creation and perpetuation of a myth-poem about the race of Man. In fact, the people who thought it was composed merely of unrelated four-line songs about the outcasts and misfits who managed to make an impression on him were dead wrong. By the time he died the poem was some 280,000 lines, most of it in free verse or nonrhyming iambic pentameter, and for the most part it was concerned with glorifying Man's sweeping expansion through the Inner Frontier. The little ballads about the outrageously colorful people were very little more than footnotes and punctuation marks in his epic, though they were the only parts of the poem that interested any of his contemporaries (except, of course, for the academics, who loved him when he was opaque and practically deified him on those rare occasions that he was obscure).

Anyway, while Orpheus wasn't especially interested in aliens, he had nothing against putting them in his poem if they were really unique—not in physical terms, since *all* species are physically unique; but unique in their relationship to Man. And in that regard, the Great Sioux Nation was a little more unique than most.

It wasn't really a nation at all. It possessed only eighty-four members, and only twice since its inception had all of them been on the same planet at the same time. They represented seven sentient races, all oxygen-breathers, each of them from a world that had been militarily conquered and economically subjugated either by the Republic or by the Democracy that succeeded it.

Some races were *so* alien that subjugation was meaningless to them; a goodly number of races resented it; but only a tiny handful *learned* from it.

Such a handful was the Great Sioux Nation.

They were outlaws and thieves, cutthroats and smugglers, playing Man's game on Man's turf—the Inner Frontier. But unlike their less enlightened brothers, they went directly to the source for their indoctrination. Each of them had served time as a member of some human band of desperadoes, and each had realized that if one was to play in Man's ballpark, he/she/it had better learn Man's ground rules.

And while they were studying the rule book, they studied the history books as well. They realized that before Man had turned to conquering and exploiting the races he had found among the stars, he had put in long centuries of practice back on his home planet. Their leader, a gold-feathered humanoid from Morioth II, found that he felt a special empathy toward the Amerinds, which had been methodically decimated on one of Man's last home-world frontiers. He took the name of Sitting Bull, though he was physiologically incapable of sitting and had no idea what a bull was, gave every member of his band an Indian name (oddly enough, Crazy Horse was the only other one derived from the Sioux), adopted certain practices of the Plains Indians, and named the group the Great Sioux Nation. Before long he had instilled in them the conviction that it was their destiny to adjust the balance of power on the Inner Frontier, while realizing a handsome profit in the process. They would commit no crime against any race except Man; they would accept no commission from any race except Man; and they would use no weapons against Man except those he had created himself.

Once Orpheus had written them up, neglecting to mention that they were aliens (though he revised it some years later), most of his audience thought they were a band of fanatics bent on revenge for injustices that had been perpetrated on the Amerinds in aeons past. Others held that they were a group of misguided idealists out to redress an imagined grievance on behalf of a small branch of humanity that had long since been exterminated or assimilated. Only the handful of people who had actually had dealings with them knew that they were simply alien outlaws and opportunists, trying their best to fit into a frontier culture that they could never fully comprehend.

But whatever the Great Sioux Nation's motivation, its efficiency was never in question. Sitting Bull's headquarters were on the mining world of Diamond Strike, some twenty-five miles south of Mother Lode, the planet's sole Tradertown. Through him, one could purchase contracts for anything from human contraband to human life.

One could also purchase information, which was why the Swagman had instructed Virtue MacKenzie's navigational computer to lay in a course for Diamond Strike.

Two days later Virtue set the ship down at the tiny spaceport just outside of Mother Lode. It was midmorning, and the distant sun glowed a dull orange through the heat-haze that blanketed the area.

The Swagman promptly walked to a local garage, where he spent the better part of ten minutes haggling with the proprietor over the rental price of a very old landcar.

"Why didn't you just pay him what he wanted?" Virtue asked irritably, opening a window to let in some air as they began driving the ancient vehicle down a narrow dirt road toward the Great Sioux Nation's headquarters. "Certainly we can afford it."

"Of course we can, my dear," he agreed amiably. "But this is Sitting Bull's world, just as Goldenrod is mine. By now he already knows we're here, and since he's not in the business of giving information away for free, it's not a bad idea to let him know that we don't always agree to pay the first price that's proposed to us."

"Will he offer a second one?"

The Swagman nodded. "And a third, and a fourth. He's a wholehearted believer in the barter system."

"He sounds like an interesting character," she commented, pulling out a handkerchief and wiping the sweat that was already starting to roll down her face.

"He's a *dangerous* character," the Swagman corrected her. "In fact I think it would be best if I did the talking and the negotiating for us."

"What makes you any better at it than me?" she demanded. "If you'd have let me bargain for the landcar, I'd have gotten us one with air-conditioning—or at least something with better shock absorbers."

"This was the only one available."

"You didn't answer my question: What makes you think you're better qualified than me?"

"Because he's an alien," said the Swagman.

"So what?"

"I was raised by aliens. I know how his mind works."

"Are you trying to tell me you were raised by members of Sitting Bull's race?" she said skeptically.

"No."

"Then what difference does it make?"

"I'm used to dealing with aliens."

"Apples and oranges," she replied. "That's like saying that since you're used to firing pistols, you'd be good with a saber." She grunted as the vehicle swerved to avoid an enormous pothole, then turned to him. "How the hell did you ever wind up living with aliens in the first place?"

"When I was three years old, my family was aboard a colony ship that crashed on Pellinath Four. There were only two survivors, and the other one died a couple of days later. The Bellum took care of me until I was seventeen."

"The Bellum?" repeated Virtue. "I've never heard of them."

"Most people haven't," replied the Swagman. "They keep pretty much to themselves."

"Why didn't they notify the Democracy that they had you?"

"Strange as it may seem to you, they didn't even know the Democracy existed. So I stayed there until a team from the Pioneer Corps landed and started charting the planet, and then they took me back with them."

"What was it like, growing up without any other members of your own race?" she asked curiously.

"Not that bad, all things considered. I think it was harder on the Bellum than on me."

"Oh? Why?"

"They were a dedicated communal society, and the concept of individual ownership wasn't very popular with them." He grinned. "Needless to say, this was a worldview that I didn't exactly share. I've been gone for close to thirty years now, and I'll bet some portions of their economy still haven't recovered.''

''I would have thought they got you young enough to properly indoctrinate you,'' commented Virtue.

''That's what *they* thought,'' he said with an amused laugh. ''But give a two-year-old child a rag doll and tell him that it's *his*, and he's got an understanding of property that even a planet filled with Bellum isn't going to shake.'' He paused. ''Anyway, I've never been very good at taking orders, so when they told me that no right-thinking entity would ever want to possess any material goods, I immediately began accumulating things at a phenomenal rate.'' He grinned again. ''I guess it carried over into adulthood.''

''Interesting,'' she said, deciding that the heat was preferable to the dust and closing her window. ''But I don't see that any of this makes you more qualified than me to speak to Sitting Bull.''

''He's an alien who's trying to act like a human,'' said the Swagman. ''That's much the same position *I* was in three decades ago.'' He paused. ''Also, I've dealt with him once before, so I know the form.''

''Form? What form?''

''He's very big on Amerind rituals. I suspect most of them never existed, but he's read a lot of books and tapes by a lot of half-baked anthropologists.''

''And *that's* what interested Black Orpheus enough to write him up?'' said Virtue, obviously unimpressed.

''He's written up less colorful characters,'' replied the Swagman. ''You and me, for instance.''

''This may come as a surprise to you, but I didn't even know I was *in* his damned song until after my verse appeared.'' She snorted contemptuously. ''I still don't know when and where he saw me, and I don't think I'll *ever* know where he got that Virgin Queen crap.''

''So you're not a virgin and you're not a queen,'' said the Swagman easily. ''*I* was never chased by a posse, either, no matter what the song says. But Black Orpheus never lets facts get in the way of truth. After all, he's a myth-maker, not an historian.''

''He's not a myth-maker *or* an historian,'' said Virtue. ''He's just a ballad-writer, and not a very good one, at that.''

The Swagman shook his head. "He may put his story in ballad form, but he's not one to let meter interfere with what he wants to say. The last time he visited me I pointed out that the meter was all wrong in his songs about Socrates and Altair of Altair and One-Time Charlie, and he just smiled and said that he'd rather have his songs ring true than scan properly."

"The man's a fool."

"If he is, then he's a very popular fool."

"You think so?" she said. "You ought to hear Cain's opinion about being dubbed the Songbird."

"Instead of complaining about it, he ought to be pleased," said the Swagman. "Orpheus has made him famous." He paused. "Hell, he's made *all* of us famous."

"You know," she said thoughtfully, wiping her forehead again, "maybe we're missing a bet here."

"In what way?"

"Maybe we ought to hunt Orpheus up and ask *him* where we can find Santiago."

"He doesn't know," said the Swagman. "He's been hunting for him for the past ten years."

"But he wrote him up!" protested Virtue. "I thought he never did that until he'd met his subject."

"Santiago's a special case. After all, an epic about the Inner Frontier that doesn't mention him just doesn't make much sense. Besides, Orpheus is like every other artist I've ever met: the further along he gets on a piece of work, the more frightened he becomes that he's going to die before it's finished and that some total incompetent will complete it for him. He wanted to make sure that the Santiago verses were done before that happened; I imagine they'll be rewritten if he ever finds him."

"Who commissioned this damned song, anyway?" asked Virtue.

"No one. He does it because he wants to."

"Then I was right the first time," she said decisively. "He's a fool."

"For doing something that makes him happy?"

"For giving it away for free."

"Maybe he's got enough money," suggested the Swagman.

She turned and stared at him. "Do you know *anyone* who's got enough money?"

The Swagman smiled. "Maybe he's a fool," he said at last.

The road suddenly dipped through a wooded hollow, and the Swagman began slowing down.

"What's the matter?" asked Virtue.

"We're almost there," he replied, pulling off to the side of the road just after it climbed out of the hollow and ran across a narrow ridge. "See that clearing about half a mile ahead?"

"What are those weird-looking structures in the middle of it?" asked Virtue, peering through the trees.

"Wigwams," replied the Swagman.

"What's a wigwam?"

"A kind of tent that Amerinds used to live in—or so Sitting Bull tells me. Personally, I doubt that anyone ever slept in anything like that. It looks much too inefficient, and it certainly doesn't afford any protection against your enemies." He shrugged. "Still, it's hardly worth arguing the point; I've got better things to do than go around researching aborigines."

He turned off the ignition.

"What now?" asked Virtue.

"Now we get out and walk," he continued, opening his door as she followed suit.

"Why? We're still almost half a mile away."

"Because Sitting Bull likes his supplicants to approach on foot. I can't really say that I blame him; there are a goodly number of ways to rig some pretty powerful weaponry to a motor vehicle, and he does have more than his fair share of enemies." He paused. "Besides, this way he gets to show off."

"I don't follow you," said Virtue.

"If the last time I came here was at all typical, we'll pick up some company along the way and march into his camp under armed guard. I imagine it makes him feel as if he's in control of the situation."

As if on cue, four aliens stepped out from behind trees and bushes. Or rather, three—tall, bald, emaciated blue beings, each carrying a multitude of weapons—*stepped* out; the fourth, which resembled a shaggy yellow caterpillar, merely *slithered*. All four aliens wore war paint and headbands. The Swagman thought they looked absolutely ludicrous, but Virtue found them interesting enough to capture with a miniaturized holographic camera that she had built into her belt buckle.

Finally one of the blue aliens, who identified himself as Cochise, pointed a sonic rifle at them. They stood motionless while the caterpillar literally sniffed out their weapons, appropriated the Swagman's two concealed pistols, and turned them over to another of the blue aliens. Finally Cochise jerked his head in the direction of the camp, and the two humans began walking toward it once again.

When they arrived, Cochise ushered them to the site of a campfire that had died sometime during the night, told them to sit down, and left them in the care of another blue alien.

"Anything out of the ordinary yet?" whispered Virtue.

"Just standard operating procedure so far," said the Swagman reassuringly.

Then the flaps of a nearby teepee were thrust apart, and Sitting Bull stepped out as Virtue surreptitiously activated her belt-buckle camera and a hidden recording device.

The first thing she noticed about him was the gold feathers. Initially she thought they were part of his costume, like the huge ceremonial headdress he wore, but she quickly saw that they were part and parcel of Sitting Bull himself.

He stood about five feet tall and was almost as broad as he was high. He covered his genitalia so inadequately with a beaded loincloth that she knew at a glance that he *was* a he and not an it; and he waddled on thick, muscular legs that were jointed so strangely that she couldn't imagine how he could possibly sit down, or even squat on his haunches.

His face, like those of the other aliens, was covered by a painted design, but seemed, if not human, at least very expressive. Virtue couldn't imagine any being with so many feathers not having a beak to go along with them, but Sitting Bull possessed a broad, flat nose and a narrow, puckered mouth. His eyes were umber, his pupils mere vertical slits. If he had ears, she couldn't spot them, but she decided that they may very well have been covered by the substantial headdress.

"Hello, Sitting Bull," said the Swagman, starting to get to his feet. "It's good to see you again."

"Remain seated," replied Sitting Bull in a harsh, croaking voice that grated on Virtue's ears; it seemed so out of place that she felt he was purposely deepening it to impress them.

The Swagman sat back down and re-crossed his legs. "Who is your companion?"

"Virtue MacKenzie," said Virtue, wondering whether to extend her hand and deciding not to. "I'm a journalist."

Sitting Bull stared at her expressionlessly for a moment, then turned back to the Swagman and cleared his throat, a grating noise that sounded like metal rubbing against metal and caused Virtue to conclude that she was hearing his normal voice after all.

"What favor do you seek from the Great Sioux Nation?"

"Information," responded the Swagman promptly.

"Will the acquisition of this information bring harm to one or more Men?" asked Sitting Bull.

"It will," said the Swagman.

The feathered alien made a sudden awkward jerking motion with his head, which Virtue took to be a nod of approval.

"Will the acquisition of this information bring harm to one or more members of any other race?"

"Absolutely not," the Swagman assured him.

"Are you aware of the penalty for lying?"

"Let us say that I can hazard a remarkably accurate guess."

"Do not guess, Jolly Swagman." Sitting Bull leaned forward and stared intently at him, and suddenly Virtue decided that he looked a lot more like an alien than an Indian. "Should any harm befall anyone other than a Man as a result of the information that you seek, you and Virtue MacKenzie will be found no matter where you try to hide. You will be brought back to Diamond Strike, you will be tortured, and eventually you will be tethered to a stake and burned to death. Is that understood?"

"Perfectly."

"Then you may make your request."

"We're looking for Santiago. Do you know where he is?"

"Yes."

There was a long silence.

"Well?" demanded Virtue.

"This I will not tell you."

"Will not or cannot?" asked the Swagman.

"I said what I said," replied Sitting Bull stoically.

"I didn't realize you were afraid of him," said the Swagman condescendingly.

"I fear no one."

"Then why won't you tell us what we want to know?"

"Because he makes war against Men. Because he brings grief to Men. Because he brings chaos to Men. Because he is Santiago."

"Cut the crap and name your price," said Virtue irritably.

Sitting Bull turned to her, his pupils dilating and contracting as he breathed. "Women do not speak in council."

"Women with money do," she replied. "How much do you want?"

"You are very irritating, even for a member of your race," said the alien. "I begin to understand why Dimitri Sokol wants you dead." He stared coldly at her. "There is no price. I will not tell you."

"You mean you haven't got the guts!" snapped Virtue.

"We fear no one," said Sitting Bull, pulling back his lips and exposing a row of bright yellow teeth. "Even the Democracy cringes in fear of the Great Sioux Nation."

"Which in turn cringes in fear of Santiago, a common criminal with a price on his head."

"Santiago is not the only Man with a price on his head," said Sitting Bull meaningfully. "You would do well to remember that."

"Is that a threat?" demanded Virtue. "If there's a price on *my* head, it was put there by a criminal on Pegasus—and if you try to cash in on it, you're going to find out just what happens to self-important aliens who go around killing human journalists! Have you got that straight?"

Sitting Bull merely stared at her and made no reply.

"Now let's talk business," said Virtue. "We're in a hurry."

The alien continued staring at her.

"Now listen, you—" she began heatedly.

The Swagman touched her arm. "That's enough," he said. "He's not trying to jack up the price; he means what he says. And in case you've forgotten, we're surrounded by his enforcers."

"Are you trying to tell me that we came all this way for nothing?" demanded Virtue. "We talk to him for thirty seconds and just give up, is that it?"

"Not entirely," replied the Swagman. "We can at least find out how the competition is doing." He turned back to Sitting Bull. "We also seek information that does not concern Santiago."

"I will listen."

"There is a bounty hunter known as the Angel. Where is he now?"

They went through the same ritual about whom such information could and could not damage, after which Sitting Bull acknowledged that he could come up with the Angel's present location in a matter of minutes. He summoned a blue alien named Vittorio, asked him something in a tongue Virtue could not identify, dismissed him, and turned back to the Swagman.

Then the haggling began. Sitting Bull demanded 20,000 Bonaparte francs; the Swagman laughed in his face and countered with 750 credits. Ten minutes later they were still at it, 236 credits apart, and finally the Swagman gave in. The negotiated bill came to 6,819 credits, payable in advance.

The Swagman dug into his pocket and pulled out a sheaf of bills. Vittorio was summoned, emerged from a nearby wigwam, said something to Sitting Bull, collected the money, and then positioned himself a few paces behind Sitting Bull, his thin arms folded across his narrow chest.

"Now we will smoke a peace pipe," announced Sitting Bull. "And then I will give you that which you have purchased."

He nodded, and a brown, sluglike creature that Virtue had thought was a log undulated over to him and produced a long, meticulously crafted wooden pipe from somewhere within the folds of its thick, crusted skin.

Sitting Bull withdrew a tiny laser device, rekindled the logs between himself and the two humans, and gestured to the yellow caterpillar, which slithered over, picked up a burning twig, and held it just above the end of the pipe. Sitting Bull took a number of deep puffs, grunted his satisfaction, and then passed the pipe to the Swagman, who filled his mouth with smoke, seemed to analyze the taste of it for an instant, and then released it.

When it was Virtue's turn, he handed it to her and whispered, "Don't inhale."

She followed his instructions, took a couple of mouthfuls of thick gray smoke, made sure nothing went down her throat, and finally blew them out.

"What is it?" she asked, making a face and handing the

pipe to the yellow alien, who ambulated away with it. "It seemed sickly sweet."

"Some kind of hallucinogenic compound," he replied softly. "It's one of his favorite parlor tricks." He grimaced. "My guess is that he insists on smoking it just so he can watch humans make asses of themselves. Get one puff of that stuff in your system and you'd still be seeing things a week from now." He turned to Sitting Bull. "May I have my information?"

"Vittorio says that the man you seek is currently on the planet of Glenovar, in the system of Zeta Halioth."

The Swagman frowned. "You're sure?"

"I am sure."

"There's no possibility of a mistake, or that you might have the wrong man?"

"None."

"All right." He paused. "I'll give you one last opportunity to talk about Santiago. We are prepared to make you a very handsome offer."

"I will not betray Santiago."

"I thought your livelihood consisted of betraying Men," interjected Virtue coldly.

"Only to the detriment of other Men," replied Sitting Bull placidly.

The Swagman stood up and helped Virtue to her feet. "Then I think it's time that we took our leave of you."

"You seek no other information?"

"No."

"Are you not curious about a shipment of anthracite sculptures in transit from Pisgah to Genovaith Four?" suggested the feathered alien, his lips curled back in what seemed to be a grin.

The Swagman smiled back at him. "I was so curious about it that I gave orders to waylay it when it passed by the Karobus system. That would have occurred, oh, about an hour ago."

"Truly?"

"Truly," said the Swagman.

"You are a very resourceful villain, Jolly Swagman," said Sitting Bull.

"In that case, perhaps I should apply for membership in the Great Sioux Nation," he replied wryly.

"You are not acceptable," said Sitting Bull. "Your weapons have been placed in your vehicle." He turned away and waddled back to his wigwam.

After the feathered alien had disappeared behind a flap in the tent, the Swagman turned to Virtue.

"We've got problems," he announced grimly.

"Oh?"

He nodded. "The Angel's a lot closer to Santiago than I thought he'd be at this time."

"Closer than we are?" she demanded.

"Probably."

"How can that be? If you know who he's seeing, why didn't we see this person first?"

"I don't know who he's seeing. What I *do* know is that there are three or four lines of pursuit for someone who's hunting Santiago. We're following the one that's tied in to his smuggling operations; if the Angel's on Glenovar, he's following a money trail." He frowned. "And he's doing a damned good job of it: he's gotten as far in four weeks as you have in almost a year—and he didn't have Cain helping him. I've got a feeling that he's within three or four worlds of someone who can probably give him Santiago's headquarters planet, and might even be able to toss in his address and room number."

"Will Altair of Altair be able to do the same for Cain?" asked Virtue.

The Swagman shrugged. "I don't know. Perhaps."

"But you doubt it."

"I really don't know," he replied.

Virtue stood up and turned to Sitting Bull's wigwam.

"Hey, Sitting Bull!" she hollered. "Come back out."

The alien emerged a moment later.

"What is your price for killing the Angel?" she asked him.

He was silent for a minute, as if weighing his expenses.

"Five million credits," he announced at last.

"Five million?" she repeated incredulously. "You must be joking! That's more than the Democracy is offering for any criminal except Santiago!"

"It will take many of my warriors, and most of them will die." He paused. "The Songbird is a killer, and he is also your partner. Why do you not ask him to kill the Angel?"

"Because I'm asking *you*," she snapped, wondering irritably if there was anyone on the Frontier who *didn't* know she had teamed up with Cain.

"I have told you my price. Will you pay it?"

"Not a chance," she replied.

Sitting Bull went back into his wigwam without another word.

"Where will the Angel be heading after he leaves Glenovar?" asked Virtue as she and the Swagman began walking back to the landcar.

He shrugged. "Who knows? The Lambda Karos system, probably. Sooner or later most money trails pass through there."

"Perhaps we should try to get there first and eliminate his contact," she suggested.

"I don't know who his contact *is*—and even if I did know, I think it's a fair assumption that from this point on, all of his contacts are pretty good at taking care of themselves. You'd need a specialist for that, someone like Cain."

"Well?" she said expectantly.

He sighed. "Out of the question. We also need him for our own line of inquiry. Of the three of us, he's the most likely to survive a meeting with Altair of Altair and some of the others who are waiting along the way. You have many wonderful qualities, Virtue—you lie and cheat and blackmail and bluff with great panache, and you're thoroughly delightful in bed— but you simply aren't a skilled professional killer."

Virtue took a deep breath, held it for perhaps half a minute, then released it explosively.

"You think the Angel is going to get there first, don't you?" she said bluntly.

He shrugged noncommittally. "The possibility exists."

Virtue stared at her companion for a long moment, and as she did so she found herself concluding that she had put her money on the wrong horse.

"Maybe I should go out to the Lambda Karos system and wait for him there," she suggested with what she hoped was the proper degree of detachment.

"Him?" repeated the Swagman. "You mean the Angel? What good would that do?"

She shrugged innocently. "Who knows? Maybe I can find some way to misdirect him, or at least slow him down." She paused. "At any rate, we'll have a clear idea of where he is and how fast he's progressing. That has to be of some use to us."

"I'm afraid you're being just a little transparent, my dear," replied the Swagman with the hint of an amused smile. "How can you possibly misdirect him if you don't know who his contact is, or what information the contact will feed him? As for having a clear idea of where he's at, that's infinitely less important than possessing a clear idea of where he's *going*." He paused, then chuckled and shook his head. "You haven't done your homework very well, Virtue: the Angel doesn't take partners. Ever."

"Who said anything about becoming the Angel's partner?" she demanded heatedly, annoyed with herself for being so obvious. "I just want to keep tabs on him, and possibly send him off in the wrong direction."

"Or accompany him in the right one," suggested the Swagman wryly.

"You're a very distrusting man," said Virtue. "I suppose it can be blamed on your upbringing."

"How about blaming it on my present company?"

"You can waste your time assessing the blame," she said. "I intend to spend mine hunting up the Angel."

"You're being foolish, my dear," said the Swagman. "Or perhaps you weren't listening to Sitting Bull as closely as you should have been."

"What are you talking about?"

"Sokol's still got a hit out on you. In fact, the only reason that Sitting Bull didn't have you killed the minute you landed is because you were with me, and I've sent a lot of business his way over the years. As soon as you go off by yourself, you're fair game again."

"Do you think I'm going to quake in terror over a squat little alien who lives in a tent?" she said with a laugh.

"It could be anyone you might meet. You don't know who Sokol may have contacted." He paused. "As for Sitting Bull, he doesn't look like much, and he doesn't surround himself with luxury, but he's a pretty formidable antagonist."

"And if I stay with you, *you're* going to protect me?"

"Indirectly. Most people don't like to offend me."

"At least Cain has had a little experience killing people."

He smiled. "I *hire* people like Cain, my dear."

They came to a fallen tree that was blocking their way and walked around it.

"What's the greatest single piece of alien artwork in the galaxy?" she asked suddenly.

He thought for a moment. "There's a mile-long tapestry on Antares Three," he said. "Forty generations of Antareans have worked on it, and it tells the history of their race in about two thousand exquisite scenes. I'd say that's about the rarest. Why?"

"What would you risk to get your hands on it?"

"Everything I have."

"Well, Santiago's the greatest single story in the galaxy, and I'll take whatever risk is necessary to find him."

"I should add that I wouldn't risk my life for that tapestry," said the Swagman.

"That's because you're not hungry anymore," said Virtue. "I still am. I want to be the best—and if seeing the Angel can help me get what I want, then I'm willing to do it."

They reached the landcar, and the Swagman picked his pistols up off the seat and put them back into his pockets.

"You're sure you won't reconsider?"

"I'm sure."

He sighed. "Then maybe I'd better go with you."

"There's no need for both of us to go out there. I'll keep you and Cain informed of his whereabouts." She paused. "I think your best course of action is to go to Altair and hook up with him there."

"Probably," he agreed reluctantly. "A question arises, however: How am I going to get there? My ship's back on Goldenrod."

"You're a resourceful man," said Virtue. "I'm sure you'll find a way." She paused. "Now please take me back to my ship."

"And if I refuse?"

"Then I'll walk, and the result will be the same, except that I'll tell Cain that you're working for the Angel and that he should kill you on sight."

The Swagman looked at her, surprised only that he felt no surprise. "I suppose you would, at that." He paused. "The nearest major planet is Kakkab Kastu Four. Can you at least drop me there?"

She considered his suggestion for a moment, then nodded.

"I suppose another few hours doesn't matter, as long as I get where I'm going." She turned to him. "But you'll pay for the extra fuel."

"We'll subtract it from your half of Sitting Bull's fee."

"I never agreed to pay Sitting Bull," she said. "I could have gotten the same information from Cain."

"If he's still alive."

"If he's not, I want half the reward if you kill Santiago."

"You're quite an operator, my dear," said the Swagman, shaking his head with mock weariness.

"One does what one must," said Virtue.

"Spare me your platitudes," he said dryly.

"I consider them words to live by."

"Only until you meet the Angel," he predicted. "Then may God have mercy on your soul, for He'll be presented with it soon enough."

Part 3

The Jolly Swagman's Book

11.

Come if you dare, come but beware,
Come to the lair of Altair of Altair.
Offer a prayer for the men foul and fair,
Trapped in the snare of Altair of Altair.

They tell a lot of stories about Altair of Altair out on the
Frontier.

Some say that, like the Jolly Swagman, she was raised by
aliens and grew up with a bitter hatred of her own race that
the Swagman somehow avoided.

Others say she wasn't human at all, but that she could
change her shape at will and enticed her victims to their
deaths with an irresistible siren song.

Homer of Troy, the self-proclaimed People's Poet who
spent half a lifetime trying unsuccessfully to write a saga of
the Frontier that would rival Black Orpheus' epic in popular-
ity, swore that she was a mutant who killed her enemies by
the use of mental thunderbolts that shattered their minds.

There was even a group on Walpurgis III, a planet colonized by covens and devil-worshipers, that believed she was a
devoted practitioner of the Black Arts who brought destruction through spells and potions.

As for Black Orpheus himself, he went directly to the
source, as always. It took him almost a month to track her
down after he'd reached the Altair system, and then he had to
wait another week before she would agree to see him. When
they finally met face to face, he took one look at her and

decided that she was the most beautiful woman he had seen since the death of his beloved Eurydice.

By the time he left some twenty minutes later, he wasn't even sure that she *was* a woman—but he knew that she was the most formidable killer he had ever encountered.

He never spoke of her again, although he did write a couple of verses about her, and when others asked about Altair of Altair he always found a way to change the subject. Nobody knows what happened during their one brief meeting, but it obviously had a profound effect upon him, one that lasted for the remainder of his life.

One of the people who wished that Black Orpheus had written a little more about her was Sebastian Cain, if only so he would have some idea of what to expect when he finally reached her.

It had taken him two weeks to discover that she did not live *on* Altair III, but rather *under* it, and now he stalked, gun in hand, through the labyrinthian network of tunnels and corridors that led to her chamber. It had cost him ten thousand credits just to find out how and where to enter the seemingly endless maze, and he had then spent the better part of two days losing the trio of men who had been tailing him since he had touched down. Finally, reasonably certain that he was no longer being followed, he had entered the subterranean world of Altair of Altair.

That had been two hours ago. Since then the temperature had dropped somewhat, and the air had become dank and stale. The corridors themselves were illuminated by diffuse blue light that gave them a surreal glow, but none of them were marked or labeled, and after he found himself back where he had started, he withdrew a small knife and began carving crude directional symbols at every intersection.

He paused, wiped some sweat from his face, and cursed under his breath. There *had* to be a quicker way into her headquarters, and he decided to give himself one more hour. If he found her by then, well and good; if not, he would retrace his steps, return to the surface, take his money back from the man who had sold him his information and possibly kill him as well, and start his search all over again from scratch. If he went back to his hotel, he was sure to pick up his troika of followers once more; possibly he would separate one from the others and find some means, painless or otherwise, of extracting the information he needed.

He began walking again, wondering if he wouldn't be better off going immediately to the surface and searching for a more direct route. Then he came to yet another intersection and found that the right-hand tunnel glowed a rich red, as opposed to the usual blue. He entered it without hesitation.

It twisted to his right, then straightened out for a few hundred feet, and finally seemed to make a sweeping semicircle to the left, never once intersecting with any other corridor. Finally it broadened out, the walls gradually forming artificially perfect right angles with the floor and ceiling, and he noticed that the illumination was considerably brighter.

Suddenly the corridor came to an abrupt end, and he found himself standing in a small vestibule that led to a large, well-lit chamber. He started to enter it, then jumped back as he discovered that his way was blocked by an electronic force field.

He approached the entrance more cautiously and looked into the chamber. It was perhaps sixty feet on a side, and its smooth stone walls sparkled like polished prisms in the artificial light. He had no idea how high the ceiling was, because the room faded into darkness some thirty feet above the floor. Lining two of the walls, to a height of perhaps eight feet, were enormous water tanks filled with alien aquatic life-forms and contained not by glass walls but by translucent energy screens.

In the very center of the room was a desk with a computer console and five small screens; one of them displayed some type of readout, and the other four seemed to show various areas of the labyrinth. Just to the left of the desk were two couches. One was empty, and on the other reclined a breathtakingly beautiful woman. Her features were human, but they were so exotic that they seemed somehow alien. Her skin was chalk white, her hair was long and black, her large eyes were almost too blue beneath her oddly arched eyebrows. Her facial features, from her full lips and delicate nose to her not-quite-pointed ears, were exquisitely chiseled. Her single garment, which was draped around her supple body like a corkscrew and exposed far more than it concealed, was made of some metallic fabric that seemed to change colors every time she breathed or moved.

"Welcome, Sebastian Cain," she said in a lilting, singsong voice. "I have been watching you work your way through my labyrinth."

"You're Altair of Altair?"

"Of course."

"I've come a long way to talk to you," he said.

"I will enjoy talking to you. We have many things in common." She paused. "That is why I allowed you to find me. You are only the third person ever to enter this chamber."

"I haven't entered it yet," he noted.

"I must protect myself," she said apologetically. "After all, I have a price on my head, and you are a bounty hunter."

"I have no professional interest in you," he assured her. "I just want to talk."

"And yet you have been carrying your gun in your hand since entering my labyrinth."

"You're not the only person who feels the need for protection," he replied. "I wouldn't be the first man you've killed."

"We are *both* killers," said Altair of Altair. "Shall we declare a truce?"

"For how long?"

"You will be warned before it is over."

"I'm willing."

"Then leave your gun in the vestibule. You can pick it up when you leave."

"Not a chance," he said.

"Will you at least replace it in your holster?"

He did so, and she rose, walked to the computer, and touched a small octagonal button.

"The shield is down," she announced. "You may enter now."

"Thank you," he said, walking gingerly through the doorway and stepping into the chamber. The floor was covered by a soft yielding substance that was more resilient than it looked and glowed with different colors every time he set his foot down.

"I have been wanting to meet you for a long time," said Altair of Altair.

"Have you?"

"Yes," she said. "Killing is a lonely profession. It is so rare that one gets to visit with one's peers."

"We're not exactly peers," answered Cain. "You're an assassin; I'm a bounty hunter."

"But many facets of our work are the same," she pointed out. "The endless waiting for the prey to appear, the moment of exultation at the kill, the distrust of confederates, the craving for solitude. Do you not agree?"

"Perhaps," he said noncommittally. "But the differences are even greater, and the fact remains that you will commit murder for anyone who pays your fee, and I kill criminals at the behest of my government."

"True," she said thoughtfully. "But then, even among bounty hunters you are a unique individual."

"Oh? In what way?"

"Most of those who make their living by killing lawbreakers were once lawbreakers themselves. Peacemaker MacDougal was a smuggler, Giles Sans Pitié and Barnaby Wheeler were bandits, even the Angel was an assassin. Of them all, only you have always operated within the law."

"You're wrong," he said. "I once had a price on my head, too."

"You were fighting on behalf of what you believed to be a legal government in exile," she replied with a smile.

"How do you know that?"

"I have been studying you for a long time," said Altair of Altair. "In our business, one does not live long without knowing the face of the enemy."

"I'm not your enemy."

"And Santiago is not yours," she replied. "Why do you want him dead?"

"What makes you think I'm after Santiago?" he asked.

"Who else could have brought you this far from Keepsake?" she replied. "I repeat: Why do you wish to kill him?"

He smiled. "Have you seen the size of the reward?"

"You are a very successful bounty hunter. You have no need of money."

"Everyone needs money."

"A man like you must have another reason," she persisted.

He stared at her, then shrugged. "It would *mean* something," he said at last.

"Ah!" She smiled. "I knew you were different!" She walked back to the couch and sprawled on it. "Do you know that not a single murder I have committed has ever meant anything?"

"What about killing the governor of Alsatia Four?" he asked.

"One second later there was a new governor, and what had changed?" She shook her head. "No, the beauty of the assassin's profession is that nothing ever means anything, and hence the perceived need for assassination never diminishes. Only you, of all the killers I know, want your actions to make a difference."

"Tell me about some of the killers you know," said Cain.

"Had you someone in mind?"

"Santiago."

"I have never met him."

"I think you have," persisted Cain.

"Why?"

"Because you killed a man named Kastartos."

"What has one to do with the other?" she asked.

"Kastartos planned to double-cross Santiago," answered Cain. "He tried to get Jonathan Stern to help him. Stern didn't think it was worth the risk, and sent word of Kastartos's plans to Santiago. It stands to reason that Santiago commissioned his death."

She stared at him pleasantly but made no comment.

"If the order came directly from him, it wouldn't be unreasonable to assume that you've met him and know where he is, would it?" he continued.

"He has never directly commissioned my services," she replied. "He works only through intermediaries."

"Who are they?"

"That is not your concern."

"If you're saying that from fear of reprisal, there's no reason for Santiago to know that we ever met."

"He already knows."

"How?"

"Because he is Santiago."

"You make him sound like some kind of superman," said Cain.

"He is just a man, and he can be killed like any other man," she replied. "You have much in common with him."

"You mean because we can both be killed?" he asked sardonically.

"That, too," she said with an enigmatic smile.

Suddenly there was a flurry of motion in one of the aquarium tanks, as a bright orange eyeless fish, slim as a dagger, burrowed into the soft sand at the bottom and emerged with a yellow-and-black-striped crustacean. The orange fish tossed the crustacean up above him and darted for its soft underbelly, guided unerringly to its most vulnerable parts by what Cain assumed was some form of sonar. The water around them turned pink with the fluid that coursed through the crustacean's veins, and instantly half a hundred other marine forms of perhaps ten different species had gathered in a feeding frenzy.

"They are beautiful creatures, are they not?" said Altair of Altair, a look of almost inhuman excitement on her face. "And savage," she continued in a singsong chant. "They kill for food, and when they are sated, they kill for the love of killing."

"Interesting," he said noncommittally.

"Fascinating," she replied with conviction. "There is one you cannot see, who lives beneath the sand. Not this clumsy shellfish, but a beautiful animal, bright as the morning sun. The others hunt for him endlessly, but they cannot find him." She smiled. "I have named him Santiago."

"And which fish is Altair of Altair?" he asked.

"None of them." She stared at him through half-lowered lids. "I kill only for recompense."

"Nobody's asking you to kill at all," said Cain patiently. "I just need to know where to find Santiago." He paused. "I'm prepared to give you a percentage of the reward if your information proves useful."

"Are you indeed?"

"Ten percent of the price on his head would keep you in fish for a long time."

"Do you know what I would do if you tried to take my very bright fish?" she asked suddenly.

"What?"

"I would kill you, Sebastian Cain. I would kill you because that fish is mine, and you would be taking something that didn't belong to you."

"Are you trying to tell me that you think you have some prior claim on Santiago?"

"Santiago is mine."

"Then why is he still alive?"

"Because the reward increases every year, and I am very patient. When it becomes large enough, then I shall kill him."

"It's large right now."

"It will become larger," she said with certainty.

"And you're not worried about someone beating you to it?"

"Do you really think it is that easy to kill him?" she asked, obviously amused. "He is *Santiago*."

"If you think he can't be killed, why not give me the information I want?"

"It would do you no good."

"In that case, it would do you no harm," said Cain.

She stared at him for a long moment, then sighed. "There are more important things than information."

"For instance?"

"The gift of life," she said. "No one who has ever entered my lair has been given it. But because I lead the solitary life of a killer, I respect all others who do as well. Pledge to return to Keepsake and fish for lesser prizes, and you may leave here alive."

"After I find Santiago," he replied, suddenly wary.

"Then you are a fool," she said. "Did you know that even as we speak, Virtue MacKenzie is racing to the Angel's side to betray you?"

He looked surprised for just an instant, then shrugged. "It won't be the first time I've been betrayed," he said. "And it won't do her any good."

"That much is true," said Altair of Altair. "For when we are through here, I must hunt down the Angel and all who stand with him."

"For poaching?" he asked wryly.

"Yes."

"If you start killing every bounty hunter who's looking for Santiago, you're going to have a full-time job on your hands."

"Most of them are insignificant specks of debris in the cosmos," she replied. "Even Peacemaker MacDougal and Johnny One-Note will never find Santiago. Of them all, only you and the Angel have the ability to find him."

"What about Giles Sans Pitié?"

"The Angel killed him last week," replied Altair of Altair.

"Giles Sans Pitié sought him out on Glenovar and proposed an alliance." She paused. "The Angel has no more use for competition than I have."

"I warned him to stay away from the Angel," commented Cain.

"You realize, of course, that I have every reason to do to you what the Angel did to Giles Sans Pitié."

"I wouldn't advise it," said Cain ominously.

"Forget your weapon, Sebastian Cain," she said, an unfathomable expression on her exotic face. "It will do you no good."

"You'll forgive me if I don't take your word for it," he said, withdrawing his gun and pointing it at her.

"How will you kill me?" she asked, her blue eyes alive with amused interest. "A bullet to the head? That *is* your trademark, isn't it?"

"I don't have a trademark."

"*All* good killers have trademarks," she replied. "With Giles Sans Pitié it was his metal fist, with Peacemaker MacDougal it is a pencil-thin beam of light, with ManMountain Bates it is his bare hands, with you it is a bullet. Only the Angel, who is adept with all weapons, slaughters with variety."

"And what is *your* trademark?" asked Cain.

"You shall see," she said softly.

And then, suddenly, he was no longer in a subterranean chamber on Altair III. Instead, he stood at the edge of a clear blue brook, the hot Sylarian sun beating down on his neck. He was barefoot, and the grass, long and swaying in the gentle breeze, felt like velvet between his toes.

He looked across the brook and saw a girl, her blond hair meticulously braided, her skin tanned and healthy. She wore a plain blue dress, and she gingerly held its skirt up to her knees as she stood ankle deep in the water.

"Help me," she said, her voice heavy with worry.

"It's shallow," replied Cain with a laugh. "Just walk across it."

"I'll fall."

"No, you won't."

"Don't tease me, Sebastian," she pleaded, reaching her hand out to him. "Please!"

"All right," he said with a smile.

It was funny, he reflected as he placed a foot in the brook and felt the cold water swirl around it. He had known her for years, had loved her from the first day he had met her, yet for the life of him he couldn't remember her name.

"It's Jennifer," she said.

"Right." He nodded. "Jennifer."

"Please hurry, Sebastian," she said. "I'm frightened."

"I'm coming."

He crossed the brook in five large steps, feeling remarkably invigorated by the water.

"You see?" he laughed. "There's nothing to it." He paused, momentarily disoriented. "Now what?"

"Now carry me across."

"Why don't I just hold your hand and lead you?" he asked.

"The stones hurt my feet," she said, half crooning the words. "Won't you please carry me?"

He sighed. "If that's what you want."

"You'll have to drop the stick first," she said.

He frowned. "What stick?"

"The stick you're carrying in your right hand. You can't lift me up if you're carrying a stick."

"Sure I can," he said, suddenly uneasy.

"It will hurt me," she said, "and it might even rip my dress. Please drop it, Sebastian."

He took a step back, still reluctant to drop the stick. "Something's wrong," he said, frowning again.

"What is it?" she asked innocently.

"I don't know," he said. "Maybe it's the dress."

The dress became a burgundy skirt and a frilly white blouse.

"Is this better, Sebastian?"

He stared at it. "I suppose so," he said at last.

"Then carry me across the brook. I'm late."

"For what?"

She giggled. "*You* know," she said with a sense of shared intimacy.

"Oh."

He stood motionless.

"Well?" she said at last.

"It's still wrong," he said, puzzled.

"What is, Sebastian?"

"I don't know. Let me think for a minute."

"We haven't got a minute, Sebastian. I'm *late*. Don't tease me like this."

He took a step toward her. "I've almost got it."

"Hurry, Sebastian!" she said, a note of urgency creeping into her voice.

He reached out to her uneasily.

"The stick, Sebastian," she chanted seductively. "Put it down."

He dropped the stick.

"Thank you," she said, a strange smile on her lips. "Are you happy, Sebastian?"

"I suppose so," he said, forcing himself to return her smile.

"I'm so glad."

"What's that in your hand?" he asked, peering at some shining object he hadn't seen before.

"A flower," she said. "A lovely silver flower."

"It's very pretty," he said, the uneasiness growing within him once again.

"Would you like a closer look, Sebastian?"

"Yes, I— *Shit!*" he muttered, diving for the stick. He grabbed it as he rolled over on the ground, pointed it at her, and squeezed it.

Suddenly there was a loud explosion, and he was once again in the subterranean chamber, and Altair of Altair lay on her back, blood pouring out from a small hole between her eyes, a silver dagger clutched in her hand.

Cain stood motionless, panting, sweat pouring down his body, trying to regain his bearings. It took his hands a full minute to stop shaking, and finally he put the gun back in its holster.

Then he walked over to Altair of Altair and looked down at her.

"There *aren't* any brooks on Sylaria," he said weakly.

He examined her to make sure there were no signs of life, then stood erect, his hands on his hips.

"Great," he muttered. "Back to square one again."

"Not necessarily," said a voice.

"Who's there?" he demanded, crouching down beside the corpse and drawing his pistol.

"My name is Schussler," said the voice, and now Cain

realized that it was coming from the computer. "If you will retrace your steps, you'll find me waiting for you at the entrance to the labyrinth."

"How will I recognize you?" asked Cain.

"You'll have very little difficulty," said the voice with a bitter chuckle. "This I promise you."

12.

He aches for the touch of flesh upon flesh,
He wonders why Fate had to end his beguine,
He longs for a woman, all virginal fresh:
Schussler the Cyborg, unhappy machine.

Black Orpheus met many unique characters during his
wanderings on the Inner Frontier. There were killers and
gamblers, preachers and bounty hunters, millionaires and pau-
pers, saints and sinners, an entire panorama of outcasts and
adventurers and misfits—but not one of them measured up to
Schussler the Cyborg, whose tragedy was that he didn't want
to be unique at all.

Father William, for example, loved the limelight; Schussler
dreaded it. Socrates enjoyed power; Schussler disdained it.
Sebastian Cain sought solitude; Schussler hated it. The Angel
had killed men almost without number; Schussler cherished
all life but his own. The Sargasso Rose had no use for human
contact; Schussler longed for it. The men and women and
aliens that Orpheus put into his song were all bigger than life;
Schussler was bigger than any of them, and wanted only to be
smaller.

Most people saw him as a miracle of science, a shining
testament to the melding of man and machine—but Black
Orpheus looked beneath the gleaming surface, past the wonders of an alien technology, straight into Schussler's tortured
soul, and wept at what he saw.

They met only once, on Altair III. Orpheus stayed with
him for a day and a night, while Schussler poured out his

strange, unhappy story. They parted the next morning, Orpheus to continue his journey among the stars, Schussler to serve his mistress and wait, without hope, for the release of death.

Things began to change when the Jolly Swagman landed on Altair. By rights he and Schussler should have had a lot in common, since one of them had been raised by aliens and the other had been rebuilt by them; but the accumulation of other people's property was the driving force in the Swagman's life—while Schussler, who *was* property, found all forms of private ownership immoral.

Still, each of them had a major stake in Cain's meeting with Altair of Altair, so they quickly reached an accommodation and awaited the outcome.

It was midafternoon when Cain emerged from the labyrinth, shielding his eyes from the pale yellow sun with his hand. He looked around the barren red landscape and saw a very small spaceship of inhuman design about eighty yards away. An elegantly dressed man was leaning against it, but when he saw Cain he immediately began walking toward him.

"I can't tell you how delighted I am that you survived!" he said with a distinct accent.

"You're Schussler?" asked Cain, starting to sweat already.

"I'm afraid not. People call me the Jolly Swagman."

"Virtue MacKenzie sent me a message that I might be running into you," said Cain. "Aren't you a little out of your bailiwick?"

"Not while you're here, I'm not," replied the Swagman easily. He looked around at his bleak surroundings. "Though one could wish for a more interesting world, I suppose. I can't imagine why anyone chooses to live here: I suspect the only things that grow on Altair Three are dust and bugs."

"Any deal Virtue may have cut with you was hers, not mine," said Cain firmly. "Where's Schussler? Aboard the ship?"

"In a manner of speaking." The Swagman grinned. "He *is* the ship."

"What are you talking about?" demanded Cain, slapping at a large red insect that had landed on his neck.

"Schussler," said the Swagman. "He's a cyborg."

Cain looked at the ship, its hull shining in the midday sun.

"There's never been a cyborg like that," he said with conviction.

"Well, there is now. Orpheus gave him three verses."

"Orpheus writes so damned much, it's hard to keep up with all of it," replied Cain.

"Maybe you should have tried," said the Swagman. "Then you'd have known about Schussler."

Cain stared at the ship again. "He's *really* a spaceship?" he asked dubiously.

"Why should I lie to you?"

"Offhand, I can think of a hundred reasons." He waved his hand at a cloud of tiny, gnatlike insects, frightening them away. "How does he communicate?"

"He's got a speaker system. It sounds just the same as a ship's intercom."

"I've got to talk to him."

"He's not going anywhere," said the Swagman, turning slightly to protect his face from the dust raised by a sudden hot breeze. "Why don't you talk to *me* first?"

"About what?"

"About Santiago."

"Not interested," answered Cain.

"In Santiago?"

"In talking to you," said Cain. "I've heard about you, Swagman."

"All lies, I can assure you," said the Swagman smoothly.

"Can you now?"

"Absolutely," replied the Swagman with an amused laugh. "Anyone who can tell you the truth about me is safely dead and buried." He pulled out a thin cigar and lit it. "If you don't want to talk about Santiago, then how about Virtue?"

"What about Virtue?"

"What Altair of Altair told you is absolutely true. She's on her way to join the Angel."

"How do *you* know what she told me?" asked Cain sharply.

"I was a spectator at your little encounter," said the Swagman, dropping an ash on the ground and just missing a ten-legged purple-and-gold Altairian beetle with it.

"How did you manage *that*?"

"With the help of our cyborg friend here," replied the Swagman easily. "He's hooked into her computer." He smiled. "I would be less than candid if I didn't confess that I knew you were here to obtain information from Altair of Altair, and based on everything I knew about her, she wasn't very likely to give it to you. So, since there was no sense in both of us risking our lives, I hunted up Schussler and gave you silent moral support while we observed you from up here.'' The Swagman paused. ''Just what did she do to you at the end there?''

''What did it look like?'' asked Cain, curious.

''Nothing special. She kept urging you to cross a brook, but we couldn't see any—and I guess she tried to convince you that your gun was a stick?'' His inflection made it a question as much as an observation.

''Something like that.''

''Well, I must say that you're every bit as good as Virtue said you were. Any bookmaker would have made Altair of Altair a ten-to-one favorite to kill you, especially on her own territory.''

''Doubtless your moral support made all the difference,'' said Cain dryly. ''What would you have done if she'd killed me?''

''There's very little I *could* have done,'' admitted the Swagman. ''With you dead and Virtue gone over to the enemy, I'd have been out of partners.''

''There are worse things than being out of partners,'' said Cain. ''Such as *not* being out of them.'' He paused. ''Why did Virtue go out after the Angel?''

''I should think that would be obvious,'' replied the Swagman. ''She's come to the conclusion that he's got a better chance to kill Santiago than you do.''

''That's what she told you?''

''Of course not. What she told me was that she planned to spy on him and perhaps feed him some false information.''

''Bullshit,'' said Cain.

''My feelings precisely. On the other hand, I wouldn't take her defection too seriously. Based on what I know of the Angel, her life expectancy once she meets him is, not to be too pessimistic about it, perhaps ten minutes.''

''She's a lot harder to kill than you might think,'' commented Cain. He was silent for a moment, then looked directly at the Swagman. ''All right,'' he said. ''So Virtue's gone off to join the Angel. What makes you think I'm looking for another partner?''

"You needn't look at all," said the Swagman with a confident smile. "I'm right here in front of you."

"And what do you think *you* can bring to this proposed partnership?" asked Cain skeptically.

"A lot more than Virtue did," replied the Swagman, pulling out a handkerchief and wiping the sweat from his face. "For one thing, I used to work for Santiago. I can identify him for you."

"I can identify him myself."

"You mean by his scar?" The Swagman laughed. "And what will you do if he's wearing gloves, or has a prosthetic hand?" His eyes narrowed. "I know other things, too," he said persuasively. "I know what world the Angel is going to run into trouble on. I know half a dozen men who are still in Santiago's employ. I know a number of his drop points for stolen goods." A satisfied smile crossed his face. "How does that compare with what Virtue MacKenzie could do for you?"

"What do you want in exchange for all this?" asked Cain, eyeing him warily.

"Nothing that would interest you," said the Swagman. "Though if you felt it incumbent upon you to give me a piece of the reward, I probably wouldn't refuse it."

"And just what is it that interests you?"

"Do you know what I do for a living?" responded the Swagman.

"You rob, you smuggle, and you kill," said Cain.

The Swagman laughed. "Besides that, I mean."

"Suppose you tell me."

"It would not be inaccurate to say that I'm an art collector. You want the reward money; I have no interest in it. I want certain of Santiago's possessions; you have no interest in them. Virtue, on the unlikely assumption that she was actually telling me the truth and hasn't tried to team up with the Angel, wants only a journalistic feature. None of our desires overlap at any point. Therefore, I see no reason why we shouldn't be able to work together."

"Why don't you go after him yourself?" asked Cain, rubbing his eye as some sweat rolled into it. "That way you'd have the reward *and* the art objects."

"I'm no killer," replied the Swagman. "As I said, I'm still not sure exactly what it was that Altair of Altair tried to do to you down there, but I'm certain that I wouldn't have survived it—and I can assure you that she was much easier to kill than Santiago will be. I'll supply the information; you'll supply the expertise. That's the deal."

"I'll take it under consideration."

"You'd better consider it quickly."

"Why?" asked Cain sardonically. "Will you find yourself another killer?"

"No," said the Swagman seriously. "You're the one I want. After all, you killed Altair of Altair. Do you know how many bounty hunters have died trying to do just that?" He slapped at a flying insect that was buzzing around his face. "But you're in a race, and every minute you delay is another minute the Angel gains on you."

"I thought you said something about a planet that's going to give him problems."

"I did," the Swagman assured him. "But he'll overcome them. He's the best."

"Then why didn't you offer your services to him?"

"Because he doesn't need them. You do." He reached out his hand. "Well, have we got a deal?"

Cain stared at his hand without taking it.

"What have you got to lose?" added the Swagman.

Cain stared at him for a long moment, then finally nodded his head almost imperceptibly. "All right—until your information proves wrong."

"It won't."

"Let's put it to the test. Where does Virtue MacKenzie plan to find the Angel?"

"Lambda Karos Three if she's lucky."

"And if she's not?"

"Either New Ecuador or Questados Four. It depends on what he learns on Lambda Karos."

Cain stared at him for a moment. "Halfpenny Terwilliger is waiting for me back at my ship. I think I'd better send him off to keep an eye on Virtue while she's keeping an eye on the Angel, just so we know where we stand."

"Can you trust him to tell you the truth?" asked the Swagman.

"I can trust him to act in his own self-interest," replied Cain. "And he'll get a lot richer by staying loyal to me than by deserting me."

"Just out of curiosity, if he's on your payroll, why wasn't he helping you against Altair of Altair?"

"For the same reason you weren't," said Cain. "He'd just have been in the way."

"Touché," said the Swagman with a chuckle. "By the way, if he's the same Terwilliger I've heard about, Man-Mountain Bates is hot on his trail."

"I know. That's another reason why he'll stay loyal to me." Cain paused for a moment while the Swagman tossed his cigar onto the red-brown dirt and ground it out with his heel. "And now, if you've got nothing further to add, I think I'd better go talk to Schussler."

"Be on your best behavior," said the Swagman, falling into step beside the bounty hunter as he headed off toward the spaceship. "He may be a little bit strange, but we need him."

"Him? You mean Schussler?"

The Swagman nodded his head. "I'm not the only one with information, and his is different from mine. He knows every place Altair of Altair has been, everyone she's seen. Even if she never met Santiago, it was almost certainly Schussler who received the order to terminate Kastartos; he has to know where it came from."

"What does one offer a spaceship?" asked Cain wryly. "He can't have any use for money."

"I'm sure he'll think of something," said the Swagman.

"I don't know," said Cain. "Any guy who wanted to become a spaceship . . ."

"I have a feeling that *want* was never the operative word."

They reached the ship and came to a halt. Suddenly a hatch door opened.

"You go ahead," said the Swagman, pulling out another cigar. "I'll join you in a few minutes."

"Why?" asked Cain suspiciously.

The Swagman held up his cigar. "He doesn't like me to smoke inside him."

Cain grimaced. "I probably wouldn't want someone smoking in *my* stomach, either, if push came to shove."

He entered the compact ship through the hatch and found himself in a brightly illuminated cabin. The control panels and terminals were like nothing he had ever seen, and even the digital readouts on the screens were in an unfamiliar language.

"Schussler?" he said hesitantly. "Are you here?"

"I am always here," replied Schussler, his melodic voice not at all what Cain had expected.

"I'm Cain."

"I know. I can see you."

"You can?" asked Cain, surprised. "How?"

"I am tied in to various sensing devices."

"So you can see inside yourself as well as outside?"

"And hear, and smell, and use senses no human can conceive of."

"It must be handy," remarked Cain.

"If one likes being a spaceship."

"Do you?"

"No."

"Then why are you one?"

"It happened seventeen years ago," said Schussler. "I was a businessman, on my way to Alpha Prego for a conference. My ship crashed on Kalkos Two."

"Never heard of it."

"It's an outpost world of a starfaring race called the Graal."

"I never heard of *them*, either," commented Cain.

"They haven't been assimilated into the Democracy yet," replied Schussler. "Anyway, I crashed, and they found me, but by the time they separated me from all the twisted metal there wasn't much left to work with." The voice stopped for a moment and was considerably shakier when it resumed. "They kept me alive, God knows how, for five months, until I came out of my coma, and then they offered me my choice: they could let me die, quickly and painlessly, or they could offer me life as a cyborg." Schussler sighed. "I was younger then, and there were many things I still wanted to see, so I chose the latter."

"But why as a spaceship?" asked Cain.

"Kalkos Two is a shipbuilding world. They used what they had."

"What about prosthetics?" persisted Cain. "I've got an artificial eye that took a day to hook up, and it sees better than the one I lost."

"They weren't human," explained Schussler.

"They could have contacted a human world."

"There wasn't enough left to work with." He paused. "Would you like to see the *real* me, the human remnant that's the driving force of this ship?"

Cain shrugged. "Why not?"

"Walk over to the computer terminal nearest the viewscreen."

"This one?"

"That's it."

"The keys don't make any sense."

"They're in the Graal's language. Touch the third from the left, top row."

Cain did as he was told, and Schussler rattled off the directions for hitting seven more keys.

Suddenly an interior wall panel slid back, revealing a small black box, no more than twelve inches on a side, with literally hundreds of wires and tubes connected to it.

"*Jesus!*" muttered Cain. "That's all that's left of you?"

"Now do you see why they didn't bother with prosthetics?" asked Schussler bitterly as the panel slid shut. "Still, they didn't do too badly, all things considered. When I try to wiggle my fingers, I alter the gyroscopes. When I feel hunger, it is assuaged by fuel for my synthetic body. When I want to speak, I activate a complex system of microscopic vibrational coils which ultimately results in what you are hearing. I am not in *control* of the ship; I *am* the ship. I monitor all my functions, navigate myself, communicate with other ships, even aim and fire weapons when the need arises. In fact, I don't yet know the full extent of my powers, since the Graal computers aren't based on binary language or any other system known to the race of Man, and I'm still learning new things about myself every day."

"It sounds like an interesting existence," said Cain without much enthusiasm.

"It is a terrible existence," said Schussler.

"Well, it's better than being dead."

"I thought so once," replied Schussler. "I was wrong." He paused. "I can analyze the air for you, break it down into so many atoms of this and so many molecules of that—but I can't breathe it. There is no meal you can conceive that I can't prepare in my galley—but I can't taste it." There was another pause, and then the beautiful voice spoke again, this time in more anguished tones. "I can count the pores in the skin on a woman's hand, give a chemical breakdown of its composition, measure the fingernails to a millionth of a centimeter—*but I can't touch it!*"

"If you're that unhappy, why haven't you killed yourself?" asked Cain. "It shouldn't be that difficult to crash into a planet, or fall right into the heart of a star."

"A *man* could choose to do that," said Schussler bitterly. "A *machine* can't."

"But you *are* a man," said Cain. "You're just wearing this ship the way other men wear clothes."

"I wish that were so, but it isn't. I am the ship and the ship is me, and when the Graal joined the two of us in this unholy alliance, they inserted two directives that are so powerful I can't override them. The first of them is to protect my own existence."

"And the other?"

"It cost the Graal a lot of money to build me. They made some of it back by selling me at auction. They explained to me that since my life expectancy is now virtually infinite, they were sure I would be happy to spend an insignificant segment of it helping them amortize my cost." He sighed, a melodic sound that somehow reminded Cain of air flowing through a pipe organ. "My other directive was to obey the commands of my owner for a period of thirty years."

"Who is your owner?"

"She was Altair of Altair," replied Schussler.

Just then the Swagman entered the ship.

"Too damned hot out there," he said, walking over to a cushioned seat and flopping down on it. He turned to Cain. "Has he popped the question to you yet?"

"What question?" asked Cain.

The Swagman laughed. "If he's got more than one, he's been holding out on me." He paused. "Well, Schussler—have you?"

"Not yet," said the cyborg.

"I repeat: what question?" said Cain.

"We still have things to discuss," said Schussler. "Then I will make my request."

"You know," said the Swagman to Cain, "I offered him good steady work back at Goldenrod, and he turned me down flat."

"I won't transport stolen goods," said Schussler firmly.

"You yourself might be considered stolen goods," noted the Swagman amiably, "since there's still thirteen years outstanding on your contract."

"I am not stolen goods," replied Schussler. "I belong to Cain for the next thirteen years."

"What?" said Cain, startled. "That's not Altairian law."

"It is one of the conditions of my contract with the Graal," said Schussler. "They understood that Altair of Altair operated beyond the scope of human law, and it was explicitly stated that should she be killed by any representative of any human government before my contract was up, I would become the possession of that representative. As a bounty hunter who will ultimately be paid by the Democracy for slaying her, you qualify as my new owner."

"I don't *want* to be your owner," said Cain.

"Just a minute," interjected the Swagman. "Let's not be too hasty about this."

"Schussler, when I was in the cavern, you indicated that you might be able to help me," said Cain, staring at the panel behind which the essential Schussler existed. "What did you have in mind?"

"I can show you where Altair of Altair has been, and who she spoke to, and many other things."

"If you'll feed it all into my ship's computer, I'll make you a free agent right now," said Cain. "I don't have any use for another ship."

"Terwilliger needs your ship, if you're really sending him to Lambda Karos," the Swagman pointed out.

"He can use yours," said Cain. "We're partners, remember?"

"It's a moot point," said Schussler. "I can't feed my information to your computer. The language my systems use is different."

"Come off it," said Cain. "You use the same language as my computer every time you receive landing coordinates. What's your real problem?"

"Please take me with you!" said Schussler suddenly, a note of desperation in his voice. "It's been so long since I've been able to *talk* with another human being!" Cain seemed hesitant, and Schussler continued: "I will serve you with complete loyalty until we find Santiago. I will guide and protect you, feed and ferry you, and I ask nothing in return except your company."

"Nothing?" repeated the Swagman meaningfully.

"Until you have found Santiago," said Schussler. "Then I have one single request to make of you."

"What is it?" demanded Cain.

"Kill me," said Schussler the Cyborg.

13.

The Songbird stalks, the Songbird kills,
The Songbird works to pay his bills.
So, friend, beware the Songbird's glance:
If you're his prey, you'll have no chance.

"Those don't belong to you," said Schussler.

The Swagman, tired of sitting in a chair that was almost comfortable, had gotten to his feet and was examining a number of alien artifacts that were attached to a wall of the command cabin.

"By the same token, they don't belong to you, either," he replied easily. He pulled at an onyx carving, breaking the magnetic field that joined it to the wall. "Interesting piece," he commented, examining it closely. "Where did your late lamented owner pick it up? Hesporite Three?"

"Neiburi Two," answered Schussler.

"Same star cluster," remarked the Swagman, with an air of satisfaction. "I wouldn't have given her credit for such exquisite taste. Do you know what this little piece is worth on the open market?"

"No," said Schussler.

"Neither do you," interjected Cain, looking up from the table where he had disassembled one of his pistols and was meticulously cleaning it. "But I'll bet you can give us its black market value to the nearest tenth of a credit."

"Touché," grinned the Swagman.

"Put it back now," said Schussler.

"I'm admiring it."

"Evaluating it, anyway," said Cain dryly.

"Force of habit," admitted the Swagman, holding the carving near the wall until the magnetic field took it from him. He began studying another piece.

"I'm still watching you," said Schussler.

"How comforting."

"You'd better not try to steal anything," continued the cyborg.

"I never steal from my friends," said the Swagman.

"I know all about you, Swagman," said Schussler. "You don't have any friends."

"It *does* simplify matters," replied the Swagman with a smile. "If it will allay your fears, I also don't steal from my partners when one of them happens to be a bounty hunter." Suddenly a small carving caught his eye, and he pulled it out of the field. "Well, well," he mused. "Life is a torrent of never-ending surprises."

"What have you got there?" asked Cain.

The Swagman held the piece up.

"It doesn't look all that special."

"As a matter of fact, it's a rather mediocre work of art," agreed the Swagman. "It's where it originated that makes it interesting."

"And where was that?"

"Pellinath Four."

"Never heard of it," said Cain.

"It's the planet where I was raised. This was carved by one of the Bellum."

"Your benefactors?" asked Schussler, interested.

The Swagman nodded, studying the carving. "I think I must have sold this thing, oh, ten or twelve years ago, out by New Rhodesia. I wonder how Altair of Altair got her hands on it?"

"What were the Bellum like?" asked Schussler.

"Not bad at all, considering that we had some serious disagreements about laissez-faire capitalism," replied the Swagman. "Still, they fed me and gave me shelter, and I'm grateful to them for that."

"Not so grateful that you didn't rob them," noted Cain wryly.

"True," agreed the Swagman. "On the other hand, if God had any serious objections to what I do, He wouldn't have made insurance companies." He paused. "Besides, I didn't take very much. They were exceptionally poor artisans. I suppose it comes from being color-blind and not having thumbs." He glanced at the piece again and replaced it on the wall, then turned to the panel that hid Schussler's essence. "Tell me about the Graal."

"They were basically humanoid," replied the cyborg, "if you consider a race humanoid because it walks erect on two legs. Beyond that, they didn't have a lot in common with Men."

"That's not too difficult to believe, given the contours of the seats in here," said the Swagman with a grimace. "What kind of art did they produce?"

The ship uttered an amused, melodic chuckle. "Nothing that would interest you. They don't have any eyes; they use a form of sonar. And while I never saw their artwork, I'm sure it would reflect their limitations."

"What a pity," sighed the Swagman. "At least *my* aliens gave me a little something to remember them by, however unwillingly."

"So did mine," said Schussler, the melody of his voice conflicting with the irony of his words.

"Where *is* this world where they put you together, anyway?" asked the Swagman. "I've never heard of the Kalkos system."

"In the Corbellus Cluster," replied Schussler.

"I was out there once," remarked the Swagman. "Ever hear of Fond Hope?"

"I've heard of it," answered the cyborg, "but I've never been there."

"I've heard of it, too," said Cain. "Didn't Orpheus write it up? Something about the Deneb Arabian, or the Delphini Arabian, or something like that?"

"The Darley Arabian," said the Swagman. "Orpheus gave him his name. In fact, he gave all three patriarchs their names." He paused. "My own modest dealings were solely with the Barb."

"I don't recall any mention of him," said Cain.

"I fear I may have left him with a certain distrust of outsiders," grinned the Swagman. "He refused to speak to Black Orpheus."

"Smart man," muttered Cain.

"I didn't understand the song," volunteered Schussler. "It sounded, well, racy."

"The Darley Arabian, tall and wild,/Has gotten another wife with child," quoted the Swagman. "I suppose that's as close to racy as Orpheus ever gets." He turned to the panel that hid Schussler from view. "Fond Hope was settled by three very large families, who immediately had a falling-out and began fighting with each other. Since this was a blood feud, none of the families wanted to import outside mercenaries. Then one day the Arabian conceived the notion of buying a couple of hundred mail-order brides and siring his own army—all in the line of duty, to be sure." He chuckled. "It took each of the other two patriarchs about a week to follow suit, and they've spent the past twenty years fighting all day and making little soldiers all night."

"What about the names?" asked Schussler.

"Orpheus found out that all the racehorses back on old Earth descended from three foundation sires, so he named the three patriarchs the Darley Arabian, the Byerly Turk, and the Godolphin Barb, after the three horses."

"What was your business with the Barb?" asked Cain.

"I knew that he had no need for mercenaries, but I thought he might be interested in purchasing a shipload of weapons to carry on the battle."

"Hot?"

"Lukewarm," admitted the Swagman. "The navy confiscated them a month after I delivered them."

"I wasn't aware that the navy ever got out to the Corbellus Cluster," said Schussler.

"They didn't—until someone thoughtlessly appropriated a few thousand laser weapons from one of their munitions warehouses."

"Is that why Santiago dropped you?" asked Cain.

"Why should you think so?"

"Because stealing from the navy isn't your style. You'd need Santiago's muscle for an operation like that. My guess is that he threw you out for selling weapons he wanted to keep."

"You couldn't be more mistaken," said the Swagman indignantly.

"Are you seriously trying to tell me that you stole those weapons yourself?" said Cain.

"Oh, it was Santiago's operation from start to finish," acknowledged the Swagman. "And yes, we did have some slight disagreement over their ultimate disposition. But we parted ways for a totally unrelated reason."

"The mind boggles," commented Cain wryly.

"I'm surprised that Santiago or the Godolphin Barb didn't commission your death," said Schussler.

"The Barb did," replied the Swagman. "Fortunately, my would-be assassin tried to attack me at my fortress on Goldenrod, where even the Angel would find it difficult to do me any damage."

"How do you know that it was the Barb who hired the assassin, rather than Santiago?" asked the cyborg.

"Because I'm still here." The Swagman wandered over to the table, where Cain had replaced the bullets in his first pistol and was preparing to clean and oil a second. "You know," he said, staring at the pieces that were neatly laid out on the table, "there's something I've been curious about ever since I observed you with Altair of Altair."

"Ask away," said Cain without looking up.

"Why do you use a projectile weapon?" said the Swagman.

"It's more accurate than laser or sonic pistols, and since it doesn't have an energy pack to begin with, it can't run out of power."

"But it makes such a loud noise."

"So what?"

"I would have thought stealth and silence were essential to your profession."

Cain smiled. "They're essential while I'm stalking my prey. Once I start shooting, I don't much give a damn who knows I'm there." He paused. "I'm not one of your menials, Swagman. I operate within the law; I don't have to sneak away when my work is done."

"A point well taken," admitted the Swagman.

"A laser gun is all right if you have to fan a large area," continued Cain. "But it's not a precision instrument. To each his own; I prefer bullets."

"I wonder what method the Angel used on Giles Sans Pitié?" mused Schussler.

Cain shrugged. "I suppose we'll find out in good time. I don't imagine Black Orpheus will be able to resist putting it into his stupid song."

"What's your objection to our friend Orpheus?" asked the Swagman.

"He's your friend, not mine."

"He's made you famous," noted the Swagman. "A century from now, that song is the only way people will know you and Schussler and I even existed. Consider it a form of immortality."

"Immortality is a greatly overrated virtue," interjected Schussler, the beautiful melodic tones of his voice ringing with bitterness.

"Most of the people I've known would disagree with that statement," said the Swagman.

"Most of the people *you've* known have spent their whole lives one step ahead of the hangman," replied the cyborg.

"Most of the people he's known have already met the hangman," commented Cain.

"Some of them have met less formal executioners," retorted the Swagman. "I'm still annoyed with you over that little affair on Declan Four."

"You had some use for Socrates?" asked Cain.

"Socrates?" snorted the Swagman contemptuously. "Of course not. There are twelve million Men on Declan Four, all of them interchangeable and infinitely replaceable." He paused. "But you destroyed a Robelian bowl that I'd been after for three years."

"It was just a bowl," said Cain. "I was there for something more important."

"*Just a bowl?*" repeated the Swagman, morally outraged. "My good man, it was one of only six such bowls in existence!"

"I've seen lots like it."

For just a moment the Swagman looked interested. Then he sighed. "I suppose one bowl looks just like another to you."

"Pretty much so," said Cain, sliding the barrel of his pistol into place and turning it gently until he felt a discernible click. "Just the way people all look alike to you."

"And it means nothing to you that there are almost a trillion people spread across the Democracy, and only six Robelian bowls of that shape and design?"

"It means you'll run out of work before I do."

"It means," the Swagman retorted, "that you have destroyed an irreplaceable work of art."

"I also destroyed a man who was in serious need of destruction," replied Cain. "On the whole, I'd say the ledger came out on the plus side."

"There wasn't even any paper on Socrates."

"Then view killing him as a service to humanity."

"I wasn't aware that you were in the philanthropy business," said the Swagman.

"There are more important things than money," said Cain.

"True—but all of them *cost* money." The Swagman raised his arms above his head, emitted a loud grunt as he stretched, and then turned to Schussler's panel. "I'm getting hungry. What have you got in your galley?"

"I have a full complement of soya products," answered the cyborg.

"Don't you have any meat?"

"I'm afraid not—but I can prepare some dishes that will be almost indistinguishable from meat."

"I've heard *that* before," muttered the Swagman.

"You might as well take what he's got," said Cain. "We're not about to divert to a planet with a grocery store."

The Swagman shrugged. "Can you come up with something that tastes like shellfish in a cream sauce?"

"I can try." Schussler paused. "What would you like, Sebastian?"

"Whatever's easy," said Cain.

"How about a steak?" suggested the cyborg.

"How about a salad?" countered Cain. "I've *had* soya steaks."

"If you'll come to the galley, your dinners are ready," announced Schussler.

"What are you talking about?" said the Swagman suspiciously. "We just ordered them."

"The Graal's technology makes meal preparation almost instantaneous," explained the cyborg. "Especially when I can work with adaptable raw materials such as soya products."

Cain and the Swagman exchanged dubious glances and entered the galley, a long narrow room in which almost all of the equipment was hidden from view.

"Where are we supposed to eat?" asked the Swagman.

"I can unfold a small table," said Schussler, "but there won't be room for both of you at it."

"We'll stand," said Cain. "Where's the food?"

"I'll have it in just a second," said Schussler. "Ah, here it comes."

A shining metal panel receded, and two nondescript plates appeared on a polished counter.

The Swagman reached out for his shellfish, then withdrew his hand and muttered a curse.

"I forgot to tell you: the plate is hot."

"Thanks," said the Swagman caustically. He reached into his pocket, withdrew a monogrammed silk handkerchief, wrapped it around his fingers, and pulled the plate over. "I could use a knife and fork."

"I wish I could help you," said Schussler apologetically. "But Altair of Altair didn't use human utensils. She preferred these."

A pair of odd-looking metal objects emerged onto the counter.

The Swagman picked one up and examined it. "Wonderful," he said. "It looks about as practical as eating soup with chopsticks."

Cain picked up the other, studied it for a moment, and then began using it on his salad.

"How did you do that?" asked the Swagman.

"I've seen these things in the Teron system," said Cain, impaling an artificial tomato and twisting a piece of artificial lettuce around it. "A Teroni bounty hunter showed me how to use it. It's not too bad once you get the hang of it."

"How are they on cream sauce?" asked the Swagman, staring at his plate.

"Try it and find out," said Cain, returning his attention to his salad.

The Swagman made three or four false starts but eventually gained a rudimentary mastery of his utensil and finally managed to get a piece of pseudoshellfish all the way to his mouth without dropping it.

"Well?" asked Schussler anxiously. "What do you think of it?"

"It isn't bad," said Cain noncommittally.

"I'll tell you what it isn't," muttered the Swagman. "It isn't Goldenrod lobster." He took another mouthful. "Still, I suppose it could be worse."

"Would you do me a favor?" asked Schussler after a moment's silence.

"It all depends," replied the Swagman. "What did you have in mind?"

"Tell me what it tastes like."

"To be perfectly truthful, it tastes like soya byproducts masquerading as shellfish in cream sauce."

"Please," persisted Schussler anxiously. "I processed it and cooked it and served it—but I can't *taste* it. Describe it for me."

"As I said: a rudimentary approximation of fish in cream sauce."

"You can't be that unimaginative!" said Schussler with a note of desperation in his beautiful lilting voice. "Tell me about the sauce: is it rich? hot? sweet? Can you identify the spices? What *type* of shellfish does it taste like?"

"It's nothing to write home about," said the Swagman. "The flavors are all rather bland."

"Describe them."

"You're forcing me to insult you. The food is barely worth eating, let alone describing," said the Swagman irritably. "You're ruining what was a totally unmemorable meal to begin with."

"You owe it to me!" demanded Schussler.

"Later," said the Swagman. "It's tasting worse by the mouthful, thanks to your nagging."

Cain sighed, reached over with his implement, and picked up a piece of the artificial shellfish, after first rubbing it thoroughly in the cream sauce. He chewed it thoughtfully, then began describing the nuances of flavor to Schussler while the Swagman picked up his plate and walked back into the command cabin to finish his meal in isolation.

Cain joined him about twenty minutes later.

"Is he still sulking?" asked the Swagman.

"Ask him yourself."

The Swagman turned to Schussler's panel. "You're not going to spend all night asking me to describe how my bunk feels, are you?"

There was no answer.

"There's a first for you—a pouting spaceship."

"You hurt his feelings," said Cain.

"Not without reason. Either we nip this behavior in the bud, or he'll be spending every spare minute asking how things taste and feel."

"It's not that much effort to tell him. He's had a rough time of it."

The Swagman stared at him. "We're growing a strange crop of killers this season," he remarked at last.

"You know," said Cain, "he could always ask you how you feel after he reduces the oxygen content in the cabin down to zero."

"Not if he wants to die on schedule, he can't," said the Swagman confidently. He paused. "Are you really going to kill him if we find Santiago's base?"

"I said I would."

"I know what you said."

"I'll do what I promised."

"But you won't be happy about it."

"I'm never happy about killing things," said Cain.

The Swagman considered that remark, as well as some of the other things Cain had said since leaving Altair III, and spent the next few minutes studying his new partner, comparing him to what he knew of the Angel, and wondering if Virtue MacKenzie had made the correct choice after all.

14.

Alas, Poor Yorick, I knew him well:
He can't climb down from the carousel.
He began with dreams, with hope and trust;
Alas, Poor Yorick, they turned to dust.

His name wasn't really Poor Yorick—not at first, anyway.
He was born Herman Ludwig Menke, and he stuck with that
name for twenty years. Then he joined a troupe of actors that
traveled the Galactic Rim, and became Brewster Moss; word
has it that he even performed for the Angel, back before *he*
became the Angel.

Anyway, by the time he was forty he had yet another new
name, Sterling Wilkes, which is the one he made famous
when he almost single-handedly brought about the Shake-
spearean renaissance on Lodin XI. It is also the one he made
notorious, due to his various chemical dependencies.

Six years later, after he'd had one hallucinogenic trance too
many before a paying audience, he was barred from the stage.
It was time for a new name—Poor Yorick seemed quite apt
this time around—and a new profession. Since he had an
artistic bent and all he knew was the theater, he turned up on
the Inner Frontier as a prop manufacturer, and in the following decade he turned out a never-ending stream of counterfeit
crowns and harmless guns, bogus jewels and bogus thrones,
almost real stones in almost valuable settings.

He also kept a sizable number of drug peddlers in business,
and when he graduated from injecting hallucinogens to chewing alphanella seeds, he was forced to supplement his income

by turning his fine forger's hand to less legitimate enterprises than the stage. As the quality of his work suffered due to his dependency, he lost his legal job and then most of his illegal commissions as well, and was reduced to selling hasty paintings of actors he had known, which were turned out during his increasingly rare periods of lucidity.

A few years later Black Orpheus came into possession of four of the paintings and instantly knew that he had stumbled onto an interesting if erratic talent.

It took him almost a year to find Poor Yorick, who was living in a ramshackle hotel on Hildegarde, still spending every credit he made to feed his habit. Orpheus tried to convince him to travel the spaceways with him and illustrate his saga, but Yorick cared more for his next connection than for posterity, and finally the Bard of the Inner Frontier admitted defeat, bought the remainder of Yorick's paintings, commissioned a painting of his Eurydice which would never be finished, and went away forever. He gave Poor Yorick only a single verse in his song; he wanted to do more, to tell his audience what a unique talent lay hidden beneath that wasted exterior, but he decided that an influx of commissions would only result in more drug purchases and hasten Yorick's death.

It must be said on Yorick's behalf that he tried to complete the painting of Eurydice, but the money he had received for it was spent within a week, and he had an ever-present hunger to feed. Since Orpheus had left him without any art to sell, he returned to forging, but every now and then, an hour here, a weekend there, he would work again on his embryonic masterpiece.

In fact, he was working on it when Schussler landed on Roosevelt III.

"Unpleasant little world," said Cain when he and the Swagman had emerged from the cyborg's interior and stood, shielding themselves from the planet's ever-present rain, on the wet surface of the spaceport.

"It's only fitting," said the Swagman, heading off for the terminal. "We're looking for an unpleasant little man." He paused. "Whoever would have thought that Poor Yorick would be Altair of Altair's most recent link to Santiago?"

"I had rather suspected *you* would," said Cain with a touch of irony. "Especially after that speech about how I needed you."

"That's why you needed both Schussler *and* me. He knew Yorick was the man we wanted, and I know where to find him."

"Isn't it about time you shared that little tidbit of knowledge with me?" suggested Cain.

The Swagman shrugged. "I can't give you an address. We'll go into the city, hunt up the cheapest hotel in the poorest area, and wait."

"And if he's not there?"

"He'll be there, or thereabouts," said the Swagman. "If we have to, we'll just follow the local dream vendor, and he'll lead us straight to him."

"What does Poor Yorick look like?" asked Cain.

"I really couldn't say. I've never met him."

"But you're sure you know where he'll be," said Cain caustically.

"I've had dealings with him before," replied the Swagman. "And I make it a habit to learn everything I can about my business associates. I know he's on Roosevelt Three, and I know that there's only one city on Roosevelt Three; finding his exact location is just a mechanical exercise."

They reached the terminal, rented a vehicle, and drove into the nearby city, which, like the planet, was named Roosevelt. Someone—an architect, a city planner, a corporate head, *someone*—had had big plans for Roosevelt once upon a time. The spaceport was built to support ten times the traffic it actually handled, the city was crisscrossed by numerous broad thoroughfares, the central square boasted two skyscrapers that wouldn't have been out of place on Deluros VIII—but some centuries back the Democracy had paused to consolidate its holdings, and when it expanded again it had been in a different direction, leaving Roosevelt III just another unimportant cog in the vast human machine, neither abandoned nor important. The proposed megalopolis became a city of diminished expectations, as modest apartment buildings, nondescript stores, unimpressive offices, and unimaginative public structures gradually encircled the two enormous steel-and-glass buildings like jungle scavengers patiently waiting for some mighty behemoth to conclude its death throes so they could partake of the feast.

The Swagman drove once around the city, then homed in

on the most dilapidated area with an unerring instinct and
brought the vehicle to a stop.

"I'd say we're within four hundred yards of him right
now," he said, handing a rainshield to Cain and activating
one himself.

"It can't get much more rundown than this," agreed Cain,
dispassionately eyeing a number of drunks and derelicts who
peered through the driving rain at them from their safe havens
inside seedy bars and seamy hotels.

"I have a feeling that I'm not properly dressed for the
occasion," remarked the Swagman, looking down at his satin
tunic, carefully tailored pants, and hand-crafted boots.

"You're not the only one who thinks so," commented
Cain, staring at an exceptionally large, barrel-chested man
who was scrutinizing them from a distance of fifty feet,
oblivious of the rain that was pouring down upon his unpro-
tected head.

"Well, we certainly don't want the riffraff rising above
their stations," said the Swagman, unperturbed. "I think
we'll make them your responsibility."

"What do you do when you find yourself in a situation like
this and there isn't a bounty hunter around?" inquired Cain
dryly.

"I'm not totally without my own resources," replied the
Swagman, withdrawing a device the size of a golf ball. He
tossed it casually in the air, caught it, and replaced it in his
pocket.

"A fire bomb?"

The Swagman nodded. "It's more powerful than it looks.
It can take out a city block, and spreads like crazy on
detonation, even in weather like this." He smiled. "Still, I'd
much prefer not to use it. It wouldn't do to fry Yorick to a
crisp before we have a chance to talk to him."

"According to you, we're within four hundred yards of
him," said Cain, looking up and down the street. "That
narrows it down to fifteen or twenty beat-up hotels and
boarding houses. How do you choose which one?"

"Why, we ask, of course," said the Swagman, walking
into a tavern. He spent a moment exchanging low whispers
with the bartender, then returned to Cain, who had been
waiting just inside the door.

"Any luck?"

"Not yet," admitted the Swagman. "Not to worry. The day's still young, if a little moist."

He sloshed through the rain to two more taverns, also without success.

"Ah!" he said with a smile as they approached yet another barroom, which had a watercolor of a large-breasted nude in the window. "We're getting close! I recognize the style."

"You collect Yorick's paintings?"

"The better ones."

The Swagman entered the building, spoke to the bartender, passed a five-hundred-credit note across the scarred wooden bar, said something else, and stepped out onto the sidewalk a moment later.

"He lives at the San Juan Hill Hotel, just up the street," announced the Swagman. "When he hasn't got enough cash for alphanella seeds, he trades paintings for drinks."

"He's not bad," commented Cain, staring at the nude.

"He's damned good, considering that he probably didn't even know his own name when he painted it. I offered to buy it, but the proprietor wouldn't sell. I got the distinct impression that it's a pretty fair representation of his girlfriend."

"Or his business partner."

"The two are not mutually exclusive," said the Swagman, heading off toward the San Juan Hill. "Especially around here."

Only one man seemed intent on stopping them, but something in Cain's face convinced him to reconsider, and they made it to the hotel without incident.

It had been a long time since the lobby of the San Juan Hill had been cleaned, and even longer since it had been painted. The floor, especially around the entrance, was filthy, and the whole place smelled of mildew. There was a small, inexpensive rug in front of the registration desk, surrounded by a light area from which a slightly larger rug had been removed at some time in the past. Miscolored rectangles on the walls marked the spots that had formerly been covered by paintings and holographs. The few chairs and couches were in dire need of repair, and the camera in the sole vidphone booth was missing.

The Swagman took one look around, seemed satisfied that this was precisely the type of place where Poor Yorick was likely to reside, and walked up to the registration desk.

The unshaven clerk, his left elbow peeking out through a hole in his tunic, looked up at his visitor with a bored expression.

"Good afternoon," said the Swagman with a friendly smile. "Terrible weather out there."

"You tracked all the way across my lobby to tell me that?" replied the clerk caustically.

"Actually, I'm looking for a friend."

"Good luck to you," said the clerk.

"His name's Yorick," said the Swagman.

"Big deal."

The Swagman reached out and grabbed the clerk by the front of his soiled tunic, pulling him halfway across the counter.

"*Poor* Yorick," he said with a pleasant smile. "I hate to rush you, but we *are* in a hurry." He twisted the tunic until the seams started to give way.

"Room three seventeen," muttered the clerk.

"Thank you very much," said the Swagman, releasing him. "You've been most helpful." He looked around. "I don't suppose any of the elevators are in working order?"

"The one in the middle," replied the clerk sullenly, pointing toward a bank of three ancient elevators.

"Excellent," said the Swagman. He nodded toward Cain, who walked across the lobby and joined him in front of the elevator. "If there's one thing I hate," he said, "it's a surly menial. You *are* protecting my back, aren't you?"

"He's not going to do anything," replied Cain.

"How do you know he hasn't got a weapon hidden behind the counter?"

"If there ever was a weapon back there, it's long since been stolen or pawned," said Cain as the doors slid shut and the elevator began ascending. "Still, I think we'll take the stairs down, just to be on the safe side."

The elevator lurched to a stop and swayed somewhat unsteadily as Cain and the Swagman emerged onto the third floor, which was in even worse repair than the lobby. Some of the rooms had no doors at all, scribbled graffiti covered the others, and the dominant smell had changed from mildew to urine.

"Three seventeen," announced the Swagman, gesturing to

the last door on the floor. "Things are obviously looking up for friend Yorick; he has a corner view."

He knocked once, and when there was no answer he punched the number 317 on the computer lock.

"I always admire a complex security system, don't you?" he commented with a grin as the door slid back into a wall.

A frail, wasted man, his teeth rotted, his complexion sallow, sat totally naked on a rickety chair by a broken window, oblivious to the rain that sprayed him after bouncing off the pane. He was working on a painting with short, incredibly swift brush strokes, muttering to himself as he continually retraced the outline of a beautiful woman's face, never quite getting the proportions correct. Scattered around the floor were cheap containers filled with artificial diamonds, rubies, sapphires, and emeralds, a complex machine for covering base metals with gold plating, and a number of jeweler's tools.

The man looked up at his two visitors, flashed them a brief, nervous smile, put a few more dabs of color onto his canvas, then casually tossed his palate onto the floor and turned to face Cain and the Swagman.

"Good afternoon, Yorick," said the Swagman. "I wonder if we might have a few minutes of your time?"

Yorick stared at him for a moment, frowned, looked back at his canvas, and then turned to him once more, a puzzled expression on his face.

"You're not in my painting," he said at last.

"No," said the Swagman. "I'm in your room."

"My room?" repeated Yorick.

"That's right."

"Well," he said with a shrug, "it had to be one or the other." He stared intently at the Swagman. "Do I know you?"

"You know *of* me: I'm the Jolly Swagman."

Yorick lowered his head, still frowning. "Jolly, jolly, jolly, jolly, jolly," he murmured. Suddenly he looked up. "I don't know you, but I know *of* you," he said with a satisfied smile. He turned to Cain. "I know *you*, though."

"You do?" said Cain.

"You're the Songbird," he said emphatically, suddenly rational. "I know all about you. I was on Bellefontaine when you killed the Jack of Diamonds. That was some shootout."

Suddenly his face went blank again. "Shootout," he said as if the word had lost its meaning. "Shootout, shootout, shootout." And just as quickly as it had come, the emptiness left his wasted face. "What are you doing here, Songbird?"

"I need a little information," said Cain, sitting down on the edge of Yorick's unmade bed.

"I need a little something, too," said Yorick with a wink and a cackle. "A lot of little somethings. Chewy little somethings, sweet little somethings."

"Maybe we can work out a trade," said Cain.

"Maybe maybe maybe," said Yorick, spitting out the words in staccato fashion. "Maybe we can." He paused, then suddenly looked alert. "How about a trade?" he suggested.

"Good idea," said Cain.

"Why is *he* here?" asked Yorick, gesturing to the Swagman.

"He likes your paintings," said Cain.

"Oh, he does, does he?" Yorick cackled. "He likes more than that. So you're the Swagman, are you?"

"The one and only," said the Swagman.

"Well, one and only Swagman," said Yorick, "did the museum on Rhinegold ever discover the one and only North Coast Princess that I forged for you?"

"It's still sitting right there in its display case under round-the-clock guard," replied the Swagman with a grin.

"And you've got the real stone?"

"Certainly."

"Certainly," repeated Yorick. "Lee-certain," he said, moving the syllables around. "Cer-lee-tain." He got to his feet and glared at the Swagman. "My courier was killed!" he said accusingly.

"Most regrettable," said the Swagman. "I hope you don't think *I* had anything to do with it."

"You guaranteed his safety," said Yorick sullenly.

"I guaranteed that he would gain safe entry to my fortress," the Swagman corrected him. "What he did after he left was his own business."

"I never got my money."

"I paid it to the courier. My obligation to you ended with that." He reached into his pocket. "However, I wouldn't want us to become enemies. Will this square accounts?" He withdrew a trio of small tan seeds.

"Give give give give give give!" murmured Yorick, snatching them out of the Swagman's hand. He raced to a dilapidated dresser, pulled open the top drawer, and tossed two of the seeds onto a pile of dirty clothing. The third he put into his mouth.

"Where the hell did you get those things?" asked Cain. "You didn't know back on Altair that we were going to see Poor Yorick."

The Swagman smiled. "What did you think I paid the bartender five hundred credits for?"

"Information—or so I thought."

"Information's worth about twenty-five credits, tops, on a dirtball like this. The rest was for alphanella seeds."

Yorick was sitting down on his chair again, his face suddenly tranquil as he slid the seed between his cheek and his gum and let the juices flow down his throat.

"Thank you," he said, his face relaxed, his eyes finally clear. "You know, sometimes I think the only time I'm *not* crazy is when I've got a seed in my mouth."

"Good," said Cain. "Just suck on it for a while. Don't chew it until we're through talking."

"Whatever you say, Songbird," replied Yorick pleasantly. "Oh, my, this is good. I don't know how I lived before I discovered this stuff."

"Responsibly," suggested Cain wryly.

Yorick closed his eyes and smiled. "Ah, yes—the killer who's hindered by a moral code. I know about you, Songbird." He paused. "You gave my friend a pass."

"A pass?" asked the Swagman, puzzled.

"Quentin Cicero," said Yorick, nodding his head, his eyes still closed. "Hunted him down and then let him go. Good man, the Songbird."

"You let Quentin Cicero go?" demanded the Swagman, turning to Cain.

"It wasn't that open and shut," replied Cain. "He had a hostage."

"That never stopped any other bounty hunter," said Yorick placidly. "So what if he'd have killed her? All the more reason for you to bring him in."

"You let him go?" repeated the Swagman furiously. "That bastard killed two of my menials!"

"I'm sorry to hear that," said Cain.

"*You're* sorry? One of them had fifty thousand credits of *my* money!"

"But the hostage lived," said Yorick.

"You see?" said the Swagman. "You go around letting hostages live and sooner or later it winds up costing a respectable businessman money!"

"I'll keep that in mind next time," said Cain.

"Who are you after now, Songbird?" asked Yorick. He paused. "I know where you can find Altair of Altair."

"I already found her."

"Was she human or not?" asked Yorick. "I could never quite tell."

"Neither could I," said Cain.

"Beautiful, though."

"Very," agreed Cain.

"How much did you get for killing her?" asked Yorick.

"Nothing."

Yorick smiled. "Then you're after Santiago." He sucked contentedly on the seed. "It's amazing how clear everything becomes after a minute or two, how absolutely pellucid. You killed her, and you talked to her ship, and now you're here."

"That's right."

"And now you want me to tell you where to go next?"

Cain nodded, and Yorick, not hearing an answer, cracked his eyes open.

"How are you going to kill him, Songbird?"

"I won't know until I find him," said Cain.

"What if *he* has a hostage?"

"Does he?"

Yorick laughed. "How would I know?"

"How would I?" answered Cain.

Yorick stared at Cain for a long moment. "You're a good man, Songbird," he said at last. "I think I'll tell you what you want to know."

"Thank you."

"And I'm a good man, so I think you'll pay me three thousand credits."

"Fifteen hundred," said the Swagman quickly.

"Shut up," said Cain, pulling out a wad of bills and peeling off six five-hundred-credit notes.

"Thank you, Songbird," said Yorick, looking for a pocket and then realizing that he was naked. He walked over to his dresser and tossed the money into the same drawer where he had deposited the two alphanella seeds. He then returned to his chair and sat down lazily. "The man you want is Billy Three-Eyes."

"I've heard of him," remarked Cain.

"Everyone out here has heard of him. There's a lot of paper on him, Songbird."

"What's his connection to Santiago?"

"He works for him."

"Directly?"

Yorick nodded. "When I forged a set of duplicate plates for New Georgia's Stalin Ruble, it was Billy Three-Eyes who picked them up and delivered them to Santiago. And the last time Santiago had an assignment for Altair of Altair, I was the go-between."

"Where is Billy Three-Eyes now?" asked Cain.

"On Safe Harbor. Ever hear of it?"

"No."

"It's a colony planet, out in the Westminster system."

"How do I find him?"

Yorick chuckled. "He'll be pretty easy to spot. Giles Sans Pitié caught up with him about eight years ago and put a notch in his forehead with that metal fist of his before he could escape. That's how Billy got his name; Orpheus thought it looked like a third eye."

"How many cities are there on Safe Harbor?"

"None," replied Yorick. "None none nine none nine none."

"Suck on the seed again," said Cain. "You're drifting."

Yorick sucked noisily, and his eyes became clear once more. "No cities at all," he said lazily. "There are two or three little villages. Most of the people are farmers. Just make the rounds of the local taverns; he'll be in one of them." He paused. "Do you need any more?"

"I don't think so."

"Good." Yorick smiled. "It's starting to wear off. It'll be gone in another couple of minutes unless I bite the seed."

Cain got to his feet. "Thanks," he said.

"Anything for the Songbird."

Cain walked to the door, then turned to the Swagman, who remained where he was, leaning comfortably against a filthy wall.

"Come on," he said.

"You go ahead," said the Swagman. "I've got a little business to talk over with friend Yorick."

"I'll wait downstairs."

The Swagman shook his head. "It could take days to consummate."

"What the hell are you talking about?" demanded Cain.

"I want to commission some paintings."

"Then do it and let's get out of here."

"You've seen him," said the Swagman. "If I'm going to get what I want, I'm going to have to nursemaid him while he works."

"Suit yourself," said Cain. "But I'm not hanging around this pigsty while you add to your collection."

"You go ahead to Safe Harbor," said the Swagman. "I'll charter a ship and join you there."

"If I walk out of this hotel alone, the partnership's over," said Cain.

"If you kill Santiago before I catch up with you, the partnership's over," agreed the Swagman. "But if I get to you before you reach him, it's in force again."

"For half the original deal."

"You have no use for what I want," said the Swagman.

"I'll *find* a use."

The Swagman looked perturbed. "Safe Harbor is just another stop along the way. You still need me."

"Not as much as you need me," said Cain. He frowned. "What brought this about, anyway? How much can his paintings be worth?"

"Not as much as Santiago, I'll admit," said the Swagman. "But Yorick's here now, and Santiago could still be years away. I'll catch up with you."

"For half."

The Swagman sighed. "For half." He paused. "If you leave Safe Harbor before I get there, leave a message telling me where to find you."

"Leave it where?"

"If you don't find anyone you can trust, have Schussler send it back to Goldenrod."

Cain turned to Yorick. "Once I leave here, nothing that happens between the two of you is of any concern to me—but I ought to warn you that leaving three thousand credits in the same room with the Swagman is like leaving a piece of meat in the same room with a hungry carnivore.''

"I resent that," said the Swagman, more amused than offended.

"Resent it all you like," said Cain. "But if you're a religious man, don't deny it or God just might strike you dead." He walked to the dresser and stood next to it. "What about having the hotel hold it for you until he leaves?''

Yorick smiled. "This hotel makes the Swagman look like an amateur.''

"Have you got any friends I can leave it with?''

Yorick shook his head.

"All right," said Cain. "What if I deposit it with the branch bank at the spaceport and tell them to release it only to you? Your voiceprint ought to be registered there.''

"That would be nice," said Yorick. "But leave a thousand credits behind. I don't want to go to the spaceport the first time I run out of seeds.''

"He'll take it from you," said Cain.

"A thousand credits? He doesn't need it.''

"That's got nothing to do with it.''

"It's *my* money. Leave a thousand credits.''

Cain opened the drawer and took out four of the five-hundred-credit notes. "I'm going to tell them not to release this to you unless you're alone.''

"Thank you, Songbird," said Yorick placidly.

"Are you sure you don't want to count the phony jewels before you leave?" asked the Swagman sardonically.

"No," said Cain. "But I'll have Schussler do a quick inventory of Altair of Altair's artwork before we take off.''

Cain turned and walked out the door. The Swagman immediately walked over to the dresser, searched around for another seed, and brought it over to Yorick.

"Here," he said. "Don't start chewing until we've talked.''

Yorick removed the first seed, now a pale yellow, from his mouth and carefully set it down on his windowsill, then inserted the new one. The Swagman stepped over to the window and stared out through the rain until he could make out Cain's figure walking back to the vehicle.

"What kind of paintings do you want, Swagman?" asked Yorick pleasantly, luxuriating in the juices of the fresh seed.

"None," said the Swagman.

"Then what was that all about?"

"Billy Three-Eyes is dead. Peacemaker MacDougal caught up with him four months ago."

"Poor Billy," said Yorick, smiling tranquilly. "I loved that notch on his forehead." He looked up at the Swagman. "Maybe you'd better go tell the Songbird."

The Swagman shook his head. "I'm just waiting for him to get off the planet before I leave."

"Well, nobody ever accused you of the sin of loyalty."

"And nobody ever will," replied the Swagman. "Just the same, I was prepared to stay with him all the way to Santiago's doorstep." He paused. "But he isn't the one."

"The one?"

"The one who can kill Santiago."

"I know," said Yorick with a euphoric smile. "That's why I told him the truth."

"What truth?" demanded the Swagman.

"About Safe Harbor. That's his next step."

"I just told you: Billy Three-Eyes is dead. Now," said the Swagman, pulling out a roll of bills and holding them enticingly before Yorick's nose, "where's *my* next step?"

"Who knows?" replied Yorick pleasantly. "Where are you going?"

"Where do you think I should go to find Santiago?"

"To *find* him?" repeated Yorick. "Go with the Songbird."

"Let me amend that," said the Swagman. "Where should I go to kill him?"

"He's my best customer," said Yorick. He paused thoughtfully. "He's my *only* customer. I don't want him killed."

"I'll buy you enough alphanella seeds so that you never need him again."

"I won't live long enough to spend the money the Songbird gave me," said Yorick placidly. "Why do I need more?"

The Swagman stared at him for a moment, then shrugged. He began walking around the room, examining the artificial gems, and finally stopped in front of the canvas.

"Are you ever going to finish this?" he asked.

"Probably not."

"I'll buy it from you if you do."

"It's already sold to your friend Black Orpheus."

The Swagman studied the portrait with renewed interest. "Eurydice?"

"I think that's what he called her. He left a couple of holographs with me, but I lost them a long time ago."

"You could have been one hell of an artist."

"I'm happier this way," said Yorick.

"What a stupid thing to say."

"My painting brings pleasure to others. My weakness brings pleasure to me."

"You're a fool," said the Swagman.

Yorick smiled. "But I'm a loyal fool. Have you got anything else to say to me, Swagman?"

"Not a thing."

"Good." He ground the seed to pulp between his molars. "I've got about a minute before it hits. Do you mind letting yourself out?"

The Swagman picked up a number of discarded sketches from the floor and carefully tucked them inside his tunic.

"Mementos," he said with a smile, walking to the door.

"Now that you've deserted your partner, where will you go next?" asked Yorick.

"I am not without prospects," replied the Swagman confidently.

"People like you never are," said Yorick, his vision starting to blur.

"People like me get what they want," said the Swagman, taking a tentative step into the room and watching for a reaction. "People like Cain don't even *know* what they want."

Yorick was beyond replying, his frail body totally catatonic. The Swagman watched him for another moment, then walked over to the dresser and took one of the two remaining five-hundred-credit notes.

"Reimbursement of expenses," he explained to his motionless host.

He took two steps toward the door, stopped, shrugged, and went back to the dresser, appropriating the final note and placing it in his pocket.

"Filthy habit, drugs," he said, staring at Poor Yorick and shaking his head with insincere regret. "Someday you'll thank me for removing temptation from your path."

A few minutes later he was on his way to the spaceport, lost in thought as he examined every angle of his situation with the cold precision of a mathematician. He finally balanced all the diverse elements and came up with a solution just before he arrived. Shortly thereafter he began making the arrangements that would once again put him back into the heart of the equation.

Part 4

The Angel's Book

15.

They call him the Angel, the Angel of Death,
If ever you've seen him, you've drawn your last breath.
He's got cold lifeless eyes, he's got brains, he's got skill,
He's got weapons galore, and a yearning to kill.

Nobody knew where he came from. It was rumored that he had been born on Earth itself, but he never spoke about it.

Nobody knew where he got his start, or why he chose his particular occupation. Some people say that he had been married once, that his wife had been raped and murdered, and that he took his revenge on the whole galaxy. Some were sure that he had been a mercenary who had gone berserk during a particularly bloody action—but no one who ever met him and lived to tell about it thought him crazy; in fact, it was his absolute sanity that made him so frightening. Others thought that, like Cain, he was simply a disillusioned revolutionary.

Nobody knew his true name, or even how he came to be called the Angel.

Nobody knew why he chose to work the Outer Frontier, out on the Galactic Rim, when there were so many more worlds within the Democracy where he could ply his bloody trade.

But there was one thing *every*body knew: once the Angel chose his quarry, that quarry's days were numbered.

In a profession where reputations could be made by a single kill—Sebastian Cain, Giles Sans Pitié, and Peacemaker MacDougal actually had a combined total of less than seventy, and Johnny One-Note was still looking for his sixth—

the Angel had hunted down more than one hundred fugitives. In a profession where anonymity went hand in glove with success, the Angel was known on a thousand worlds. In a profession where each practitioner carved out his own territory and allowed no trespassing, the Angel went where he pleased.

Orpheus met him only once, out by Barbizon, the gateway to the Inner Frontier, three weeks before he killed Giles Sans Pitié. They spoke for only ten minutes, which was more than enough for Orpheus. His audience had expected him to give the Angel no less than a dozen verses—after all, he had given three to Cain and nine to Giles Sans Pitié—but with the insight that had established him as the Bard of the Inner Frontier, Orpheus wrote only a single stanza. When asked for an explanation, he simply smiled and replied that those four lines said everything there was to say about the Angel.

Virtue MacKenzie wished he had written a little more, if only so she'd have a better idea of what to expect if she ever caught up with the Angel. She had reached the Lambda Karos system two days after he had departed, and missed him again on Questados IV. She arrived on New Ecuador three days later, checked for word of his whereabouts at the local news offices, received only negative answers, and finally returned to her hotel, where she took a brief nap, showered, changed her clothes, and went down to the main floor restaurant for dinner.

Three hours later she was sitting at a table in the back of The King's Rook, a tavern that served as the gathering place for local journalists. Two men and a woman—all newspeople—and another man, a prospector who had hit it rich in the asteroid belt two planets out from New Ecuador, sat around the table, staring at the exposed cards in front of Virtue.

"It's up to you," said the prospector impatiently.

"Don't rush me," said Virtue, sipping her whiskey and staring at her hole card until it came back into focus. "I'm thinking." Finally she pushed a one-hundred-credit note across the worn felt to the center of the table. "Call," she said.

The prospector and one of the men dropped out, the woman raised the pot another fifty credits, the other man folded, and Virtue, after still more consideration, matched her bet.

"Read 'em and weep," grinned the woman, turning her hole card face up.

"Damn!" muttered Virtue, tossing her hole card onto the table. She grabbed a nearby bottle and poured herself another drink. "You didn't learn to play from a little rodent called Terwilliger, did you?"

"Anyone for quitting?" asked one of the men, staring directly at Virtue.

"Not when I'm down almost two thousand credits," she replied pugnaciously.

"Anyone else?"

"Hell," said the prospector. "If she wants to keep on playing, I'm willing to keep on taking her money."

"I don't plan to keep losing," said Virtue

"Then you'd better cut back on the booze," said the prospector. "She had you beat on the table."

"When I want your advice, I'll ask for it," said Virtue, trying to remember exactly what the winner's cards were.

"More power to you." He shrugged. "Whose deal?"

"Mine," said a journalist. He began shuffling the cards.

A well-dressed man entered the tavern just then, looked around, and walked directly over to the five cardplayers. They paid no attention to him until he stopped a few feet away.

"I beg your pardon," he said, "but I wonder if I might join you?"

The four locals stared at him and made no reply.

"Suit yourself," said Virtue.

"Thank you," he said. "By the way, I'm told that there is an excellent game that's in need of players."

"Oh?" asked the prospector nervously. "Where?"

"Right there," he said, pointing to an empty table at the far end of the room.

The prospector and the three journalists almost fell over each other racing to the other table. Virtue, confused, rose to join them, muttering, "What the hell's wrong with *this* table?"

"Not you," said the man firmly, seating himself on one of the hastily vacated chairs.

She stared across the table, studying him in the dim light of the tavern. He was tall, though not as tall as Cain, and quite well built without being heavily muscled. His hair was so blond that it appeared almost white, and his eyebrows were barely visible. It was impossible to guess his age. His cold, penetrating eyes were not quite blue, not quite gray, practically clear. The rest of his face was unmarked and rather handsome, but it was the almost colorless eyes that instantly commanded attention.

He was dressed in a dark gray outfit that seemed black at first glance; it was severely cut and exquisitely tailored. He wore a conservatively styled silver tunic beneath his coat, and his boots, while lacking the embellishments of the Swagman's, nonetheless seemed more expensive. On the small finger of his left hand was a platinum ring that housed a truly fabulous diamond.

"You're the Angel," she said. It was not a question.

He nodded his head.

"I thought you'd look different," she said at last, trying to buy time while everything came into sharper focus.

"In what way?"

"More like a killer."

"What does a killer look like?" asked the Angel.

"Leaner and hungrier," she said. Suddenly a thought occurred to her. "Are you here to kill me?"

"Probably not," he said, pulling out a long, thin cigar and lighting it. "You don't mind if I smoke?"

She stared into his colorless eyes and shook her head.

"Good," he continued. Suddenly he leaned forward. "You've been following me for more than a week. Why?"

"What makes you think anyone's been following you?" replied Virtue.

The Angel smiled—a cold, lifeless smile. "You reached Lambda Karos Two two days after I left and began asking questions about me. Your next stop was Questados Four. Again you inquired into my whereabouts. Now you're here. What am I supposed to think?"

"Coincidence?" she suggested lamely.

He stared at her until she began fidgeting uncomfortably.

"I must appear very stupid for you to make such an answer," he said at last. "Now, let me ask you once more: Why are you following me?"

"I'm a journalist," said Virtue. "You're a romantic figure. I thought you might make a good story."

He stared at her again, without expression, without passion, and again she found herself increasingly uneasy.

"I'm only going to ask you one more time," he said, "so I want you to consider your answer very carefully."

"You're making me very nervous," said Virtue self-righteously.

"Being followed makes *me* very nervous," replied the Angel. "Why have you been doing it?"

"I wanted to meet you."

Virtue noticed that her glass was empty and reached for the bottle, but the Angel was faster and placed it on the far side of the table.

"Why did you want to meet me?" he persisted.

"I think we may be able to help each other."

He stared at her, offering no reply, and finally she resumed speaking.

"You're after Santiago. So am I."

"Then we're competitors."

"No," she said hastily. "I'm not after the reward. All I want is the story." She paused. "And I really *could* use a story on you as well."

"I have no interest in your journalistic aspirations," said the Angel. "Why should I let you come along?"

"I have information that you may not have," said Virtue.

"I doubt it."

"Can you afford to take the chance?"

"I think so." He paused and stared at her again. "But I don't know if I can take the chance that you'll return to Sebastian Cain and tell him where I am and where I'm going next."

"Who's Sebastian Cain?" she asked innocently.

"He's a very foolish man who has taken on too much excess baggage," replied the Angel. "Did you offer him the same deal you offered me—he gets the reward and you get the story?"

"Yes. Except that the Swagman gets something, too. Santiago's art collection, I think."

"And Cain sent you here to spy on me?"

She shook her head. "Coming here was my own idea." He stared silently at her, and again she felt herself compelled to say more than she had intended. "I've sized up the candidates, and I'm going with the winner. If anyone can kill Santiago, you're the one."

"And you'll remain completely loyal to me?" he said sardonically. "Until you hear of someone else who's even better, that is?"

"That's unfair."

"But selling out your partner isn't?" he asked, a note of distaste in his voice. "I wonder what it is about Cain that makes people desert him. The Jolly Swagman has left him, too, you know."

"Who told you that?" asked Virtue, genuinely surprised.

"I have my sources. I expect him to contact me any time now to see if I've changed my mind about not requiring a partner." He paused. "I will tell him that I haven't."

"Is that what you're telling me?" she asked, suddenly apprehensive about what happened to would-be partners. She looked around for support or comfort, only to discover that one by one the customers were quietly leaving the tavern, casting frightened glances at the Angel as they did so.

"I'm not sure," he said. "You possess some information that might prove useful to me."

"I told you so," she said smugly.

"Not about Santiago," he replied disdainfully. "You know less than nothing about him."

"Then what are you talking about?"

"Sebastian Cain," said the Angel. "I'm getting close to Santiago. Three or four more worlds, another week, another month, and I'll be there." He took a puff of his cigar. "Cain is getting close, too. He's got that cyborg ship, and he's already visited the drug addict on Roosevelt Three." He paused. "And he killed Altair of Altair," he added with a touch of admiration.

"I can tell you all about him," said Virtue triumphantly.

"I know."

She paused. "What's in it for me?"

"Exclusive coverage of Santiago's death."

"And a series of features on you," she added quickly.

He stared at her once more. "Don't push your luck. I'd *like* information about Cain; I don't *need* it."

"One feature?"

He made no reply, but his cold clear eyes seemed to bore into hers.

"All right," she said at last.

"You've made a wise decision," said the Angel.

"Well, now that we're going to be traveling together, where are we bound for next?" asked Virtue.

"I'll know in a few minutes."

"Based on something I'm going to tell you?" she asked skeptically.

He shook his head. "I've already told you: you don't possess any useful information about Santiago—but there's a man on New Ecuador who does. I expect him to stop by our table momentarily."

"Why?"

"Because I asked him to."

"Does everyone do what you ask them to?" she inquired with a trace of resentment.

"Most people do," said the Angel.

"And those who don't?"

"They soon wish they had." He paused for a moment. "I think it's time you started telling me about Cain."

"Right now?"

"As soon as you sober up," he replied, signaling to the bartender, who hurried over, bowing obsequiously.

"The lady would like a cup of black coffee," said the Angel.

"And yourself, sir?"

"A white wine, I think," said the Angel. "Not too sweet. Perhaps something from Alphard."

"Right away, sir," said the bartender, scurrying off. He returned a moment later, placed a large cup of coffee in front of Virtue, and offered a glass to the Angel.

"This isn't an Alphard wine," said the Angel, taking a sip from the glass.

"No, sir," said the bartender nervously. "We don't have any. But it's from Valkyrie, which has excellent vineyards. It's a fine vintage, truly it is."

The Angel took another taste while the bartender watched him apprehensively, and finally nodded his approval. The bartender immediately signaled to an assistant, who brought the bottle to the table.

"What do I owe you?" asked Angel.

"It's on the house, sir."

"You're sure?"

"Yes, sir. It's a pleasure to serve you."

"Thank you," said the Angel, dismissing them and watching as they rapidly retreated to their posts behind the bar.

"This isn't very fair," said Virtue.

"What isn't?"

"I'm drinking coffee and you're drinking wine."

"Were you under the impression that life was fair?" asked the Angel ironically.

"I could be drinking whiskey and playing cards," she continued sullenly, glancing over toward the reporters, who were casting furtive glances in her direction.

"They don't want your company."

"What makes you think not?" demanded Virtue.

"Because you've been sitting here talking to me. They'll wait for what they think is a proper interval—perhaps another five minutes—and then leave before you can rejoin them."

"You're sure?"

"Absolutely."

"This happens all the time?" she continued.

"Yes."

"You must be a very lonely man."

"There are compensations," he replied dryly. "Surely Sebastian Cain has said as much to you."

"I'm not certain that he agrees with you."

"Then why is he a bounty hunter?" asked the Angel, suddenly interested.

"He wants to do something important," she said with a cynical smile. "Or meaningful. Whichever comes first."

"God save us from moral men with good intentions," said the Angel. He took another sip of his wine and relit his cigar, which had gone out.

"I can see where an abundance of them might put you out of business," commented Virtue.

"I don't foresee that as an imminent danger," said the Angel. "Let's get back to Cain. The money trail is a lot easier to follow than the smuggling trail; why did he choose the latter?"

"That was where he got his first hard information."

"Information's not that difficult to come by."

"Maybe you're better at extracting it than he is."

"You make him sound something less than formidable," remarked the Angel. "This is contrary to my assessment of him, especially considering how far he's gotten."

"Bounty hunters aren't all alike," replied Virtue, reaching into her satchel and withdrawing a cigarette. "For example, I have a hard time envisioning Cain killing anyone—and I have an equally hard time picturing you letting anyone live."

"You misjudge me. I only kill fugitives."

"What about Giles Sans Pitié?"

"And fools," he amended.

"I've heard a lot of things, good and bad, about him," said Virtue, "but I never heard anyone call him a fool before."

"That's because most people were afraid of him."

"Why *did* you kill him?"

"He proposed an alliance. I refused. He threatened me." He smiled mirthlessly. "*That* was foolish."

"You killed him because he *threatened* you?"

"You doubtless feel it would have been more sporting to wait until he'd taken a few swings at my head with that metal fist of his?" suggested the Angel.

"How do you know he wasn't bluffing?"

"I don't. But when a man takes a position, he must be prepared to live—or die—with the consequences of his actions. Giles Sans Pitié threatened to kill me. There was only one possible consequence."

"How did you kill him?" she asked curiously.

"Efficiently," he replied. "Now reach into your satchel and turn your recorder off. We're supposed to be discussing Cain, not creating a biographical feature on me."

"Can't blame a girl for trying," she said nonchalantly while deactivating the recorder.

The Angel poured himself another glass of wine as the four cardplayers silently left the tavern.

"What was Cain's reaction when he found out that he would have to confront Altair of Altair?"

"He wasn't scared, if that's what you mean," said Virtue.

"That wasn't what I meant. Any man who's been in our profession as long as Cain has learned to master his fear." The Angel leaned forward slightly. "Was he excited?"

"Not much excites him. Resigned is the word I'd use."

"What a pity."

"Why? Does killing people excite you?"

"Killing most people is just a job to be done as quickly and efficiently as possible," said the Angel. "But killing someone like Altair of Altair . . ." His face came alive. "The highest levels of competition in *any* field of endeavor are indistinguishable from art—and I find art exciting."

"Then that's why you're after Santiago?" asked Virtue. "Because he affords you the greatest competition?"

He shook his head. "I am hunting Santiago because I need the reward. The challenge he presents is merely an added bonus."

"Come on," said Virtue skeptically. "I know your record. Do you really expect me to believe that you're after still more money?"

"What you believe is a matter of complete indifference to me," replied the Angel.

"But you've made tens of millions of credits!" she persisted.

"My creditors have expensive tastes," he said.

Suddenly his attention was taken by a small, portly, balding, red-faced man who cautiously entered the tavern. The man looked around uneasily, saw the Angel, and walked over to the table.

"Mr. Breshinsky?" said the Angel.

The man nodded, sweat dripping off his face as he did so. "I was told you wanted to see me," he said in a wary voice.

"You were also told what information I needed."

"I regret to inform you that I don't have access to it," said Breshinsky nervously.

"You *are* the account officer of the New Ecuador branch of the Bank of Misthaven, are you not?"

Breshinsky nodded again.

"Then you know on which world Dimitrios Galos initially established his business account."

"I'm forbidden by law to tell you that," protested Breshinsky. "That's privileged information."

"Which you are now going to give to me," said the Angel, staring intently at the uncomfortable banker.

"It's out of the question!"

"If it were out of the question, you wouldn't have shown up."

"I came because nobody says no to the Angel."

"Then don't say no now, or I could become very annoyed with you," said the Angel gently.

"This could cost me my job!"

"This could cost you considerably more than your job."

Breshinsky seemed to shrink within himself.

"Who is your companion?" he asked at last. "I can't

divulge sensitive information like this in front of a third party."

"I personally guarantee her silence."

"You're sure?" asked Breshinsky, staring at Virtue.

"I just gave you my word."

There was another uncomfortable pause.

"Can we at least discuss some compensation?" asked Breshinsky, his hands trembling noticeably. "My entire future is at stake if this should get out."

"Of course," said the Angel. "I'm not an unreasonable man."

"Good," said Breshinsky, pulling out a silk handkerchief and mopping his forehead. "May I sit down?"

"That won't be necessary," replied the Angel. "I never haggle. I'll make one offer, and you can take it or leave it."

"All right," said Breshinsky. "What's your offer?"

"Your life, Mr. Breshinsky," said the Angel calmly.

The portly little man gasped, then emitted a nervous giggle. "You're joking!"

"I never joke about business."

Breshinsky stared at him for a long moment, then uttered a sound that was halfway between a sigh and a sob. "The account was initiated on Sunnybeach."

"Thank you, Mr. Breshinsky," said the Angel. "You've been most helpful."

"May I leave now?"

The Angel nodded, and the little banker walked rapidly to the door.

"Would you really have killed him if he hadn't told you what you wanted to know?" asked Virtue.

"Of course."

"I thought you only killed fugitives."

"And fools," added the Angel. "Eventually one comes to the realization that everyone is one or the other."

"Including Santiago?"

"*Almost* everyone," he amended.

"You're a very cynical man," she said.

"It must be the company I keep," he replied. He noticed that his cigar had gone out again, and unwrapped and lit a fresh one. "We'll leave for Sunnybeach at sunrise tomorrow morning."

"Then I'd better go back to my hotel and start packing," said Virtue. She paused. "What will I do with my ship?"

"That's not my concern," said the Angel.

"Thanks a lot."

"If you're unhappy with the arrangements, you can always remain on New Ecuador," said the Angel.

"Not a chance," she replied. "We're partners now. I'm staying with you."

"We are *not* partners," he corrected her. "We are traveling companions, nothing more. And you'll stay with me only so long as you prove useful." He stood up. "Meet me at my ship at sunrise."

"How will I know which one it is?" she asked as he began walking toward the doorway.

He stopped and turned to her.

"You're an investigative reporter," he said. "You'll find it."

Then he was gone, and Virtue MacKenzie found herself sitting alone in the almost deserted tavern. She remained motionless, lost in thought, for a number of minutes, trying to assimilate what she had seen and learned of the Angel. There was no longer any question in her mind that he would find Santiago, and very little that he would succeed in killing him. But for the first time since she had begun her search, she felt unsure of her course of action; the Angel frightened her as no other man she had ever met.

She reviewed her various options, which included finding and teaming up with Cain or the Swagman once more, proceeding on her own, or chucking the whole thing and living on the remainder of her unspent advance, compared them against remaining with the Angel, and finally concluded that while she hadn't made the safest decision, she had made the right one.

She stood up, walked to the far side of the table where the Angel had placed her bottle, downed two large swallows, and headed back to her hotel, trying to come up with various facts about Cain and Santiago that would make her of continuing value to the Angel.

16.

Come to the lair of the cold Virgin Queen!
Come and see sights that have never been seen!
Money that's piled as high as the sky,
And a bandit queen anything other than shy!

People used to ask Black Orpheus about that verse, since it seemed so different from his original stanza about Virtue MacKenzie. At first he was genuinely puzzled—after all, he hadn't written it—but after a while he put two and two together, figured out who wrote it and why, and decided to let it stand, probably to further confuse the academics who had made careers out of continually misinterpreting him.

Once the Angel had let drop that he had a constant need for money, Virtue decided to convince him that she had access to it—so she jotted down the four lines, spread some untraceable cash around, and made sure that the verse continually came to his attention.

She was guilty of overwriting a bit more than usual; at any rate, it didn't have quite the effect she had anticipated. The first time the Angel heard it he remarked that Orpheus must have discovered a second Virgin Queen; he never referred to it again. When it reached the Swagman's ears, he concluded that money wasn't the only thing Virtue was capable of piling as high as the sky. As for Cain, who heard it after he'd reached Safe Harbor, he grimaced and commented to Schussler that some of the sights referred to had been seen altogether too often. Of all the men and aliens Virtue had met on the Inner Frontier, only Sitting Bull, chief of the Great Sioux

211

Nation, assumed that the verse had actually been written by Black Orpheus, and he found himself in full agreement that shyness was not exactly one of the Virgin Queen's more noticeable traits.

In truth, the only positive effect it ever did have was that Virtue gained another little piece of immortality when Orpheus incorporated it into his ballad.

In the meantime, it was business as usual during the two-day voyage to Sunnybeach. The Angel questioned her thoroughly about every aspect of Cain's character, every portion of his past, every hope he may have expressed for his future. She answered with the truth when she could and lied when she couldn't.

Even though he assumed that her knowledge of Cain was fragmentary at best, the picture that emerged puzzled and disturbed the Angel. He understood men who killed for profit, and men who killed for hatred, and even men who killed for ego—but Cain seemed to fall into none of those categories. And, as with anything that ran counter to his experience, he distrusted it, as he now distrusted Cain.

For her part, Virtue tried to learn more about the Angel, especially his past and his reasons for becoming first an assassin and then a bounty hunter. He didn't overtly refuse to answer her; he merely ignored her questions, and when he stared at her with his colorless eyes, she felt disinclined to force the issue.

Finally they reached Sunnybeach, which handled considerably more traffic than she had expected. On most Frontier worlds one simply decelerated and landed, but the procedure here was not unlike that back in the heart of the Democracy.

First a voice came over their radio and asked them to identify themselves.

"This is the *Southern Cross*, two hundred eighty-one Galactic Standard days out of Spica Six, William Jennings, race of Man, commanding," replied the Angel.

"Registration number?"

The Angel rattled off an eleven-digit number.

"Purpose of visit?"

"Tourism."

"Are you equipped to land planetside, or will you require use of an orbiting hangar?"

"I can land in any spaceport rated Class Seven or higher."

"Please maintain your orbit until we can confirm you," said the voice, breaking the connection.

"Who is William Jennings?" asked Virtue.

"I am—until we pass through customs."

"I assume the ship's point of origin and registration number are phony, too."

"They're untrue," said the Angel. "Which is different from being phony. I can prove they're what I say, just as I can prove that I'm William Jennings."

"Why not tell them who you really are?" asked Virtue. "It's not as if bounty hunting is illegal."

"It tends to scare off one's prey and alert one's competition."

"Then why ever identify yourself at all?" she persisted.

"I don't care who knows I've been to a world once I've left it," replied the Angel disdainfully.

The radio came to life again.

"Attention, *Southern Cross*. We need to know how many other sentient entities are aboard your ship."

"One other, besides myself," replied the Angel.

"Please identify."

"Virtue MacKenzie, passenger, race of Man, who boarded at New Ecuador two Standard days ago."

"What was your business on New Ecuador?"

"Tourism."

"Proposed length of stay on Sunnybeach?"

"I have no idea," said the Angel.

"I require a definite answer," said the voice petulantly.

"I propose to stay here for ten days."

"The Sunnybeach economy is based on Plantagenet sovereigns. Will you require the use of a currency exchange?"

"All I require is a clearance to land my ship."

"Please maintain orbit," said the voice, and again the connection was broken.

"I feel like I'm right back in the Democracy," commented Virtue.

"It's a bother," he agreed. "When I have my own planet, I won't tolerate this bureaucratic nonsense."

"Your own planet?" she repeated.

He nodded.

She laughed. "Are you laboring under the delusion that a grateful Democracy is going to give you your very own planet just for killing Santiago?"

"No."

"Then what are you talking about?"

He turned to her, and for just a moment she thought he might put a forceable end to her unwanted questioning then and there. Instead, he instructed his ship's computer to create a hologram of a cross section of the Galactic Rim.

"Do you see this?" he asked, indicating a glowing yellow star.

She nodded.

"It's a G-Four star with eleven planets, the fourth of which is named Far London. Its population has grown to almost three hundred thousand since it was initially colonized." He paused. "Far London has been ruled by a hereditary monarchy, the last descendent of which died a few years ago and left a considerable debt. The government has advertised for a new monarch."

"The stipulation being that you'll pay off the late lamented family's debts?" asked Virtue.

"In essence," said the Angel.

"How much more do you need?"

"Killing Santiago should just about do it."

"And then you'll retire to a quiet life of ruling the peasants?" she asked.

"I've always wanted to have my very own world to rule."

"Well," she said, "at least there'll be one world where we don't have these idiot delays before we can land." She paused. "Have you thought about what other improvements you'll make?"

"No. But I think I can make one guarantee."

"Oh? What is that?"

"It will be safe to walk the streets of my city."

"I don't suppose I'd like to be a lawbreaker in your city," she agreed. "What does the populace think of this idea?"

"Given the previous few monarchs, they'll approve."

"And if they don't?"

"Then they'll learn to adjust," he said softly.

Suddenly the radio crackled with static.

"*Southern Cross,* you are cleared for landing. We will now feed the coordinates into your computer." There followed two seconds of high-pitched humming, after which the ship began decelerating and heading downward toward the surface of Sunnybeach.

"I trust your passport is in order," remarked the Angel. "I don't suppose customs will be any less pompous and self-important."

"Of course," she replied.

But when they landed, she found herself the object of some ten minutes' worth of mild harassment, since her passport hadn't been scanned or registered since Pegasus. When they finally released her, the Angel was nowhere to be seen, and she walked rapidly through the spaceport, looking for him. She passed a handful of human vendors, as well as a number of aliens selling everything from indigestible sweets to incomprehensible wood carvings, and eventually found the bounty hunter at a tobacco stand, purchasing a fresh supply of cigars from a pink, tripodal being from Hesporite III.

"This place is simply lousy with aliens," she remarked. "I didn't know Sunnybeach was so cosmopolitan."

"It isn't," said the Angel. "They're not allowed to leave the free trade zone around the spaceport."

"By the way, I want to thank you for all your help back there at the customs desk," she said sarcastically.

"*My* papers were in order," he replied.

"You could have waited."

"Partners wait. Traveling companions don't."

He paid for the cigars, placed them in a lapel pocket, and began following the signs to the ground vehicle rental area. Virtue fell into step beside him.

When they arrived, he stopped and turned to her.

"You're not coming with me. Find your own transportation, and register at the Welcome Inn."

"Why can't we go into town together?" she asked. "It'll be more convenient."

"Because you're feeling followed."

"*What?*"

"You heard me."

"I didn't see anybody," Virtue protested.

"I did."

"Then how do you know that *you're* not the one who's being followed?"

"Because when I left customs, he stayed behind and waited for you."

"What does he look like?" asked Virtue.

"He's not that clumsy," replied the Angel. "I've only gotten two brief glimpses of him."

"How do you know he's following me if you've only had two glimpses of him?"

"I know," he said calmly.

"And now you're just going to leave?" she demanded.

"He's not after *me*," said the Angel.

"I hope they're not expecting a chivalrous king on Far London."

"They're not," said the Angel, walking toward a rental vehicle.

"Wait!" said Virtue. "What should I do about this guy?"

"That's entirely up to you. But if I were you, I'd try to find out what he wanted before I led him to my hotel."

"It's *your* hotel, too," she said desperately. "If you don't help me lose him, he'll know where you're staying. That might be worth quite a bit of money to someone."

"It's not my hotel," he answered.

"It isn't? Then where will you be staying?"

"That's not the sort of information I share with traveling companions."

"Then how will I find you?"

"*I'll* find *you*," he replied. "I'll meet you in the Welcome Inn's lobby at sunset."

"If I'm still alive," she said bitterly.

"If you're still alive," he agreed.

He tossed his single piece of luggage into the back of the vehicle, climbed into the driver's seat, registered it to his account with an identification card, and drove off.

Virtue waited for ten minutes, casting frightened glances into the shadows, then rented her own vehicle and drove out into the bright Sunnybeach sun. When she was halfway to town she realized that she'd left her overnight kit at the spaceport, but decided not to return for it.

Her initial idea upon reaching the nearby city, which, unsurprisingly, bore the same name as the planet, was to walk up and down the streets, window-shopping, until she got a glimpse of her pursuer. That resolve lasted about thirty seconds. Whoever had named the planet had possessed a mordant sense of humor: Sunnybeach was a desert world, with about five hundred miles of beach for every foot of seashore. The heat, once she left the confines of her air-conditioned vehicle, was oppressive, and she got the feeling that the only variation in the weather was an occasional sandstorm.

She had almost collapsed from the simple exertion of walking half a block when she came to a small, elegant restaurant. She entered it, requested a table that faced the front door, and pretended to study the menu while keeping a watchful eye on the doorway.

Some five minutes later a familiar bearded face, topped by a shock of unkempt red hair, peered in through the window, and an instant later Halfpenny Terwilliger entered the restaurant and walked directly to her table.

"Goddamn it!" she snapped, both relieved and annoyed. "Are *you* the one who's been following me?"

"Yeah," he said breathlessly. "We've got to talk."

"I've got nothing to say to you."

"You've got more to say than you think," said Terwilliger, watching the door as intently as Virtue had been doing a moment earlier. He signaled to the waiter. "Has this place got another room?"

"Another room, sir?"

"One that can't be seen from the street," explained Terwilliger.

"We don't open it until dinnertime," said the waiter.

Terwilliger waved a one-hundred-credit note in front of him. "Open it now," he said. "And close it as soon as we're seated."

The waiter took the note with no sign of embarrassment and led them through a doorway into a smaller room which possessed only six lace-covered tables.

"Take money for two beers out of that and keep the rest," said the little gambler when he and Virtue had been seated.

The waiter arched a supercilious eyebrow and left the room.

"What the hell are you doing here?" demanded Virtue when they were alone.

"Waiting for you," replied Terwilliger. "I was going to give you two more days to show up, and then hop over to Hallmark."

"Why were you skulking after me like some kind of criminal?"

"I have my reasons," he said.

"You mean the Angel?" asked Virtue. "He doesn't give a damn who I talk to."

"I'm not worried about the Angel."

"Then what *are* you worried about?"

"ManMountain Bates."

"Is he still after you?"

"The man simply will not let bygones be bygones!" complained Terwilliger peevishly. "He's chased me halfway across the Inner Frontier."

"You seem to have done the same to me," remarked Virtue. "Were you on New Ecuador, too?"

The little gambler shook his head. "I followed you as far as Questados Four. Then Bates started breathing down my neck again, so I decided to jump a few worlds ahead of you, just in case he was using you to find me." He paused for breath, then continued. "The Swagman told me that the Angel would probably pass through Sunnybeach or Hallmark, depending on what he learned on Lambda Karos, and I came here first. It sounded like a vacation planet." He grimaced. "They ought to draw and quarter the guy who named it. Hanging's too good for him."

"Why were you looking for me in the first place?"

"Cain sent me."

"To spy on me?"

"Well, now, *spy* is a pretty ugly word," said Terwilliger, pulling a deck of cards out of his pocket and nervously starting to shuffle them. "Besides, if I was really spying on you, I'd stay in hiding. You'd never know I was around."

"I'd just listen for the sound of a spine snapping," she said nastily.

He winced. "Don't remind me."

"All right," she said. "You're not spying. You're just here to sample Sunnybeach's delightful climate." She paused. "What *else* are you here for?"

"To appraise the situation."

"And what's your appraisal?"

"That's pretty obvious," said Terwilliger. "You've jumped ship. You're working with the Angel now."

"And you're going to run back and tell that to Cain?"

"I don't have any choice."

"Of course you do," said Virtue. "You can choose *not* to tell him."

"And risk losing my ten percent of the reward?" said Terwilliger. "Not a chance."

The waiter entered the room then and placed a glass and a container of beer in front of each of them.

"Thank you," said Virtue, immediately filling her glass.

"May I take your orders now?"

"This is all we're having," said the gambler.

"Allow me to point out that this is a restaurant, not a tavern," said the waiter officiously.

Terwilliger pulled another hundred-credit note out of his pocket and handed it to the waiter. "Point it out again in another hour," he said.

The waiter pocketed the money, picked up his tray, and pivoted toward the door in one graceful and well-practiced motion. A moment later they were alone again.

Virtue drained her glass and turned back to the gambler. "How far has Cain gotten?"

Terwilliger shrugged. "Who knows? I haven't been in touch with him since I left Altair Three."

"The Angel mentioned his having obtained some information from a drug addict on Roosevelt Three."

"It's news to me," said Terwilliger.

"If you don't know where he is, how the hell are you supposed to contact him?"

"Through Schussler."

"Schussler?" repeated Virtue. "Who's he?"

"Schussler's more of an *it* than a *he*," answered Terwilliger.

"That cyborg ship I heard about?"

He nodded.

"Schussler belonged to Altair of Altair, didn't he?"

"Yes."

"So he'd probably have had access to any information in her computer banks?"

"I don't know," said Terwilliger. "I suppose so."

"Then that means that Cain's got still another source of information," she mused aloud. "He might be closer than we thought." Suddenly she turned to Terwilliger. "Why did the Swagman leave him?"

"I didn't know that he did."

"You're not exactly a fount of information," she said caustically.

"I'm supposed to be gathering it, not dispensing it," replied the gambler.

There was a momentary silence.

"Maybe he threw him out," she suggested thoughtfully.

"Maybe *who* threw *who* out?"

"Cain," she said. "Maybe he decided he didn't need the Swagman any longer. Maybe he's come to the conclusion that this cyborg holds the key."

The waiter entered the room again.

"I thought I told you to leave us alone," said Terwilliger irritably.

"I know, sir, but if you are Mr. Terwilliger, I have a message for you."

The gambler's face turned pale. "Was it given to you personally?"

"No, sir. It came from the spaceport."

"Get out."

"But the message, sir."

"I don't want to hear it!" snapped Terwilliger.

The waiter stared at him for a moment, then shrugged and left.

"Damn!" muttered the gambler.

"What was that all about?" asked Virtue.

"ManMountain Bates," said Terwilliger. "He's landed on Sunnybeach—and he's got someone keeping tabs on me, or he wouldn't have known I was here."

"Your friend Bates isn't very long on brainpower," commented Virtue, pouring her beer into a glass. "Why announce his presence if he's hunting for you?"

"You haven't seen him," said Terwilliger unhappily. "There's no way he can *hide* his presence."

"But calling ahead, for God's sake!" she snorted contemptuously.

"He's just letting me know that he knows I'm here," said Terwilliger. "It's his idea of a joke. He thinks it'll terrify me." He paused and smiled wanly. "He's right."

"What are you going to do about him?"

He laughed nervously. "I'm going to have a couple of drinks, and then I'm going to run so fast it'll make your head spin."

"Back to Cain?"

"He's my guardian angel." He paused thoughtfully. "Unless . . ."

"Unless what?"

"Cain's a few thousand light-years from here, and you've got an angel of your own. I'll forget about my report if you'll get him to protect me."

"For how long?" she asked.

"Until I'm safely out of this system."

"There's one condition."

"What?" he asked suspiciously.

"Before you leave, you contact Cain and tell him that I'm delaying and misleading the Angel, and that I'm still loyal to him," said Virtue.

"Just in case he gets there first?" asked the gambler sardonically.

"It's always a possibility."

"I don't know," said Terwilliger dubiously. "If he finds out, I'll lost my piece of the action."

"Bates is between you and your ship," she pointed out. "What's ten percent to a dead man?"

He stared at the backs of his cards for a moment, then nodded. "It's a deal," he said at last. "You *can* get the Angel to protect me, can't you?"

Virtue flashed him a confident smile.

"He'll do anything I say," she assured him.

17.

He's bigger than big, he's taller than tall,
He's meaner than mean, and that isn't all—
He drinks straight from morning right through to the night,
He's ManMountain Bates, and he's anxious to fight.

His real name was Hiram Ezekial Bates. He was born on
the colony planet of Hera, and when he was eight years old
he stood six feet two inches tall.

His parents consulted with numerous specialists. The incompetent among them suggested that he had merely done his
growing early; the others knew he had a pituitary system gone
berserk, but after subjecting him to countless examinations and
tests could recommend nothing to stop it. Finally, when he
was twelve years old—he stood seven feet three inches tall by
then—they found a doctor who could arrest his growth.

The problem was that nobody had asked Hiram *his* opinion, and the fact of the matter was that he relished the notion
of being the biggest human being in the galaxy. When they
finally took him to the doctor, he dislocated four vertebrae in
the poor man's back, broke both of his legs, and quite
literally tore his office apart.

That was the day that he became ManMountain Bates.

They put him in a home for disturbed juveniles. He battered down the brick wall with his bare hands and took off for
points unknown, surfacing some five years later on the Inner
Frontier. By then he had finally reached his full growth—
eight feet seven inches, and close to 575 pounds of burly,

rock-hard muscle— and he worked his way through a number of menial jobs before he chucked it all and became a gambler.

He was close to thirty years old the first time that Black Orpheus saw him. He was sitting in a poker game in the back room of a bar on Binder X, surrounded by five rugged miners. He'd been losing pretty heavily, and he was none too happy about it. Finally he glared around the table and announced in a loud, belligerent voice that his luck had just changed and he intended to win the next few hands.

The pot reached six thousand credits on the ensuing hand when Bates finally slammed his cards down on the table. He had a pair of sixes. Two of his opponents had flushes and one had a full house; all tossed their cards into the middle of the table, face down, and opined that they had nothing that could beat him. In a manner of speaking, they were right.

Two more such displays followed, and when Bates had recouped his evening's losses he took his money and left the game, heading deeper into the Frontier. It made a lasting impression on Black Orpheus.

Their paths crossed once more, about five years later, on Barios IV. Orpheus was attracted by the sounds of a barroom brawl and upon arriving at the scene found that ManMountain Bates had challenged the entire clientele of a sleazy spaceport bar. They were a hard-living, hard-drinking lot, prospectors and cargo hands and traders, but Bates threw them around the barroom as if they were so many toothpicks, laughing all the while in his deep bass. One after another was tossed through windows or into walls, until only Bates and Orpheus remained standing.

"Write *that* in your goddamned song!" he bellowed happily, tossing enough money on the bar to pay for the damages and walking off into the hazy night.

Orpheus took him at his word and gave him six verses. He also tried to line up a fight between Bates and Skullcracker Murchison, who was the unofficial freehand heavyweight champion of the Inner Frontier, but Murchison did a little checking up and decided he wanted no part of ManMountain Bates.

As he stood in the lobby of the Welcome Inn, staring apprehensively out into the street while Virtue MacKenzie registered at the front desk, Halfpenny Terwilliger found himself in complete agreement with Murchison.

"All right," said Virtue, walking over to him. "I'm all set."

"Good," replied the little gambler. "Let's go up to your room and wait for the Angel there."

"He's supposed to meet me right here."

"How soon?"

"At sunset."

"That's another two hours or more," complained Terwilliger. "Hell, Bates could walk here from the spaceport by then."

"Nobody walks in this climate."

"Damn it! You know what I mean!" He tried to regain his composure. "I'm not going to sit around this idiot hotel's idiot lobby for two hours. I might just as well stand out in the street with a bull's-eye painted on my forehead."

"Okay," assented Virtue. "Send the message and you can hide in my room."

"Message? What message?"

"To Cain."

"Right now?" he demanded.

"Whenever you want to," replied Virtue sweetly. "But you can't go up to my room until you do it."

Terwilliger glared at her, then uttered a sigh of resignation. "You win. Where do I send it from?"

"I'm sure the hotel has a subspace tightbeam transmitter. Just ask at the desk."

"What's your room number?"

"Why?" asked Virtue suspiciously.

"I'm going to have to bill it to your room."

"The hell you are."

"But I don't have any money."

"Come on, you little rodent," said Virtue. "I saw you bribing the waiter back in the restaurant."

"That was Cain's money," he said lamely.

"I don't give a damn whose money you spend, as long as it isn't mine."

"Are you sure you don't want to pay for it?" he persisted. "It seems kind of immoral to use his money to send him a phony message."

"Not as immoral as lying to me about your finances," she said firmly. "Now reach into your pocket and dig."

He shrugged, approached the desk, had the tightbeam booth pointed out to him, and began walking across the lobby to it.

"I'm sure you don't mind if I come along," said Virtue, joining him.

"You're very distrusting," said the gambler. "It'll turn you into a grouchy old lady."

"A grouchy, *rich* old lady," she corrected him with a smile.

It took him about two minutes to compose the message and another minute to issue routing and coding instructions so that Schussler would receive it. Then he paid his charges at the desk and turned to Virtue.

"Are you satisfied now?" he asked. "Or would you rather I stood on the street with a bunch of signs pointing to me?"

"Don't tempt me," she said, heading off toward the elevators. He followed her, and a minute later they were walking down the corridor of the fourth floor.

"Here we are," she said, pressing her thumb up against the lock mechanism. It took less than a second to scan her print and check it through the front desk's computer, and the door receded into the wall.

"Nice," commented Terwilliger, stepping into the room ahead of her. "Very nice."

"Not bad," she agreed, entering the room and ordering the door to slide shut behind them.

The room was large and airy, some twenty-five feet on a side, with a plush carpet, a king-sized bed, and a pair of very comfortable chairs. One wall housed a recessed cabinet which contained a holographic entertainment system that was currently displaying an assortment of paid advertisements for Sunnybeach's rather mundane night life. A small table between the chairs had instructions for expanding it into a gaming table, with boards for chess, backgammon, and *jabob*, an alien card game that was all the rage in the trendiest human gambling establishments.

"I haven't stayed in a place like this since I made my second fortune!" exclaimed Terwilliger.

"Your *second* fortune?" repeated Virtue. "What happened to it?"

He grinned ruefully. "The same thing that happened to my first one."

She looked at him, sighed, shook her head, and walked over to the closet.

"Open," she muttered.

Nothing happened.

"Open," she repeated.

Still nothing.

"Damn! It's on the blink. If I had anything to put in it, I'd call the desk and complain."

"Just a minute," said Terwilliger. "I've seen one of these before."

He walked up to the ornate door and reached his hand straight through it.

"What the hell did you do?" she asked.

"Nothing," he answered. "There's no door here. It's a holographic projection." He smiled and pointed to a pair of well-camouflaged holo lenses. "It's cheaper than actually installing a hand-carved door like that, and once you get used to it it's more convenient, too. And," he added, "you get to redecorate for the cost of a couple of new image tapes."

"How much else is fake, I wonder?" said Virtue, pacing around the room and touching various objects. "Just the closet door, I guess," she concluded.

"Try the bathroom," he suggested.

She walked to the door, tried to pass through it, and bounced off.

"I didn't mean the door," he said, ordering it to open. "But I'll bet you credits to pebbles that those gold-spun curtains around the dryshower aren't really there."

"A dryshower?" she said irritably. "Shit! I was planning to take a long hot bath tonight."

"On a desert world?" he said. "Hell, I'll bet even their suites don't supply any water except from the drinking tap."

"Oh, well," she said, returning to the bedroom and walking to one of the chairs. "We might as well relax and wait for the Angel."

"Suits me," assented Terwilliger, sitting down opposite her. He pulled out his cards and began shuffling them on the table. "Care for a little game of chance?"

"No, thanks."

"You're sure?"

"If you played games of chance instead of games with predetermined results, you wouldn't be hiding here right now," she replied.

"You can deal," he offered.

"Blackjack," she said promptly, taking the cards from him. "Ten credits a hand. Dealer wins all ties."

"Fine—as long as you'll accept my IOUs if I lose."

"You can play with Cain's money," she said. "After all, we're all partners, so we'll be keeping it in the family, so to speak."

"What the hell," he said with a shrug. "Why not?"

They played for almost two hours, during which time Terwilliger won four hundred credits without ever once being allowed to deal. Finally Virtue looked out the window, handed the deck back to him, pulled four hundred-credit notes out of her satchel, placed them on the table, and got to her feet.

"It's just about time," she said.

"Why don't you meet him and bring him back up here?" suggested Terwilliger nervously.

"What if he's been delayed and I bump into your friend first?" she replied. "Do you really want to be stuck up here in a room that has only one exit?"

"You've got a point," he admitted begrudgingly, following her to the door.

They descended to the lobby, which was considerably more crowded as dinnertime approached, and Virtue quickly scanned the faces that were assembled there.

"Is he here yet?" asked the gambler.

"No."

"Then what do we do?"

"We wait," she said.

"What if somebody has killed him?" asked Terwilliger, a blind panic starting to overwhelm him.

"If someone has killed the Angel, you'd better get down on your knees and start saying your prayers," said Virtue, "because I guarantee you that Judgment Day is at hand. Now stop shaking, and try not to wet your pants."

Terwilliger was too busy peering through the lobby windows into the darkened street beyond to make any reply.

"You can relax now," said Virtue a moment later as the Angel walked through the doorway. "He's arrived."

Terwilliger exhaled loudly with relief, and she wondered idly just how long he had been holding his breath.

"Did you learn anything useful?" she asked as the Angel crossed the lobby and approached her.

"A bit," he said noncommittally. "I'll have to see one more man tomorrow." He paused. "Who's your friend?"

"Halfpenny Terwilliger."

"Is he the one I spotted at the spaceport?"

"Yes. He works for Sebastian Cain."

The Angel stared at Terwilliger and said nothing.

"Well, actually, that's not an operative statement," said the gambler nervously. "My services are currently on the open market."

"Good luck with them," said the Angel. "Now go away."

"What?" demanded Terwilliger.

"I know all about you. You're a crooked gambler who hooked up with Cain on Port Étrange and left him on Altair Three. You have nothing that I want."

Virtue turned to Terwilliger. "Sorry," she said.

"Now just a minute!" he shouted, drawing stares from all over the lobby. "We had a deal! I kept my end of it. Now he's got to protect me!"

"Any deal you made, you made with *her*," said the Angel in level tones.

"No!" said Terwilliger desperately. "I need *you!*"

The Angel stared at him silently.

"Don't you understand?" said Terwilliger. "ManMountain Bates is coming here to kill me!"

"Not without cause, or so I've been told," said the Angel.

The gambler turned to Virtue. "You get him to protect me, or I'll tell him what you had me do."

"He might be useful to us, after all," said Virtue carefully.

"I gather he's already been useful to you," replied the Angel dryly. "He is of absolutely no use to me."

"I can tell you things about Cain," said Terwilliger urgently. "Where he's been, where he's going, things like that."

"I already know where he's been and where he's going."

"I can tell you where Santiago is!"

"You don't know where Santiago is," replied the Angel. "Now go away."

"But I—"

Suddenly Terwilliger froze, his eyes fixed on the hotel's doorway. There was an awed murmuring throughout the lobby, and Virtue and the Angel turned to see the cause of the commotion.

Standing just outside the door was a huge mountain of a man. His shaggy brown mane swirled down to his shoulders, his teeth gleamed white through his thick beard, and his blue eyes glared balefully at Halfpenny Terwilliger. He was dressed in a handmade outfit composed entirely of the cured pelts of animals he had killed with his bare hands, and his boots, except for the steel heels, were also made of animal skins.

"I want *you!*" bellowed ManMountain Bates, pointing his finger at Terwilliger.

The desk clerk quickly touched his computer panel, and the thick front door slid shut.

"You've got to help me!" pleaded Terwilliger.

"You got yourself into this situation," said the Angel. "Get yourself out."

Terwilliger began cursing in frustration and terror, his eyes glued to the door. There was a sudden thudding noise, which was repeated at regular intervals of about five seconds apiece, and he knew that ManMountain Bates was attempting to hammer the door down with his fists.

"Can't you do *some*thing?" asked Virtue.

"There's no paper on him," replied the Angel emotionlessly.

The door began buckling, and a moment later it caved in entirely. The customers and staff scuttled for positions of safety as Bates entered the room.

"I'm ManMountain Bates!" he roared. "My father was a whirlwind and my mother was a lightning bolt! I'm Leviathan, the great beast of the murky deep!" He began pacing back and forth in front of the terrified Terwilliger. "I'm half cyclone and half tornado! I'm Behemoth, the giant hellcat of the Frontier! I was spawned in a supernova and baptized in a lake of lava! I can outfight and outdrink and outfuck and outswear any man or alien that was ever born or whelped or hatched!"

Terwilliger, tears running down his face, turned to the Angel, who had moved a few feet away from him.

"*Please!*" he whined.

"You think this midget is going to help you?" demanded Bates. He threw back his huge head and laughed. "Why, I'd crush him like an insect! I'd bite off his arms and legs and spit out the bones!"

The Angel stared at him with an expression of mild interest but made no comment.

"I've traveled half the galaxy to find you, you skinny little worm!" shouted Bates, turning his attention back to Terwilliger. "I've gone without food and without sleep and without women, just waiting for this moment."

He reached out with surprising swiftness for so large a man and grabbed the gambler by the front of his tunic, pulling him close.

"Now you're going to learn what happens to anyone who thinks he can cheat ManMountain Bates!"

He lifted Terwilliger high above his head with a single hand.

"Virtue!" wailed the gambler. "For God's sake, make him *do* something!"

The Angel watched, expressionless, as Bates wrapped his immense arms around Terwilliger and squeezed. There was a single agonized shriek, followed by a sharp cracking noise, and then Bates threw the gambler's lifeless body onto the lobby floor.

The huge man glared at the faces around the room, then placed a foot on Terwilliger's neck.

"I'm ManMountain Bates, and I've claimed my just and terrible vengeance!" he bellowed defiantly. "Now you've all got something you can tell your grandchildren about!"

He pivoted slowly until he was facing Virtue and the Angel.

"You!" he thundered, pointing an enormous finger at her.

"Me?" asked Virtue.

"He called to you," said Bates. "Why?"

Virtue tried to formulate an answer, found that her mouth was too dry to speak, and shrugged.

"He owed me two hundred thousand credits. What's your connection to him?"

"I hardly knew him," she managed to say.

"Who are you?"

"Oh, nobody very important," she said, taking a frightened step backward.

"If I find out that you've lied to me, I'll be back for you," he promised.

She swallowed once and nodded.

"Well?" he demanded, turning to glare at the desk clerk.

"Well what, sir?" asked the man, his voice shaking.

Bates pointed to the corpse at his feet. "Aren't you going to clean this mess up?"

"Yes, sir," said the clerk, pressing the Maintenance code on his computer. "Right away, sir."

"Good. I wouldn't want people to think that a classy hotel like this caters to ugly little worms like *that*." He emphasized the last word by spitting on Terwilliger's body, then looked up again. "All right! Everyone go on about your business."

Nobody moved.

"I mean *now!*" he roared.

Suddenly the lobby became a beehive of activity as people raced for exits and elevators. In another moment no one was left except Bates, Virtue, the Angel, the desk clerk, and two recently arrived maintenance men who were preparing to remove the little gambler's twisted body.

ManMountain Bates took a couple of steps toward Virtue and the Angel.

"You, too!" he said. "Get out."

The Angel began walking toward the front door.

"I've never seen anything like him!" whispered Virtue. "He's like some kind of primal force!"

"He talks too much," said the Angel.

"I heard that!" said Bates ominously.

The Angel continued walking, and Bates strode over, grabbed him by the shoulder, and spun him around.

"Nobody walks out on me when I'm talking to them," said Bates, a nasty smile on his face.

The Angel twisted free and met his gaze.

"I don't like to be touched," he said softly.

"You don't, eh?" Bates grinned, laying his hand on the Angel's shoulder again.

The Angel slapped his hand away. "No, I don't."

Bates suddenly shoved him on the chest, sending him careening backward into a wall.

"Leave him alone!" said Virtue. "He hasn't done anything to you!"

"He insulted me," said Bates, taking a menacing step toward the Angel. "Besides, my blood's up now! There's nothing like breaking a back to get a man's juices flowing."

"Angel, tell him you're sorry and let's get the hell out of here!" said Virtue desperately, visions of wealth and fame departing as she imagined the Angel's body lying in a crumpled heap next to Terwilliger's.

"You're the Angel?" demanded Bates, a look of uncertainty momentarily flickering across his face.

"That's right."

"Then why did you say I talked too much?"

"Because you do," replied the Angel.

"I don't care who you've killed!" bellowed Bates, suddenly enraged again. "You're going to apologize, or I'm going to be known as the man who killed the Angel with his bare hands."

The Angel stared coldly at him for a long moment. Finally he spoke.

"I'm sorry that you talk too much."

"That's it!" growled Bates. "You're a dead man! There's going to be one more angel in hell tonight!"

He took two more steps forward and was within arm's reach of the Angel.

"You can still stop," said the Angel. "There's no paper on you."

Bates roared a curse, reached back, and swung a haymaker at the Angel's head. The Angel ducked, and the huge man's fist went right through the wall. While he was trying to extricate his hand, the Angel reached forward, made two incredibly quick motions with his right hand, and stepped aside.

Bates bellowed another curse as he tried once again to pull his hand out of the wall. Then a curious expression spread across his face, and he slowly looked down to where his innards were spilling out through the slash in the front of his coat.

"I don't believe it!" he muttered, trying to hold himself together with his free hand.

The Angel retriggered his weapon to the mechanism hidden beneath his sleeve.

"But I'm ManMountain Bates!" murmured the giant incredulously, and died.

"My God!" exclaimed Virtue, staring with morbid fascination at Bates, who still hung from the wall by his hand. "What did you cut him with?"

"Something sharp," replied the Angel calmly. He walked

over to the registration desk. "You'd better call the police," he said.

"I hit the alarm the second that guy broke down the door," answered the clerk, his face pale and sweating. "They'll be here any minute now."

"I trust that you'll be willing to testify that I killed him in self-defense," continued the Angel.

"Absolutely, Mr. . . . ah . . . Mr. Angel?"

The Angel stared at him for a moment, then turned to Virtue.

"This was your fault, you know," he said.

"Mine?" she repeated.

He nodded. "If you hadn't promised Terwilliger that I'd protect him, he wouldn't have waited around here until Bates showed up."

"Then Bates would have killed him two hundred feet away from here, or half a mile, or at the spaceport," said Virtue. "Don't go blaming me for that."

"But *I* wouldn't have had to kill Bates," explained the Angel patiently. "It was just wasted effort. He's not worth a credit anywhere in the Frontier."

"*That's* all he represents to you?" said Virtue unbelievingly. "Just a wasted effort? My God, he was Leviathan himself, just like he said!"

"He was just a man. He bled like any other."

The police arrived then, and the Angel spent the next couple of minutes recounting the events to a very respectful officer, who had the good sense not to ask him to produce his passport.

Finally, after he finished making his statement, and the officer was interviewing the desk clerk, and two more policemen were trying to remove Bates's hand from the wall, the Angel walked over to Virtue once again.

"By the way, exactly what was it that Terwilliger did for you in exchange for my protection?"

"Nothing."

"I asked you a question," he said. "I expect an answer."

"He sent a totally unnecessary message to a man I'm never going to see again," said Virtue earnestly, staring in awe at the huge corpse of ManMountain Bates.

"Cain?" he asked.

She turned to him and smiled.

"Who's Cain?"

18.

Simple Simon met a pieman going to the fair;
Simple Simon killed the pieman on the thoroughfare.
Simple Simon likes the taste of his new outlaw life:
It's not for pies that Simon needs his shining steel knife.

He never used a knife; that was just a case of Black
Orpheus practicing a little poetic license.

And he was anything but simple.

In fact, he had degrees in mathematics and laser optics and
two or three of the more esoteric sciences, and he taught at
one of the larger universities on Lodin XI for the better part
of a decade. He was heavily invested in the commodities
market when a bumper crop of *kirtt,* the Lodinian equivalent
of wheat, sent prices plummeting down and wiping out his
life's savings. It was shortly thereafter that he decided a
professor's salary would never buy him all the things that he
wanted.

So he left the Democracy and set out for the Inner Frontier,
where he embarked on a new course of studies, which included a major in murder and a minor in bigamy. He killed
his first four wives and managed to collect the insurance on
three of them before it occurred to him that there was a lot
more money to be made if he didn't limit his killing to his
spouses.

He forthwith became a free-lance killer for hire. Because
he had a scientific turn of mind, he favored laser weapons of
his own creation; and because he had a healthy respect for
those with greater physical skills than himself, he tended to

specialize in meticulously devised deathtraps rather than in personal confrontations.

His new profession forced a certain degree of modesty upon him, so much so that he took on the protective coloration of the scientific illiterate. Orpheus saw right through him, of course—seeing through façades was one of the things he did best—and named him Simple Simon as a private joke. The name stuck, and before long Simple Simon's holograph was gracing the walls of the Inner Frontier's postal stations.

The Angel stood in the spaceport's post office, glancing briefly at Simon's face while checking to see if there were any new fugitives worthy of his attention, while Virtue, her satchel slung over her shoulder, stood in the doorway and waited for him.

"I thought you were closing in on Santiago," she said as he rejoined her. "Why bother studying a bunch of second-rate villains?"

"Force of habit," he replied, heading off down the corridor that led to his spaceship. "Besides, for all I know Cain or somebody else has already killed him—and I've still got a planet to buy."

"So in effect, the post office wall is your professional trade journal," commented Virtue.

"I never thought of it that way."

"That's because you're not a journalist," she said.

There was considerably less red tape this time than during their last trip through the spaceport—Virtue guessed that the local authorities had issued orders to get the Angel off the planet as swiftly as possible—and a few minutes later they were in one of the three dozen rental hangars for private spacecraft, climbing into the ship.

"Something's wrong," said the Angel, inspecting the auxiliary control panel that was just inside the hatch.

"What do you mean?"

"The security system's been tripped. Don't touch anything."

"Is it going to explode?" she asked apprehensively.

He shook his head. "I doubt it. If they'd planted a bomb, you'd have triggered it the moment you set foot on the ship."

"Is that why you let me go through the hatch first?" she demanded.

He made no reply, but looked carefully around for another

minute without moving farther into the ship, then turned back to her.

"All right," he said. "Let's get back on the ground—carefully."

She followed him through the hatch, and a moment later she was standing some fifty feet away, staring at the ship, while the Angel was speaking to spaceport security on an intercom.

"Nothing's happening," she said when he rejoined her.

"If it didn't blow up while you were walking around in it, it's not likely to blow up just because you're looking at it," he said.

"Then what was done to it?" she asked.

"That's what I intend to find out."

A moment later a harassed-looking security officer appeared.

"What seems to be the problem?" he asked.

"Someone's been in my ship since I landed," said the Angel.

"Oh? Who?"

"That's what I'd like to find out."

The security officer walked to the intercom, asked for an office extension, whispered in low tones for a moment, and then returned to the Angel.

"From what I understand, your mechanic came by just before sunrise."

"I don't carry a mechanic."

"They tell me that his papers were all in order, and that he even had a work order with your signature on it."

"Which signature?" demanded the Angel sharply.

"The Angel, I suppose," responded the officer. "Your identity isn't exactly a secret since last night."

"How did they know it was my signature?" said the Angel. "What did they compare it against?"

"How the hell do I know?" asked the officer. "My guess is that they didn't bother to check it against anything. The man works for a reputable firm. They probably took him at his word."

"What repairs did he say he planned to make?"

"I haven't the slightest idea," said the security officer.

"Why not?"

"Look—I've spent the last five hours helping the shipping department trying to track down a missing animal that was supposedly flown in from the Antares Sector. I can find out what you want to know, but I'll have to check with security and maintenance and whoever the hell else is likely to have his work order on file.''

"Do so immediately," said the Angel. "Then check with his employer and see if they've ever heard of him. And then get a mechanic that you can personally vouch for and have him check my ship over from top to bottom."

"Where can I reach you?" asked the security officer.

"I'll be in the restaurant, waiting for your report."

"It may take a while."

"See that it doesn't."

The Angel headed off down the corridor, followed by Virtue. They passed several souvenir shops and a pair of alien restaurants and finally came to a large restaurant that catered to Men. The bounty hunter looked around, then walked past a number of empty tables until he came to one in the corner of the room that suited him.

"Why here?" asked Virtue, sitting down opposite him.

"Somebody sabotaged my ship," he said. "I feel more comfortable sitting with my back to the wall."

"But you don't mind having *my* back facing a doorway?" she demanded.

"Not in the least," he replied.

"Were you always this considerate of others, or did it just come with maturity?" she asked sarcastically.

"Sit anywhere you want," he said, indicating a number of empty tables. "It makes no difference to me."

She sighed. "Let's change the subject. Did you learn anything useful this morning?"

"I learned the name and location of the next world we'll be visiting."

"Would you care to share that little tidbit of information, or are we going to play guessing games?"

"I'll tell you once we've left Sunnybeach."

"This is silly!" she snapped. "Even if you tell me what planet we're going to, I don't know who or what you're looking for there. Do you really think I'll book passage out of here while you're waiting for the mechanic to check out your ship?"

"No."

"Then why are you being like this?"

"Because for a man in my profession, the most important single virtue is not the mastery of weapons or physical combat, but meticulous attention to detail."

"What has that got to do with what we're talking about?"

"Listen carefully, because I'm only going to explain it once," said the Angel, lighting up a thin cigar. "If I tell you the name of our next port of call, there are only two things you can do with that information: ignore it or use it. If you ignore it, as you almost certainly will, you didn't need it in the first place—but if you use it, you will use it to my detriment."

"But you told me back on New Ecuador that we'd be coming to Sunnybeach next," she pointed out.

"My ship was operational on New Ecuador," he replied. "If you had acted independently on that information, you would never have lived to see Sunnybeach."

"I can't tell you how touched I am by such trust," she said cynically.

"My trust isn't lightly given," he responded. "You've done nothing to earn it."

"What are you talking about? I told you all about Cain, didn't I?"

"Betraying a partner is not exactly the sort of behavior that inspires confidence," said the Angel. He paused. "Did I mention that I stopped by the information center of your hotel while you were still asleep this morning?"

"Oh?"

He nodded. "I was curious about the message you had Terwilliger send to Cain yesterday afternoon. The person on duty was kind enough to show me a copy of it."

"He's not allowed to do that!"

"Once I discussed the alternatives with him, he seemed more than happy to accommodate me."

"I told you about it last night," said Virtue defensively. "It doesn't mean a damned thing. I was just hedging my bets—but you're the one I've put my money on."

He stared at her and made no reply.

"Look," she continued. "I could have stayed at the spaceport yesterday after you left for town and caught the next ship out of here. I didn't. That ought to prove something to you."

"It proves that you have a well-developed sense of self-preservation," he replied.

"I don't know why I waste my time talking to you!" she snapped.

"Because you want to find Santiago," said the Angel, signaling to a waitress and gesturing for her to bring two coffees. "The problem," he continued, "is that *he* seems to have found *us* first."

"You think Santiago sabotaged the ship?" asked Virtue.

"Not personally, of course. But I suspect that he ordered it done."

"Why didn't he just have you killed?"

"I'm a little harder to kill than you might think," he said quietly.

"But what purpose could be gained by messing around with the ship?" she persisted. "It can't be a warning. He must know he can't scare you off."

"That's what disturbs me," said the Angel. "It doesn't make any sense—and Santiago is not a stupid man."

"Maybe it was ordered by Cain or the Swagman," she suggested. "They certainly have a stake in delaying you."

He shook his head. "They have an even greater stake in *stopping* me."

"Just because it hasn't exploded yet doesn't mean there's not a bomb."

"Nobody is going to mourn or avenge either of us," replied the Angel. "If there was a bomb, it would have exploded the instant we entered the ship."

"Speak for yourself!" she snapped. "I've got lots of friends."

"I doubt it," said the Angel.

The coffee arrived, and they waited until the waitress was out of earshot before speaking again.

"Could it have been a friend of ManMountain Bates?" asked Virtue.

"I doubt that he had any friends," replied the Angel. "Besides, one doesn't avenge a friend's death by damaging his killer's ship." He frowned. "It's got to be Santiago's doing. I just wish it made a little more sense to me."

A woman dressed in mechanic's clothing entered the coffee shop, looked around, and approached their table.

"Are you the . . . Are you Mr. William Jennings?" she asked hesitantly.

"Yes."

"I've just taken a look at your ship," she said. "I'll have to go over it much more thoroughly before I can give you a complete damage report, but you were right: someone's been tampering with it."

"I assume there were no explosives?"

She shook her head. "Not that I've been able to find. It doesn't look like anyone was out to kill you, just to keep you here for a few days."

"How many?"

"Based on what I've found so far, I'd guess that it'll take two or three days to get the parts shipped in and installed." She paused. "It could come to a lot of money. Do you want an estimate first?"

The Angel shook his head. "Just do whatever's necessary to get it working."

"Where can I contact you when it's ready?" she asked.

"You can't," he said. "But I'll be checking in a couple of times every day. Who should I ask for?"

She gave him her name and identification number, then left the coffee shop.

"You still look disturbed," observed Virtue.

"I still am," he replied. "What does Santiago think he gains by tying me down here for two or three days? I can't be that close to him yet."

He finished his coffee and ordered another.

"Why don't we go to the bar?" suggested Virtue, staring distastefully at her coffee.

"Because we want to keep our heads clear until we figure out what's going on," replied the Angel with equal distaste.

She glared at him for a moment, then shrugged and sipped from her half-empty cup.

They sat in silence for another five minutes, and then the security officer sought out the Angel.

"I've been checking up on the mechanic . . ." he began.

"His company never heard of him, and you can't find him in the directory," said the Angel. It was not a question.

The officer sighed and nodded. "Somebody really screwed up on this one." He pulled out a two-dimensional copy of the mechanic's identification card. "This is the guy. Does he look familiar to you?"

The Angel studied the photograph, which appeared just above the man's signature and thumbprint.

"No," he said. "Do you mind if I keep this?"

"Not at all," said the officer. "It's in the computer if we need another copy." He paused. "We'll keep checking from this end, and I assume that you have . . . ah, certain private sources?"

The Angel made no reply.

"Well, then," said the officer, "if you'll excuse me, I've got to get back to work."

"On the saboteur?"

He shook his head. "The scanner's broken down at one of the passenger terminals," he said apologetically. "Just one of those days. But I'll make sure that the office follows up on your mysterious mechanic."

The Angel stared at him.

"If they haven't got it solved by tomorrow morning, I'll take charge of the investigation myself," he promised with a nervous smile. He backed away, stumbled against a table, apologized, then turned and walked rapidly out of the coffee shop.

"Mind if I take a look?" asked Virtue.

"Be my guest," said the Angel, handing the card to her.

She stared at the bearded face. "Five'll get you ten that he's clean-shaven by now—if all that hair was real in the first place."

She returned the card to him. He took one last look at it, then slipped it into a pocket, threw a couple of coins on the table, and got to his feet.

"Let's go," he said.

"Where to?"

"We're not going to come up with answers hanging around here," said the Angel. "And the spaceport's bureaucracy isn't going to be of any use to us." He paused. "In a way, this may have been a blessing in disguise."

"How do you figure that?" she asked.

"Because if I can find the man who sabotaged my ship, I may be able to get a direct line to Santiago. It could save us a couple of weeks."

"Where will we start looking for him?"

"*We* aren't looking for him; *I* am," he said firmly. "You're going back to your hotel to wait for me."

"The hell I am!"

He stared coldly at her. "If I wouldn't tell you our next

port of call, you may be sure that I won't allow you to come with me if there's a chance that I might actually find out where Santiago is.''

She was about to protest again, but something in his colorless eyes made her decide against it.

They walked silently through the spaceport to the vehicle rental area. When they arrived, Virtue turned to the Angel.

"Separate transportation again?" she asked caustically.

He shook his head. "We'll go together."

"It can't be courtesy, and we've already ruled out chivalry," she said suspiciously.

"I want to make certain that you go directly to your hotel."

"Are you going to stand guard outside my door to make sure I stay there?"

"Once you've walked in the front door, I don't much care what you do, as long as you don't try to follow me."

The Angel rented a vehicle, and as they began the ten-minute journey into town, it became apparent that the air-conditioning system had seen better days. Virtue decided not to complain about it until he did, and was amazed to find that his face was as dry at the end of the trip as it had been within the spaceport, while she herself was soaked to the skin.

The Angel pulled up to the entrance of the Welcome Inn, where workmen were busily replacing the door ManMountain Bates had broken down, and turned to face her.

"I won't be in touch with you until tomorrow, unless I find what I'm looking for. I warn you once again not to follow me. Since I don't know where to begin, I'm going to start with the lowest examples of the local criminal element and work my way up. They're not likely to prove a very friendly or accommodating lot, and there's very little likelihood that I can protect you if you're skulking around in the shadows—so just go to your room, have dinner, and relax."

"And you think you can find out who sabotaged the ship by intimidating a bunch of small-time crooks?" she said sardonically.

"Probably not," he admitted. "Most likely the man who worked on the ship is long gone from Sunnybeach. But I'm stuck here for the next few days, and I've got to start *some*-where, so—"

Suddenly he stopped speaking and stared intently out the window at a shabbily dressed panhandler who was begging for coins some fifty feet away.

Finally the Angel smiled.

"Now it all makes sense," he said softly.

"What does?"

"Never mind." He turned back to her. "When you go into the hotel, find yourself a nice, comfortable seat in the lobby."

"What are you talking about?"

"You heard me."

"I'm hot and I'm tired, and as long as I'm stuck in this hellhole, I intend to go to my room, take a dryshower, and change my clothes."

"I wouldn't advise it," said the Angel.

"I'm getting a little bit sick and tired of taking orders from you!" snapped Virtue.

"All right," he said with a shrug. "Do what you want."

"*Why* shouldn't I go to my room?" she demanded, suddenly unsure of herself.

"Because I was operating under a false premise," he explained. "I thought someone was out to stop me. It's *you* he's after." He reached forward to the control panel and hit the door latch. "Now walk into the lobby and don't look around you."

Suddenly Virtue found herself stepping out onto the sidewalk, oblivious to the intense heat, as the Angel pulled away and sped off into the distance. Forcing herself to look straight ahead, she walked past the desk, then turned left and found a chair that was partially hidden from the doorway.

She sat absolutely motionless, afraid to call any attention to herself, and wondered what to do next. She began furtively studying the people in the lobby, trying to determine which of them looked like killers, and came to the uneasy conclusion that they *all* did.

Finally, after what seemed an eternity, the Angel entered the lobby, accompanied by the panhandler, who looked terribly confused. The bounty hunter glanced in her direction and jerked his head.

She stood up immediately and gestured questioningly toward herself. He nodded, and as she joined them on their way to the elevator she noticed that the Angel had a small hand weapon pressed against the panhandler's back.

"I keep telling you, sir—you're making a terrible mistake," whined the panhandler when the three of them were alone in the elevator, ascending to Virtue's floor. "I've never seen you before in my life, honest to God I haven't."

"But *I've* seen *you*," replied the Angel grimly. "Staring out at me from the post office wall."

"I've never even been to the post office."

The Angel made no reply, and a few seconds later the elevator came to a stop.

"Who is he?" asked Virtue as they stepped out into the empty corridor.

"His name's Simple Simon," said the Angel, prodding the panhandler with his weapon until the man began walking. "And he's just a little more sophisticated than he appears to be."

"Well, there you are, sir," said the panhandler. "My name's not Simon at all. It's Brubaker, sir, Robert Brubaker. I have my identification with me."

"Keep walking," said the Angel.

"If he's really a wanted killer, how did he get past customs?" asked Virtue.

"The same way William Jennings did," said the Angel. "If I wanted, I could come up with ten authentic passports proving that *I* was Robert Brubaker."

"I suppose you could, at that," acknowledged Virtue.

"But I *am* Robert Brubaker!" protested the panhandler. "I'm an honest, hardworking man, I am."

"Hardworking, anyway," said the Angel as they came to Virtue's room. "Stop here."

The panhandler came to a halt.

"All right," said the Angel, backing about fifteen feet down the corridor. "Virtue, open the door and then step aside. *You*," he continued, gesturing toward the panhandler with his weapon, "walk in first."

"Then can I go home?" asked the man.

"Then we'll talk about it."

Virtue extended her hand, let the computer lock scan her thumbprint, and jumped back as the door slid into the wall. The panhandler, shaking his head and looking as if he truly believed he had fallen into the company of a madman, sighed and stepped into the room.

Nothing happened.

The Angel walked to the doorway.

"Go over to the window," he commanded.

The panhandler did as he was told.

"Now sit on each chair and then on the bed."

The Angel waited while the panhandler followed his orders, then nodded to Virtue. She entered the room, and then the Angel stepped inside the doorway.

"You must have been wrong," commented Virtue.

"Close the door and be quiet," said the Angel, scrutinizing the room.

"Hey!" said the panhandler irately. "You promised to let me go!"

"I promised that we'd talk," said the Angel, walking carefully around the perimeter of the room, his gaze darting from one piece of furniture to another. "Are you ready to tell me where it is?"

"Where *what* is?" demanded the man.

"My closet!" exclaimed Virtue suddenly.

"Open it," the Angel ordered the panhandler.

"It's already open," said Virtue, starting to back away from it. "This is just a holographic projection."

"How do you turn it off?"

"I don't know."

"Call down to the desk and tell them to disconnect it," said the Angel.

She did as he ordered, and a moment later the closet flickered out of existence, leaving a single metal rod stretched along a four-foot length of wall.

"That's a relief!" she breathed. "You had me believing you for a minute there."

The panhandler walked up to the Angel. "I've got a wife and three kids depending on me," he said plaintively. "Can't I go now?"

The Angel pushed him down into a chair. "You're dead meat, Simon," he said. "The only question is whether I kill you now or later."

"But my name isn't Simon!" shouted the man desperately. "I'm Robert Brubaker!"

"Shut up," said the Angel quietly. He continued his methodical inspection of the room. When he came to the bathroom door he stopped and turned to the panhandler with a smile on his face.

"Smart," he said admiringly. "Very smart, Simon."

"I don't know what you're talking about."

"The way you rigged it."

"I didn't rig anything!"

"You couldn't be sure a maid wouldn't enter the room before Virtue did, so you couldn't rig it to kill the first person to walk through the door or reach into the closet."

"Look," said the panhandler. "If I walk into the bathroom, *then* will you let me go?"

"Yes," assented the Angel. "But you look hot and uncomfortable. I think maybe you'd better treat yourself to a dryshower, first."

"I don't need a dryshower. I just want to leave."

"But I insist."

"Damn it!" yelled the panhandler. "You pull a weapon on me, drag me up here, accuse me of being someone I never heard of, and threaten to kill me! Isn't that enough? Can't you just leave me alone now?"

"After your dryshower," said the Angel.

"I'm not getting undressed in front of a strange woman."

"You can keep your clothes on."

"Ma'am?" he pleaded, turning to Virtue. "Can't you make him leave me alone? I'm just a street beggar who never did anyone any harm!"

"She's not in charge here," said the Angel, reaching out and grabbing him firmly by the wrist. "Let's get on with it."

The panhandler pulled back, and the Angel released him.

"All right," muttered the panhandler. "You win."

"Then he really *is* Simple Simon?" exclaimed Virtue.

"I told you he was."

"Why the dryshower?" she asked.

"It's the one thing a maid could reasonably be expected to leave alone, even if she cleaned the bathroom," said the Angel. "And on a planet where the average temperature is somewhere around a hundred and twenty-five degrees, it's the first thing you'd head for once you came back here." He turned to Simon. "Am I right?"

Simple Simon nodded his head wearily.

"Explosives or lasers?" asked the Angel.

"Lasers."

"Why do you want to kill *me*?" demanded Virtue.

"There's a guy on Pegasus who's put out a hit on you," replied Simon.

"Dimitri Sokol?" she said, surprised.

"Yeah, that's the one."

"But he already tried on Goldenrod," said Virtue. "I thought that was all over."

"This isn't a game, and it's not played by gentleman's rules," interjected the Angel. "Just because Sokol's failed once doesn't mean he's going to give up." He paused. "When I spotted our friend here standing outside the hotel, I realized that I had been wrong about Santiago sabotaging the ship. Simon had to scout the place out last night in order to learn your number, so he had to know that I wasn't staying here. The fact that he was here anyway meant it was *you* he was after. He was just waiting around so that he could confirm your death. Probably Sokol required a holograph, or maybe even your body itself." The Angel turned to Simon. "Obviously you sabotaged my ship to keep her on Sunnybeach until you could kill her—but why go to such elaborate lengths? Why not just pick her off when we landed at the spaceport?"

Simon made no reply.

"If I have ask again," said the Angel softly, "you'll wish you had answered the first time."

Simple Simon stared into his colorless eyes and decided that he was telling the truth.

"Sokol passed the word that she travels with bounty hunters—first the Songbird, then Father William, and now you. That meant if I tried for a hit out in the open, I'd have to go for you, too, and I didn't like the odds. So I figured the safest way to go about it was to damage your ship and kill her when she came back here. Believe me, Angel," he said sincerely, "I never intended to kill you. I did everything I could to keep you out of the way while I went about my business."

"You make it sound as if killing *me* is perfectly acceptable!" snapped Virtue.

"Well, you must have done *something* to him, or he wouldn't have ordered the hit," said Simon.

"What I did is between him and me," said Virtue.

"Not anymore, obviously," commented the Angel. He turned to Simple Simon. "I've got one last question to ask you: How much did Sokol offer?"

"Fifty thousand credits."

"That much?" said Virtue, impressed.

"Virtue, I want you to remember that figure," said the Angel. "All right, Simon. It's time for that dryshower."

"But I didn't try to kill you!" said Simon desperately.

"You're a wanted man, with a price on your head."

"Dead or alive!" protested Simon. "Contact the police and turn me over to them!"

"The dryshower," said the Angel emotionlessly.

"But why? I'm worth the same to you either way!"

"I'm in a race, and you cost me three days."

"And you're going to kill me for that? This is crazy!"

The Angel pointed his weapon at Simple Simon. "Start walking or I'll kill you right where you're sitting."

Simon, very real tears of fear streaming down his face, reluctantly got to his feet and walked into the bathroom. The Angel followed him, and a moment later Virtue heard a single shriek of utter agony. Then the Angel emerged.

"Good riddance," said Virtue. "Imagine! The son of a bitch didn't see anything wrong with killing me!"

"After I collect the reward, I think I'll inform your friend Sokol that I expect him to pay for the repairs to my ship."

"He'll never do it."

"I have ways of encouraging him," said the Angel dryly. "Now I want you to take a look at Simple Simon."

"Why?"

"Because I said to."

She shrugged and walked into the bathroom. Simple Simon lay on his back, his face and part of his torso burned away by the hundreds of tiny laser beams that had struck him when the Angel activated the dryshower. There was a smell of cooking flesh, and thin streams of black smoke rose from a number of his wounds.

Virtue resisted the urge to vomit and staggered back into the bedroom.

"God, he looks horrible!" she admitted.

"He died a horrible death," replied the Angel calmly.

"Couldn't you have turned him over to the police?" she asked. "Nobody deserves to die like that."

"I could have."

"Then why didn't you?"

"Because you needed an object lesson."

"*He* died because you wanted to give *me* an object lesson?" she said incredulously.

"He was always going to die, whether I killed him or the government did," replied the Angel. "Don't waste too many tears on him. He murdered more than twenty-five men and women, and the death he died was meant for you."

"What am I suppose to have learned from all this?" asked Virtue.

"You are a reasonably courageous and resourceful woman," began the Angel.

"Thank you," she said sardonically.

"But you are also completely unimaginative," he continued. "You act rashly, without any thought of consequences. I wanted you to see Simon's corpse, because I want you to know that you're associating with people for whom this is not an exciting adventure but a deadly serious business."

"I already know that."

"I wanted to reinforce that knowledge," said the Angel, "before I told you what I have to say next."

"And what is that?" she asked apprehensively.

"I have had to kill two men in the past twenty-four hours. Neither of them had any argument with *me*."

"Bates didn't have any argument with *me*, either," she interrupted. "He was after Terwilliger."

"Who in turn was here to see you," said the Angel. "You have caused me a great deal of inconvenience, and have cost me three days in my pursuit of Santiago."

"What are you leading up to?"

"Up until now I was perfectly willing to let you go your own way whenever you wanted," he said. "But after our stay on Sunnybeach, you *owe* me, and when we reach Santiago's planet you're going to pay off."

"How?"

"I'll let you know when we get there. But if you try to leave me before then, or disobey my orders once we're there, then I promise you that I'll accept Dimitri Sokol's commission and kill you myself."

As she looked into his cold, lifeless eyes, she knew that he was telling her the truth, and that knowledge terrified her more than anything Sokol or even Santiago could ever threaten to do to her.

Part 5

Moonripple's Book

19.

Moonripple, Moonripple, touring the stars,
Has polished the wax on a thousand bars,
Has trod on the soil of a hundred worlds,
Has found only pebbles while searching for pearls.

Beneath the grease stains and the tattered clothes, she was actually quite a pretty girl. She had blue eyes that had seen too many things and shed too many tears, square shoulders that had borne too many burdens, slender fingers that would have been soft and white in a gentler life.

If she had any name other than Moonripple, she couldn't remember it. If she had ever called any world home, she couldn't remember *it*, either.

She was nineteen years old, and she had already met Black Orpheus four times. He even began joking that he'd wander into the least likely bar on the least likely planet he could think of, and there would be Moonripple, scrubbing floors, cleaning tables, or washing dishes. The highlight of her brief life was the single verse he created about her one evening on Voorhite XIV, when he was playing his lute and singing his ballad to keep his mind off the storm that was raging through the chlorine atmosphere just beyond the human colony's domed enclosure.

She fascinated him, this waif with a future that seemed no more promising than her past. Where did she come from? How many worlds had she been to? What was she searching for? Had she no higher aspiration than to be a barmaid to the galaxy? She tried to help him, but she truly didn't know any of the answers.

The last time he saw her was on Trefoil III. She was waiting on some twenty-five tables by herself and falling increasingly behind. When her employer began yelling at her and threatening to beat her if her performance didn't improve, Orpheus stepped forward and stated that since she couldn't remember when she had been born, he was officially declaring this to be her seventeenth birthday and was taking her out to dinner. The crowd was thirsty and ill tempered, and probably not even Sebastian Cain or Peacemaker MacDougal could have taken the tavern's only barmaid away and emerged unscathed, but because he was Black Orpheus they let him lead her out of the bar without a word of protest.

He fed her, and bought her new clothes, and even offered to take her with him until he could find her a permanent job on some other world. She replied with disarming sincerity that she bore her employer no ill will and had no desire for any other type of work. Orpheus got the feeling that she was afraid to form any bond, either emotional or financial, that might tie her down to a particular world until she finally found the as-yet-undefined thing she was searching for. They talked far into the morning, the Bard who took such pleasure in the endless variety of Men and worlds he visited, completely unable to understand the wanderlust of one who seemed to take no pleasure in anything.

Finally, when it was time for him to leave, he offered her a few hundred credits, enough to book passage to another planet with another tavern, but she refused, explaining that it rarely took her more than a month or two to save enough money to move on to the next world, and that she would feel guilty about taking money from a man who had already done so much for her.

As Orpheus left for his next port of call, he was convinced that he would regularly encounter her every couple of years—but they never met again, for while he continued his aimless journey, immortalizing men and events, Moonripple finally came, after many false starts and digressions, to the colony world of Safe Harbor, which was where Cain first encountered her.

He wandered into the Barleycorn, the larger of the two local taverns, shortly after Schussler landed in late afternoon.

It was totally empty. He checked the sign on the door, which proclaimed "We Never Close," shrugged, and sat down at a table.

"I'll be with you in just a moment, sir," said Moonripple, coming out of the kitchen with a huge pitcher of beer, which she carried over to a large table across the room.

She smiled at him, disappeared again, and returned half a minute later carrying an enormous roast, which she set down next to the pitcher.

"That looks like real meat," remarked Cain.

"It is," she said proudly. "We grow our own beef on Safe Harbor." She approached Cain's table. "May I help you, sir?"

"It's a possibility," he replied. "I'm looking for someone."

"Who?"

"Billy Three-Eyes. Ever hear of him?"

She nodded. "Yes, sir."

"Do you happen to know where he is?"

"He's dead, sir."

Cain frowned. "You're sure?"

She nodded again.

"When and where?"

"He was killed right out there," she said, indicating the street, "by a man called MacDougal."

"*Peacemaker* MacDougal?" asked Cain.

"Yes, sir. That was his name."

"Shit!" muttered Cain. He looked up at the girl. "Did he have any friends here?"

"Mr. MacDougal?"

"Billy Three-Eyes."

"Oh, yes," she said. "Everybody liked Billy."

"We must not be talking about the same man."

"I'm sure we are, sir," said Moonripple. "After all, how many men could have been called Billy Three-Eyes?"

"He had a big scar on his forehead?"

"Right above the bridge of his nose. Yes, sir."

"And everybody *liked* him?" continued Cain, surprised.

"Yes, sir," replied Moonripple. "He was always telling funny stories. I was very sorry when he died."

"Who would you say was his closest friend on Safe Harbor?"

She shrugged. "I don't know, sir. I only saw him when he was in here."

"Did he usually come alone?"

"Yes, sir. But once he got here, he talked to everybody."

"I see," said Cain. He sighed. "Well, I might as well stick around and talk to some of the people *he* talked to. Bring me a beer, will you?"

"Yes, sir," said Moonripple. She walked to the bar, held a glass under a tap, and returned to him.

"Thanks," said Cain.

"I should tell you, sir, that hardly anybody will show up for another three or four hours."

"How about the group that's coming by for dinner?" asked Cain, pointing toward the roast.

She smiled. "Oh, that's not a group. It's just for one man."

"There's got to be four or five pounds of meat there," said Cain. "Do you mean to tell me that one man is going to eat it all?"

Moonripple nodded. "Oh, yes, sir. And the chocolate cake that's in the oven."

Cain stared at the roast again. "Is he doing it on some kind of a bet?" he asked, curious.

"No, sir," answered Moonripple. "He has the same meal every day."

"He wouldn't happen to be eleven feet three inches tall, with orange hair, would he?" asked Cain, only half joking.

The girl laughed. "No, sir. He's only a man."

"If he can pack that much food away, there's nothing *only* about him," replied Cain. He paused. "By the way, how long has Billy Three-Eyes been dead?"

"Four or five months, sir." She paused. "Oh!" she said suddenly. "I forgot the potatoes!"

"You ought to change your sign out front," commented Cain. "I thought this place was just a tavern."

"It is."

"But you're serving food," he observed.

"Only to Father William. He's kind of a special customer." She turned to go to the kitchen, but Cain grabbed her arm.

"Father William's on Safe Harbor?" he demanded.

"Yes, sir. He'll be by in just a few minutes."

"How long has he been here?"

"I'm not sure, sir," said Moonripple. "Maybe a week."

"I didn't see his tent on my way into town."

"Tent, sir?"

"He's a preacher."

"I know, sir, but he says he's on vacation."

Cain frowned. "Did he ask about Billy Three-Eyes, too?"

"No, sir." She looked uncomfortable. "You're hurting my arm, sir."

"I'm sorry," said Cain, releasing the girl. "You're sure he didn't say anything about Billy Three-Eyes?"

"Not to me, sir." She began walking to the kitchen. "Excuse me, but I have to get his potatoes."

"Did he mention Santiago?" asked Cain.

"Why should he do that?" asked Moonripple, stopping a few feet short of the kitchen door.

"Because he's a bounty hunter as well as a preacher."

"What does that have to do with Santiago?"

Cain stared at her, amazed by her ignorance. "He's the most wanted outlaw on the Frontier."

"You must be wrong, sir," said Moonripple, leaning forward so that the door could sense her presence and slide back to admit her. "Santiago is a hero."

"To who?" asked Cain.

She laughed as if he had just told a joke, and before he could question her further she was inside the kitchen, leaving him to sip his beer thoughtfully and stare at the door that quickly hid her from view.

She emerged a moment later, carrying a large serving dish filled with potatoes au gratin.

"Tell me about Santiago," said Cain as she walked over to Father William's table.

"I don't know him, sir," said Moonripple.

"What makes you think he's a hero?"

"Everybody says so."

"Who's everybody?" persisted Cain.

"Oh, just lots of people," she said with a shrug. "Can I get you another beer, sir?"

"I'd rather you talked to me about Santiago," said Cain.

"But I don't know him," protested Moonripple.

"He's eleven feet tall and he's got orange hair," said a deep voice from the doorway. "What else do you want to know?"

Cain turned and saw a large, extremely heavy black-clad man, his twin laser pistols clearly visible, standing in the doorway.

"You're Father William?" he asked.

"At your service," said Father William, walking over and extending a huge hand. "And you are . . . ?"

"Sebastian Cain," said Cain, surprised by the strength in the pudgy fingers.

"Ah!" said Father William with a smile. "You're Virtue MacKenzie's friend!"

Cain nodded. "And you're the man who saved her life back on Goldenrod."

"The Lord was her savior," replied Father William. "I am merely His instrument."

"What's His instrument doing on an out-of-the-way little world like Safe Harbor?" asked Cain.

"You wouldn't believe me if I told you," said Father William with a smile.

"Probably not—but suppose you tell me anyway and let me make up my own mind."

"Well, the truth of the matter is that when I found out what wonderful food this child cooks"—he smiled at Moonripple— "I decided that it was time to take a vacation, and since I'm a man who likes his comforts, what better place than right here?"

"Do you really cook the food yourself?" asked Cain.

"Yes, sir," said Moonripple.

He turned back to Father William. "You still haven't told me what you were doing here in the first place."

Father William smiled again, and the fingers of his right hand drifted down toward the hilt of a pistol. "I wasn't aware that I was obliged to do so."

"Just trying to make conversation," said Cain with a shrug.

"As long as you aren't insisting, then I have no objection to telling you," said the preacher. "I set down here a few days ago because my ship needed some minor repairs." He walked over to his table. "I'll be happy to continue our conversation, but it would be sinful to let this magnificent repast get cold. Will you join me?"

"I'll sit with you," said Cain, getting up and walking over. "But I'm not very hungry."

"What a shame," said Father William insincerely. He picked up an oversized napkin, tied it around his neck, pulled the serving platter toward him, and sliced off a few large pieces of meat. He then impaled one of the pieces on his fork, brought it to his mouth, and began chewing noisily. "Perhaps you'll allow me to ask *you* the same question you asked me: What is a famous bounty hunter like Sebastian Cain doing on Safe Harbor?"

"Just sitting around drinking beer."

"God has little use for liars, Sebastian," said Father William. He turned to Cain. "And *I* have even less."

"I came here looking for Billy Three-Eyes."

"Was there paper on him?"

"Probably," answered Cain.

"Probably?" repeated Father William, wolfing down still more food and following it up with a large glass of beer.

"I don't know. I wasn't here to kill him; I was after some information."

"About Santiago?"

"Why should you think so?" asked Cain.

"Because you were talking about him when I came in."

"I thought everybody out here talks about Santiago."

"I also know of your partnership with Virtue MacKenzie," Father William pointed out. He finished the last of the meat he had sliced, considered giving himself a second helping of potatoes au gratin, decided against it, and attacked his roast with renewed vigor. "What did you think you could learn from Billy Three-Eyes?"

"Where to find him."

"So you plan to be the man who kills Santiago?" asked Father William between mouthfuls.

"I plan to try," answered Cain. He paused. "I have a feeling that I'm getting pretty close to him."

"What makes you think so?"

"Because the worst crime anyone is likely to commit on Safe Harbor is robbing a store—but three bounty hunters have landed here in the past four months: you, me and Peacemaker MacDougal. That must mean *some*thing."

Father William frowned. "MacDougal? Is *he* here?"

"Not anymore. He killed Billy Three-Eyes."

"Well, there you have it," said the preacher decisively.

"There I have *what*?"

"Coincidence. You and MacDougal were both after Billy Three-Eyes, and I'm here because my ship had a problem."

"Why was Billy Three-Eyes here?" asked Cain.

Father William shrugged. "Who knows?"

"Somebody must," said Cain. "He was a killer. What was he doing on a world like Safe Harbor?"

"Hiding out, in all likelihood." Father William took a final mouthful of meat. "Moonripple!" he called out.

"That's her name?"

The preacher nodded. "Lovely, isn't it? It evokes images of stardust and ethereal beauty."

"I've heard it somewhere before," said Cain, frowning.

"Yes, sir," said Moonripple, emerging from the kitchen.

"I think it's time for the cake, my child," announced Father William.

Moonripple stared at his plate and frowned. "I keep telling you, sir, that if you insist on finishing your meal this fast, you'll make yourself sick."

"Who says I'm through?" Father William laughed. "I've still got most of the potatoes and half a pitcher of beer. But the cake would make a pleasant change of pace."

"Wouldn't you rather rest a bit and give yourself time to digest what you've eaten?" asked Moonripple.

"It'll be digested by the time you return with the cake." He paused. "You layered it with that fudge frosting we talked about yesterday, didn't you?"

"Yes, sir."

He tossed a platinum coin to her. "That's my girl!"

She caught the coin, placed it in a pocket, and went back into the kitchen to fetch the cake.

"Delightful child," said Father William. "She's wasting her time here. I've offered her a job as my personal cook, but she turned me down flat."

"Maybe she thinks you're not likely to provide long-term employment at the rate you put food away," commented Cain dryly.

"Nonsense!" said the preacher. "The Lord's got important work for me, Sebastian. I plan to live a long, long time—which," he added, "is more than can be said for bounty hunters who try to kill Santiago."

"You're a bounty hunter, too," Cain noted.

"Ah, but I'm one of the smart ones. I'm not after Santiago."

"Why not? The price on his head could build a lot of churches."

"People have been trying to find him for thirty years or

more without any success," replied Father William. "He's not worth the effort."

Moonripple reemerged from the kitchen, carrying a rich-looking chocolate layer cake.

"This has been a very interesting afternoon," remarked Cain as she set the cake down on the table.

"Has it indeed?" asked the preacher, looking down at the cake with the happy air of a child opening a present.

Cain nodded. "Yes, it has. So far I've met two people on Safe Harbor. One of them thinks Santiago is a hero, and the other is a bounty hunter who has no interest in him whatsoever."

"Moonripple, my dear," said Father William, ignoring Cain's comment, "do you think if you looked high and low you might be able to find me some ice cream to go with this luscious cake?"

"I think you finished all our ice cream yesterday, sir," she replied.

He looked crestfallen. "Check anyway, just in case."

She shrugged and headed off to the kitchen.

"Moonripple," repeated Cain. "Didn't Orpheus write her up a couple years ago?"

Father William nodded. "She's told me about him. I gather *he* offered her a job, too, and she didn't take it. She's a very independent young lady."

"And a very well-traveled one, too," said Cain. "I wonder what she's doing here?"

"Why don't you ask her?" suggested Father William, finishing his beer. "As for me," he added, rubbing his pudgy hands together, "I don't think I can wait for her to find that ice cream." He picked up a knife. "Would you like me to cut you a piece?"

"No, thanks," said Cain as the preacher cut a third of the cake away and placed it on his plate.

Father William stared at the cake for a moment, then picked up a piece and tasted it.

"Sebastian," he said, his face reflecting an ecstasy usually reserved only for his communications with God, "you don't know what you're missing!"

. "Twenty thousand calories, at a rough guess," said Cain.

"I preach hard and I kill hard," said Father William seriously. "God understands that I've got to eat hard, too.

You can't have a weakling doing the Lord's work, not out here on the Frontier.''

"*I* believe you," said Cain. "I just hope your heart and kidneys do, too.''

"The Lord is my shepherd,'' said the preacher, attacking the cake in earnest. "I'll make out just fine.''

Moonripple approached the table again.

"I'm sorry, Father William, but there really isn't any ice cream left.''

"You'll remember to get some by tomorrow, won't you?'' asked Father William with childlike urgency.

"I'll try.''

"Good girl!'' he said, returning his attention to the cake.

"Would you like me to take the potatoes away now, sir?''

He placed a huge hand over the container. "I'll get to them, child, never fear.''

"Have you ever thought of becoming a chef for the navy?'' asked Cain with a smile.

"Oh, no, sir,'' replied Moonripple seriously. "I like my work just as it is.''

"Father William suggested that I ask why you came to Safe Harbor,'' said Cain.

"I don't know,'' she said with a shrug. "I'd heard about it, and it sounded like a nice place.''

"How long have you been here?''

She stared at the ceiling and moved her lips silently, totaling up the days and months.

"Two years next week, sir.''

"That's a long time for you to spend in one place, isn't it?''

"What do you mean, sir?''

"Orpheus says you've been to more than a hundred worlds.''

"He was a very nice man,'' she said. "He put me into his song.''

"And he said you liked to travel all over the galaxy.''

"I do.''

"But you stopped here,'' Cain pointed out.

"I like this world.''

"And you disliked all the others?''

She shrugged. "Some of them.''

"And the rest?''

"They were nice enough, I suppose. I just like this one better."

"What's so special about it?" asked Cain.

She looked puzzled. "Nothing."

"Then why do you like it better?"

"I don't know. The people are nice, and I like my job, and I have a nice place to live."

"That's enough," said Father William.

"You told me to ask her," replied Cain.

"There's a difference between asking and badgering. Leave her alone now."

Cain shrugged. "I'm sorry if I've upset you, Moonripple."

"You haven't, sir," she replied. "You and Father William have both been very nice to me."

An elderly man entered and walked over to a table next to the one Cain had left, and Moonripple went off to wait on him.

"Well, Sebastian," said Father William, finishing the piece of cake on his plate and cutting the remaining two-thirds in half. "I guess you'll be on your way, now that the man you came to see is dead."

"I guess so," said Cain.

"Well, it's been a pleasure meeting you and talking to you."

"How long will you be staying here?" asked Cain.

"The way that girl cooks, I could stay forever," replied Father William. "But I think I'll be on my way in another two or three days. There are still a lot of souls to be saved out here—and a few that need to be sent on ahead to Satan."

"But not Santiago's?"

Father William smiled. "I suppose if I were to bump headfirst into him, I might give some serious thought to it," he answered. "But I've got better things to do than chase all over the galaxy after a will-o'-the-wisp."

"To each his own," said Cain, getting to his feet.

Father William extended a chocolate-smeared hand, and Cain took it.

"You're an interesting man," said Cain. "I hope I'll see you again someday."

"Who knows?" replied the preacher. "The Lord works in mysterious ways."

Darkness had fallen when Cain walked out into the humid

Safe Harbor atmosphere, and it took him a moment to get his bearings. The planet's three tiny moons were clearly visible but provided very little illumination, nor was there any lighting on the deserted street.

The town, such as it was, was only about five blocks square, and Schussler had been able to set down less than two miles away. Once the bounty hunter ascertained which way he had come, he set about retracing his steps and spent the next ten minutes walking down a dirt road that fronted an enormous field of mutated corn stalks, each some ten to twelve feet high and holding an average of twenty ears apiece.

In the distance he could hear a calf bleating. Logically he knew that imported embryos had to be born and raised before they could be slaughtered, but while Father William's roast hadn't seemed out of place to him, somehow the sound of a calf growing up on an alien world untold trillions of miles from where it had been conceived struck him as highly incongruous.

He continued walking, and after another fifteen minutes he came to Schussler, who had recognized him when he was still a few hundred yards away and opened the hatch for him.

"Did Billy Three-Eyes have anything useful to say?" asked the cyborg when Cain had seated himself in the command cabin.

"He's dead," said Cain. "Peacemaker MacDougal took him four months ago."

"I'm sorry to hear that," said Schussler. There was a momentary pause. "I'll bet the Swagman knew it all along!" he exclaimed suddenly.

"I wouldn't be surprised."

"Where will we go next?"

"Nowhere," said Cain. "There's something funny going on right here."

"Funny?"

"I ran into Father William."

"What was he doing?" asked Schussler.

"He said he was taking a vacation."

"Curious," murmured Schussler. "Still, I suppose it's possible."

"Anything's possible," said Cain. "But why here, and why now?"

"It *does* seem peculiar that so many bounty hunters have

recently visited an innocuous little agricultural world," admitttted Schussler.

"And I met a girl named Moonripple."

"The name is unfamiliar to me."

"She's just a barmaid," replied Cain. "Not very pretty, not very smart. Maybe twenty years old, tops."

"Then why does she interest you?"

"Because Orpheus wrote her up."

"Orpheus has written up thousands of people."

"And four of us are within two miles of each other on a little colony world in the middle of nowhere," said Cain.

"I hadn't looked at it that way," said Schussler. "That's very interesting."

"I'd say so."

"*Very* interesting," repeated the cyborg.

"Anyway, according to Orpheus, Moonripple has been to one hundred planets."

"I myself have been to more than three hundred," said Schussler. "What's so unusual about that?"

"Nothing. But it means she had to hit better than a world a month since she was ten or eleven years old—and now, for some reason, she's stayed on Safe Harbor for two years. What made her stop traveling?"

"A good question," agreed the cyborg. "What's the answer?"

"I don't have one—yet."

"Did you learn anything else about her?"

"Yes," said Cain. "She thinks Santiago is a hero."

"Why?" asked Schussler.

"I don't know," said Cain. "But I sure as hell intend to find out." He paused. "Can you get some information for me?"

"What kind?"

"I know they don't have any spaceports on this planet, but there has to be some regulatory agency that cleared you for landing and gave you the proper coordinates."

"Yes, there is."

"Contact them and see if you can find out how long Father William has been here."

Schussler had the information thirty seconds later. "He's been on Safe Harbor for almost a month."

"He told me he landed here with engine trouble a week ago. Moonripple said the same thing."

"I can double-check if you like."

"It's not necessary." Cain stared at the wall and frowned. "I wonder what he's waiting for?"

"We're getting close, aren't we?" asked Schussler, a note of anticipation momentarily driving the mournful tone from his musical voice.

"Very." said Cain softly.

20.

One-Time Charlie makes mistakes,
But never makes them twice.
His heart is black as anthracite,
His blood is cold as ice.

It was the name that did it.

Certainly Black Orpheus had no other reason to put him into the ballad. He wasn't a hero or a villain, a gambler or a thief, a cyborg or a bounty hunter; in fact, he wasn't anything colorful at all. He was just a drifter named Charles Marlowe Felcher, who wandered from one agricultural world to another, drinking a little too much to make up for not working quite enough.

He had a mean streak, but he wasn't a very imposing physical specimen, and his mastery of fisticuffs and self-defense left a lot to be desired. He felt no enormous compulsion to pay his debts, but since that was common knowledge nobody ever gave him a line of credit, and especially not bartenders. He carried an impressive sonic pistol on his hip, but he wasn't very accurate with it, and more often than not he forgot to keep it charged.

But he had that name, and Orpheus couldn't let it pass without putting it into a verse.

Since he wasn't a very loquacious man, nobody knew exactly *why* he was called One-Time Charlie. Some people said it was because he had been married once in his youth, left his wife behind when he came out to the Frontier, and swore he would never live with a woman again. Others

267

created a complex legend about how he had served time for some crime or another and vowed that he would commit every criminal act in the book just once, so that the police would never again be able to find a pattern to his behavior. A third story had it that he caused such havoc on his binges that he never returned to a world he had visited. A few of his enemies—and he certainly had a number of them—said it was a name created by Flat-Nosed Sal, one of the more notorious prostitutes of the Tumiga system, after he paid for an entire weekend of her time but could only perform once.

Orpheus wasn't concerned with the origin of his name, but only with the fascinating images it evoked; and since he caught him on a bad day, when he had been drinking pretty heavily and wasn't in one of his friendlier moods, the verse came out the way it did.

One-Time Charlie's verse was a recent addition to the canon, and as a result very few people on Safe Harbor had heard it—which was probably all for the best, since sooner or later someone who had heard the song and the stories would start asking him about Flat-Nosed Sal, and as often as not he and his questioner would both wake up in the local jail or the local hospital.

He arrived on a typical Safe Harbor day—warm, sunny, somewhat humid—and spent the next few hours looking for work at the larger farming combines. He was still making the rounds when Cain awoke, shaved, showered, and walked into town.

The place had the flavor of a small village back on old Earth, with rows of frame buildings and houses divided into neat little rectangles. Even the styling was similar, with many of the houses possessing dormer windows and huge verandas. He paused to examine one of them and wasn't surprised to find that beneath the woodlike veneer was a layer of a titanium alloy, and that the house ran on fusion power.

He walked another block and saw the figure of Father William sitting on the front porch of his small hotel, swaying gently back and forth on the oversized wooden rocking chair. He shaded his eyes as he watched the bounty hunter approach.

"Good morning, Sebastian," he said. "Lovely day, isn't it?"

Cain nodded. "That it is. Good morning, Father William."

"I thought you'd be off in pursuit of Santiago this morning," said the preacher.

"There's no hurry," said Cain. "I thought I'd sample some of Moonripple's cooking myself." He paused. "Besides, Santiago's been out there for thirty years or more. Another couple of days can't hurt."

"I hear tell that the Angel is closing in on him."

"That's what they say."

"And that doesn't worry you?"

"I'm trying not to lose any sleep over it," answered Cain.

"You're a confident man, Sebastian Cain," said Father William. "If it was me, I'd have taken off from Safe Harbor last night."

"But it's not you," said Cain.

"True enough," agreed the preacher. "Well, enjoy your stay. Possibly you'd like to join me for dinner tonight?"

"Perhaps."

"You seem singularly unenthused," noted Father William.

"You eat so damned fast, you're likely to swallow my arm before you realize you've made a mistake," said Cain with a smile.

Father William threw back his head and roared with laughter. Finally he regained his breath. "I like you, Sebastian! I truly do!" Suddenly he became serious. "I hope we never have to confront each other as enemies."

"Are you planning on breaking the law?" asked Cain.

"Me?" snorted Father William. "Never!"

"Neither am I."

Father William stared at him for a long moment. "Would you care to come up here and sit beside me for a spell?"

"Later, perhaps," said Cain. "I've got to buy some supplies."

"Go in peace, Sebastian," said the preacher. He looked up at the sky. "A beautiful day—the kind of day that makes a man forget how much evil there is abroad in the galaxy."

Cain nodded to him and continued walking down the street until he came to a small general store. He entered it and was momentarily chilled by the rush of cold air.

"Good morning, sir," said the proprietor, a portly, middle-aged man who had meticulously combed his thinning hair to cover a bald spot and succeeded only in calling attention to it. "May I help you?"

"Possibly," said Cain, looking down the various aisles. "Do you carry any books or tapes here?"

"Safe Harbor doesn't have a newstape," he said. "Nothing very exciting ever happens here," he added with an apologetic smile. "But we do have a selection of tapes and magazines from nearby worlds. Is there anything in particular you're looking for?"

"Yes," said Cain. "Have you got material about Santiago?"

"Nothing worth looking at," said the shopkeeper. "Just the usual stupid speculations written by incompetents who have nothing better to do with their time." He sighed. "You'd think somebody would tell the truth about him after all these years."

"What *is* the truth?" asked Cain.

"He's a great man, a *great* man, and they keep treating him like some kind of common criminal."

"I don't mean to seem rude," said Cain carefully, "but none of the stories I've heard about him make him sound like anything but an outlaw."

"You've been listening to the wrong people."

"Are you one of the right ones?"

"I beg your pardon?"

"What can you tell me about Santiago?"

"Oh, nothing very much," replied the shopkeeper.

"Just that he's a great man," said Cain.

"That's right, sir," said the shopkeeper briskly. "You'll find our magazines and tapes in the middle of aisle three, just past the computer supplies."

"Thank you," said Cain. He wandered over to the tape section, browsed for a couple of minutes, and walked out.

His next stop was the barber shop, where he got a shave while listening to the barber tell him with a straight face that he had never heard of anyone named Santiago.

Cain spent the rest of the morning wandering through the small village, striking up conversations wherever he could. The people were divided almost equally: half of them thought Santiago was a saint, and the other half seemed not to recognize his name.

Finally he returned to Father William's hotel. The preacher was still rocking lazily in the sunlight, sipping a tall iced drink through a straw.

"Hello, Sebastian," he said. "Have you decided to join me?"

"For a couple of minutes, anyway," said Cain, pulling up a chair.

"A couple of minutes is all I've got," replied Father William. "It's getting on toward lunchtime." He paused. "Did you have a successful morning?"

"An interesting one, anyway," responded Cain.

"I notice that you're not overburdened by supplies," remarked the preacher with a lazy smile.

"I decided to carry them back after the heat of the day," lied Cain.

"Good idea," said Father William. "Will you be leaving then?"

Cain shrugged. "Perhaps."

"Where will you be going next, Sebastian?"

"I haven't decided yet. How about you?"

"Szandor Two, perhaps, or possibly Greenwillow. It's been a few years since I've preached to either of them." He paused. "I suppose I'll stop by a post office somewhere along the way and make up my mind after I've seen the latest Wanted list."

"Haven't they got any post offices on Safe Harbor?" asked Cain.

Father William shook his head. "Not a big enough planet. The mail gets delivered every three weeks to the local chemical company. The townspeople pick it up when it arrives, and the rest of it gets passed out when they deliver fertilizer and insecticides to the farms."

"How many mail deliveries have you been here for?"

"Two," said Father William.

"Last night you told me you'd only been here a week," said Cain.

"Last night you hadn't told that unholy ship of yours to check with the local authorities," replied the preacher easily. "That was unwise, Sebastian, challenging the word of a servant of the Lord."

"Isn't lying supposed to be a sin?" inquired Cain mildly.

"God can be very understanding," answered Father William.

"Is He equally understanding of all the people who lied to me this morning?"

"Nobody lied to you, Sebastian."

"More than a dozen men told me that they had never heard of Santiago."

"*Almost* nobody," amended Father William.

"When is he due to show up?" asked Cain.

"Who?"

"Santiago."

Father William chucked. "You're letting your imagination run away with you, Sebastian."

"I thought we were going to talk," said Cain.

"We're talking right now," said the preacher.

"One of us is talking," Cain corrected him. "And one of us is still lying."

Father William smiled. "You're lucky I'm on vacation, Sebastian. I've taken men's scalps for less than that." His smile vanished. "However, I wouldn't press my luck if I were you."

"Am I to assume that our conversation is over?" asked Cain caustically.

"Not at all," said Father William, rising to his feet. "But I think we'll continue it over lunch. I'm famished!"

He walked across the unpaved street to the tavern, and Cain fell into step beside him.

Moonripple had already laid out a huge spread for Father William and looked somewhat distressed when she saw Cain enter with him.

"I didn't know you were coming, sir," she said apologetically. "I haven't made anything for you."

"He can have one of my sandwiches," said the preacher magnanimously.

Cain looked at the table. "Are you sure seven of them will be enough for you?" he asked wryly.

"God tells us that we must make sacrifices," said Father William, tying a napkin around his neck and sitting down. He turned to Moonripple. "Did you remember to buy the ice cream, my child?"

"Yes, sir," said Moonripple.

"Excellent! By the way, Mr. Cain will be my guest for dinner."

"Mr. Cain?" she repeated, staring at Cain. "Are you the one they call the Songbird?"

Cain nodded. "It's not my favorite name."

"I've heard about you all over the Frontier," she continued

enthusiastically. "Black Orpheus gave you three verses!" She paused, embarrassed. "I'm sorry about not knowing who you were last night."

"There's no reason why you should have known me," replied Cain.

"But you're so famous!"

"No more so than you and Father William," said Cain. "We're all in the damned song."

She looked concerned. "Don't you like Orpheus' song?"

"Not especially," he said. Moonripple looked like she was about to cry, and he quickly added: "But the verse he did about you was lovely."

"Do you really think so?" she asked, smiling again.

He nodded. "Have you ever found those pearls that he claims you were looking for?"

"I wasn't really hunting for pearls," she replied. "That was just a thing to say."

"What *were* you looking for on all those worlds?" asked Cain.

She shrugged. "I don't know."

"Maybe we were both looking for the same thing," he suggested.

"Maybe," she agreed. "What are you looking for?"

"Santiago."

"I've never met him, sir."

"Do you know anyone who has?"

"I really couldn't say, sir," she replied. "I mean, if *you* had met Santiago, you'd hardly be likely to tell someone like me, would you?"

"Would you like to meet him?"

"A great hero like that?" she said. "He wouldn't have time for someone like me, sir."

"Moonripple, my child," said Father William, who had been eating with feverish haste during their conversation, "I think I'm ready for another pitcher of beer."

"Right away, sir," she said, walking behind the bar and holding a fresh pitcher under the tap.

"You'd better dig in, Sebastian," said Father William, "or there won't be anything left for you."

"You go ahead," said Cain. "I'm really not very hungry."

"You weren't hungry last night, either," remarked the preacher. "No wonder you're so gaunt. Don't you ever eat?"

"Aboard my ship," answered Cain.

"You couldn't get me into that unholy melding of man and machine," said Father William devoutly. "I'm surprised God allowed it to happen."

"If God didn't want Men to become spaceships, He wouldn't have created the Graal," said Cain with a smile.

Father William looked up sternly from his food. "Sebastian, you can ask all the questions you want about Santiago— but when you make fun of the Lord, you're walking on very thin ice. Do you understand what I'm saying to you?"

"I apologize if I've offended you," said Cain.

"It's not *me* you have to worry about offending," said the preacher. "It's the Lord."

"Then I apologize to both of you."

Father William stared at him for a long moment, trying to decide if Cain was making fun of him, then nodded a terse acceptance and returned to his meal.

Moonripple brought Father William's beer over to him. Cain was about to start questioning her again when the door opened and Charles Marlowe Felcher walked in, strode up to the bar, and ordered a beer and a whiskey. He looked hot and discouraged, as indeed he was.

"Good afternoon," he said, nodding to Cain and Father William.

"Greetings, neighbor," said the preacher. "I think it's still morning for a few more minutes, though."

"It feels like afternoon," One-Time Charlie replied, downing the whiskey and going to work on the beer. "I've been making the rounds all morning, looking for work."

"There's not much to be had on Safe Harbor," offered Father William.

"So I've been finding out." He signaled to Moonripple and held up his whiskey glass. "Keep this thing full, honey." He looked back to Father William. "I didn't know this joint was a restaurant, too."

"It isn't," said the preacher. "I'm a friend of the family."

"You live around here?"

"Just vacationing."

"You, too?" he asked Cain.

"Just drinking beer," replied Cain.

"What's your name, friend?" asked Father William.

"Felcher, Charles Felcher," was the reply. "But most people call me One-Time Charlie."

"Orpheus told me about you," said Moonripple disapprovingly.

"Well, whatever he told you, it was probably a lie," said One-Time Charlie. "After all, that's what he gets paid for doing, isn't it?"

"He doesn't get paid at all," she said.

"Then he's a bigger fool than I thought," laughed Charlie, downing a second whiskey and holding his glass out for a refill.

"He's not a fool!" she said hotly. "He's a great artist!"

"Didn't anyone ever tell you that the customer is always right?" said One-Time Charlie.

"Not when he says bad things about Black Orpheus, he isn't," she replied defiantly.

"Have it your way," he said with a shrug. "I'm just here to have a drink and cool off."

Father William returned to his repast, while Cain sipped his beer thoughtfully and decided not to question Moonripple any further until One-Time Charlie had left or passed out. He decided that the latter was more likely, given the rate at which he was putting away whiskey and washing it down with beer.

"Moonripple, my girl, I think I could use another two or three sandwiches before you bring out my dessert," announced Father William when he had emptied his plate. "And put a little more cheese on them this time."

"Yes, sir," she said, heading off to the kitchen.

"That looks like a nice job, being a friend of the family," commented One-Time Charlie, looking up from his drink.

"It has its advantages," agreed Father William. "Especially for a man of the cloth who donates all his money to charitable causes."

Charlie grinned. "Are you a preacher?"

"I am privileged to serve the Lord in that and other capacities," replied Father William.

"Can't be much work for you on a little backwater world like this."

"As I told you, I'm on vacation."

"Stupid place to come for a vacation."

"Ah, but *I'm* vacationing," said Father William with a smile. "Are *you* working?"

"I'm working on this bottle, is what I'm working on," said One-Time Charlie, his words starting to slur.

Moonripple returned with the sandwiches and placed them down before Father William, then went back to her post behind the bar.

"Those sandwiches look pretty good," said One-Time Charlie. "I think I'll have some, too."

"I'm sorry, sir, but they're not one of our services," said Moonripple.

"If you can make them for a preacher, you can make them for an honest worker," said One-Time Charlie irritably.

"Really, I can't, sir," said Moonripple. "These come from the owner's private kitchen."

"I don't give a damn where they come from!" growled Charlie. "If *he* can have them, so can I."

Moonripple looked across the room at Father William, who nodded almost imperceptibly.

"All right, sir," she said to One-Time Charlie. "I'll be right back with your sandwiches."

She went into the kitchen, and he turned triumphantly to Father William and Cain.

"You just have to know how to talk to these people," he said smugly.

Both of them stared silently back at him, and after a moment he returned to his drinking.

Moonripple emerged a few minutes later, carrying two platters. She set one of them down on the bar in front of One-Time Charlie and carried the other, which held Father William's dessert, to the preacher.

"Ah!" he exclaimed happily. "You found strawberries for my cheesecake! You are truly an angel, my girl!"

"That's really good cheesecake?" asked One-Time Charlie sullenly.

"The best!" enthused Father William. "The girl is an absolute artist in the kitchen!"

"I'll have a piece, too," he told Moonripple.

"I'm afraid there isn't any more," she replied.

"We're not going to go through all that again, are we, honey?" he said. "I told you I wanted a piece of cheesecake."

"She's telling you the truth," said Father William. "She only makes one a day. I prefer them fresh."

"Then make another one," said One-Time Charlie.

"I can't, sir," answered Moonripple. "I buy the makings each morning. Father William doesn't like me to use frozen ingredients."

"You're Father William?" asked One-Time Charlie, surprised.

"That's right."

"The bounty hunter?"

"When God so wills it."

"Is this girl any relation to you?"

"No."

"Then you've got no interest in anything I say to her." One-Time Charlie turned back to Moonripple. "Go out and buy some more makings."

"I'm not allowed to leave, sir."

He grabbed her arm as she walked by.

"I thought we decided that the customer was always right."

"You're hurting me!" said Moonripple, trying to twist free.

"I'm going to do a lot more than that if we don't figure out who's the boss here," he said nastily.

"Let her go," said Cain softly.

"Another party heard from," said One-Time Charlie, turning to glare at him without relinquishing his grip on the girl. "Who asked you to butt in?"

"I'm another friend of the family," said Cain.

"Yeah?" said One-Time Charlie pugnaciously. "Well, you and your goddamned family can go fuck yourselves."

"You've had too much to drink," said Cain, getting slowly to his feet. "Now let her go and get out of here."

"Are you a bounty hunter, too?" asked Charlie sarcastically.

"As a matter of fact, I am."

"Have you got a name?"

"Sebastian Cain."

"The Songbird?" said One-Time Charlie, frowning. "What have we got, some kind of convention going on here?"

"What we've got is a drunk who's asking for trouble," said Cain ominously.

"Come on," laughed One-Time Charlie. "Everybody knows you guys don't kill anyone who's not wanted by the law. This is a private discussion between me and this little girl; why don't you just keep your nose out of it?''

"Just let her go and walk out, and nobody will get hurt," said Cain slowly.

Suddenly One-Time Charlie twisted Moonripple's arm behind her and produced a knife with his free hand, pressing it against the girl's throat. "Take one step toward me and I'll slice her!" he snarled.

"Do you suppose there's any paper on One-Time Charlie?" asked Cain, never taking his eyes off the man.

Father William nodded, pulling his coat back and revealing his laser pistols. "A sinner like him? There's got to be paper on him somewhere, Sebastian."

One-Time Charlie started to realize that he was in over his head, but in his drunken state of mind he couldn't find any way out of his situation. He tightened his grip on Moonripple and began edging slowly toward the door, keeping her between himself and the two bounty hunters.

"Make a move and I'll kill her!"

Cain shrugged and turned to Father William as if to say something else. Then, in one blindingly swift motion, he spun around, drew his pistol, and placed a bullet between One-Time Charlie's eyes. The room reverberated with the sound of the gunshot.

Moonripple screamed as One-Time Charlie fell to the floor, and Cain walked over to her and put an arm around her.

"It's all right," he said gently. "You're safe now."

"Very nice work," said Father William admiringly. "You're as good as they say you are." He walked over to One-Time Charlie's body and studied his face closely. "He doesn't look familiar," he said after a moment. "But you can never tell."

"If you want him, he's yours," offered Cain.

"You mean it?"

"View it as my belated contribution to church," said Cain wryly.

"Praise the Lord, I've got another convert!" laughed Father William, pulling out his skinning knife.

"Come outside," said Cain to Moonripple. "You don't want to watch this."

"What is he going to do?" she asked, staring at the preacher with horrified fascination.

"Nothing that concerns us," replied Cain, walking her to the doorway.

She went out into the street with him, still trembling, as the townspeople poured out of their stores and houses to converge on the tavern. Cain ignored them and kept walking until he and Moonripple were well clear of the crowd.

"Will you be all right, or would you like me to take you to a doctor?" he asked.

"I'm fine, sir," she said.

"You're sure?" he asked as the sound of Father William's voice came out of the tavern, reassuring the onlookers that no crime had been committed and that another sinner had been sent to Satan a few years ahead of schedule.

"Yes, sir," said Moonripple. "I'm all right, really I am."

"Good. That was a pretty close call."

She looked up at him. "You saved my life. Why?"

"I like you," replied Cain. "And I've never been very fond of people like One-Time Charlie."

"What can I do to repay you?" she asked.

"You can tell me the truth about Santiago."

She considered his request silently for a moment, then nodded.

"If that's what you want," she said.

"Father William is waiting for him. When is he due to show up?"

"He's already here," said Moonripple.

"Santiago's on Safe Harbor right now?" asked Cain, startled.

"Yes."

"How long has he been here?"

"For years, I guess," answered Moonripple. "He lives here."

"Well, I'll be damned!" muttered Cain. "Can you take me to him?"

"No. But I can introduce you to someone who can."

"When?"

She shrugged. "Right now, if you'd like."

Cain was suddenly aware of Father William's presence and turned to find the preacher standing some twenty feet away, his grisly trophy in his hand.

"You're very persistent, Sebastian Cain," he said. "I admire that in a man."

"If he's been here all along, why haven't you gone after him yet?" asked Cain.

"I don't want him."

"Why not?"

"I have my reasons," said Father William.

"Well, I have mine for wanting to find him."

"So I've been given to understand."

"I've got nothing against you," said Cain seriously. "But if you try to stop me, I'll kill you."

"I wouldn't dream of it," said Father William, holding his hands out from his laser pistols.

"Do you plan to be here when I get back?" asked Cain.

"*If* you get back," the preacher corrected him.

"I'll see you then," said Cain. He paused. "Aren't you going to wish me luck?" he added ironically.

"God be with you, my son," said Father William sincerely.

Then Cain was following Moonripple down the street, half expecting to feel the searing pain of a laser in the small of his back. He was mildly surprised when he turned the corner intact and unharmed, with Father William's parting words still echoing in his mind.

21.

Silent Annie never speaks,
Never murmurs, never shrieks,
Doesn't whisper, doesn't call—
But someday, someday, she'll tell all.

Orpheus had a feeling about her.

There was an indefinable *something*—a look, an attitude, a way of carrying herself—that made him think she carried some enormous secret within her.

He had no idea how right he was.

Her name was Silent Annie. She wasn't mute, but she might as well have been.

All anyone knew about her was that something pretty bad had happened when she was eleven or twelve and living on Raxar II. She spent two years in the hospital, and when she emerged she was physically recovered—but she never spoke again. She was *capable* of speech, her doctors said; but the experience she had undergone had traumatized her, possibly forever.

She turned up in some mighty odd places over the years—Altair III, Goldenrod, Kalami II—but she never stayed for long. Nobody knew what she did on those worlds, and very few people knew that she called Safe Harbor home.

"Silent Annie?" repeated Cain when Moonripple told him where she was taking him. "She's here, too?"

"Yes, sir."

"It seems like half the people Black Orpheus ever wrote about are on Safe Harbor," he said.

"Not really, sir," replied Moonripple. "There's just you, and me, and your ship, and Father William, and Silent Annie."

"Didn't Orpheus say that she was a deaf-mute?"

"She doesn't talk, but she can hear everything you say."

"What's her link to Santiago?"

"She works for him, sir," said Moonripple.

"You're sure?"

Moonripple nodded her head. "Yes, sir."

"By the way," said Cain, "you can stop calling me sir. My name's Sebastian."

"Thank you, sir. It's a very pretty name."

"You think so?" he asked dubiously.

"Yes, I do. Don't you?"

"I suppose it's better than Songbird," he said. He looked around. "Does Silent Annie live in the middle of a cornfield?" he asked.

"Of course not," laughed Moonripple.

"Well, that's just where we're headed," he noted. "We're almost a mile out of town."

"She has a little house about half a mile up the road, sir."

"Sebastian," he corrected her.

"Sebastian."

"How did you meet her?"

Moonripple shrugged. "I don't even remember. At church, probably. It couldn't have been in the tavern, because she doesn't drink."

"And you're good friends with her?"

"Not *best* friends," she said, accentuating the word. "I've never had a best friend."

"How well do you know her?"

"Sometimes she stops by in the morning and we have tea together, and once in a while I visit her on my day off," answered Moonripple.

"What makes you think she'll take me to Santiago?" persisted Cain.

"Why wouldn't she?"

"Because I'm a bounty hunter."

"Santiago knows that, sir."

"Santiago knows about me?" asked Cain, startled.

"Santiago knows everything," she said.

He stared at her but made no comment, and they spent the next few minutes walking in silence.

"There it is, sir," she said, pointing to a small structure set in about fifty feet from the road.

"It looks empty," said Cain.

"Oh, she's home, sir," said Moonripple decisively.

"What makes you so sure?" he asked.

"Where else would she be?"

"Beats the hell out of me," answered Cain, turning off the road and following a narrow path up to the front door.

He waited for the security system to scan the two of them, and just as he was sure that he had been right about the home being deserted, the door slid back into the wall and he found himself facing a small, slender woman dressed in a very old military daysuit.

She was perhaps thirty years old, and her features were sharp and stark. She had a scar that began on her forehead and ran through her right eyebrow and down her cheek, which even cosmetic surgery had been unable to hide. She wore no makeup, which made her thin lips seem even thinner.

"Hello, Annie," said Moonripple. "This is Sebastian Cain. He'd like to meet you."

Silent Annie motioned for them to enter the house, and Cain followed the two women through a small foyer into a living room that was larger than it appeared from the outside. The walls were covered by shelving units, which in turn were covered by disorganized stacks of books and tapes. A dust-covered computer sat on a battered desk in one corner, and Cain could see from the text on the screen that she had been reading when they had interrupted her.

The furniture matched the decor of the room: old, not very comfortable, and arranged without any concern for design or order. Silent Annie pointed first at Cain and then at the largest of the chairs, and he sat down, while Moonripple sat cross-legged on the floor next to him.

Silent Annie made a pouring gesture.

"Yes, I'd love some tea," said Moonripple. "What about you, sir?"

"Tea will be fine," said Cain.

Silent Annie forced a smile to her lips, then left the room for a moment and returned with a chipped porcelain pot and three cups carried on a plastic tray.

"Thank you," said Cain, taking one of the cups.

Silent Annie made a squeezing gesture with her hand.

"I don't understand," said Cain.

"She wants to know if you'd like a slice of lemon," said Moonripple.

"No, thanks," said Cain as Moonripple reached out and took a cup for herself.

Silent Annie walked over to a couch that was covered by a blanket, placed the tray on a nearby table, and sat down, staring questioningly at Cain.

"He wants to meet Santiago," volunteered Moonripple. She paused for a moment. "I told him you'd take him there."

Silent Annie arched an eyebrow.

"I promised him, Annie," said Moonripple.

Silent Annie made a gesture with her hands that Cain could not interpret.

"Because he saved my life."

Another gesture.

"A very mean man came into the tavern and tried to hurt me, and he stopped him."

Silent Annie stared at Cain, appraising him.

"Will you take him, Annie?"

Silent Annie sat motionless for a moment, then nodded her head.

"Thank you!" said Moonripple happily. "I knew you would!"

Silent Annie continued to stare at Cain, who met her gaze. Finally she turned back to Moonripple and made another gesture with her hands.

Moonripple turned to Cain. "She wants me to leave now."

"How will I talk to her?"

"She's very good at making herself understood," Moonripple assured him.

"Let's hope so," he said. "I didn't know what the hell she was doing when she spoke to you with her hands."

"She's been teaching me sign language, but she has other ways of communicating."

"Then I thank you for your help," said Cain, getting up and helping her to her feet. "I hope we meet again."

"You're a very nice man, Sebastian," she said, standing on her tiptoes and kissing his cheek. Then, suddenly embarrassed, she turned and scurried out of the room.

"How soon can we start?" asked Cain.

Silent Annie held up her hand, palm outward, signaling

him to wait, then walked to the window. When Moonripple reached the road and began heading back toward the village, she turned back to him.

"Soon," she said.

"What?" said Cain, startled.

"We'll start soon enough," she replied in a firm voice. "But first I think we'd better have a little speak."

"I thought you couldn't speak."

"I can, when I have something to say, Mr. Cain," said Silent Annie.

"Why do you pretend to be mute?" he asked.

"So I won't have to answer stupid questions." She sat down and sipped from her cup of tea. "You've come to kill him, haven't you?"

"Yes, I have."

"Why?"

"There's a price on his head."

"And that's the only reason?"

"How many more do you need?" replied Cain.

"I had rather hoped for something more meaningful," said Silent Annie. "I would hate to think that we had misjudged you."

"Misjudged me?" repeated Cain.

"We've been waiting for you, Mr. Cain, ever since Santiago told Geronimo Gentry to start you off on the trail that eventually led you to Safe Harbor."

"Let me get this straight," said Cain, confused. "Are you saying that Santiago *wanted* me to find him?"

"That is precisely what I am saying."

"I don't believe it."

"Believe whatever you want," said Silent Annie with a shrug. "How do *you* think you got here, after all those years of virtually no progress?"

He stared at her and said nothing.

"I shouldn't imply that he made it easy for you," she continued. "That wouldn't have served his purposes. But he did make it possible; he decided to give you the initial impetus."

"Why?"

"He's been studying you for a long time, Mr. Cain," continued Silent Annie. "Ever since you came out to the Frontier."

"Still why?"

"Because he studies everyone."

"But he doesn't allow everyone to find him."

"No," she replied. "You are only the second."

"Who was the first?"

"It doesn't matter," said Silent Annie. "He's dead now."

"What about Father William?" asked Cain.

"What about him?"

"*He* found Santiago."

"You're wrong, Mr. Cain," replied Silent Annie. "He's not hunting for Santiago."

"Then what's he doing here?"

"I'm not sure you'd believe it if I told you," she said.

"Perhaps not," agreed Cain. "But why don't you tell me anyway, and let me make up my own mind?"

"He's here to *protect* Santiago."

"From me?" asked Cain skeptically. "Then why didn't he take me on when he had the chance?"

"He's not worried about you."

Cain was silent for a moment. "The Angel?" he asked at last.

She nodded. "He'll be here before too much longer."

"I take it that he's gotten this far without any help from Santiago."

"That is correct."

"And that Santiago doesn't want to be found by the Angel?" continued Cain.

"I doubt that he's given it any thought whatsoever," replied Silent Annie. "Protecting him is Father William's idea, not his."

"Why would Father William help a man with a price on his head?" asked Cain.

"That's what I hope to show you before you meet Santiago," said Silent Annie, finishing her tea and pouring herself another cup.

"Where does Moonripple fit into all this?"

"She's just a very pleasant little barmaid, nothing more."

"But she knew Santiago was on Safe Harbor," he pointed out.

"So did everyone else you spoke to this morning."

"And no one's tried to turn him in for the reward?"

"Actually, five or six people have," said Silent Annie.

"You'll find them buried in various cemeteries around the planet."

"Let's get back to Moonripple for a minute," said Cain, trying to assimilate everything Silent Annie had told him. "She's been hitting a world a month for most of her life. Why did she come here?"

"Just chance, nothing more."

"And why has she stayed?"

"For the same reason I have," said Silent Annie.

"All right," said Cain. "Why have *you* stayed?"

"Because Santiago is a great man."

"Santiago is a thief and a murderer."

"It's all a matter of viewpoint," she said.

"Viewpoint's got nothing to do with it," replied Cain. "The man has been killing and plundering since before you were born. The Democracy's managed to implicate him in almost forty murders, and there have probably been more than a hundred they don't know anything about. And I have it on good authority that he's got warehouses filled with stolen merchandise all over the Inner Frontier."

"May I assume that your authority is the Jolly Swagman?"

"He wouldn't be risking his life if he didn't know they existed," answered Cain.

"I'm not arguing their existence," said Silent Annie. "Merely your interpretation of them." She paused. "And incidentally, I don't see the Swagman risking his life at this moment."

"Is *he* a part of this, too?"

"Absolutely not," she replied. "He was once, but Santiago dismissed him."

"A falling-out between thieves?" suggested Cain.

"There was only one thief involved," she replied sternly. "And he no longer works for us. I argued in favor of killing him, but Santiago chose to let him live."

Cain leaned back and sighed. "All right," he said at last. "I've heard a lot of talk from you and Moonripple about how Santiago is a great man. Suppose you tell me why you think so."

"Fair enough," said Silent Annie. "You tell me that Santiago is responsible for the deaths of a hundred and forty men. Let me begin by telling you that the actual figure is closer to eight hundred."

"That makes him a great man?" said Cain ironically.

"How many men have *you* killed, Mr. Cain?"

"That's not at issue here," said Cain.

"Tell me anyway."

"Thirty-seven."

"You're lying, Mr. Cain," she said with a smile.

"The hell I am."

"I happen to know that you killed more than five thousand men and women on Sylaria alone."

"That was war," he said.

"No, Mr. Cain. That was revolution."

"Are you trying to tell me that Santiago is a revolutionary?" he asked skeptically.

"Yes, I am."

"A woman named Sargasso Rose suggested the same thing," he said. "I didn't believe her, either. Who is he supposed to be revolting against?"

"The Democracy."

Cain laughed out loud. "Are you seriously suggesting that he expects to overthrow the Democracy?"

"No, Mr. Cain. The Democracy controls tens of thousands of worlds, and hold some ninety-eight percent of the human population in the galaxy. There are more than thirty million ships in its navy, and it has inexhaustible wealth and resources to draw upon. It would be foolish to dream of overthrowing it."

"Well, then?"

"He seeks only to neutralize it on the Frontier, to eradicate its more heinous abuses."

"By stockpiling artwork and murdering small-time smugglers like Duncan Black?"

"Duncan Black was a traitor," she said coldly. "He was executed, not murdered."

"The end result was pretty much the same," commented Cain.

"Have you never executed anyone for deserting what you thought to be a just cause, Mr. Cain?" she demanded.

He was silent for a moment.

"Yes, I have," he admitted at last. "Keep talking."

"*You* talk about stockpiling artwork, but it's the Swagman that I hear speaking," continued Silent Annie. "In point of fact, he and Santiago had their falling-out because Santiago refused to keep certain pieces that the Swagman wanted, but sold them through the black market, where the Swagman would have had to pay competitive prices for them."

"To pay the troops?" suggested Cain.

"Were you paid on Sylaria or the other worlds where you fought?" she asked.

"No."

"Neither are we," she said. "The troops, as you call them, work for free, Mr. Cain."

"Then what does he need all that money for?"

"You shall see."

"When?"

"Soon."

"Why not now?" he insisted.

"Because you caused a bit of a commotion back in the village when you killed One-Time Charlie," said Silent Annie.

"Moonripple didn't mention anything about my killing him."

She smiled. "I'm not totally isolated here, Mr. Cain. Father William contacted me and told me what had transpired before you had covered half the distance to my house." She paused. "At any rate, while you were totally justified in your actions, it was impossible to keep your identity a secret."

"I never tried to," he interjected.

"Let me amend that," she said. "It was impossible to keep your *occupation* a secret. That was unfortunate."

"Why?"

"Because a number of the townspeople are willing to lay down their lives to protect Santiago. When Father William is certain that none of them are coming here to try to stop you, he'll contact me again, and then we can leave."

"If one of them shows up, I intend to defend myself," said Cain.

"That won't be necessary," she said. "If need be, Father William will warn them off."

"Why?"

"Because Santiago wants you intact, and Father William will honor his wishes."

"Even if it costs Santiago a couple of followers?"

"It almost certainly won't—but yes, even so."

"You're not exactly making him sound like a saint," remarked Cain.

"He's not. He's a man who has been forced to make more life-and-death decisions than any one human being should ever have to make."

"That was his choice."

"That was his calling," she corrected him.

"What makes *me* so important to him?" demanded Cain.

"I should think that would be obvious to you," said Silent Annie.

Cain stared at her for a very long moment. Finally he spoke.

"Why should I want to join him?"

"Because you yourself were once a revolutionary."

"The galaxy is lousy with men who were once revolutionaries," he said.

"Most of them have adjusted. You haven't."

"I've adjusted better than most," Cain replied with a touch of irony. "I took what I learned and put it to a new use. I used to kill men for free." He smiled mirthlessly. "Now I do it for a living."

"He's not interested in you because of the men you've killed."

"Then why *is* he interested in me?"

"Because of the men you *haven't* killed," said Silent Annie.

He frowned. "I don't think I understand you."

"You let Quentin Cicero live."

"He had a hostage."

"You've given out other pardons, too," she continued. "You spent ten weeks hunting down Carmella Sparks, and let her walk away."

"She had three kids with her," said Cain uncomfortably. "One of them was still nursing. They would all have died."

"That wouldn't have stopped Peacemaker MacDougal or the Angel," she said.

"Then maybe Santiago ought to be talking to them instead of me."

"He has no interest in men who have forfeited every last vestige of their humanity. It is *because* you are still capable of acts of compassion that he wants you."

"Yeah," said Cain. "Well, I don't know if I want *him*."

"You will," she said confidently. "He is the greatest man I know."

"How did you meet him?"

"I grew up on Raxar Two," she said. "It had a large alien population, and we had a military government in order to keep them properly pacified." The muscles in her jaw twitched slightly. "When I was eleven years old, I was beaten and raped by three soldiers. The Democracy was having trouble getting more military funding, and they didn't want any incidents that might embarrass them and cost them their money, so they covered it up. The three men were transferred to another world, and were never punished. I spent two years in the hospital."

"Is that where you got the scar?" asked Cain.

"That's just the one you can see," said Silent Annie bitterly. "Anyway, Santiago heard about what had happened, and—"

"How?" interrupted Cain.

"He's been out here a long time," she replied. "He has sources everywhere. Once he learned what they had done to me, he had the three men killed." She forced a grim smile to her face. "I believe the late Altair of Altair was my particular angel of vengeance."

"And then you joined him?"

"Wouldn't you have?" she replied.

"I'd have killed them myself."

"Not all of us are killers, Mr. Cain," she replied. "It requires a certain primal instinct that not everyone possesses."

"Does Santiago?"

"I don't know for a fact that he has ever personally killed another human being."

"Given the number of deaths that he's decreed, that might be construed as cowardice in certain circles," remarked Cain.

"I won't dignify that remark with an answer," Silent Annie said coldly.

"How did you find him?" asked Cain, declining to apologize for his comment.

"He makes it very easy, when he wants to be found."

"I think I'd be willing to debate that," he said wryly.

"Do you honestly think you could have found him if he hadn't wanted you to?" she asked.

"Based on what you've told me, no," he admitted.

"He makes the way more difficult for some than for others," she continued.

"I'll testify to that, at least," said Cain.

"For Moonripple, it was perhaps easiest of all."

"I thought you said she landed here by chance."

"It was pure chance that she landed on Safe Harbor when she did," explained Silent Annie. "But sooner or later she was bound to arrive."

"Why?"

"Her parents worked for Santiago. The Democracy captured and killed them when she was only four years old." She paused. "He couldn't reach out for her then, because there was too great a chance that she was being watched. So he became her guardian angel. Wherever she went, whatever world she worked on, there was always someone watching over her, protecting her. Finally, when we were sure that the Democracy had given up on her, it was subtly suggested that her wanderings should take her in the direction of Safe Harbor. When she finally arrived, we waited to make absolutely sure she hadn't been followed, and then she was told the truth."

"By you?"

Silent Annie shook her head. "She doesn't know I can speak."

"By Santiago himself?" asked Cain.

"She's never met him." Silent Annie paused. "She's a very sweet girl, but our battle isn't hers. She's already suffered enough casualties. The less she knows, the better."

"Then why did Santiago endanger himself by letting her know anything at all?"

"He wanted her to stay on Safe Harbor, where he could better protect her should the need ever arise."

"And if she wants to leave?" asked Cain.

"She's free to go."

"Even knowing that this is Santiago's world?"

"Even so."

Cain lowered his hand, lost in thought. Finally he looked up at Silent Annie.

"I'd like to meet him," he said.

"You shall."

"I'm also aware that this could be a trap."

"Why would we use such an elaborate one?"

"I don't know," he admitted. "But if you've been lying to me, he's a dead man."

"I'm not lying." She walked over to a communicator. "Father William should have given us the all-clear signal before this. I'd better check in at the tavern and see what the problem is."

"Maybe you'd better let me," volunteered Cain. "Moonripple might answer, and you're supposed to be a mute."

Silent Annie smiled. "If she answers, I'll just ask for Father William. Since she's never heard my voice, she's hardly likely to identify it."

"I stand corrected," said Cain.

Silent Annie spent a moment speaking in low tones, then broke the connection and turned to Cain.

"It's all right," she announced. "We can leave now."

"What was the holdup?"

"He got to drinking beer and consuming food, and totally forgot about us," she said with a semitolerant smile.

"It sounds like him," agreed Cain. Suddenly he frowned. "We'll have to put this off for an hour or so."

"What's the matter?" she asked.

"There's something I have to do first."

"Does it have to do with Santiago?" she asked suspiciously.

"Indirectly. There's a promise I have to keep."

"To whom?"

"To a friend." He walked to the door. "I'll be back."

She nodded, and he left her small house and began walking down the road that led through the little village. Within half an hour he had arrived at his destination.

"You look unhappy," said Schussler as he came through the hatch.

"I am," answered Cain.

"Then you were wrong about Safe Harbor?"

He shook his head. "I was right."

"Santiago's coming?" asked Schussler excitedly.

"He's here now."

"Thank God!" said Schussler with a sound that was as close as a thing of metal and machinery could come to a sigh of relief.

There was a momentary pause.

"Do you remember our bargain?" asked the cyborg.

"That's why I'm here."

"You're an honorable man, Sebastian."

"How do I go about it?" asked Cain, walking over to the

panel that hid Schussler's essence from view. "Is there a way I can disconnect you without causing you too much pain?"

"I can't feel pain," said Schussler. "If I could, I might even choose to live."

"That's a stupid thing to say."

"Only to a man who can feel, Sebastian."

"All right," said Cain, touching the code that exposed Schussler's tiny enclosure. "What do I do now?"

"I am compelled to obey your orders, even at the cost of my own existence," said Schussler. "Simply order me to cease functioning and I'll die."

Cain stared at the small box. "You mean that's all there is to it?"

"Yes."

"I could have done that at any time."

"But we had an agreement," said Schussler. "I was also compelled to fulfill my end of it."

"Are you ready?" asked Cain.

"Yes. . . . Sebastian?"

"What?"

"I've put down on oxygen planets, and chlorine, and methane. I've been to Deluros Eight, and to the most obscure dead worlds on the edges of the Frontier. I've flown faster than light, and twisted my way through meteor storms."

"I know."

"There's one thing I've never done, one place I've never been."

"Where is that?"

"I've never seen the inside of a star."

"Nobody has."

"Then I'll be the first," said Schussler. "What a beautiful image to carry with me into eternity!"

"Then I so command it," said Cain unhappily.

"Thank you, Sebastian," said the cyborg. "You'd better leave me now."

"Good-bye, Schussler," said Cain, walking to the hatch.

"Watch for me, Sebastian," said Schussler. "It will be twilight soon. I'll wait until then, so that you can see me." He paused. "I'll be the first shooting star of the evening."

"I'll be watching," promised Cain.

And an hour later, as he and Silent Annie were finally setting out on their quest, he stopped to look up. For a moment he saw nothing out of the ordinary; and then—and it was probably just his imagination, for the sun was still quite brilliant and Schussler was some eighty million miles distant—he thought, for a fleeting instant, that he could see an unbelievably bright form streaking toward Safe Harbor's golden sun. It moved faster and faster, and then flickered gratefully out of existence.

Part 6

Santiago's Book

22.

His sire was a comet,
His dam a cosmic wind.
God wept when first He saw him,
But Satan merely grinned.

An even forty verses: that's what Black Orpheus gave him.
Nobody else ever got more than a dozen—but then, nobody
else was Santiago.

Orpheus was faced with a moral and artistic dilemma when
he finally confronted the subject of Santiago, for all of his
verbal portraits were based on firsthand knowledge, and he
had never seen the notorious outlaw. (In point of fact, he had
seen him on five separate occasions over the years, and
spoken to him twice, but he didn't know it, then or ever.)

On the other hand, he knew that any ballad that aspired to
describe the men and events that had shaped the Inner Frontier would be laughably incomplete if it didn't include a major
section on Santiago.

So he compromised. He gave him forty verses, but he never
once referred to him by name. It was his way of saying that
the Santiago stanzas were somehow incomplete.

Sebastian Cain was fast coming to the conclusion that the
legend of Santiago was as incomplete as the ballad. He sat
beside Silent Annie as her vehicle sliced between lush fields
that seemed to writhe and ripple in the dim light of Safe Harbor's moons, finally coming to a halt in front of a small barn.

"First stop," she announced, opening the door and getting
out.

"A barn?" asked Cain as the warmth and humidity hit him full force.

She smiled. "I was rather hoping that you'd learned not to judge anything associated with Santiago by its appearance."

She walked up to the prefabricated structure, tapped out a combination on the lock, and the door slowly opened inward.

"Come along, Mr. Cain," she said, uttering a low command that illuminated the darkened building.

Cain followed her into the cool interior of the barn and found himself facing a row of drying bins, each filled to the brim with ears of mutated corn. High above him was a loft that had once contained hay but looked as if it hadn't been used in the past twenty years.

"Well?" he said.

"Take a look in the third bin."

He walked over and stared at it.

"It looks like corn," he said.

"That's what it's supposed to look like," she replied. "Look a little more closely."

He reached in with both hands, tossing ears of corn aside, and came to a gold bar.

"The Epsilon Eridani raid?" he asked, laboriously lifting the bar with both hands and studying it.

She nodded. "We've got about forty of them left."

"All in this bin?"

"Yes."

"What happened to the rest of it?" asked Cain. "I saw one bar with Jonathan Stern back on Port Étrange, but no one seems to know what became of the others."

"Most of them have been dispersed," she replied. "Would you like to know where?"

"Why not?" He shrugged.

"Follow me."

Silent Annie walked into the barn's tiny office, which contained two vidphones, a pinup calendar printed on real paper, a small wooden desk, an ancient swivel chair, and a computer. Everything except one phone and the computer was covered by a layer of dust.

She activated the computer, waited for it to identify her retina pattern and thumbprint, and then ordered it to bring up the details concerning the Epsilon Eridani gold.

Cain studied the readout as it appeared on the small screen.

"I see that Father William got about a third of it," he noted.

"He's one of the conduits Santiago uses to feed the hungry and medicate the sick. The bulk of the Epsilon Eridani gold was sold on the Kabalka Five black market."

"Kabalka Five? That's an alien world, isn't it?"

"It doesn't take aliens long to find out what men will do for gold," she replied.

"What became of the money you got for the gold?"

She called up another chart on the screen.

"*All* of it went to hospitals?" he asked.

"Not quite. It also sponsored a raid on Pico Two."

"What the hell is on Pico Two? It's just a little dirtball of a world, out by the Quinellus cluster."

"Some of our friends were incarcerated there."

"So you got them out?"

She shook her head. "That was impossible."

"Then what?"

"We blew up the jail."

"With your friends inside it?"

"The Democracy will stop at nothing to find Santiago," replied Silent Annie. "These were loyal men, but they would have talked. If torture didn't work, there are drugs that would have."

"So much for loyalty," said Cain dryly.

"He's not a god and he's not a saint," she said. "He's just a man, and he's fighting against the most powerful political and military machine in the galaxy. Our people know what might befall them when they go out on a mission."

Cain made no comment.

"Secrecy is our only weapon," she continued. "It must be preserved at all costs." She paused, searching for the words to drive home her point. "How do you think he's kept his identity and his whereabouts hidden all these years?" she said at last. "We return from our missions, or we die—but we do not allow ourselves to be taken prisoner."

"Then what happened to your men on Pico Two?"

"They were taken by surprise, before they could destroy themselves." She stared at him levelly. "You look disapproving, Mr. Cain. I should think that you of all people would know that revolution is not a gentleman's sport and is not played by gentleman's rules."

"True enough," he said after some consideration. "I just don't like the thought of killing one's own people."

"I hope you don't think *he* does," replied Silent Annie. "This is a grim business. There's nothing romantic about harassing an overwhelming power with no hope of winning."

"If he knows he can't win, why does he do it?"

"To avoid losing."

"That sounds profound, but it doesn't make a hell of a lot of sense," said Cain.

"I'm sure he'll be happy to expand upon it for you."

"When?"

"Soon," she replied, deactivating the computer and heading back toward the vehicle. "Come along, Mr. Cain."

He fell into step behind her, and a moment later they were once again driving through the humid night air on a single-lane country road.

"Was he born on Safe Harbor?" asked Cain after a momentary silence.

"No."

"How long has he been here?"

"Safe Harbor has been his headquarters for about fifteen years now, though he spends about half his time off-planet."

"Have I ever seen him?" he asked, curious.

"I really couldn't say," she replied. "It's possible." She smiled. "Black Orpheus has, though he doesn't know it."

"There are a lot of things that damned folksinger doesn't know," said Cain.

"You're a very disapproving man, Mr. Cain," said Silent Annie. "Your life must have been filled with disappointments."

"No more than most," he answered. Then he smiled wryly. "On the other hand, there has been a noticeable lack of triumphs."

"Let's have no false modesty. You're a very successful bounty hunter."

"You've been watching too many video fictions," he said. "I don't call villains out to fight in the midday sun. There's nothing very challenging about walking up to a man who's never seen you before and blowing him away before he knows what you're up to."

"And is that what you did to Altair of Altair and the Jack of Diamonds?" she asked with a smile.

"No," he admitted. "I was careless in one case and clumsy in the other."

"What about Alexander the Elder? He had six men protecting him when you took him."

"Four," he corrected her.

"You're evading the point."

"I thought the point was that you were interested in me because of the people I *didn't* kill."

"That's true. But you're a man of many talents, and I'm sure Santiago can make use of all of them."

"We'll see," he said noncommittally.

They rode in silence for another half hour, the corn and wheat fields broken only by an occasional methane production plant, where the waste of Safe Harbor's farm animals was converted into energy. Finally she turned off the road and approached a row of silos.

"More spoils of conquest?" he asked as the vehicle came to a halt.

"A medical center," she replied.

"Why camouflage it?" he asked. "The Democracy has got better things to do than make raids on hospitals."

"Because Safe Harbor's population isn't large enough to support a facility of this size," explained Silent Annie. "A complex like this would draw unwanted attention to ourselves."

He got out of the vehicle and followed her into one of the silos. She led him to an elevator, and after a brief descent he found himself in a white, sterile environment some sixty feet beneath the ground.

"How big is this place?" he asked, looking down the polished corridors that radiated in all directions.

"I don't know the square footage," she replied, "but it extends beneath the entire silo complex. We have twenty-three laboratories, half a dozen observation wards, a pair of surgeries, and four isolation wards. There's also a commissary, as well as extensive staff quarters so that our people aren't seen arriving and leaving every day."

They began walking past the laboratories, each with its white-frocked medics and scientists, and finally came to the first of the observation wards. Cain paused to look in through a thick, one-way glass and saw nine men and women lying in beds, plugged in to life-support and monitoring units. They reminded him of burn victims, with blackened skins that blistered and peeled away from their bodies.

"What happened to them?" asked Cain, staring at an elderly woman whose cheekbones were both exposed.

"They're from Hyperion."

"Never heard of it."

"It was opened up five years ago," she said. "There were about five thousand initial settlers, all of them members of an obscure religious sect."

"They look like they believe in walking through fire," he commented.

She shook her head. "They believe in living in peace with their neighbors. In this particular case, their neighbors were a very aggressive humanoid race, and it took them almost two years to reach an accommodation—but they finally did." She paused. "Then the Democracy decided that Hyperion was strategically desirable as a military base. There were a couple of incidents involving the native population, and Hyperion was declared off limits to civilians. The colony, which had made its peace, refused to leave."

"And the navy did *this* to them?"

"Indirectly," she replied. "After the navy came to the conclusion that pacifying the native humanoids was more trouble than it was worth, they released a chemical agent in the atmosphere which killed off the entire race. It's far from the first such instance out here." She looked through the glass at the nine humans. "Unfortunately, it also caused a bacterial mutation that resulted in a virulent skin disease among the colonists. Since they had been warned to leave, the navy refuses to take responsibility for them."

"How many colonists survived?" asked Cain.

"Of the original five thousand, a little less than half of them are still alive."

"And how many of them are here?"

"Just those that you see. We haven't the room or the money to treat them all, so we brought a representative sample here to see if we could effect a cure. If we can come up with a serum or a vaccine, we'll ship it back to Hyperion with them."

"And you do this for how many worlds?"

"As many as we can."

"It must cost a small fortune to run this kind of operation," he commented:

"A *large* fortune," she corrected him. "We have four other facilities on the Inner Frontier."

"All functioning covertly?"

She nodded. "If the Democracy knew about them, they'd be that much closer to finding Santiago." She looked directly at him. "And if they find him, the people of Hyperion and a hundred other worlds of the Inner Frontier will have no place to turn."

They walked out into a corridor leading to the next ward, and Cain immediately stepped back to allow an orderly to wheel an enormous, elephantine being into one of the surgery rooms.

"What the hell was *that?*" he asked.

"A native of Castor Five," she replied.

"You work on aliens, too?"

"Her race is sentient, and it has been oppressed by the Democracy. We have no third qualification."

"You start treating all the aliens the Democracy has oppressed, and you won't be able to build enough hospitals to hold them," said Cain.

"I know," she said. "But we do what we can. It's just a gesture, but a very important one." She eyed him carefully. "Or are you of the opinion that it is Man's manifest destiny to rule the galaxy alone?"

"I never gave it much thought," he answered. "I suppose if might makes right, he's got a jump on the rest of the field."

"*Does* might make right?" she asked.

Cain shrugged. "No. But it makes it pretty difficult for anyone to tell you you're wrong."

"But not impossible," she pointed out. "And that's precisely what we're doing—by example." She stared at him again. "I hope this is making some impression on you, Mr. Cain. It's very important that you understand exactly what we're fighting for."

"It's making an impression," he said noncommittally.

"I hope so," she repeated.

They walked through the remainder of the complex in silence, then returned to the elevator.

"How many more public works do I have to see before I get to meet Santiago?" asked Cain as they ascended to the surface.

"There aren't any more," said Silent Annie. "At least, not on Safe Harbor. We don't want to do anything that might call attention to this planet."

She stepped out into the interior of a silo, and he followed her as she made her way to the vehicle. A moment later they were once again speeding across the countryside.

"How much farther?" he asked after a few minutes.

"About fifteen miles," she replied. "It's been dark for almost three hours now. Are you getting hungry?"

"I can wait."

"I can signal ahead and have dinner waiting for you when we arrive."

"It's not necessary."

"Do you still intend to kill him?" she asked suddenly.

"I don't know."

She made no further comment, and they drove the next twenty minutes in silence. Then she took a hard left turn and began driving down a bumpy dirt road. In the distance Cain could see a white prefabricated house with a huge veranda that seemed to circle it completely.

"That's it?" he asked.

"That's it."

"He's not very well protected," he commented. "I've only spotted three sensing devices since we turned onto this road."

"You're not supposed to see *any.*"

"It's my business to see them."

She shrugged. "It's dark out. Probably some of them have escaped your attention."

"I doubt it."

"You must also remember that he has no enemies on Safe Harbor," said Silent Annie. "Except perhaps for you."

"Just the same, his security's lousy," said Cain. "That guy on the roof stands out like a sore thumb."

"What guy?"

"The one with the laser rifle. He let the moonlight glint off his infrared scope a minute ago."

"I don't see anyone," she said, peering into the darkness.

"He's there, big as life—and twice as easy a target. It's going to take more than this to keep the Angel out."

"Is that your professional opinion?"

"It is."

"I'll tell him you said so."

"I'll tell him myself," said Cain.

They pulled up to the house and climbed out of the vehicle.

Silent Annie led the way to the front door, which slid back into the wall before she reached it, letting out a burst of cool dry air in the process.

Cain followed her into the foyer, which was empty, and then into the large living room. There were a number of slightly shabby, very comfortable chairs and couches arranged in little groupings, and a heatless pseudofire roared in a brick fireplace. There was also a portable bar, a large holo screen, and a trio of elegantly framed mirrors—but it was the books that overwhelmed everything else in the room. They were everywhere—stacked neatly in floor-to-ceiling cases, piled on tables, casually tossed onto window seats, spread open over chair and sofa arms, even laid out on the hearth.

The only person in the room was a man dressed in a tan lounging suit. He sat on an easy chair, reading a leather-bound book and sipping an Alphard brandy.

He appeared to be in his late forties or early fifties. His hair was brown and thinning, and had started to turn gray at the sides. His eyes, too, were brown, and stared curiously at Cain from under long, thin eyebrows that sloped gently upward, giving him a perpetually questioning look. His nose had been broken at least once, possibly many times, and his teeth were so white and straight that Cain immediately decided they weren't his own. There was an S-shaped scar on the back of his right hand.

He was a burly man who was starting to put weight on a once powerful figure, but when he stood up he did so with an athletic grace.

"I've been waiting a long time to meet you, Sebastian," he said in a deep voice.

"Not as long as *I've* been waiting to meet *you*," said Cain.

Santiago smiled. "And now that you're here, which do you propose to do—talk or shoot?"

"We'll talk first," said Cain. He looked around the living room. "You've got quite a library. I don't think I've ever seen so many books in one place before."

"I like the heft and feel of a book," replied Santiago. "Computer libraries are filled with electronic impulses. Books are filled with *words*." He patted his book fondly and tossed it onto his chair. "I've always preferred words."

"You've also got a lot of mirrors," noted Cain.

"I'm a vain man."

"Tell whoever's behind them not to get overeager. I could have taken them out the second I entered the room."

Santiago laughed. "You heard him," he said, turning to the mirrors. "Leave us alone." He turned back to Silent Annie, who had been standing quietly behind Cain. "You can leave us, too. I'll be quite safe."

"You're an optimist," said Cain as Silent Annie left the room.

"A realist," said Santiago. "If you kill me, you'll do it in such a way that you live to spend the reward." He paused. "Can I offer you some brandy?"

Cain nodded, and Santiago walked over to the bar and poured out a glass while the bounty hunter studied him.

"Here you are," said Santiago, approaching him and handing him the brandy.

"You're too young," said Cain.

"Cosmetic surgery," replied Santiago with a smile. "I told you I was a vain man."

"You're also a *wanted* man."

"Only by the Democracy," said Santiago. "Let me suggest that sometimes it's not a bad idea to judge a man by his enemies."

"In your case it's an absolute necessity," said Cain sardonically. "I've *met* your friends."

Santiago shrugged. "One works with what's at hand. If I could have enlisted better allies than Poor Yorick and Altair of Altair and the others, I assure you I would have." He paused. "In fact, that's why you're here."

"So I've been told."

"We're very much alike, Sebastian. We hold the same values, we fight against the same oppression, we even subscribe to the same methodology. I very much want you on my side."

"I've retired from the revolution business," said Cain.

"You fought for the wrong causes."

"The causes were right," said Cain. "The *men* were wrong."

"I stand corrected."

"What makes you any better than they were?"

Santiago stared at him for a moment.

"I have a proposal," he announced at last. "You've had a long, hard day, Sebastian. You've killed a man, you've seen things that no member of the Democracy has ever seen, and you've finally come face to face with the most wanted man in the galaxy. You must be hot and tired and hungry." He paused. "Let's declare a truce for tonight. We'll have dinner, we'll get to know each other a little better, and tomorrow morning, when you're feeling rested, I promise that we'll talk business—mine *and* yours."

Cain stared at him impassively, then nodded. "I think I'll skip dinner, though," he said.

"You've only had one sandwich all day."

"You're very well informed," remarked Cain.

"And *you're* worrying needlessly," said Santiago. "I've had numerous opportunities to kill you since you landed on Safe Harbor. I didn't permit you to come all this way just to poison you."

"Makes sense," admitted Cain.

Santiago led him into the dining room, which was as cluttered with books as the living room.

"I trust you'll be a little easier on my pantry than Father William," said Santiago. He shook his head wonderingly. "The way that man eats, I don't know why he isn't dead by now."

"A lot of people are wondering the same thing about you," said Cain, seating himself across from Santiago.

"A lot of people think I *am* dead," said Santiago. Suddenly he chuckled. "You wouldn't believe some of the stories they tell about me, Sebastian. I've heard that I was killed three different times last year, and that I laid waste to a little world called Silverblue out on the Galactic Rim. One story even had me assassinating some diplomat on Canphor Seven."

"You're also eleven feet tall and have orange hair," remarked Cain wryly.

"Really?" asked Santiago, interested. "I hadn't heard that one." He shrugged. "Well, I suppose that's the price of anonymity."

"I'd hardly call you anonymous," said Cain. "There are hundreds of men making full-time careers out of trying to hunt you down and kill you."

"And here I am, alive and well," said Santiago. "I'd say that's a pretty good definition of living anonymously."

"If you really want to be anonymous, why not scotch some of these myths and legends that have sprung up about you?"

"The more crimes the Democracy thinks I've committed, the more manpower they'll divert from people who can't defend themselves," he replied. "But here we are, talking business again, after I promised to let you relax."

"I don't mind," said Cain.

"We'll have ample time for it tomorrow," said Santiago. "Shall we talk about literature?"

Cain shrugged. "Whatever you like."

"Good," said Santiago as a pair of young men emerged from the kitchen and began serving them. "Have you ever read anything by Tanblixt?"

"I never heard of him."

"He's an *it*, not a *him*," said Santiago. "A Canphorite, in fact—and an absolutely brilliant poet."

"I've never been interested much in poetry," said Cain.

"Excellent soup," commented Santiago, sipping a spoonful. "Father William drinks it by the gallon."

"It's very good," agreed Cain, taking a taste.

"I've also been rereading a number of novels written in the days when we were still Earthbound," continued Santiago. "I've developed a special fondness for Dickens."

"*David Copperfield*?" suggested Cain.

"Ah!" Santiago smiled. "I *knew* you were a learned man."

"I just said I'd read it," replied Cain. "I never said I liked it."

"Then let me recommend one I've just finished: *A Tale of Two Cities*."

"Maybe I'll give it a try tomorrow," said Cain. "*If* we're still talking."

"We will be," Santiago assured him. "A few minutes ago you asked how I differed from all the other revolutionaries you've fought for. We'll discuss it in detail tomorrow, but I'll give you a hint right now, if you'd like."

"Go ahead."

"My cause was lost before I ever joined it," replied Santiago with an enigmatic smile.

Cain was still considering that remark when he got up from the dinner table and went off to discuss literature with the King of the Outlaws.

23.

He lives on a mountain, a mountain of gold,
With a temper that's hot and a heart that is cold.
He issues his orders, makes known his demands,
Then sits back to watch while his empire expands.

It wasn't a mountain of gold, of course—but it was as beautiful a farm as Cain had ever seen.

There were some 1,800 acres, divided equally between wheat, mutated corn, soybeans, and livestock, crisscrossed with streams, dotted here and there by ponds.

"Actually, the ground rolls a little too much to be truly efficient farmland," remarked Santiago as the two men sat on the veranda, looking out over the sloping fields. "It's a fact that realtors all over the galaxy have learned to appreciate: the prettier the landscape is, the harder it is to farm it effectively. Proper farmland is flat." He sighed. "But I took one look at this place and fell in love with it."

"It's restful," agreed Cain.

"It broke my heart to bulldoze the trees that were in the field. I kept the prettiest grove intact, and erected the house right next to it." Santiago pointed to a pair of nearby trees. "I have a hammock that I tie between those two," he said. "I love to lie on it, sipping an iced drink and feeling just like a proper country gentleman."

"You're an odd kind of revolutionary," remarked Cain.

"I'm fighting an odd kind of revolution," replied Santiago.
"Why?"

"Why is it odd?" asked Santiago.

311

"Why are you fighting it?"

"Because somebody has to."

"That's not much of a reason."

"It's the best reason there is," said Santiago. "The first
duty of power is to perpetuate itself. The first duty of free
men is to resist it."

"I've heard this song before," said Cain dryly.

"Ah, but it was sung by people who wanted power themselves, people who wanted to remake their worlds or even the
Democracy."

"And you don't want to do that?"

"Remake the Democracy?" said Santiago. He shook his
head. "The second you attain power, you become what you've
been fighting against." He paused. "Besides, I'm enough of
a realist to know that it can't be done. The Democracy has
more ships than I've got men. It will still be abusing its
power a millennium after you and I are dead."

"Then why persist?" asked Cain.

Santiago stared at him thoughtfully for a moment.

"You know, Sebastian, I have a feeling that you'd be
happier if I were a gentle, white-haired old man who called
everyone 'my son,' and told you that utopia was just around
the corner. Well, it isn't. I persist in fighting because I see
something that's wrong, and the alternative to fighting is to
submit."

Cain made no comment.

"If you want a philosophic justification, you'll find it in
my library," continued Santiago. "I've got a much simpler
explanation."

"What is it?"

He smiled a savage smile. "When someone pushes me, I
push back."

"It's a good feeling," admitted Cain. "But . . ."

"But what?"

"I'm tired of losing."

"Then join me, and fight on my side," said Santiago.

"You've already admitted you can't win."

"But that doesn't mean I have to lose." He paused. "Hell,
I wouldn't want to overthrow the Democracy even if I could."

"Why not?"

"First, as I said, because I don't want to become part of
the establishment that I'm fighting. And second, because the

Democracy isn't truly evil, or even especially corrupt. It's simply a government that, like all governments, makes its decisions based on what will result in the greatest benefit for the greatest number. From their point of view, and given their constituency, they're a moral and ethical institution. They undoubtedly feel that they have every right to plunder the Frontier and abrogate the rights of its citizens—and in the long run, if it strengthens their position in the galaxy, they may even be correct." He paused. "On the other hand, those of us who bear the brunt of these abuses don't have to stand idly by and hope that everything will work out for the best. We can fight back."

"How?" asked Cain, staring intently at him.

"By understanding the nature of the enemy," said Santiago. "This isn't some planetary military machine we're talking about. This is the *Democracy*. It encompasses more than a hundred thousand worlds, and it's not going to change—not overnight, not ever." He paused. "But if we harass and harry them enough, we can convince them that it's less expensive in terms of money and human life to leave us alone than to continue to oppress us." He took a deep breath and exhaled it slowly. "After all, what do we really have that's worth such an expense? We're a mass of insignificant, underpopulated worlds."

"To say nothing of disorganized," commented Cain.

"That's part of our strength."

Cain arched an eyebrow.

"You look skeptical," noted Santiago.

"I never thought lack of organization was a virtue."

"It never was before. But if we organized, if we had an army and a navy and a chain of command, the Democracy would know where to strike, and we would be decimated within a week. In fact, the nature of the enemy makes it impossible for a leader to emerge from the masses and rally men to his banner."

"Except for you."

Santiago chuckled. "I'm not a leader," he said. "I'm a lightning rod. I raid and I loot and I kill, and the Democracy wrings its hands and offers rewards for the King of the Outlaws." A satisfied smile crossed his face. "If they *knew* why I was doing this, if they had the slightest inkling what I was financing with the spoils of my conquests, they'd have fifty million men out here, scouring every inch of every world for me." He paused. "I'm good at hiding, but I'm not *that* good. I'd much rather be thought of as a successful villain than a successful revolutionary."

"*Are* you a successful revolutionary?" asked Cain.

"You were at the medical center," replied Santiago. "You've seen what we're trying to do."

"Any team of doctors could do the same thing."

"True," admitted Santiago. "But any team of doctors couldn't pay for the facility, and they certainly couldn't mine the area where the navy plans to build its base on Hyperion."

"Silent Annie says it was an accident."

"Was it also an accident that they killed off a native population of millions of sentient beings?" demanded Santiago. "That scenario has been played over and over again all across the Inner Frontier. I'm trying to convince them that there's a better way—and failing that, I'll damned well convince them that there's a less painful way."

"Is it working?"

"It depends on your point of view," answered Santiago. "Hundreds of colonies exist that would have been decimated. Tens of thousands of Men are alive who otherwise wouldn't have been. A handful of alien races who hated all Men have learned that some of us are a bit less hateful than others." He smiled. "It's a matter of proportion. I would say it's working; the Democracy would probably wonder why we had wasted so many lives and so many years to produce such insignificant results."

A man in his early thirties, with a streak of white running through his coal-black hair, emerged from the interior of the house just then and approached them.

"Yes?" said Santiago. "What is it?"

The man looked at Cain hesitantly.

"This is Sebastian Cain," said Santiago. "While he is my guest, I have no secrets from him." He turned to Cain. "Sebastian, this is Jacinto, one of my most trusted associates."

Cain nodded a greeting.

"I am pleased to meet you, Mr. Cain," said Jacinto, inclining his head slightly. He turned back to Santiago. "Winston Kchanga has refused to deliver our merchandise to us."

"I'm sorry to hear that," said Santiago, frowning. "Has he offered any reason?"

Jacinto snorted contemptuously.

"I'm afraid Mr. Kchanga has outlived his usefulness to us," said Santiago.

Jacinto nodded and went back into the house.

"I suppose I should explain."

"It's none of my business," replied Cain.

"Hopefully it will be before much longer. Winston Kchanga is a smuggler operating out of the Corvus system. He made a commitment to us, money was exchanged, and he has elected not to honor that commitment. He doesn't know that *I* am involved, but that's neither here nor there." He sighed. "Regrettable."

"Not *that* regrettable," said Cain. "There's paper on him."

"Perhaps I should clarify my statement," said Santiago. "I find it regrettable that one of the people we are fighting for should try to swindle us. I have no regrets whatsoever about ordering his death." He looked sharply at Cain. "I'm fighting a war, and whenever one fights a war there are going to be casualties. My main concern is that they aren't innocent ones."

"From what I hear, there's wasn't a hell of a lot that Kchanga was innocent of," said Cain. He paused. "There's paper on your friend Jacinto, too. He used to go under the name of Esteban Cordoba."

"Jacinto hasn't left Safe Harbor in seven years," said Santiago. "You have a remarkable memory, Sebastian."

"It's that white streak in his hair," replied Cain. "It's pretty hard to forget."

"He's the most trusted associate I have," said Santiago. "He's served me loyally for almost fifteen years." He stared at Cain again. "What do you propose to do about him?"

Cain shrugged. "Nothing."

A broad smile spread over Santiago's face. "Then you're joining us?"

"I didn't say that. We've got a lot more to talk about."

Santiago got to his feet. "Shall we walk while we talk?" he suggested. "It's too beautiful a day to just sit in the shade."

"Whatever you want."

"Then come with me, and I'll show you the farm while we speak."

Cain followed Santiago down off the veranda.

"Are you a fisherman, Sebastian?" asked Santiago.

"No."

"You should try it sometime. I've stocked three of the ponds."

"Maybe someday I'll take it up."

"You should. It's very relaxing." He began circling one of the ponds. "I believe you had some questions to ask me?"

"A few," said Cain, falling into step beside him. "For starters, when did you decide you needed a bodyguard?"

"Is that what you think I have in mind for you?"

"If it isn't, then it should be," said Cain. "The Angel can't be too far away."

"I already have bodyguards."

"They couldn't stop me if I decided to kill you right now."

"True—but I know that you won't. And I have no intention of giving the Angel a tour of my farm."

"I assume that you haven't helped *him* to find you?"

Santiago frowned and shook his head. "No. He's a remarkable man."

"And as I said last night, you're a wanted one."

"He won't get past Father William."

"He's gotten past better men than Father William," said Cain.

"There *are* no better men than Father William," replied Santiago.

"If you don't want me as a bodyguard, just why *am* I here?" asked Cain.

"I've been a very fortunate man, Sebastian," said Santiago. "But nobody lives forever. I would like to think my work will go on after I'm gone. It can't do that unless I leave good people behind me—people like Jacinto and Silent Annie, and people like you."

Cain stared at him. "You *do* think he's going to kill you."

Santiago shook his head. "No, I truly don't. But I can't conscript men to my cause the way the navy can. I have to study them carefully and then try to convince the best of them to join me."

"Why now?"

"It took me this long to be sure you were the man I wanted."

"How many others have you asked?"

"Recruiting people is nothing new. Sebastian. I've been doing it ever since I came out here. You're the most recent, but you're not unique."

"How many of them have I met?"

"More than you might suppose," replied Santiago. "How else would I have known about you?"

"I know Geronimo Gentry is one of them."

"That's correct."

"What about Terwilliger?"

Santiago shook his head. "No."

"Stern?"

"No." Suddenly Santiago laughed. "I suppose I'll have to recruit him if I ever want to organize the *fali*."

"He says he met you when you were in jail on Kalami Three."

"Then I suppose he did."

"You don't match his description of you."

Santiago shrugged. "As I told you, I've had cosmetic surgery."

"Did it take four or five inches off your height?"

"That was many years ago, and Stern has been with the *fali* for a long, long time—and he was a much smaller man than you are." He looked amused. "Or are you suggesting that I'm an imposter?"

"No," said Cain. "Are you suggesting that *I* become one?"

"I don't think I follow you."

"I looked at your *Tale of Two Cities* last night," said Cain. "It occurs to me that the Angel has never seen either of us."

"And you think I want you to impersonate me if and when he arrives?"

"Do you?"

"Absolutely not. I fight my own fights." He paused. "Other than that, how did you like the book?"

"Other than that, it was pretty boring."

"I'm sorry that you didn't enjoy it."

"I had other things on my mind," said Cain. "I still do."

"Such as?"

"Such as whether or not I can believe you," replied Cain. "I've killed an awful lot of people for men I believed in, and I've always been disappointed."

"I'm not asking you to kill anyone for *me*, Sebastian,"

said Santiago. "That would be presumptuous. I'm asking you to help me *protect* people from the abuses of a distant government that couldn't care less about them."

"Not ten minutes ago you ordered Jacinto to kill someone for you," Cain pointed out.

"That was for the cause, not for me," answered Santiago. "Since I can't fund my operation through legitimate means, I must resort to questionable tactics. Winston Kchanga cannot be allowed to cheat us and escape punishment for his actions. If word got out that we didn't protect our interests, it wouldn't be long before the criminal element preyed upon us just as the Democracy does." He turned and began walking alongside a field containing row upon row of huge, mutated corn. "Revolution is no place for the squeamish. Surely you must understand that."

"I understand that," said Cain. "How many men will you want me to kill?"

Santiago stopped and met his gaze levelly. "I'll never ask you to kill anyone who doesn't deserve killing."

"I do that now, and I get well paid for it."

"If you come with me, you'll continue doing it. You'll get paid nothing, there will be a price on your head, and even the people you're fighting for will want you dead." Santiago smiled wryly. "That's not much to offer, is it?"

"No, it isn't."

"Then let me sweeten the pot," continued Santiago. "You'll have one benefit that you don't have in your present occupation."

"What?"

"The knowledge that you'll have made a difference."

"It would be nice to have, just once," said Cain sincerely.

"Nobody will know it but you," said Santiago.

"Nobody *has* to."

There was a momentary silence.

"What are you thinking, Sebastian?"

"That I'd like to believe you."

"Do you?"

"I haven't made up my mind." He paused in the shadow of a twelve-foot-high cornstalk. "What if I decide not to?"

"I'm unarmed, and my bodyguards are back at the house."

"I was more concerned with what *you* might do to *me*."

"We'll worry about that when the time comes."

"You'll have to kill me," said Cain. "Or try to, anyway. I know what you look like and where to find you."

"There are a few others who do, too," said Santiago. "It would make things much less complicated if you joined me, though."

They continued walking, Santiago listing his grievances against the Democracy, telling Cain of the actions he had taken and the people he had saved and failed to save. Cain listened thoughtfully, asking an occasional question, making an occasional observation.

"It's the judgment calls that age you," said Santiago as they walked alongside a stream that made a natural boundary between two of the fields. "There's an enormous amount of work to be done, and we have very little money and man-power. Do we spend it on salvation or retribution? Do we put everything we have into patching up the Democracy's victims and sending them back to be stomped on again, or do we let them lie where they've fallen and take steps to see that the same thing doesn't happen to their neighbors?"

"You prevent it from happening again," said Cain firmly.

"Answered like a bounty hunter," replied Santiago. "Unfortunately, it's easier said than done. The Epsilon Eridani raid was atypical. We don't have the firepower to stand up to the navy." He sighed. "Oh, well, that's what keeps it challenging. We do what we can, where we can. It's a balancing act—saving people when it's possible, punishing others when we can get away with it, and financing the whole thing with enterprises and associates that make the Swagman look honorable by comparison."

"How did you miss killing Whittaker Drum?" asked Cain.

"Socrates?"

"Yes."

"Because I'm not some kind of phantom avenger, righting all the wrongs of the galaxy," said Santiago. "I knew what he had done on Sylaria, even before I knew that you had fought for him." He turned to Cain and stared at him. "But that was twenty years ago, and Sylaria is thousands of light-years away. Socrates was useful to me, so I used him, just as I've used hundreds of men who are far worse than him."

He stopped and inspected an enormous ear of corn.

"Three more weeks and it'll be ready to harvest," he announced. "Four at the most. Have you ever been on a farm at harvesttime, Sebastian?"

Cain shook his head. "No, I haven't."

"There's a sense of accomplishment, of nature fulfilled and renewed," said Santiago. "Even the air smells better."

Cain smiled. "Maybe you should have been a farmer."

"I suppose I am, in a way."

"I meant full-time," said Cain. "I wasn't referring to this."

"Neither was I," replied Santiago. "Saint Peter was a fisher of men. I'm a sower of revolution." He seemed pleased with himself. "I rather like that."

They walked another quarter mile or so. The cornfields were supplanted by long rows of soybeans, which in turn dwindled into nothingness as they reached the top of a ridge.

"What's that down there?" asked Cain, pointing to a neatly manicured clearing within a small dell. There was a wooden bench facing a pond that was dotted by colorful water plants.

"My very favorite place," said Santiago, leading him over to it. "I often come here to read, or simply meditate. You can even see some of the livestock from here." He took a deep breath, as if even the air tasted better in this clearing. "I've planted some flowers, but they've already blossomed and died; they won't bloom again for another five or six months."

"Flowers aren't all you've planted," commented Cain, gesturing to two mounds of earth.

"They were two of the best men I ever knew," said Santiago quietly.

"Then why put them in unmarked graves?"

"Nobody ever comes here except me, and I know who they are," replied Santiago.

Cain shrugged, then noticed a flash of motion out of the corner of his eye. Turning, he saw a man walking toward them. The sun caught the white streak in the man's hair, and Cain realized that it was Jacinto.

"I thought I'd find you here," said Jacinto when he finally joined them. He turned to Cain. "Rain or shine, he spends a couple of hours a day here."

"It's a pretty place," said Cain.

"Are you just visiting?" asked Santiago.

Jacinto shook his head. "Father William is at the house."

"It's unusual for him to come out to the farm. I suppose he's just making sure that Sebastian hasn't killed me."

"He *did* say that he's here to talk to Mr. Cain," said Jacinto.

"He's about as subtle as an earthquake," remarked Santiago. He stepped away from the graves. "Well, I suppose we shouldn't keep him waiting."

He began walking back toward the house, and Cain and Jacinto fell into step behind him.

"Will you be staying with us for any length of time, Mr. Cain?" asked Jacinto.

"It's a possibility," replied Cain.

"I hope so. We've needed someone like you."

"We need about a thousand people like him," said Santiago. "However, we'll settle for the one we've got."

"May I ask a question that requires your professional expertise, Mr. Cain?" said Jacinto.

"Go ahead."

"What do you think of our security?"

"It stinks."

Jacinto shot a triumphant smile at Santiago. "That's what I've been trying to tell *him* for months." He turned back to Cain. "How would you change it?"

"Triple your manpower and put them on round-the-clock watches, for starters. And try to explain to them that if *they* can see in the dark, so can the Angel."

"You see?" Jacinto demanded of Santiago.

"We've been through all this before," said Santiago irritably. "I won't be a prisoner on my own planet." He increased his pace, and Cain and Jacinto lagged behind.

"I apologize for involving you in this argument," said Jacinto softly. "But he simply will not bring any more men back to Safe Harbor."

"How many has he got here?" asked Cain.

"You mean on the planet?"

"Not counting doctors and technicians and the like."

"Perhaps fifty."

"And on the farm?"

"Fifteen, counting myself."

"That won't stop the Angel."

"I know. Hopefully you will be all that we need."

"I haven't said I'm staying."

"Then perhaps Father William . . ."

"I doubt it." Cain paused. "By the way, there's one other bit of professional advice I can give you."

"Yes?"

"If you ever leave Safe Harbor, dye your hair."

Jacinto looked surprised. "I will," he said. "Thank you."

They caught up with Santiago shortly thereafter, and the three men walked the remaining distance to the house together, Santiago pointing out various facets of the farm to Cain as they passed them. Father William was waiting for them on the veranda.

"Good morning, Santiago," said the preacher. "Jacinto." He turned to Cain. "Hello again, Sebastian. Have you enjoyed your stay?"

"It's been interesting," replied Cain.

"Are you getting along well with your host?" he asked sharply.

"So far."

"I'm glad to hear it."

"I was sure you would be."

"I understand you want to talk to Sebastian," said Santiago. "If you wish, we'll leave you two alone."

"That won't be necessary," said Father William with a curious smile. "Actually, I'm just here to deliver a message from a new arrival."

"The Angel?" asked Cain, suddenly tense.

Santiago shook his head. "He's out by the Cantrell system."

"Who is it, then?" persisted Cain.

"Why don't you just read this?" said Father William, handing him a folded sheet of very expensive stationery.

Cain saw that it was written in an elegant, near calligraphic script, and read it aloud:

> *"The Jolly Swagman sends Greetings and Felicitations to his Partner, Sebastian Cain, and cordially invites him to the Barleycorn Tavern for aperitifs at four this afternoon, at which time they will renew their Friendship and also discuss certain Matters of Business."*

Cain tossed the note onto a table. "That's the Swagman, all right," he said.

"Silent Annie urged me to kill him while I had the chance," said Santiago. "I think she may have been right."

"Is there any reply?" asked Father William, still amused.

"I'll deliver it in person," said Cain grimly.

24.

He robs and he plunders, he kills and he loots,
He stealthily sneaks up and suddenly shoots.
He never forgets and he never forgives;
He never relents while an enemy lives.

One of the things Black Orpheus never understood was why the Jolly Swagman, who was his friend, refused to give him any information about Santiago, denying him even a physical description. He was sure the Swagman knew Santiago, had overheard two of his associates say as much, but that was the one subject upon which the loquacious criminal refused to speak.

It made a lot more sense from the Swagman's point of view. What nobody understood about him, not Orpheus, not even Father William or Virtue MacKenzie, was that money was just a tool, a means to an end—and that end was his collection of alien artwork. He kept his own counsel about Santiago not out of any loyalty or friendship for him, but simply because Santiago alive and free was plunderable, if he could just come up with a method, whereas Santiago captured and incarcerated was the property of the Democracy, as were all his possessions.

The third alternative was Santiago dead, and that was what he had come to Safe Harbor to discuss.

He sat in the tavern, sipping an iced mixture of exotic liqueurs from Antares and Ranchero, a small alien puzzle-game in his hand. He manipulated the oddly shaped pieces with a sureness that came from long hours of practice, look-

324

ing up every now and then to admire Moonripple's face and figure—what he could distinguish of them beneath her unkempt hair and the ragged clothing.

Finally he tired of the puzzle, put it back in the pocket of his elegantly tailored satin tunic, pulled out a small, transparent cube from another pocket, and spent the next few minutes admiring the tiny blue-and-white beetlelike insect, crusted with jewels, that resided there.

He had just put it away when Cain and Father William entered the tavern and approached him.

"Good afternoon, Sebastian," said the Swagman with a friendly smile. "I see you got my message."

Cain sat down opposite him. "What the hell are you doing here?"

"In a moment," said the Swagman, holding up his hand. "First I have a gift for your chauffeur."

"I assume you're referring to me," said Father William, amused.

"That I am. Moonripple!"

"Yes, sir?"

"Father William's present, if you please."

She went into the kitchen and emerged a moment later carrying an enormous tray, which contained a large roasted waterfowl in a cream sauce. It was surrounded by dumplings and potatoes.

"Where shall I put it, sir?" asked Moonripple.

"As far from this table as possible." He smiled apologetically at Father William, who was eyeing the waterfowl greedily. "I'd like to speak to my partner privately. This will give you something to do with your mouth."

"I'm not even going to take offense at that remark, given the magnitude of this thoroughly Christian gesture," said Father William, rubbing his hands together and walking over to the table where Moonripple had placed the tray. He signaled to the girl. "I think I'm going to need a pitcher of beer to wash this down, my child." She began to protest, but he held up a finger for silence. "I know what we discussed last night, but God understands that the flesh is weak. I'll begin my diet next Monday."

"For sure this time?"

"Unless Providence intervenes."

She looked her disbelief but brought him his beer, and a

moment later he was attacking his dinner, oblivious to the rest of the universe.

"It's good to see you again, Sebastian," said the Swagman, lowering his voice just enough so that it wouldn't carry across the room.

"I wish I could say the same," responded Cain. "What are you doing here?"

"Simple. You followed a smuggling trail and the Angel followed a paper trail." He grinned. "I decided to follow the easiest trail of all—bounty hunters."

"There are a lot of worlds with more bounty hunters than this one."

"True," admitted the Swagman. "But they don't have you and Father William on them. You killed a man yesterday, but you didn't leave—and Father William has been here for more than a month."

"Santiago's not here," said Cain.

"Allow me the courtesy of asking if he is, before you start lying to me," said the Swagman. He paused. "If he *isn't* on Safe Harbor, Orpheus must be having a reunion of all the killers he's ever written up. You know that the Angel's on his way here, don't you?"

"How close is he?" asked Cain.

"Two or three days away," replied the Swagman. "And he's got another of your partners with him."

"Virtue or Terwilliger?" asked Cain.

"Hadn't you heard? Terwilliger, alas, has gone to that great gambling parlor in the sky."

"Who killed him—the Angel?"

The Swagman shook his head. "ManMountain Bates finally caught up with him."

Cain shrugged. "He shouldn't have cheated him."

"I knew you'd be heartbroken," said the Swagman with a chuckle. "If it'll make you feel any better, the Angel avenged his death."

Cain frowned. "There wasn't any paper on Bates."

"I guess the Angel must be one of nature's noblemen," commented the Swagman. "He gives work to incompetent journalists and he avenges crooked gamblers." He scrutinized Cain from beneath half-lowered lids. "Have you met any similarly public-minded citizens lately?"

"Who did you have in mind?" asked Cain expressionlessly.

"You know who," said the Swagman. "Has he enlisted you in the Great Crusade yet?"

"I don't know what you're talking about."

"If you play the fool, Sebastian, we're never going to get anywhere. I know he's here, and I can't believe that you've been on this world for two days without finding him."

Cain stared at the Swagman for a long moment.

"I found him," he said at last.

"And of course you didn't kill him."

"No, I didn't."

The Swagman smiled. "I knew you wouldn't. So did Yorick." He shook his head. "I would have thought you'd have gotten all that idealism out of your system after getting the hell pounded out of you in your impetuous youth."

"I thought so, too," admitted Cain.

"There's no drunk like an old one," said the Swagman. He signaled to Moonripple, who had just brought Father William a pan of hot biscuits. "A refill, if you please."

"Yes, sir." She looked at Cain. "Will there be anything for you, sir?"

"Maybe a change in company."

"I beg your pardon?"

He sighed. "I'll have a beer."

"Right away, sir."

"I can't imagine what Orpheus saw in her," commented the Swagman as he watched Moonripple walk to the bar.

"No, I don't suppose you can," said Cain.

The Swagman smiled. "I have a feeling that I've just been insulted."

Cain stared at him and made no reply.

"By the way," continued the Swagman, "I didn't see Schussler on my way into town."

"He's dead."

"That was stupid, Sebastian. You receive an absolutely free spaceship with an enormous bank of interesting information, and you destroy it? How wasteful."

"I gave him my word."

"I sincerely doubt that a promise given to a machine is legally binding."

"All the more reason for keeping it," said Cain.

"You're sounding more like him every day," said the Swagman, amused.

"Like Schussler?" asked Cain, puzzled.

"No. Like *him*."

Moonripple arrived with their drinks.

"I want to thank you once again for saving my life, sir," she said to Cain.

"I was happy to do it," he replied.

"I hope Silent Annie was able to help you."

He nodded.

She smiled. "I'm glad. That means I've done something good for you, too."

"Yes, you have."

She smiled again and went back into the kitchen to work on Father William's dessert.

"That's a very touching mutual admiration society you two have going," commented the Swagman.

"If you say so."

"If *I* save her life, will she take *me* to see Santiago, too?"

"I very much doubt it."

"What commitment have you made to him?"

"None, as yet."

"But you will?" he persisted.

"Perhaps."

The Swagman grimaced and shook his head sadly. "Stupid. Just plain stupid."

"Then I suggest you don't join him," said Cain dryly.

"The man is sitting on the biggest collection of artwork on the Frontier!" said the Swagman in exasperation. "And nobody seems to care about it except me!"

"He's also sitting on the biggest collection of bluefever vaccine," answered Cain calmly.

"Who the hell cares about vaccine?" demanded the Swagman. "We're talking about irreplaceable objects of art!"

"Talk about them a little more softly," said Father William from across the room. "You're spoiling my digestion."

"You're a bigger fool than *he* is," said the Swagman, lowering his voice and nodding his head toward Father William. "At least he thinks he's serving the Lord."

"Maybe he is," said Cain.

"You're in danger of becoming a bore, Sebastian," said the Swagman distastefully. "A newfound sense of purpose is one thing; a newfound religious conviction is another."

Cain stared across the table at him. "Just what the hell is it that you want, Swagman?"

"You know perfectly well what I want."

"You'll have to get it yourself."

"Nonsense. We're partners."

"Our partnership is dissolved."

"That doesn't change a thing," said the Swagman.

"Oh? Just how do you figure that?"

The Swagman leaned forward. "Santiago is a dead man, Sebastian. If you don't kill him, the Angel will. It's as simple as that." He withdrew the cube from his pocket and began examining the jewel-encrusted beetle again. "Why let *him* pick up the reward for doing what you can do right now?"

"He won't."

The Swagman smiled. "Who's going to stop him—Father William?" He chuckled. "Killing run-of-the-mill sinners is one thing; killing the Angel is another." He stared intently at Cain. "Or do you think that *you're* going to stop him?"

"It's a possibility."

The Swagman snorted contemptuously. "You haven't got a chance."

"I didn't have a chance against Altair of Altair, either."

"This is different," said the Swagman earnestly. "He's the *Angel*."

"I'm getting tired of hearing about him," said Cain.

"You're going to get a lot more tired of it when everyone starts talking about how he killed Santiago."

"Santiago has stayed hidden for the past three decades," Cain pointed out. "He strikes me as a man who can take care of himself."

"What are you talking about?" demanded the Swagman. "Do you think you're the first bounty hunter to set foot on Safe Harbor?"

Cain shook his head. "Peacemaker MacDougal was here four months ago. He killed Billy Three-Eyes right in front of this tavern." He smiled grimly. "But of course you knew that, didn't you?"

"I'm not talking about Peacemaker MacDougal!" snapped the Swagman. "Hell, half a dozen bounty hunters have gotten this far. Two of them even made it out to his farm."

"What farm?" asked Cain innocently.

"The goddamned farm where Father William gave you my

note," said the Swagman, holding the cube up to the light. "I told you: I'm not totally without resources."

"You didn't even know he lived on Safe Harbor when I left you two weeks ago," said Cain, unimpressed.

"Not until yesterday," admitted the Swagman. "But I knew that he lived on a farm, and I knew that he buried the two bounty hunters who found him out there in one of his wheat fields. I just didn't know where the farm was."

"Who told you that?"

"Someone who worked for him and saw the graves."

"That bespeaks a certain ability to defend himself, doesn't it?"

"If ordinary bounty hunters could get that close, the Angel will kill him," said the Swagman. He paused. "Unless you kill him first."

"Not interested," said Cain.

The Swagman smiled. "You haven't let me make my offer yet."

"Make it and then leave me alone."

"Half," said the Swagman with a confident grin.

"Half of what?"

"Half of the artwork. You keep all the reward and we split the artwork fifty-fifty."

"Stop playing with that damned beetle and go away," said Cain.

"Do you realize what I'm offering you?" asked the Swagman, putting the cube back in his pocket.

Cain nodded. "Do *you* realize that I'm rejecting your offer?"

"You're crazy!" snapped the Swagman. "Even after I take the pieces I want, the rest of it is worth millions on the black market!"

"Maybe I'm just not an art collector."

"You've made a very foolish career decision, Sebastian."

"Is that a threat?" asked Cain.

The Swagman shook his head. "Just a prediction."

"All right. You've made your offer, I've turned it down. Now what?"

"Now we wait."

"For what?"

"For you to change your mind."

"I'm not going to," said Cain.

"Then we wait for the Angel to kill Santiago."

"*He* won't deal with you, either."

"Probably not," agreed the Swagman. "But he also won't know where the artwork is, and I've got as good a chance of finding it as he does."

"Then why make an offer to me at all?" asked Cain, puzzled.

"Because you're a reasonable man, and we've already got a partnership agreement, whether you choose to acknowledge that fact or not. The Angel might take a different view of my confiscating the artwork."

"Then let me set your mind to rest," said Cain seriously. "If you try to take anything that belongs to Santiago, whether he's alive or dead, I'll kill you myself."

The Swagman stared at him. "He *has* made an impression on you, hasn't he?" he said, amused.

"You heard what I said."

The Swagman sighed. "Then I guess I'll just have to check into the boarding house where Father William is staying and await developments."

"Like a scavenger waiting around a kill," commented Cain distastefully.

"An apt comparison," agreed the Swagman with no show of anger. "You'd be surprised how few scavengers die hungry when they follow the right predators."

Cain turned to Father William, who had finished his fowl and was just in the process of polishing off the various side dishes with great enthusiasm.

"We're through talking, if you'd like to join us now," he said in his normal voice.

"Or you could continue to pretend you weren't listening," said the Swagman.

Father William looked across the room and smiled.

"*I* was eating. *God* was listening." The preacher spent another moment sopping up the last of the cream sauce with a piece of a biscuit, then walked over to join them. "Did you conclude your business?"

"We agreed to disagree," said the Swagman.

"Are you planning to leave today, or are you going to blacken your immortal soul still further?" asked Father William.

"Oh, I think I'll stay around for a few days." The Swagman suddenly grinned. "Nice place for a vacation."

"Much as I like you, Swagman, if you lift a finger against

Santiago, I'll hunt you down like an animal," said Father William.

The Swagman chuckled. "You'll have to stand in line. Everyone seems to have become terribly single-minded."

"Just remember: there's paper on you."

"But not for murder," said the Swagman.

"Don't count on that saving your sinful scalp," said the preacher. "You wouldn't be the first man who got killed for resisting arrest."

"Arrest?" repeated the Swagman with a laugh. "Since when did you become a minion of the law?"

"What do you think bounty hunters are?" demanded Father William. "Out here on the Frontier, we're all the law there is. We may not keep the peace, but we punish the lawbreakers—and even that leads to a proper respect for the law after a time."

"I never looked at it that way," admitted the Swagman. "Still, I suppose there's some truth to it."

"More than you know, Swagman," said Father William seriously. "I suggest that you keep it in mind."

"Maybe you'd better tell my partner here," said the Swagman. "He's thinking of helping a wanted criminal."

"You know," said the preacher, "it might be best for all parties concerned if you just went back to Goldenrod and admired your ill-gotten gains."

"I thought it might be more fruitful to try to add to them."

"The only reason you're still alive is because *he* hasn't told me to kill you yet," continued Father William. "This is his world, and you're trespassing."

"I'll try not to lose any sleep worrying about it," said the Swagman.

"Maybe you'd better *start* worrying about it," suggested Cain.

"Kill me, and *Santiago* had better start worrying," retorted the Swagman confidently. "If I don't report in to Goldenrod every day, one of my robots will tell my menials where I am."

"They won't care," said Cain.

"They will when the robot informs them that this is Santiago's world." The Swagman grinned. "You don't really think I'd come here without taking some precautions, do you?"

"I've seen your menials," said Father William. "They're not much."

"But they talk incessantly," replied the Swagman. "You know, for years I've been trying to figure out how to get them to keep a secret. Now I'm glad that I never found an answer."

Father William and Cain exchanged glances.

"All right," said the preacher after some consideration. "You can stay."

"How hospitable of you," said the Swagman ironically.

"But you'd better be on your ship five minutes after we kill the Angel, or you're a dead man." He paused. "Santiago wasn't born on Safe Harbor; he doesn't have to live out his life here, either. If I were you, I'd keep that in mind before I did anything rash."

"Well," said the Swagman, getting to his feet. "I hate to drink and run, but I think I'd better arrange for my accommodations." He turned to Cain. "Once you've calmed down, I trust that you'll reconsider my offer."

"I wasn't excited the first time I heard it," said Cain.

"Think about it," urged the Swagman, walking to the doorway. "Fifty percent."

"Go away," said Cain, turning his back on him.

The Swagman shrugged and walked out the door.

"Well, Sebastian," said Father William, leaning back on his chair, "I must say that I'm proud of you."

"Oh?"

"You looked into the face of the enemy and didn't blink."

"*He's* not the enemy," said Cain. "He's what you're fighting to protect."

"A sobering thought," admitted Father William with a grim smile.

"How much worse can the Democracy be?" mused Cain.

"It's not how much worse," replied the preacher. "It's how much more powerful—and hence, how much more capacity for harm?"

Cain nodded. "I know."

"Things aren't as clear-cut as they were when you were a young man, are they?" chuckled Father William.

"No, they're not."

"It's easy to decide to remake a world," said the preacher. "It's more difficult to choose between evils."

Cain sighed. "It is that," he agreed. He paused. "How did *you* meet him?"

"Santiago?"

"Yes."

"He recruited me, just like he recruited you."

"You knew that was why I was here, didn't you?" asked Cain.

Father William nodded. "I knew almost a year ago that he had decided he wanted you." He chuckled again. "I'll confess I had my doubts when I learned that you were hooked up with the Swagman and that young woman."

"Virtue?"

"That's the one."

"She's an interesting lady," said Cain. "Sometimes I have the feeling that she's going to come out of this better off than anybody."

"She knows how to get what she wants, I'll grant her that," said the preacher.

"And now she's got the Angel," said Cain.

"I have a feeling that she's going to learn that he's a little *more* than she wants," said Father William, not without a note of satisfaction.

"Tell me something," said Cain.

"If I can."

"Who's buried in those two graves?"

"Two men who gave their lives to Santiago's cause."

"The Swagman said they were bounty hunters."

"Once upon a time they may have been. I really couldn't say."

"He told me they were after Santiago, and they made it all the way out to the farm before they were killed."

"The Swagman's wrong," said Father William firmly.

"What were their names?"

Father William shrugged. "Who knows? Nobody uses their real names out here—and especially not if they work for Santiago." He paused. "Why are you so curious about them?"

"Inconsistencies bother me."

"Then don't talk to the Swagman. He's never seen the farm in his life. Santiago has no reason to lie to you; the Swagman has no reason to tell you the truth." He leaned forward. "What did he offer you?"

"Half of the artwork."

"That's very generous," said the preacher. "I wonder how he planned to cheat you out of it?"

"I'm sure he's given it considerable thought," said Cain.

Moonripple emerged from the kitchen and approached Father William.

"How soon will you be wanting your dessert, sir?" she asked.

"Right now," said Father William. "Will you join me, Sebastian?"

"Why not?" said Cain.

"You're sure?" asked Father William, surprised.

"I could use a little snack."

Father William looked as if his heart was about to break. Finally he turned to Moonripple. "My child, how long will it take you to cook up another chocolate cake?"

"I have three more in the kitchen, sir," she replied.

"Good. Bring two of them out here." He turned to Cain. "That way neither of us will leave the table hungry."

"Moonripple's right, you know," said Cain.

"About what?"

"You're going to eat yourself to death."

"I need energy for the work ahead," answered Father William seriously.

Cain shrugged. "It's your life."

"No, Sebastian. It belongs to the Lord, just as yours belongs to Santiago now."

"What makes you think it does?" asked Cain.

"I don't think so," replied the preacher. "I know so."

"I don't know any such thing."

"Yes, you do, Sebastian," said Father William. "He chooses his recruits very carefully, and he's never been wrong about one yet. You could have killed him last night or this morning and cashed the biggest reward you ever dreamed about; you didn't. You could have dealt with the Swagman just now; you didn't." His booming voice became almost gentle. "Your mind may be undecided, but your heart knows where you stand."

Cain looked momentarily surprised.

"I suppose it does, at that," he said thoughtfully.

25.

A riddle inside an enigma,
Wrapped up in a puzzle or two.
What man fits these specifications?
The King of the Outlaws—that's who!

"How did your meeting with the Swagman go?" asked Santiago, looking up from his book as Cain joined him on the veranda.

"About as expected."

Santiago seemed amused. "He was that obvious?"

"He was that hungry," replied Cain.

"By the way," said Santiago, "I sent one of my men to Silent Annie's house for your belongings. I hope you don't mind."

"It's all right," said Cain, sitting down and looking out over the vast expanse of farmland. "I'll be staying."

"I'm delighted to hear it."

"You knew it all along."

"Yes, I did," admitted Santiago. "But I'm glad that you know it, too. We can use you, Sebastian."

"Sooner than you think," replied Cain. "The Swagman says that the Angel will be here in two or three more days." He paused. "It might be a good time to select a target and go off on a raid."

"Somewhere far away?" asked Santiago with a smile.

"The farther the better."

"I thank you for the thought, Sebastian, but Safe Harbor is

my home. I don't propose to run away from it at the first sign
of danger."

"*Is* it the first sign?" asked Cain. "The Swagman told me
that half a dozen bounty hunters had made it this far."

"He was wrong," said Santiago. "The actual number is
four—and if I didn't run from them, you may rest assured
that I won't run from the Angel. Besides," he added, "would
you want to serve a leader who flees from his enemies?"

"I don't suppose it's any worse than serving a leader who's
got a death wish," said Cain seriously.

"Believe me, Sebastian—it will take more than the Angel
to kill Santiago." He gazed at the horizon and sighed contentedly. "Look at that sunset. Isn't it glorious?"

"If you say so."

"I do." Santiago turned to Cain. "I assume the Swagman
is staying on Safe Harbor?"

Cain nodded.

Santiago chuckled. "He's not as inspiring as the sunset,
but he's every bit as predictable. What did he offer you to kill
me—a third of his profits in addition to the reward?"

"Half."

Santiago looked amused. "Well, why not? He doesn't
intend to pay you anyway."

"I know," replied Cain. He paused. "How did you ever
get mixed up with him in the first place?"

"The same way you did, I suspect. He had something that
I needed."

"What?"

"Certain business contacts."

"And he asked to join your organization in exchange for
them?"

Santiago shook his head. "That was *my* idea."

"Why?" asked Cain, puzzled.

"Some men have a lean and hungry look about them,"
replied Santiago. "If you're going to have any dealings with
them, it makes sense to put them where you can keep an eye
on them."

Cain smiled ironically. "If that's your criterion for employment, I'm surprised you don't have a standing army of ten
million."

"If there were ten million Swagmen out there who could
help me accomplish my goals, rest assured that I would hire

them all," said Santiago. "However, it has been my experience that truly competent criminals are almost as rare as truly competent heroes." He stood up suddenly. "But where are my manners? Here it is evening, and you haven't eaten yet. Come into the house."

Cain stood up and followed him inside. "I'm not really hungry," he said. "Watching Father William demolish a ten-pound bird can kill anyone's appetite." He grimaced. "I'm surprised he left the bones."

Santiago laughed. "I know the feeling." He paused. "Well, at least let me offer you a drink to celebrate your joining us."

Cain nodded his assent, and they walked to the living room, where Jacinto was sitting on a couch, reading one of Santiago's books.

"Have you heard the news?" Santiago asked him. "Sebastian has decided to stay with us."

"I know," replied Jacinto. "Father William told me when he dropped him off a few minutes ago."

Santiago walked over to his bar and studied the array of bottles. "Something special," he muttered, half to himself. Suddenly his face lit up. "Ah! The very thing." He reached up and grabbed a bottle. "Korbellian whiskey," he said, displaying the label. "It's made from a plant very similar to barley that they have growing up the sides of their mountains. There's nothing else quite like it." He poured out three glasses and began passing them around. "What do you think of it?" he asked as Cain took a tentative sip.

"Unusual," replied Cain. He took another taste. "Interesting, though. I think I like it."

"You *think* you like it?" laughed Santiago. "Sebastian, you've been on the Frontier too long."

Cain downed his drink and held out his glass for a refill. "I'll need another to make up my mind."

"Happy to," said Santiago, filling his glass again. "But be careful. It packs quite a wallop."

Cain finished the second, and suddenly, for the first time in years, felt a little light-headed. "I see what you mean." He grinned. "I think I'd better quit while I'm ahead."

"Good," said Santiago. "I like a man who knows his own limitations."

"Maybe you should suggest that to Father William the next time he comes to dinner," said Jacinto sardonically.

"As far as his capacity to put away food is concerned, the man *has* no limitations that I've been able to discern," replied Santiago. He shrugged. "Well, I suppose bounty hunters, like revolutionaries, come in all shapes and sizes."

"I suspect that his size gives him an added advantage," said Jacinto.

"Oh?" asked Cain, interested. "What is it?"

"He looks like he's too slow and fat to draw those laser pistols of his. It breeds overconfidence in the enemy."

"I doubt it," said Cain. "What you have to remember is that any man who carries a gun out here is undefeated. You can't afford to get overconfident in this business."

"That's probably why you're still alive when so many men who view things differently are dead," said Santiago.

"Perhaps."

"Have you another explanation?" asked Jacinto.

"When I was a very young man I wasn't afraid of death, and that gave me an advantage over the men I fought. As the years went by, I realized that there was nothing fair or reasonable about death, that it could come to anyone, so I became very careful; that gives me an advantage of a different kind."

"Which you've used with remarkable success," interjected Santiago. "I suppose all good bounty hunters do."

"There *are* no bad bounty hunters," replied Cain. "Just good ones and dead ones."

"Why did you become a bounty hunter in the first place?" asked Jacinto.

"When I realized that I wasn't going to make the galaxy a better place to live in in one bold stroke, I decided to try doing it one small step at a time."

"Have you ever regretted it?"

"Not really," replied Cain. "We all make choices; most of us get pretty much what we deserve." He paused thoughtfully. "I used to think, years ago, that someday I'd like to settle down. I was always going to find the right woman when I got a little spare time." He smiled ruefully. "I never even began looking for her." He shrugged. "I suppose if it had meant more to me, I would have."

Santiago nodded knowingly. "With me it was children. I'd been an only child, and a very lonely one at that. I always wanted a house filled with kids." He chuckled ironically.

"So now I have one filled with killers and smugglers. Every now and then I stop and wonder how the hell it happened."

"People don't come out to the Frontier to raise families," said Cain.

"Unless they're colonists," agreed Santiago. "Or shop-keepers. Or merchants. Or farmers." He sighed ironically. "Or anyone but us."

"It's just as well," said Jacinto. "None of us expects to die of old age."

Santiago turned to Cain. "Second-guessing himself is not one of Jacinto's strong points." He smiled. "As for dying of old age, I personally plan to live forever. There's too much work yet to do to worry about dying."

"Then don't take foolish chances," replied Cain.

"You're referring to the Angel again?"

Cain nodded.

Santiago sighed. "How can I ask my supporters to risk their lives if I'm not willing to do the same thing?" he said seriously.

"The operative word was *foolish*," said Cain.

"He can't run from the Angel," said Jacinto.

Cain turned to him. "I thought you were the one who wanted to tighten his security."

"I still do," replied Jacinto. "But if word gets out that Santiago can be frightened off, then before long everyone we deal with will be surrounding themselves with killers and refusing to honor their commitments to us." He paused. "We don't do business with honorable men, Mr. Cain. It is their fear of Santiago that keeps them in line, nothing more."

"It's probably all for the best that you don't have children," remarked Cain ironically. "Being the most feared man on the Frontier isn't much of a legacy to leave them."

"It *would* be more satisfying to lead my troops into glorious battle," agreed Santiago. "Unfortunately, that's not the kind of war we're fighting—and my troops, for the most part, are a bunch of misfits, reprobates, and criminals who don't even know they're involved in financing a revolution."

"How often do you deal with them directly?" asked Cain.

"Very seldom. Things seem to work much more smoothly when they think I'm some kind of unapproachable demigod. Even in this day and age there's a considerable amount of primal mysticism in the human soul; it would be foolish not to capitalize on it." He paused. "This doesn't mean that I don't take a very personal interest in my operation. I'm away from Safe Harbor about half the time—but since only a handful of people know what I look like, I can usually check up on my employees without any danger of disclosure."

"No one's ever suspected you?"

"Let's say that no one's ever been so bold as to voice their suspicions to my face," replied Santiago with a satisfied smile. "Every now and then I let them know—always well after the fact—that they've been in my presence without being aware of it; it helps to convince them that I'm a mysterious criminal kingpin from whom nothing can be kept hidden." He paused. "I would say that takes up most of my time abroad."

"And the rest of it?"

"I do have other business to conduct," answered Santiago. "I search for potential recruits, look for weak spots in the Democracy's defenses, and try to determine which worlds can best use our money and our manpower."

"Always without their knowledge, of course," added Jacinto. "If we let them know, then the Democracy would realize what Santiago really is."

"So it's like a chess game," said Cain. "Move and countermove."

"I really couldn't say," said Santiago. "I've never played chess."

"Never?" asked Cain sharply.

"Never," replied Santiago. "You say it like I've committed some kind of sin."

"I apologize," said Cain. "I was just surprised."

"No offense taken," said Santiago. He paused. "You're sure I can't offer you some dinner?"

"In a little while, perhaps."

"Or another drink?"

Cain shook his head. "No, thanks. I'd like to ask you a question."

"Go right ahead."

"Were you ever in jail on Kalami Three?"

"I think if you'll go there and check the records, you won't find any mention of me," replied Santiago.

"That isn't what I asked."

Suddenly Santiago grinned. "I've got it!" he announced. "Stern told you that I played chess with him!"

"Did you?"

"I've already told you: I don't play chess."

"Why would he have said you did?"

"Probably to embellish a story for which he was receiving a considerable amount of money."

"But you *were* imprisoned on Kalami Three?"

"For a very brief period. My memory of Stern is that he bragged about the men he'd swindled and killed, and kept relating grandiose schemes about how he intended to find a solar system of his own to rule. It seems to me that we played cards until one of the prison attendants took away his deck." Santiago smiled. "As I recall, he still owes me money from that game." He looked at Cain. "Were there any other questions you wanted to ask?"

"Just two."

"Ask away."

"First, now that I've joined you, there's no sense keeping me here on Safe Harbor once we've taken care of the Angel. What will you be wanting me to do next?"

"To tell you the truth, I haven't decided," replied Santiago seriously. "There's the little matter of getting our money back from the late Mr. Kchanga's heirs. The sooner we do it, the sooner we can purchase food and ship it to Bortai."

"Bortai?" asked Cain.

"A mining world about two hundred light-years from Bella Donna," replied Santiago. "They've only got a three-week supply of food remaining."

"Can't they import more?"

Santiago shook his head. "The Democracy's tied up their funds."

"Why?"

"Because a month ago they sold two hundred tons of iron ore—perhaps a week's output, certainly no more than that—to a pair of alien worlds that have refused to join the Democracy's economic network. This is the Democracy's way of telling them never to do so again." A savage expression crossed his face. "In the meantime, more than a hundred and fifty human children stand an excellent chance of starving to death."

"When do I leave?"

"*If* you leave, it will be in about a week," answered Santiago. "We'll give Kchanga's associates every opportunity to honor his commitment first."

"That's cutting it awfully close," said Cain. "Once I get the money, you'll still have to buy and ship the food."

"I know. As I told you before, it's a balancing act. It's worth the delay if we can find someone in Kchanga's organization that we'll be able to deal with in the future. And if not," he added with a quiet ferocity, "we'll show them what it means to play fast and loose with Santiago."

"And if they *do* come up with the money?"

"What do you think, Jacinto?" asked Santiago.

"Zeta Piscium," answered Jacinto promptly.

Santiago shook his head. "Too risky."

"What about Zeta Piscium?" asked Cain.

Santiago studied the bounty hunter for a long moment, and then began speaking. "The navy has a large base on the fourth planet of the Zeta Piscium system. We have a number of reports on it somewhere." He paused. "All their supplies for the entire Quartermaine Sector are purchased through the Zeta Piscium office and routed through the supply base there."

"And?"

"If someone were to destroy their computer system, it would be months before they could bring their records up to date," explained Jacinto. "Arms shipments couldn't be forwarded, payrolls couldn't be processed, they couldn't purchase so much as a cup of coffee until their accounting department was able to determine how much money was in their various accounts." He paused. "We would have to lay the blame elsewhere, of course: Santiago is a criminal, but he cannot be perceived to be a revolutionary."

"Everyone knows he was responsible for the Epsilon Eridani raid," Cain pointed out.

"But that was a gold robbery," explained Jacinto with a smile. "He was merely a cunning criminal who robbed the navy of its bullion." He paused. "But no conceivable profit will accrue from destroying the computer complex at Zeta Piscium Four. Therefore, he can't be associated with it."

"What's their security like?" asked Cain.

"Very tight," said Santiago. "That's why I'm not inclined to try it, despite Jacinto's enthusiasm."

"But think of the lives we'll be saving if we can disrupt their system for even two months!" urged Jacinto.

Santiago stared at him. "I appreciate your arguments, but passionate advocacy is no excuse for rashness. The odds are hundreds to one against success."

"But—"

"We can't join *every* battle," interrupted Santiago. "Our purpose is to perform meaningful actions, not to die with poetic futility. The subject is closed." He turned back to Cain. "You had a second question, Sebastian?"

"It's not quite of the same magnitude," said Cain apologetically.

"Good. One question of that magnitude is all I really care to discuss before dinner. What was it that you wished to know?"

"I was curious about that scar on your hand."

Santiago held up his right hand, staring at the S-shaped scar on it. "I wish there was a heroic story to go along with it, but the simple truth is that I caught it on a fishhook when I was a small boy."

"I would have guessed that it was a knife wound."

Santiago chuckled. "Nothing so exciting. Shall we adjourn to the dining room now?"

"I haven't asked my question yet."

Santiago looked puzzled. "I beg your pardon. What, exactly, did you wish to know about it?"

"Why do you still have it?" asked Cain. "It's the only physical feature of yours that seems to be known beyond Safe Harbor. Why didn't you get rid of it when you underwent your cosmetic surgery?"

Santiago stared at his hand for another moment, then laughed. "I'll be damned if I know," he replied. "It's been a part of me for so long that I never even mentioned it to the surgeon."

"I hope you wear gloves when you're traveling incognito," said Cain.

"I always do. I was born in the Democracy; my fingerprints are on file there somewhere. I wear contact lenses that distort my retina pattern for the same reason." He rose to his feet. "Shall we eat now?"

They went off to the dining room and spent the rest of the evening talking about Santiago's immediate and long-range plans for the future. Cain went to bed with another book—

Tanblixt's poetry, which he found totally incomprehensible—and continued his discussion with Santiago and Jacinto the next day, his enthusiasm for their enterprise growing by the hour.

Then, just before sunset, Virtue MacKenzie showed up on Santiago's doorstep, and all of the revolutionary's plans for the future were forcibly put on hold.

26.

He burns brighter than a nova;
He stands taller than a tree;
He shouts louder than the thunder;
He flows deeper than the sea.

"Actually," Santiago was saying as he leaned back in his easy chair and sipped his brandy, "I'm told that he was the patron saint of the oppressed Spanish nobility. They used to invoke his spirit before doing battle to drive the Moors out of their country."

"Santiago means Saint James in Spanish, a language they used to speak on old Earth," added Jacinto, who was sitting on a large, comfortable couch with Cain.

"Not quite as biblical as your own name, Sebastian," remarked Santiago.

"It's my middle name that bothers me," said Cain. "I should never have let Orpheus know what it was. Then I wouldn't have to put up with this Songbird nonsense." He sighed. "Still, I suppose we can't choose our names."

"Everyone out here does just that," noted Santiago.

"Those are names for the Frontier," replied Cain. "They're not official."

"If you stay on the Frontier, they're official enough."

Suddenly the security system warned them that a vehicle was approaching. It was identified as Silent Annie's, and a moment later the door slid back to reveal her slim figure.

"Annie—what a pleasant surprise!" said Santiago, getting to his feet. "To what do we owe the pleasure of this visit?"

"We have a bit of a problem on our hands," replied Silent Annie, remaining in the doorway.

"Oh?"

Silent Annie nodded her head. "She's sitting in my vehicle."

"Who is it?" asked Santiago.

"Virtue MacKenzie."

Cain stood up and walked to a window, saw Virtue sitting blindfolded inside the vehicle, then turned to Santiago and nodded. "Where's the Angel?" he demanded.

"In orbit," replied Silent Annie.

"Why did you bring her out here?" asked Santiago, more curious than annoyed.

"She landed a couple of hours ago, found Father William, and told him that she had a message for you from the Angel." Silent Annie paused. "He figured that if she was telling the truth, you'd probably want to hear what it is."

"And if she's lying?" asked Cain.

"Then she'll never leave Safe Harbor alive," promised Silent Annie coldly.

"Why didn't Father William bring her himself?" asked Santiago.

"He wants to be in town when the Angel lands," answered Silent Annie.

"It's a big planet," said Cain. "What makes him think the Angel will land near the town? I wouldn't."

"You *did*," replied Silent Annie.

"But I didn't know Santiago was here," Cain pointed out.

"He'll land there because he'll need Virtue to guide him to me, and she landed there," said Santiago.

Cain considered the statement for a few seconds, then nodded. "You're probably right," he conceded.

"Well, let's not keep our guest waiting," said Santiago to Silent Annie. "Bring her in."

Silent Annie went back outside and returned a moment later with Virtue MacKenzie. Her blindfold was removed, and she looked around the room, studying each of the three men confronting her.

"Hello, Cain," she said at last.

Cain nodded a greeting but said nothing.

She looked at Jacinto. "You're too young," she said decisively and turned to Santiago. "It must be *you*."

Santiago smiled and bowed. "At your service. Won't you sit down?"

"Can I have a drink first?" she asked.

"Of course. What would you prefer?"

"Anything with alcohol."

Santiago turned to Silent Annie. "Would you do the honors, please?"

She nodded and walked to the bar, while Santiago escorted Virtue to a chair.

"You're a very courageous woman to come here by yourself," said Santiago, sitting down opposite her.

"After you've traveled with the Angel, not much else can scare you," she replied sincerely.

"Just a minute," said Cain, walking over and taking her satchel from her.

"Hey!" she snapped, grabbing futilely at it. "What's the idea?"

"You're delivering a message," said Cain, reaching in and withdrawing a small recording device, "not getting an interview." He held the bag up to a light, examined it minutely, then returned it to her with his hand outstretched. "Where is it?"

"I don't know what you're talking about," said Virtue.

"You've got to have a camera hidden somewhere. You can hand it over or I can strip you naked. There's no third way."

"I don't have to put up with this!"

Cain turned to Jacinto. "Hold her," he ordered.

Jacinto took a step in her direction and Virtue held up a hand. "All right," she said. "Just a minute." She fumbled with her jacket and plucked off a large button, handing it to Cain. "Are you satisfied now?" she demanded.

"For the moment," he said, deactivating the incredibly miniaturized holographic mechanism and putting it in his pocket.

"I'll want that back when I leave," she added.

"We'll see," said Jacinto ominously.

"What's this 'we'll see' shit?" said Virtue heatedly. "I came under a flag of truce!"

"As a message carrier, not a journalist," responded Jacinto.

"You have my word that your property will be returned to you," said Santiago. "And now," he added, glancing firmly at Cain and Jacinto, "if my friends can control their enthusiasm, I would be interested in hearing what you have to say."

"The Angel wants to meet you tomorrow morning," she said.

"I'll just bet he does," said Silent Annie, returning with Virtue's drink.

"The Angel wants to kill me," said Santiago. "Why should I care to present myself to him?"

"He's willing to discuss it," said Virtue.

Santiago looked amused. "To discuss killing me?"

"To discuss *not* killing you," she replied.

"A subject near and dear to my heart," replied Santiago. "What does he propose to say?"

"That he's willing to be bought off," said Virtue.

"For how much?"

"It's negotiable," answered Virtue. "I get the feeling that he's talking in the neighborhood of two or three million credits."

"The reward for me is up to twenty million credits. Why should he settle for so much less?"

She grinned. "Nobody knows what you look like. He can turn in the body of the first derelict he finds, claim that it's you, and still get the reward."

"I'm sure it's been tried before," said Santiago.

"Probably," she agreed. "But people tend not to argue with the Angel."

Santiago studied her thoughtfully. "Where does he want to meet me?"

"A place called the Barleycorn Tavern."

"How did he find out about it?"

"It's where Peacemaker MacDougal killed Billy Three-Eyes," replied Virtue. "It's the only location on Safe Harbor that he knows."

"What time does he want to meet me?" asked Santiago.

"Nine o'clock."

"You're not seriously considering meeting with him?" demanded Cain.

"I haven't decided yet," said Santiago.

"It's a setup," said Cain.

"Perhaps," agreed Santiago.

"Then don't go. Make him come out here."

"And kill ten or twelve of my men?" said Santiago with a smile. "I can't spare them."

"They can't spare *you!*" snapped Cain.

"Possibly the Angel really wants to make a deal," said Santiago. "After all, twenty-three million credits is better than twenty."

Cain shook his head vigorously. "He'll have to go into the Democracy to collect it—and they won't give a damn if he's the Angel or God Himself. They're going to want proof."

"How soon does he need an answer?" Santiago asked Virtue.

"I'm supposed to contact him tonight and let him know your decision," she replied.

"And if I decide against meeting with him?"

She shrugged. "Then I suppose he'll come out here and kill you."

"What do *you* get out of all this?" asked Jacinto.

"I'm a journalist. I get a story." She turned to Santiago. "Perhaps you'd like to give me an interview right now?" she suggested.

Santiago chuckled. "I admire your dedication."

"Then you'll do it?" she persisted.

He shook his head. "I'm afraid not."

"If you'll give me an interview, I'll tell the Angel you're not here."

"She's lying," said Cain.

"The hell I am!" snapped Virtue irately.

Cain turned to her. "Come on," he said. "You tell him that, and the second the interview appears, he'll come after you and hunt you down."

"He'll never find me."

"If he could find Santiago, he can find a journalist who'll be making the most of her publicity."

"I'll take my chances," replied Virtue.

"No you won't. You'll take your interview, and then you'll tell the Angel everything you saw and heard."

Santiago cleared his throat.

"I'm going to take a little walk," he announced, "and consider the Angel's proposition. I'll give you my answer when I return."

"I'll go with you," said Silent Annie.

He shook his head. "I'd rather go alone. I'll be back in a few minutes."

He walked out the door.

"Where is he going?" asked Cain.

"Down to the dell," answered Jacinto. "He always goes there when he wants to think."

"What the hell is there to think about?" said Cain, puzzled. "He can't actually be considering going through with this!"

Jacinto shrugged. "Who knows?"

Cain walked over to Virtue, grabbed her by the wrist, and yanked her to her feet.

"Come on," he said.

"Where are you taking her?" demanded Jacinto.

"Out to the veranda," said Cain. "I want to talk to her."

"You can talk to her right here."

"Alone," said Cain.

Jacinto stared at Cain for a moment, then nodded his head.

Cain led Virtue through the dining room and out onto the veranda, then commanded the door to close behind him.

"I can't believe it!" she said, her face flushed with excitement. "I've finally found him!"

"And now you're going to kill him," said Cain.

"I'm not killing anyone," she said. "I'm just a journalist." She look at him sharply. "But while we're on the subject, how come *you* haven't killed him?"

"The situation has changed," said Cain. "I've joined him."

"How much is he paying you?" she asked, curious.

"Nothing."

She stared at him disbelievingly. "Are you going to give me all that crap I heard from Silent Annie about what a great man he is?"

"I don't know if he's a great man," said Cain slowly. "But he's a *good* man—better than I'll ever be, anyway. And he's working for a good cause."

"He's a goddamned outlaw."

"He's a good man," repeated Cain. "And I'm not going to let him be killed."

"I seem to remember that we made a deal back on Pegasus," said Virtue.

"You broke it when you joined the Angel."

"Didn't you get Terwilliger's message?"

Cain nodded. "Was it sent before or after ManMountain Bates killed him?" he asked sardonically.

She glared at him. "It was the truth!"

"Then why are you running the Angel's errands?" he shot back.

"Because he got Dimitri Sokol to take the hit off me," she replied.

"And when do you stop working for him? When he kills Santiago?"

"He's just going to talk to him."

"That's a bunch of shit and you know it," said Cain. "This thing's got trap written all over it."

"What difference does it make?" demanded Virtue defiantly. "I've got a story to get, and you've sold out to the enemy. If I can't get an interview, I'll cover his death."

"The enemy isn't Santiago," said Cain. "It's the Angel."

"The Angel is a bounty hunter who's working within the Democracy's law. Santiago is a criminal who's broken it time and again."

"It's not that simple," said Cain.

"It's precisely that simple," she said triumphantly. "You've joined a gang of killers and bandits, and you're castigating me for working with the man who's trying to bring their leader to justice."

"You never gave a damn about justice in your life!" snarled Cain. "All you care about is your goddamned story and what you think it will do for you."

"Don't you go getting high and mighty with *me*, Cain!" she snapped back at him. "I know how many men you've killed—and not just as a bounty hunter, either. There's still a price on your head back on Sylaria." She paused to catch her breath. "We both set out to find Santiago. You were going to kill him, and I was going to get my story. It's hardly my fault that you've forgotten what you're supposed to be doing here!"

"I'll give you a story to take home with you," he said savagely. "You can cover the death of the Angel."

She glared at him, and then her expression changed as all the rage seemed to drain from her.

"You can't kill him," she said, shaking her head slowly. "Don't throw your life away trying."

"I won't let him kill Santiago," said Cain doggedly.

"Nobody can stop him. Believe me, Cain—I've seen him in action. I know what he can do." She suppressed a shudder. "He's inhuman!"

Cain stared at her. "If you're that afraid of him, why are you working for him?"

"Because he can get what I need," she said with a tight smile. "And because I'm that afraid of him." She stared directly into Cain's eyes. "Have you got anything else to say, or can I have another drink?"

He stared back at her, seemed about to speak, thought better of it, and led her back inside. Jacinto and Silent Annie were still in the living room, waiting for them.

"Is he on his way back yet?" asked Jacinto.

"I didn't see him," said Cain. "What's he doing out there, anyway—communing with the dead?"

"That's in very bad taste, Mr. Cain," said Jacinto. "The men in those graves were fine men."

"Then maybe *they'll* talk a little sense to him," said Cain. "He's got to know this is a trap."

"He knows."

"Then what's the problem?"

Jacinto sighed wearily. "Billions of people in the Democracy may fear his name, but there are tens of thousands out here who practically worship it, who know that he's the only thing that stands between them and their oppressors. He's all they've got, he and the myth that has grown up around him—and he doesn't want them to think that he's betrayed their faith in him by becoming a coward."

"There's nothing cowardly about running away from a fight you can't win," said Cain.

"When you're Santiago, there is."

"No one will ever know."

Jacinto nodded toward Virtue. "We'd have to kill *her* to keep the story from spreading, and he won't do it."

"Then you and I will have to stop him," said Cain decisively.

"How?"

"By force, if necessary."

"You'll do whatever Santiago tells you to do," interrupted Silent Annie. "He's your leader."

"We're trying to *keep* him our leader," answered Cain.

She stared harshly at him. "When you make a commitment to follow a man, you make a *total* commitment. You don't just obey those orders you approve of, and disregard the rest." She paused for emphasis. "Whatever he decides, we'll support it."

"We'll see," said Cain noncommittally.

There was an uneasy silence which Virtue finally broke.

"Does anyone mind if I pour myself a drink?"

Jacinto gestured toward the bar. "Fix it yourself."

She walked over and began inspecting the rows of bottles. "This is a pretty well-stocked little bar," she said, impressed. She noticed one bottle in particular and picked it up. "Korbellian whiskey!" she exclaimed. "I haven't had any of this in, oh, it must be five years!" She poured herself a glass and took a quick swallow. "He's got good taste, I'll give him that."

"I consider that a great compliment," said a voice from the dining room doorway, and they all turned to see Santiago standing there.

"Well?" said Cain, looking at him.

Santiago walked across the room to where Virtue was standing, glass in hand.

"Tell the Angel I'll be there," he said.

"You're crazy!" exploded Cain.

"Nevertheless, that's my decision." He turned back to Virtue. "If you'll wait in the vehicle that brought you, I'll have one of my men take you back to town. I'm sorry, but I'll have to tell him to blindfold you again."

"And my camera?"

"It will be returned to you after we've destroyed whatever it recorded here."

Virtue finished her whiskey and walked to the door. "Cain's right, you know."

"Thank you for your opinion," said Santiago, dismissing her.

She shrugged and left the house. Santiago nodded to Silent Annie, who went off to find a driver.

"You can't do it!" said Cain.

Santiago smiled. "Are you giving me orders, Sebastian?"

"She as much as said that the whole thing is a setup," continued Cain. "If you really feel you've got to give the Angel a crack at you, stay here at the house, and at least make him work for it."

"To what purpose?" asked Santiago. "If he truly intends to kill me, why let him kill all of you as well? He's good enough to do just that, you know."

"He won't kill *me*," promised Cain.

"Even you, Sebastian," said Santiago. "I've followed his career as closely as I have your own. I don't mean to hurt your pride, but you haven't got a chance against him."

"If that's true, then you've got even less of a chance," said Cain as Silent Annie rejoined them.

"*If* he wants to kill me," said Santiago. "There's a chance that he only wants to talk."

"There's two chances—slim and none."

"Then," said Santiago calmly, "perhaps he'll discover that it's harder to kill me than he thinks."

"You're just flesh and blood like anyone else," said Cain.

"No, Sebastian," said Santiago. "I may be flesh and blood, but I am also myth and mystery and legend."

"It won't do you any good."

"It has before."

"You've never faced anyone like the Angel before," said Cain.

"If it ends, it ends," said Santiago. "I've led a satisfying life. I've seen hundreds of worlds, I've had the pleasure of owning this farm—and, in some small way, I've made a difference." He shrugged and forced a smile to his lips. "And before you go writing my epitaph, I wish at least one of you would consider the possibility that I might not die."

"I beg you not to do this," said Jacinto earnestly.

"I appreciate your concern," replied Santiago, "but my decision has been made."

"Then let me go in your place," said Cain suddenly. "The Angel has never seen either of us. At least I'll have a chance against him."

"I thought we decided that you didn't want to become Sydney Carton," noted Santiago.

"I've changed my mind."

"Well, I haven't changed mine," said Santiago. "I appreciate your offer, Sebastian, but I have more important things in mind for you."

"What could be more important than saving your life?" demanded Cain.

"There's still work to be done, whether I'm here or not," said Santiago gently. "And now, if no one minds, I think I'd like to have dinner."

Cain and Jacinto spent the entire meal trying to argue

Santiago out of his position, but he remained adamant. When he had finished eating he went out to the dell by himself and returned at about midnight, seemingly content. He invited Silent Annie to spend the night in one of the guest rooms, bade the three of them good night, and went off to bed.

Cain retired to his room, pulled two pistols out of his luggage, and spent the next hour oiling and cleaning them. He set his alarm for twenty minutes before sunrise and was totally dressed and checking his ammunition when he heard a knock at the door.

"Open," he commanded in a low voice, and Santiago and Silent Annie entered the room.

"I was afraid of this," said Santiago, staring at the pistols that Cain had laid out on the dresser. "Sebastian, what are you doing?"

"I'm going into town," replied Cain, making no attempt to hide his weapons.

"I've told you not to."

"I know what you told me," said Cain. "I'm going anyway."

"Annie?" said Santiago, stepping aside, and suddenly Cain was looking down the barrel of a sonic pistol.

"What the hell is this?" demanded Cain.

"I appreciate what you want to do, Sebastian," said Santiago, "but I can't allow it." He turned to Silent Annie. "I'm leaving in ten minutes. You'll keep him here?"

She nodded.

"Good-bye, Sebastian," said Santiago.

He walked down the hall, and the door slid shut.

"You know he's going off to get killed, don't you?" said Cain bitterly.

She stared unblinking at him. "Santiago can't be killed."

"Santiago could do with a few more realists in his organization, and a few less fanatics." He got to his feet. "If you let me pass, I can still stop him."

"Stay where you are," she warned him.

"You're letting him drive off to his death!" snapped Cain. "Why?"

"Because it's his decision, and I plan to abide by it."

"Why the hell is he doing it?" said Cain, still mystified.

"To save the lives of everyone here," she replied. "If the Angel wants to kill him, he'll kill him wherever he is."

"We could have tightened our security."

"In one night?" said Silent Annie, shaking her head and smiling sadly.

"We could have laid a trap for him." He glanced desperately at the door. "We still can."

"The die has been cast."

"That's a feeble thing to say," replied Cain. "He's going off to face the Angel, and all I get from you is platitudes!"

She stared at him. "He rescued me from a life of despair, and gave meaning to it. I love him more than you ever could. If I can let him do what he has to do, then so can you."

Cain heard the sound of Santiago's vehicle starting off down the farm's long, twisting driveway.

"He's gone," he said, his emotions draining away. "And you've helped to kill him."

"I told you: Santiago cannot die."

"Be sure you write that on his tombstone!"

"Why are you so enraged?" she asked, honestly curious. "You've only known him for two days."

"I've been searching for him all my life," said Cain bitterly. "And now, thanks to you, I've lost him."

She smiled. "He would approve of that answer."

"He's not going to be around to approve of anything much longer."

They sat there in silence for the next five minutes, Cain glaring at her with a growing sense of futility and frustration, Silent Annie watching his every movement with a fanatical intensity.

Suddenly there were footsteps in the hall, and then they heard Jacinto's voice.

"Are you in there, Annie?"

Silent Annie turned her head toward the door for just an instant—and in that instant Cain dove across the room and sent the pistol flying against a wall. She leaped toward it, but he was faster, grabbing her and hurling her roughly onto the bed.

"What's going on in there?" demanded Jacinto, pounding on the door.

Cain picked up the sonic pistol, disconnected the charge, and tossed it onto the dresser. Then he picked up his own guns and loaded his pockets with ammunition, never taking his eyes off her. Finally he walked to the door and commanded it to open, only to find himself confronted by Jacinto, whose face was streaked by tears.

"I'm going into town," Cain announced.

"I know," said Jacinto. He took a step forward, and Cain saw that he held a wicked-looking knife in his hands.

"Don't try to stop me," Cain growled ominously.

"That was never my intention."

"Then let me pass."

"There is one thing that I must do first," said Jacinto, still approaching him.

27.

There are those who will say he's a sinner,
There are those who will say he's a saint;
There are those who will swear he's as strong as a bear,
But whatever they tell you—he ain't!

Black Orpheus wasn't so much prophetic as he was just plain lucky. He wrote that verse for pretty much the same reason that he wrote Silent Annie's—because he had a feeling that there was a lot more to his subject than met the eye.

He never knew just how right he was.

Virtue MacKenzie was already seated in the tavern when Father William and the Swagman showed up. The preacher greeted her coldly, then sat down at his usual table and asked Moonripple to prepare some breakfast for him, while the Swagman walked over and joined her.

"Good morning, my love," he said. "I knew we were destined to meet again."

"It's a little early in the day for you, isn't it?" she responded, setting her 360-degree holographic camera on the table and checking her microphone.

"What would life be without new experiences?" he said with a smile. "I've always wondered what the world looked like before noon."

"Which world?" she inquired dryly.

"*Any* world."

"Pretty much the same, I'd imagine." said Virtue.

"Blurrier," he replied, blinking his eyes. "Where's your traveling companion?"

"He'll be along," she assured him.

"Well, in his absence, I suppose it wouldn't hurt to talk a little business," said the Swagman.

"I've got nothing to discuss with you," said Virtue, inserting the microphone into its slot in the camera.

"We *do* have an agreement concerning the disposition of the artwork," persisted the Swagman.

"That agreement's only valid if Cain kills Santiago," replied Virtue. "And in case you hadn't heard, Cain has joined him."

"Then put in a good word for me with the Angel."

She stared at him. "Swagman, I don't know any good words about you."

"This is no time to deal in acrimony," said the Swagman. "Neither you nor the Angel knows how to dispose of the artwork; I do. You need me."

"I don't care about the artwork," she said. "I'm getting what I want."

"You think so?" asked the Swagman, amused.

"The Angel wants the reward money, I want the story. Our interests don't overlap."

"Ah, Virtue," he said with a sigh, "I wish you were as bright as you think you are."

"What are you talking about?"

"Do you really think he's going to let you live?" asked the Swagman.

"Why shouldn't he?"

"Because Dimitri Sokol's put a price of one hundred thousand credits on your pretty little head."

"The Angel had him take the hit off," she said.

He shook his head. "The Angel had him stop advertising it. There's a difference."

"Then why hasn't he killed me already?" she demanded.

"Because he needed you to get Santiago to come here. Once he kills Santiago, he doesn't need you for anything— unless you can convince him that he can make a healthy profit by letting you and me dispose of the artwork."

"You and me?" she repeated skeptically. "Why are you suddenly being so generous?"

"Because he knows you, whereas my reputation has been besmirched by numerous small-minded parties who are jealous of my success." He leaned forward. "I'll cut you in for ten percent."

"Ten percent?" she said with a harsh laugh. "Your generosity knows no bounds."

He shrugged. "All right—fifteen. And you'll still have your story."

"Not a chance."

"You're making a big mistake," said the Swagman.

"Somehow, as frightening as the Angel is, I find him more trustworthy than you."

"It's your funeral," he replied. "Just think about what I said." He signaled to Moonripple, who emerged from the kitchen carrying Father William's breakfast on a huge tray. "A cup of coffee when you get the chance, my dear."

"Right away, sir," she answered.

"Coffee?" asked Virtue, grinning.

"They tell me it contracts the pupils," said the Swagman. "I'm certainly willing to give it a chance."

"It steadies the nerves."

"Whatever," he shrugged. Suddenly he noticed that Father William had clasped his hands before him and lowered his head. "I've never seen you do that before," he said.

"I pray all the time," replied Father William.

"Not before a meal, you don't," said the Swagman. "Usually you just dig in like you're trying to break a speed record."

"Maybe he's nervous," suggested Virtue.

Father William stared sternly at her. "I was praying for the Angel's soul. I plan to remand it to Satan's custody this morning."

"Maybe you'd better put in a good word for yourself, if you plan to go up against him," said Virtue.

"I don't ask the Lord for personal favors," said Father William. He continued staring at her. "I think I'd better pray for you next. You've done a wicked thing, Virtue MacKenzie."

"Don't you go blaming *me* for this," she said defensively. "I never even heard of Safe Harbor until yesterday. The Angel found this place without any help from me."

"But you convinced Santiago to meet him."

"All I did was deliver a message," she replied. "Hell, I told him he was crazy to come."

"I'll pray for you anyway."

"While you're at it," said the Swagman, "you might say one for me, just to be on the safe side."

"It wouldn't do any good," answered Father William.

Moonripple arrived with the Swagman's coffee, while Father William said a brief prayer for Virtue and then attacked his meal with even more gusto than usual.

Moonripple placed the tray behind the bar, then hesitantly approached Father William.

"Excuse me, sir," she said tentatively.

"Yes, my child?"

"I realize it's none of my concern, but I couldn't help overhearing what you said, and I just wanted to know if it was true?"

"That the Swagman's going to hell?" replied Father William. "Absolutely."

"No," she said. "That wasn't what I meant." She paused, nervously fidgeting with her apron. "Is it true that *he* is coming here today?"

"I hope not," said Father William.

She started to ask something more, then shook her head and retreated to the kitchen while Father William returned his attention to the diminishing pile of food on his plate.

Virtue busied herself rechecking her equipment, while the Swagman sipped his coffee and tried unsuccessfully to pretend that it was Cygnian cognac.

Then the door opened and the Angel, clad in a strikingly somber outfit, stepped into the tavern. His pale, no-color eyes surveyed the room, missing no detail.

"You're a few minutes early," said Virtue.

He made no answer but chose a table that was next to a windowless wall and walked to it, elegant and catlike, never taking his eyes from Father William. When he reached it he pulled out a chair and sat down.

"I assume from your demeanor that you're the Angel?" said the Swagman cordially.

"I am."

"Good. They call me the Jolly Swagman. I have a mutually beneficial business proposition to put to you."

"Later," replied the Angel.

"It could mean a lot of money to you," continued the Swagman persuasively.

"I said later."

The Swagman looked into the Angel's cold, lifeless eyes.

"I'll tell you what," he said hastily, getting to his feet and keeping his hands in plain view. "I think I'll just go across the street and relax for a little while. We'll talk later."

The Angel paid no attention to him as he hurried out the door, but stared intently at Father William.

"I won't let you kill him," said the preacher, glaring at him while continuing to eat.

"I'm only here to talk to him," replied the Angel.

"I don't believe you."

The Angel shrugged. "Believe what you want—but don't do anything foolish."

Father William continued glaring at him as Moonripple came through the kitchen door and approached the Angel.

"May I help you, sir?" she asked.

The Angel shook his head, never taking his eyes from Father William.

"He should be here any minute," said Virtue.

"Will Cain be with him?" asked the Angel.

"No." She paused nervously. "I have to ask you a question."

"Go ahead."

"Has Dimitri Sokol still got a hit on me?"

"No."

"You're sure?"

"Who told you otherwise?" asked the Angel.

"I was just curious."

"It was the Swagman," said the Angel.

"Was he telling the truth?"

"Does he ever?"

"Damn it!" snapped Virtue, her anger overcoming her fear. "I want an answer!"

He turned his head toward her slightly, still keeping Father William in his field of vision. "I already answered your question. If you didn't believe me the first time, you won't believe me now."

They sat in silence for another minute. Then Father William finished the last of his breakfast, took the napkin he had tied around his neck, wiped his mouth off, and tossed it onto the table.

"You've had your warning," growled the preacher ominously.

"You don't have to die," said the Angel. "There's no paper on you."

"The Lord is my shepherd, I shall not want!" intoned Father William, rising to his feet, the handles of his laser pistols glinting in the tavern's artificial light.

Suddenly Moonripple, her eyes wide with horror, took a step toward the Angel.

"You can't kill Father William!" she said in hushed tones. "He's a servant of the Lord!"

"It's his choice," replied the Angel calmly, his gaze never leaving the preacher's hands.

"Stand back, child!" said Father William.

"You can't!" she repeated, rushing toward the Angel.

Father William reached for his pistols, and three long metal spikes appeared in the Angel's right hand as if by magic. Moonripple hit his arm just as he was hurling them, but all of them found their way into Father William's massive body before he could draw his pistols, and he collapsed with a surprised grunt.

The Angel got to his feet and swept Moonripple aside with his arm. She careened off the wall and fell to the floor, motionless.

"See if she's still alive," he ordered Virtue while he walked across the room and crouched down next to Father William. One of the spikes was buried in his chest, another protruded from his right arm, and the third was lodged in the left side of his neck, but he was still conscious.

"You were lucky," said the Angel dispassionately, appropriating Father William's pistols. "You owe your life to that child. Try not to move too much and you may not bleed to death."

"Kill me now!" rasped Father William. "Or as God is my witness, I'll hunt you down to the very depths of hell!"

"Stupid," muttered the Angel, shaking his head. He frisked the preacher for concealed weapons, carefully withdrew the three spikes, stood up, and walked over to Moonripple.

"She's breathing," said Virtue. "But she's got a hell of a bump on her head."

He felt her head and neck with expert hands. "She'll be all right," he said.

"What about Father William?"

"He's in better shape than he has any right to be," replied the Angel. "That fat gives him a lot of protection."

"Will he live?"

"Probably."

"Shouldn't we get the pair of them to a doctor?"

"Later," said the Angel.

She looked at the semiconscious preacher. "He's bleeding pretty badly."

"You do what you want," replied the Angel, returning to his chair. "I'm here to meet Santiago."

She stared at Father William for another moment, then shrugged and went back to her recording equipment.

They sat without speaking for a few minutes, the silence broken only by Father William's hoarse breathing and occasional curses. Then the door slid open once again, and Santiago entered.

"What's been going on here?" he demanded, kneeling down next to Father William.

"Are you Santiago?" asked the Angel.

"I am," replied Santiago without looking up.

"Your associate made an unwise decision."

"Is he alive?"

"I'll outlive *that* spawn of Satan!" rasped Father William, regaining consciousness.

Suddenly Santiago saw Moonripple.

"What have you done to the girl?"

"She'll be all right." The Angel gestured toward the chair opposite him. "Take a seat."

"In a minute," said Santiago, walking over and examining Moonripple. His hands found the swelling on the side of her head. "That could be a fracture there." He turned to Virtue. "Have you summoned a doctor?"

"All in good time," interjected the Angel. "We have business to discuss first."

Santiago glanced back at Father William, then turned to the Angel.

"I want your word that you won't kill them, however our negotiations turn out."

"You have it."

Santiago sighed. "All right," he said, sitting down. "Let's get on with it."

"You realize that you are the most wanted man in the galaxy," began the Angel.

"I do."

"This is because you are the most successful criminal in the galaxy," he continued.

"Get to the point," said Santiago.

"The point is simply this: A criminal who has been as successful as you have been undoubtedly has accumulated a considerable amount of money. I wonder if you would be interested in spending some of it to purchase your continuing good health?"

"How much did you have in mind?"

"The reward is currently twenty million credits," said the Angel. He paused thoughtfully. "I should think that thirty million will do nicely."

"Thirty?" exclaimed Virtue. "I thought you were talking about three!"

The Angel smiled mirthlessly. "That was talk," he said. "This is business." He stared directly into Santiago's eyes. "The amount is payable in full before you leave this table."

Santiago smiled grimly. "You never had any intention of making a deal, did you?"

"I am a man of my word," replied the Angel. "I said that if you came here I would make you an offer, and I have. What is your answer?"

"You go to hell," said Santiago.

The Angel reached out with an incredibly swift motion, and an instant later Santiago fell out of his chair, blood spurting from his throat. He was dead before he hit the floor.

Father William emitted a hideous gutteral yell, tried to get to his feet, and actually got one leg planted before he grabbed at his chest and collapsed, panting heavily.

Virtue closed her eyes and fought the urge to vomit as the Angel got to his feet, walked over to Santiago's body, and looked down at it, studying the contorted face.

"Well, you've got your story," he said at last.

"It was gruesome!" she said weakly.

He turned to her. "Death usually is."

Suddenly a single gunshot rang out.

For a moment nobody moved. Then the Angel, a trickle of blood starting to run out of his mouth, turned to the door, swaying slightly.

"Fool!" said Cain softly. "Do you think Santiago can be killed that easily?"

He fired another shot, and the Angel dropped to his knees.

Father William laboriously raised himself onto his elbows. "You poor dumb bastard!" he rasped with a derisive laugh. "You murdered the wrong man!"

Cain advanced slowly across the room.

The Angel, puzzlement and pain reflected on his face, tried to speak, coughed up a mouthful of blood, and finally forced the words out.

"Then who is Santiago?"

Cain held up his right hand and displayed an S-shaped wound that was still oozing blood.

"*I* am now," he said.

"Poor sinner!" grated Father William. "Everybody knows that Santiago can't die!" He roared with laughter and was still laughing when he passed out.

The Angel reached inside his coat for a sonic weapon, and a third shot rang out. He flew backward as if hit by a sledgehammer, then lay still.

Cain turned to Virtue. "Go get a doctor," he ordered.

She got up and began putting her camera into her satchel.

"Leave it," said Cain.

"Not a chance," she said, glaring at him. "I risked my life to get what's in there."

"It'll still be there when you get back."

"Then why can't I take it?"

"Because I want to make sure you return. We've got things to discuss."

She looked at the camera, then back at Cain again. "You promise you won't touch it?"

"Unless someone dies because you stood here arguing," he replied. "If that happens, I swear to you that I'll blow it to pieces."

She seemed about to argue with him, then turned and went out the door. Cain briefly examined the four bodies on the floor, two of them living, two of them dead, then walked to the bar, poured himself a drink, and waited.

Virtue returned alone about two minutes later, her face flushed from running.

"There's quite a crowd gathering outside," she remarked.

"Where's the doctor?" asked Cain.

"I told him he was going to need a lot of help," she replied. "He's getting his staff together, and hunting up a vehicle that can transport everyone to the hospital."

"How soon will he get here?"

"I don't know. About five minutes, I suppose."

"Wait here," he said, walking to the door. He stepped out onto the street and found himself facing about twenty onlookers.

"There's been some trouble," he said, "but it's under control now. There will be a medical team arriving shortly. I think it would be best if all of you would go back to your homes."

Nobody moved.

Cain held up his right hand and turned it so they could see the wound on the back of it.

"Please," he said.

They stared at his hand, and then, one by one, they began dispersing. One man lagged behind the others, then walked up and asked if there was anything he could do to help; Cain shook his head, thanked him, and sent him on his way.

"That was pretty impressive," said Virtue when he came back into the tavern. "How long is this charade going to continue?"

"What charade?" he asked.

"Pretending to be Santiago."

He stared at her expressionlessly. "I'm not pretending."

"What about the reward?" she asked.

"I imagine it'll go up," he replied. "The Angel was working for the Democracy."

She met his gaze and was surprised at what she saw there. "You're serious, aren't you?"

He nodded silently.

"Then what about my story?" she asked.

"What story?"

"I've got a recording of the Angel killing Santiago."

He shook his head. "*I'm* Santiago. You have a recording of a bounty hunter killing an imposter."

"We'll let the viewers judge for themselves."

Cain shrugged. "It's a pity, though," he said softly.

"What is?" she asked suspiciously.

"That your story has to end here."

She looked at him curiously.

"And that you never got your interview," he added.

"Oh?"

"There were so many things you could have learned," he continued. "Enough for ten pieces."

"Enough for a book?" she asked meaningfully.

"Who knows?"

"I'll have to think about it," said Virtue.

The door opened and a doctor, flanked by three assistants, entered the tavern.

"Not for too long," Cain told her.

The medics carried Father William and Moonripple out on air-cushioned stretchers, and the doctor walked over to Cain.

"I'll be back for the other two later," he said. "But I'm going to have to work fast to save Father William."

Cain nodded. "Just come back for this one," he said, gesturing to the Angel. "I'm taking the other home with me."

The doctor looked down at Santiago, then at Cain, and nodded his head.

Cain waited until he and Virtue were alone again before speaking.

"I'd better pull my vehicle up and load him into it," he said. He walked to the door, then turned to her. "I'll need your decision before I go."

He turned back and found himself facing the Jolly Swagman.

"I saw everyone else leaving, so I decided that this might be an opportune time to come over," he said with a smile. "I'm glad to see you're still alive."

He walked past Cain and stared at the two corpses.

"Well, I'll be damned!" he muttered. "Both of them!" He turned back to Cain. "I thought I saw two bodies being carried out."

"Father William and Moonripple," said Cain. "They're still alive."

"I'm glad to hear it. I've got a sneaking fondness for that fat old man." He rubbed his hands together. "Well, here we are—the Three Musketeers! Who would have thought that we'd actually make it?"

"What do you want?" asked Cain.

"What do you mean, what do I want?" laughed the Swagman. "You've got the reward, Virtue's got her story—I want the artwork."

"No deal," said Cain.

The Swagman frowned. "What are you talking about, Songbird?"

"My name's not Songbird."

"All right—Sebastian."

"It's not Sebastian, either."

"Well, what *do* you want to be called?"

"Santiago."

The Swagman laughed heartily. "He's got *that* much stashed away?"

"What I have is none of your business."

"All right," said the Swagman. "This has gone far enough. We made a deal. The artwork's mine!"

"You made a deal with a man who no longer exists," said Cain.

"Now listen to me!" said the Swagman. "I don't know what kind of double cross you're trying to pull, but it's not going to work. You've got the reward; I want the artwork."

"What you want doesn't interest me."

"Do you think that just because you're the one who killed him you're entitled to everything?" demanded the Swagman. "It doesn't work that way, Sebastian!"

"His name's Santiago," said Virtue.

"You, too?" he said, turning to face her.

"I'm his biographer," she said with a smug smile. "Who knows Santiago better than me?"

The Swagman turned back to Cain. "I don't know what kind of scam you two have worked out, but you're not getting rid of me that easily. I've put as much work into this as you have; I deserve something for my time."

"Some alien artwork?" suggested Cain.

"Of course some alien artwork! What the hell do you think I've been talking about?"

"All right," said Cain. "You're entitled to something."

He walked to Santiago's body, knelt down, and removed a gold ring from one of his fingers.

"Here you are," said Cain. "Now go away."

The Swagman looked at the ring, then hurled it against the wall.

"I'll tell what I know," he said threateningly.

"Do whatever you think you have to do," said Cain.

"I'm not bluffing, Sebastian. I'll tell them he's dead."

"And next month or next year another navy convoy will be

robbed, and everyone will know that Santiago is still alive," replied Cain calmly.

The Swagman stared at Cain. "This isn't over yet," he promised.

"I know," said Cain. "For one thing, you're going to be protecting me."

"What are you talking about?"

"There's still a price on my head, and you know I live on Safe Harbor. If any bounty hunter makes it this far, I'm going to assume that you told him where to find me." He smiled grimly. "I would take a very dim view of that."

"How can I keep tabs on every bounty hunter who's looking for Santiago?" demanded the Swagman in exasperation.

"You're a clever man," said Cain. "You'll find a way."

The Swagman seemed about to protest, then sighed and turned to Virtue.

"You're really going along with this deception?" he asked.

"What deception?" she replied innocently.

"Wonderful," he muttered. "You know," he added thoughtfully, "it occurs to me that you've run through most of your advance already. You're not going to do much more than break even."

"Have you any suggestions?"

He smiled with renewed self-confidence. "Hundreds of them, especially for a famous art critic like yourself."

"We'll talk about it later," she said, unable to completely hide her interest.

"I'll be at the boarding house for a few more days. That is," he added sardonically, "if it's all right with Santiago?"

"Two days," said Cain.

"Then, if there are no further objections, I think I'll take my leave of you," he said, walking to the door. "I crave the company of honest men and women."

"I doubt that the feeling is mutual," said Cain.

The Swagman chuckled and left the tavern.

"I was afraid that you were going to kill him," remarked Virtue.

"Cain might have. Santiago will find a use for him."

"But all he has to do is tell the navy where to find you."

"But he won't," said Cain confidently as he walked to the door. "If the navy kills me, the Democracy will appropriate all my belongings, including the artwork."

It took Cain another five minutes to load Santiago's body into his vehicle. Then he and Virtue drove the fifty miles out to the farm.

Jacinto was waiting for him, and while Virtue remained at the house, the two men gently carried Santiago down to the dell, where a third grave had been dug that morning.

"He loved this place," said Jacinto after they had filled in the grave. He looked around. "It *is* beautiful, isn't it?"

Cain nodded.

Jacinto stared down thoughtfully at the unmarked grave. "He was the best of them all."

"Was he a bounty hunter, too?" asked Cain.

Jacinto shook his head. "He came here as a colonist almost twenty years ago, and built the Barleycorn Tavern."

"What about the one before him?"

"A professor of alien languages."

"And a chess player?" asked Cain.

Jacinto smiled. "A very fine one."

Cain walked to a shaded area beneath a gnarled tree. "When you bury me, I want it to be right here," he said.

Jacinto drew himself up to his full height and looked into Cain's eyes. "Santiago cannot die," he said firmly.

"I know. But when you bury me, remember what I asked."

"I will," Jacinto promised.

Cain walked back to the three graves.

"Go on up to the house," he said. "I'll join you in a little while."

Jacinto nodded and began walking away, while Cain lowered his head and stared at the three mounds of earth. He stood there silently for almost half an hour, then sighed deeply and returned to the house.

Virtue was waiting for him on the veranda, camera in hand.

"Are you ready?" she asked eagerly.

"In a minute. I've got to say something to Jacinto first." He turned to her. "By the way, there's a condition."

"What is it?"

"You're to take no holograph of my face. You'll use the little camera I took from you yesterday and aim it at my hands." He paused. "That's my ground rule. Do you agree to it?"

"Of course," she replied easily. "It may actually extend my term as your biographer."

"I'm glad we understand each other."

He sought out Jacinto and asked for a status report on Winston Kchanga's organization.

"We've had no reply from them," said Jacinto.

"And the Democracy is still freezing Bortai's funds?"

Jacinto nodded.

"Then I'm going to have to pay our associates a little visit," said Cain grimly. "Load their coordinates into my ship's navigational computer. I'm leaving tomorrow."

"Yes, Santiago."

He returned to the veranda.

"All right," he said. "Let's begin."

"Suppose you start by telling me about this movement of yours," said Virtue, focusing her camera on the back of his right hand. "Who are you fighting against?"

"Movement?" he repeated, puzzled. "I don't know anything about any movement." She opened her mouth to protest. "But I can tell you about the seventeen men and women that I robbed and killed on Silverblue."

She grinned and activated the microphone, and he spoke far into the night, telling her the bloody history of the most notorious criminal in the galaxy.

EPILOGUE

Some say that he's a hundred,
Some say that he is more;
Some say he'll live forever—
This outlaw commodore!

That was the last verse Black Orpheus ever wrote.

Shortly after setting the words down, he landed on the fourth planet of the Beta Santori system. It was a beautiful world, a pastoral wonderland of green fields and cool clear streams and sturdy ancient trees, and the moment he stepped out of his ship he decided to spend the rest of his life as its only inhabitant.

He named it Eurydice.

Of course, even without Black Orpheus, life—and death—continued on the Inner Frontier.

Geronimo Gentry, Poor Yorick, and Jonathan Stern were all dead within a year—one from old age, one from too many alphanella seeds, and one from a plethora of sins that still had no names.

The Sargasso Rose remained a lonely and bitter woman, cursing Sebastian Cain nightly for not fulfilling his promise to her. Skullcracker Murchison lost his unofficial title, regained it, and finally retired after taking one blow too many to the head.

Peacemaker MacDougal hunted down Quentin Cicero and Carmella Sparks, then went deeper toward the core of the galaxy in search of Santiago. Dimitri Sokol served as ambassador for two years on Lodin XI, resigned when he felt he had accumulated enough political favors, and moved to Deluros VIII, where he ran successfully for a minor office and later was offered a major post within the government.

Father William was slow to heal from his wounds. He remained in the hospital for the better part of six months, invoking the wrath of God upon all the doctors who refused to release him until he had lost half his body weight. The day he walked out he began regaining his lost bulk with a vengeance, but his stamina was gone, and he finally settled on Safe Harbor, the pastor of that planet's only church.

As for the Swagman, he actually did team up with Virtue MacKenzie for a brief period. After they had yet another falling-out, he returned to Goldenrod and sat down to write his memoirs. His enthusiasm soon waned, though he never completely abandoned the project, and before long he had hired a new batch of menials and was once again adding to his collection in his inimitable way.

Virtue had left the Democracy in obscurity, but she returned as a celebrity. Her series of interviews with Santiago won her three major awards, and her biography of the notorious bandit made her wealthy. She returned to the Inner Frontier every couple of years for fresh material on the King of the Outlaws and never failed to come up with it. She drank too much, slept with too many men, and spent too much money—and enjoyed every minute of it.

Cain carried on his campaign for nine more years, spending what his network of illicit enterprises accumulated where it would do the most good, fighting only that handful of battles he knew he could win, and spreading the myth of Santiago even farther across the Frontier.

He had always felt that when the end came it would be at the hands of Peacemaker MacDougal—but it was Johnny One-Note, making only his ninth kill, who finally hunted him down. He was sitting on his veranda, gazing tranquilly across the rolling fields of corn and wheat, when it happened, and he never knew what hit him. Johnny One-Note got to within half a mile of his ship before they tracked him down and killed him.

That afternoon there was a fourth unmarked grave in the small dell by the pond—under the gnarled tree, as Cain had requested. In the evening Moonripple came all the way out from town on foot.

A slender man, with sad eyes and a brilliant streak of white running through his dark hair, stood on the front porch and watched her approach.

"Yes?" he said.

"I've come to see Santiago."

"Why?" he asked.

"I've been a barmaid all my life," she replied. "Father William says that it's time to do something more." She paused uneasily. "He says that Santiago might be able to help me."

"It's possible."

"Where can I find him?" asked Moonripple.

"Come, child," he said gently, reaching out his bandaged right hand to her. "I am Santiago."